I0662230

BOOKS BY OLIVIA ASH

Dragon Dojo Brotherhood

Reign of Dragons

Fate of Dragons

Blood of Dragons

Age of Dragons

Fall of Dragons

Death of Dragons

Queen of Dragons

A Legend Among Dragons

The Nighthelm Guardian Series

City of the Sleeping Gods

City of Fractured Souls

City of the Enchanted Queen

Demon Queen Saga

Princes of the Underworld

Wars of the Underworld

Blackbriar Academy

The Trials of Blackbriar Academy

The Shadows of Blackbriar Academy

The Hex of Blackbriar Academy

The Blood Oath of Blackbriar Academy

The Battle of Blackbriar Academy

Sentinel Saga

By Dahlia Leigh and Olivia Ash

The Shadow Shifter

STAY CONNECTED

Join the exclusive group where all the cool kids hang out... Olivia's secret club for cool ladies! Consider this your formal invitation to a world of hot guys, fun people, and your fellow book lovers. Olivia hangs out in this group all the time. She made the group specifically for readers like you to come together and share their lives and interests, especially regarding the hot guys from her novels.

Check it out! Everyone in there is amazing, and you'll fit right in.

https://www.facebook.com/groups/LilaJeanOliviaAsh/

Sign up for email alerts of new releases AND an exclusive bonus novella from the Nighthelm Guardian series, *City of the Rebel Runes*, the prequel to *City of Sleeping Gods* only available to subscribers.

https://wispvine.com/newsletter/olivia-ash-email-signup/

Enjoying the series? Awesome! Help others discover the Dragon Dojo Brotherhood by leaving a review at Amazon.

http://mybook.to/DDB1

BLOOD OF DRAGONS

Book Three of the Dragon Dojo Brotherhood

OLIVIA ASH

I'm not the girl I used to be, and the world is no longer as it was.

The magic I possess—the magic I'm quickly *mastering*— it can destroy whole cities. Start wars. Change the tides of a battle.

As the dragon vessel, pretty much everyone wants me either locked up or dead.

Out of the shadows comes a new threat—a fighter who reminds me a little too much of my mentor.

He wants to take my old place at Zurie's side. And the only way he can get it, apparently, is to kill me.

Dragons and humans alike just won't leave me alone. In the end, that's going to be their fatal mistake.

Because I don't go down quietly.

Those who come after me die early deaths, and none of these fools will take my magic—or my beautiful newfound freedom—from me.

Blood of Dragons is a full-length novel with a badass heroine, a riveting storyline, and an alternative relationship dynamic. Get ready for a heart-pounding story filled with a dragon shifter romance unlike anything you've read before.

Buckle in for heart-pounding action, breathtaking magic, deadly assassins, four drop-dead gorgeous leading men, lots of toned muscles, **and most importantly—a young woman's journey of justice, self-discovery, and freedom.**

READ THE WHOLE SERIES

The Dragon Dojo Brotherhood: a riveting and addictive dragon shifter fantasy romance series.

Book 1: Reign of Dragons
   Book 2: Fate of Dragons
   Book 3: Blood of Dragons

Book 4: Age of Dragons (June 2019)

Publisher's Note: The Dragon Dojo Brotherhood is an adult urban fantasy series with explicit scenes and is meant for mature readers who enjoy spellbinding stories with a few fan-your-face moments in their fantasy fiction.

CONTENTS

Important Characters & Terms   XV

Chapter One   1
Chapter Two   14
Chapter Three   28
Chapter Four   42
Chapter Five   66
Chapter Six   85
Chapter Seven   93
Chapter Eight   101
Chapter Nine   111
Chapter Ten   127
Chapter Eleven   135
Chapter Twelve   143
Chapter Thirteen   151
Chapter Fourteen   164
Chapter Fifteen   171
Chapter Sixteen   176
Chapter Seventeen   187
Chapter Eighteen   194
Chapter Nineteen   205
Chapter Twenty   227
Chapter Twenty-One   237
Chapter Twenty-Two   252
Chapter Twenty-Three   259
Chapter Twenty-Four   269
Chapter Twenty-Five   277
Chapter Twenty-Six   289
Chapter Twenty-Seven   298
Chapter Twenty-Eight   307
Chapter Twenty-Nine   322

Chapter Thirty   329
Chapter Thirty-One   340
Chapter Thirty-Two   348
Chapter Thirty-Three   358
Chapter Thirty-Four   374
Chapter Thirty-Five   384
Chapter Thirty-Six   395
Chapter Thirty-Seven   405

Author Notes   413
About the Author   419

IMPORTANT CHARACTERS & TERMS

CHARACTERS

Rory Quinn: a former Spectre and the current Dragon Vessel. Rory was raised as a brutal assassin by her mentor Zurie. After her first taste of freedom, Rory never wants to go back to the life Zurie forced upon her... even though Zurie is hellbent on dragging her back.

Andrew Darrington (Drew): a fire dragon shifter. Drew is one of the heirs to the Darrington dragon family. With no real regard for rules or the law in general, Drew tends to know things he shouldn't and isn't fond of sharing that intel with just anyone. Though he originally intended to kidnap Rory and use her power for his own means, her tenacity and strength enchanted him. They have a pact: if he doesn't try to control her, she won't try to control him. Drew sees her as an equal in a world where he's stronger, smarter, and faster than nearly everyone else.

Tucker Chase: a weapons expert and former Knight. Tucker's a loveable goofball who treats every day like it's his last—because it well might be. His father is William Chase, current General of the Knights terrorist organization. Tucker was originally assigned to hunt Rory down and turn her in to his father, but as he spent more time with her, she became the true family he never felt he had. After he fed false intel to his father to protect her, the Knights branded him as a traitor.

Levi: an ice dragon shifter and feral dragon. Not much is known of Levi or his past, and no one but he knows what turned him feral. Rory saved him from a snare trap on the edge of the Vaer lands, and he has been by her side ever since. She's determined to turn him human again, but the clock is ticking... and not even Levi thinks they can do the impossible.

Jace Goodwin: a thunderbird dragon shifter and master of the Fairfax dojo. Jace grew up in high society and has the vast network to prove it. A warrior, he operates as the General of the Fairfax army—and his only soft spot is for Rory. His dragon marked her as its mate and will accept no substitute. Unfortunately, Rory and Jace butt heads more than they get along. If she dies, his dragon will go feral, so he has quite a bit at stake since his woman insists on running off and putting herself in harm's way.

Irena Quinn: Rory's sister and current heir to the Spectre organization. A brutal fighter, Irena's only purpose in life is to keep her sister safe. A powerful bio-weapon created by the Vaer has left her in a coma after a mission-gone-wrong, and Zurie knows more about that night than she's letting on.

Zurie Bronwen: current leader of the Spectres and former mentor to Rory and Irena. Zurie is a brutal assassin and holds the title of the Ghost. Cold-hearted, calculating, and clever, Zurie is determined to bring Rory back under her control. She'll do whatever it takes to get the girl back and reprogram the insubordination out of her brain using drugs and isolation.

Diesel Richards: a former Knight turned Spectre. With Irena indisposed and Rory out of the picture, Diesel would become the Ghost if Zurie dies. His incentive is to get rid of Zurie, Rory, and Irena. He's helped Rory once and tried to kill her on other occasions, so Rory isn't sure what Diesel really wants. Honestly, no one knows...

Harper Fairfax: a thunderbird, the Boss of the Fairfax dragon family, and Jace's cousin. Harper is friendly and bubbly, full of life and joy, but Rory knows a fighter when she sees one. The young woman is smart and cunning. As much as Rory enjoys Harper's company, she can't bring herself to let her guard down.

Guy Durand: an ice dragon and former second-in-command to Jace Goodwin at the dragon dojo. Guy has always wanted power. When he lost the challenge to Jace for control of the dojo, he joined the Vaer and gave over sensitive secrets about Rory and the dojo itself. The last time he and Jace met, each man swore to kill the other.

Ian Rixer (deceased): a fire dragon, Kinsley Vaer's half-brother, and a master manipulator. Ian was smarmy, elitist, and arrogant. He was often referred to as honey-coated evil for his ability to speak so calmly and kindly, even while torturing his prey. He treated everything like a game, and playing with Rory cost him his life.

Mason Greene (deceased): a fire dragon and sadistic Vaer lord tasked with dismantling the Spectre organization. Someone betrayed Zurie, Irena, and Rory by giving him access to their sensitive intel. His attempt to kill Rory backfired massively and ultimately cost him his life.

Jett Darrington: a fire dragon, the Boss of the Darrington family, and Drew's father. Wants Rory for reasons not even Drew fully knows, but everyone's certain it can't be good. Cut Drew off when he wouldn't hand Rory over, but promised Drew everything he could ever dream of—including ruling the Darrington family—if he turns Rory over.

Milo Darrington: a fire dragon, Drew's brother, and current heir to the Darrington family line purely because he's older than Drew. Not much of a fighter, but an excellent politician and manipulator.

Isaac Palarne: a fire dragon and the Boss of the Palarne family. A skilled warrior and empowering speaker, Isaac can rally almost anyone to his cause. He's a deeply noble man, but there's something unnerving about his eagerness to get Rory to come to the Palarne capital.

Kinsley Vaer: an ice dragon shifter and the Boss of the Vaer family. Her power and cruelty make grown men tremble in fear. She's absolutely ruthless, cruel, vindictive, and vengeful… the sort to kill the messenger just because she's angry. She's increasingly frustrated that Rory has slipped through her fingers so often, and she's determined not to let it happen anymore.

OTHER TERMS

The Dragon Gods: the origin of all dragon power. The three Dragon Gods are mostly just lore, nowadays. No one even remembers their names. But with the Dragon Vessel showing up in the world, everyone is beginning to wonder if perhaps they're a bit more than legend...

Dragon Vessel: According to legend, the Dragon Vessel is the one living creature powerful and worthy enough to possess the magic of the Dragon Gods. Rory Quinn was kicked into an ancient ceremony pit—the one Mason Greene didn't know was used to judge the worthiness of those who entered. With that ritual, Rory unknowingly brought the immense power of legend back to the world.

Castle Ashgrave: the legendary home of the dragon gods, said to be nothing more than ruin and myth.

Mate-bond: The connection only thunderbirds can share that connects two souls. The mate-bond is not finalized until the pair make love for the first time. Even before it's finalized, however, the mate-bond is powerful. The duo can vaguely feel each other's whereabouts and, if one should die, the other would go feral.

Spectres: a cruel and heartless organization that raises brutal assassins and hates dragonkind. The Spectres specialize in killing dragons and are known as some of the fiercest murderers on the planet, in part thanks to their highly advanced tech that no one else has yet to duplicate. They're a spider web network that spans the globe, all run by the Ghost. Often, Spectres are raised from birth within the organization and are never given the choice to join. Once a Spectre, always a Spectre— quitting comes with a death sentence.

Override Device: a bit of Spectre tech. Very frail and easy to break, it fits into most USB ports and can grant access to sensitive files. Though imperfect and obscenely expensive to create, it usually works.

Voids: a bit of Spectre tech. Fired from a gun with special attachments, a void can force a camera to loop the last 10 seconds and allow for unseen access to secured locations.

The Knights: an international anti-dragon terrorist organization bent on eradicating dragons from the world. Run by General William Chase, they'll do anything and kill anyone it takes to further their mission. There are some rebel Knights organizations that think the current General is too soft, despite his brutal rampage against dragons and his willingness to kill his own family, should the need arise.

Fire Dragons: the most common type of dragon shifter. Fire dragons breathe fire and smoke in their dragon forms. They're found in a wide array of colors.

Ice Dragons: uncommon dragons that can freeze others on contact and breathe ice. Usually, ice dragons are white, pale blue, or royal blue. The only known black ice dragons belong to the Vaer family.

Thunderbirds: dragon shifters that glow in their dragon forms and possess the magic of electricity and lightning in both their dragon and human forms. They're the most feared dragons in the world, and also the rarest.

Seven Dragon Families: the seven dragon organizations that are run like the mob. Each family values different things, from wealth to power to adrenaline. Usually, a dragon is born into a dragon family and never leaves, but there are some who betray their family of origin for the promise of a better life.

Andusk Family: sun dragons who prefer warm climates, almost all of which are golden or orange fire dragons. They're notoriously vain, focused on beauty and being adored. Somewhat materialistic, the Andusk dragons hoard wealth and gems and exploit those in less favorable positions.

Bane Family: dark fire dragons who deal mainly in illegal activities. They view laws as guidelines that hold others back, while they aren't stupid enough to follow others' rules. They like to see what they can get away with and push the limits.

Darrington Family: the oldest and most powerful family. Darringtons are mostly fire dragons, and angering them is considered a death sentence. They're well situated financially, with a vast network of natural resources, governments, and businesses across the globe. They're notorious for thinking they're above the rules and can get away with anything... because they usually do.

Fairfax Family: a magical family known as the only one to have thunderbird dragons. They have innate magic and talent, but sometimes lack the drive it takes to use those abilities to obtain greater power. They prefer to think of life as a game, and the only winners are those who have fun. To the Fairfax dragons, adrenaline is more important than money, but protecting each other is most important of all.

Nabal Family: wealthy fire and ice dragons. Money and information are most important to the Nabal, and they have an eerie ability to get access to even the most secured intel. Calculating and cunning, the Nabal weigh every risk before taking any action.

Palarne Family: noble fire and ice dragons known for their honor and war skill. Ruled by the dragon code of ethics, the Palarne family operate as a cohesive military unit. Their skills in war are unparalleled by any other family.

Vaer Family: a secretive family of fire and ice dragons, they're known to be behind many conspiracies and dirty dealings in the world. Some see them as brutal savages, but most fear them because they have no ethics or morals, even among themselves.

CHAPTER ONE

As I watch my sister sleep in her hospital bed, I can't help but think she looks like a corpse.

It's freaking me out.

I sit in the private room Jace secured for her, my elbows on my knees as I try to shake the morbid thoughts from my brain. With the door closed, no one knows I'm in here—except maybe Jace.

There's a bit more color to Irena's cheeks now, and her vitals are better than the first time I saw her strapped to a slab in Ian Rixer's fortress. I bristle at the thought of the bastard keeping her hostage, but he isn't a threat to us anymore.

That's what happens when people threaten what I love. They die.

At least Irena is safe—well, mostly. I try to keep

perspective. There's improvement in her vitals, but I just can't bring myself to hope too hard. After all, she's been in a coma for a long time.

Jace wouldn't like that I'm here. He hates it any time I leave the dojo, but today is important.

Risk-my-life important.

When I entered the secluded room, I unsurprisingly found a camera and switched it off to give me a few minutes alone with my sister. By now, Jace knows I'm gone—hell, I wouldn't be surprised if he himself were monitoring the camera feed when I disabled it.

Being here is risky, but this is my last hurrah.

"We might not get to talk again for a while, Irena," I say softly, shoulders tense as I study the screens above her.

Heart rate—normal.

Brain activity—normal.

Blood pressure—normal.

And yet, she still hasn't woken up.

For all intents and purposes, it really does look like she's asleep, rather than in a coma. I wonder if she can hear me, or if this will all filter through her subconscious and be forgotten.

Honestly, I'm not sure which to hope for.

If Irena wakes up, there's a chance she could use all of this against me. We're sisters until the bitter end, and she loves me. No question. She will love and protect *me*, but I don't know how she'll feel about the magic in my blood, or about Zurie hunting us both. We've been trained to hunt dragons, after all.

I've become what I once hunted.

"It's not just about me anymore," I say to her. "Not even just about us. It's bigger than either of us."

All my life, I operated out of self-preservation. It was me and Irena against the world. Family first.

But my family is bigger now.

Tucker, Drew, Levi, and even Jace—they're a part of my life, for better or worse, forever. All of them, including Jace's soldiers, would die for me.

I can't just think about myself anymore.

"It's time I give Jace an ultimatum," I tell Irena, pretending for the moment that she can hear me. "He and I have been butting heads pretty much since we met, and he's been trying to keep me behind locked doors for almost as long. But we can't keep fighting, not when so many people are after us both." I drum my fingers on my thigh. "After all of us."

Like it or not, he and I are tied to each other. The two of us can never be safe while the other is in danger.

That's why Jace and I need a truce.

A real one. One I can stake my life on.

And that puts Irena at risk. It's why I'm here— because my conversation with Jace might backfire. He's so unpredictable, so hard-headed, and I have no idea how he'll react. He could negotiate with me or bar me from seeing Irena for the length of her hospital stay. He could even lock me in a cell—I have no idea.

But he holds the cards here, and he controls my access to Irena as long as she's unconscious. It's what I didn't want, but I had no other choice. Even if it means risking a run-in with the people who are after me, I need at least one moment alone with Irena. I've fought tooth and nail to save her—and, in a way, this is goodbye.

For now. Just in case.

Part of me wants to wait for Irena to come out of her coma before I start all this with Jace, but I can't delay. The tunnels below the dojo pose a huge threat to everyone in it, and every second I delay puts me and them all at risk.

In the past, I wouldn't have cared. They're dragons, after all. But I'm not who I was—and after everything I've witnessed in the dojo, I won't be held accountable for another attack. Especially not because I wanted a way out of the dojo in case the dojo master tries to lock me in my room.

These fleeting few moments with Irena, right now —depending on how Jace reacts—may be the last time I talk to her for a while.

Maybe ever, depending on how much he and I piss each other off.

I don't for one moment think he would kill her to spite or control me—he's a better man than that. Besides, I would hate him for life and make his world a living hell, and he knows it.

But he might use her as leverage against me in an ill-advised attempt to get me to behave.

Besides, to date, I haven't gotten a moment alone with my sister. Jace has always been nearby, every time. I suspect if he had it his way, that's what my life will be like.

Jace, always nearby.

Jace, always watching.

I grit my teeth at the thought, hating the way it makes me feel controlled. Contained. Restrained.

"I let my pride get the best of me," I admit to Irena. I clench my fist, and white light briefly swirls over my skin as I dip into my magic. "My fear of trading one master for another. Zurie controlled everything about our lives, and I thought Jace might try to do the same." I sigh, rubbing my hands together as I stare at the tacky green carpet beneath my feet. "But I have to face the facts, Irena. I have to at least try to understand where he's coming from. If I die, he goes feral. So, as much as I hate to admit it, I kind of get where his need to keep me locked away comes from. I won't let him *do* it, but still—I can at least understand. It's progress, I guess."

I stand and run my hand through my hair, brain

buzzing with thoughts and concerns as I pace Irena's bedside. We used to work through things like this together, brainstorm and plot our strategies when we were backed into corners.

It's tough when she doesn't talk back, but it helps all the same. To see her pulse—to know her heart's still beating—gives me a sense of tranquility I didn't have before I walked in here tonight.

I didn't realize how much I needed that reassurance —to know she's still fighting, that she hasn't given up.

But I can't stay here much longer.

It's nearly time.

As long as Drew has access to the tunnels, the dojo is at risk. Not because Drew would do anything malicious, but because the fact that he could hide such a glaring flaw from Jace reveals a chink in the dojo's armor that can be exploited. It undermines the entire dojo's strength, and I don't want that burden on my shoulders anymore. If the dojo's attacked again, it puts Jace and all his people in immense danger.

I'll just have to see to it that Jace doesn't make me regret giving up my way out.

I lean against the wall and shut my eyes, preparing myself for what's to come.

Send me into battle and I'll grab a gun on my way out the door. Challenge me to a duel and I'll rarely say no.

But talking—sharing *feelings*—dragon gods, kill me now.

So, this is it, my last hurrah. My last daring escape into the night with no one else the wiser. I had to get one last little adventure in before I turned over the keys to my only means of escape from the dojo, should Jace get a little too comfortable ordering me around.

Footsteps echoed down the hallway—two people, one walking with thudding steps and the other at a light patter. One man, one woman.

That's my cue.

I switch on the camera sitting on the shelf nearby and tug sharply a red hardcover book beside it. As I pull it back, the book tilts on a hinge and activates a secret door in the wall. Jace told me this place was commissioned by the dojo itself, which granted him certain control over the blueprints. I figure adding a few secret doors and heavily monitored back entrances was a wise move—and I was noticing a distinct pattern in Jace's design choices.

The secret door slides open, silent as a whisper, and I duck inside the dimly lit tunnel. A few taps on the keypad in the metallic wall of the secret corridor close it behind me, and I tilt my head toward the wall to listen as the two newcomers enter Irena's room moments later.

The muted creak of a door opening filters through the wall, and the click of high heels softens as a woman's shoes hit the carpet. "...would be so much easier if we knew who this was," the woman says, her voice muffled. "We have nothing to go on. No family history, no—"

"Stop asking questions," a man says sharply.

There's a moment of silence, and I imagine the woman shooting him a glare. "She's *human*, Doctor. In a facility equipped for *dragons*. None of this makes any sense."

The doctor sighs. "I picked you for this assignment because you're the best damn nurse I have. I'm trusting you, Doreen," he says quietly. "Don't make me regret that."

I tense, wondering if he's going to spill the beans. Because if he does, I might have to open this door and break some necks. No one can know Irena's connection to me or the Spectres—if they do, it's a death sentence for her, and maybe for me as well. She's one of the few people I would go to hell to save, and my enemies know it.

With my hands pressed against the door, I can barely breathe as I wait for his next words.

"The person who put her here is powerful," he says, his voice barely audible. "That means you need to keep your head down, do what you're told, and stop asking questions."

"But—"

"No questions, Doreen," he snaps. "I don't like it,

either. Do you know how strange this whole mess is? The bio-weapon, the antidote, the results from my tests. Nothing here is right. Nothing here is *simple.* But there's a reason she's up here, out of sight, in a secured wing."

"I assumed as much," the woman says with a huffy sigh. "I've never seen that many armed guards in the hospital before."

"There are more than you see," the Doctor says. "Between you and me, I noticed a few new faces yesterday, and I suspect they're undercover agents of some sort. They're everywhere, and any one of them would write you up in their report if they hear you talking about this girl."

"Fine," the nurse snaps. The sound of fingers on a keyboard filter through the door, and it sounds like Doreen has shifted to the screens.

I don't like the idea of this woman watching over my sister. It raises the wrong sort of flags for me.

"Ready for the next dose," Doreen says in an annoyed tone.

"I'll inject it," the man says. "Hand it over."

There's a pause, but the shuffle of fabric makes me think she eventually obeyed.

"Can I at least ask about this antidote?" The muffled thud of heels over the carpet approaches the door, and I figure she's probably five feet from me at most. I might be able to open the door and grab her before the doctor even notices she's missing, depending on how involved he is with his injection.

But I refrain. Jace probably wouldn't like me going around, killing his hospital staff.

"Try to keep your questions to a minimum," the doctor says absently. "But if you're only going to ask about the antidote, then sure, go ahead."

The beep of the heart rate monitor accelerates, and my hand instinctively hovers above the pad that will let me back in the room. A few keystrokes, and I would be in.

It takes everything in me not to barge in on them.

The woman's footsteps rush away from me, toward the bed. "Doctor, is she—"

"She's fine," he snaps. "That happened during the last two injections as well."

"But her pulse—by the gods, how is she alive?"

There's a long pause, and all I can hear is the racing beep of the heart rate monitor. "I don't know," the doctor admits after a while, his voice tense.

"How many more does she need?"

"Two more," he says simply. "Wait for it. Wait— there." The heart rate monitor slows to normal, and he lets out a relieved sigh. "Sets me on edge every time. I can't have this girl dying on me."

Even though he can't see me, I nod.

Damn right.

"Good gracious," the woman says softly. "Look at that."

"Every time," the doctor says, and I can envision him nodding. "She gets a little more color in her face with each dose. By the fifth one, I suspect she'll wake up."

"And if she doesn't?"

There's another long pause, and I'm tempted yet again to hurl this door open to get more information and clues as to what is going unsaid. Expressions. Body language. Anything more than just the muffled conversation.

Eventually, the barely audible clatter of a needle dropping into a sharps container filters through the secret door. "Then we will do everything in our power to wake her up another way."

"And if that fails?"

"It won't," he says simply. "I won't allow it."

I relax, if only slightly. This doctor is every bit as dedicated as Jace promised he would be. The thought calms me a little, though I'm not altogether fond of his nurse. Whatever they went through for him to trust her so explicitly, I'm not sure it's enough for me to put blind faith in the woman.

"Those scars," Doreen says breathlessly. "How could she even get scars like these, and so young?"

"Doreen, damn it," the doctor says through gritted teeth.

"Sorry."

To me, Doreen doesn't sound the least bit sorry, and that seals her fate. I think it's time for me to dig a little into Doreen's past and find out just who is looking over my sister—and perhaps find a way to give the woman a new assignment.

As for me, I need to go. I can't stand in this passageway all night, even though I want to stay by Irena's side. The secret walkways, only just wide enough for two people to walk side by side, are controlled by access panels and heavily fortified. The only reason I was able to get access at all is likely because Jace didn't lock me out, and I suspect his soldiers are well aware I'm here. They're probably monitoring me through the cameras lining the hall-ways, and I'm honestly surprised they haven't arrived *en masse* to escort me back.

I brought my gun and voids, but with so few left, I didn't want to risk using them. Once I run out of voids, I'm done—there's no getting more. I need to save them for an emergency.

Jace's soldiers will probably march through the tunnels at any moment, which would suck. Frankly, I would like to make it back on my own and enjoy the tail end of my last hurrah while I can.

Part of me is simply dreading the looming conver-sation I can no longer avoid.

I groan, kind of wishing the earth would just

swallow me whole instead. This won't be fun—because either the controlling and stubborn Jace Goodwin will relax his tight grip on my life, or I will have to leave the dojo forever.

I'm honestly not sure how this could possibly work in my favor, but I'm going to try.

CHAPTER TWO

I slip through the evening shadows several miles from the hospital, looking for a car to steal. The random Jeep I borrowed to get here is too risky to take back, since I can't risk anyone recognizing it or me.

Honestly, the thought of taking someone's car is making me feel guiltier than it ever has in the past, and I've walked past three perfect opportunities so far because all the clues suggested it was the person's only car.

I don't want to screw anyone over—I just need a ride home.

My growing morals are kind of getting in my way, but I guess it's a small price to pay in the end.

Surprisingly, no one greeted me at the exit of the hospital wing. I had expected a full entourage, a small army to guide me to a helicopter and whisk me back to the dojo, but it had been quiet as I exited the building into the warm night.

Color me surprised. I'm not sure what game Jace is playing, but he certainly has me intrigued.

Now, I need to go with my backup plan—find my own way to the dojo. Not a problem. I've been on my own before.

As I weave through the houses in this suburban area, I notice several upstairs lights click off. Bedrooms, probably. The sun set roughly two hours ago, and I imagine dozens of kids being tucked into their beds, living the kind of fairytale childhoods I never got.

I silently drop from a tree and creep through the small grassy stretch between two of the houses. With a brief peek at the road, I scan the dozens of driveways before me.

There—four houses down is a house with three cars. All local plates, and I figure this late on a Tuesday night, they probably don't have guests over. With that many brand-new cars, they'll likely have good insurance. That means I'm not screwing them over if I take one.

This house looks like fair game.

Before I can move, the hair on my neck stands on end.

Deep down, my intuition flares in warning. There's

a sudden urge to hide, one that's fueled only by my primal sense of self-preservation.

Running purely on instinct, I press my back against the hard siding of a nearby house as something whizzes past my face. It digs deep into a nearby tree.

A tranquilizer dart.

Freaking *awesome*.

I knew this was a risk of coming here, and in the end, it was worth it. I just can't let them catch me.

With adrenaline buzzing through me, I bolt. There's no time to assess, no time to counter. Trapped in a tight alley between two houses, I don't have much leverage against an attacker—especially not one that's trying to snipe me out with tranquilizer darts. If one of those hits me, I'll only have a few precious minutes to either take out my opponent or find a place to hide—neither of which is likely to happen before I fall unconscious.

As I run, I keep to the shadows and let my natural stealth take over. A lifetime of Spectre training kicks in, fueling me forward, keeping me out of sight. Every moment I can, I survey my surroundings, looking for my attacker.

There's no one.

I'm running from someone I can't even see.

And when I find them, they're going to *die*.

My first thought is that Zurie has found me—but

that's not possible. If she had, the tranquilizer wouldn't have missed.

My second thought is Diesel is coming after me, likely to do Zurie's bidding as always. But he doesn't possess this kind of finesse. He usually punches his problems in the face.

Whoever is after me now, they're not a Spectre. This is someone else.

With the immediate threat avoided, I switch from prey to predator. Someone who could sneak up on me has to be talented, with enough of a grasp on stealth to go unheard. That means they'll still be tracking me, and I can lure them into a trap.

First, I need to find higher ground.

As I leap the next fence, I come across a large backyard littered with toys. A jungle gym sprawls across one corner of the yard, complete with a slide and built-in wooden fort. Behind it, a thick row of trees and hedges hide most of the back fence. A three-story house looms above me, with a wooden stairwell leading from the ground up to a deck on the second floor. A lone light at the sliding glass door casts thin shadows across the grass, leaving most of the yard in darkness.

Higher ground. Limited hiding places. Low light. Open field. Obstacles. Few places to run without giving me a clear shot to the back of their head.

It's perfect.

As I run toward the jungle gym, I pull out a small dagger from the belt at my waist and toss it into the middle of the yard, where I know it'll glint in the light as my new enemy runs by.

It's my bait—and all I need to spring my trap is for my new opponent to pause long enough to study it.

I jump into the jungle gym's small fort and draw my gun, keeping to the shadows as I train my barrel at the dagger in the yard.

And I wait.

Thankfully, I don't have to wait long. Seven minutes later, a tall man jumps the fence after me, landing in the grass without even a whisper of noise. He's tall and well built, and I can even see his biceps in his silhouette. His chest rises and falls a little too quickly, suggesting he doesn't have my stamina or speed, but he's still kept a surprisingly close tail on me.

Well, at least he's talented. If he was a thundering idiot, I would've been disappointed in myself for letting him nearly catch me. In fact, the way he moves reminds me of Tucker. The tilt of the shoulders, the way he holds his head.

For a moment, my heart races at the thought of Tucker tailing me—but it can't possibly be him. Tucker would never hurt me. This man must also be a Knight, and maybe he and Tucker trained together.

As the man walks into a beam of light, I don't

recognize him. My heart slows, and I let out a relieved breath.

This strange man steals through the yard, scanning the ground as he sprints across the grass. As he passes the dagger, he slows, his head bent toward the ground.

I press my finger over the trigger, taking aim.

The rush of a glass door sliding open interrupts us.

A little girl giggles. "Daddy, come on!"

Without moving anything but my gaze, I look up at the deck as a little girl, maybe seven, tugs on a man's arm. They rush down the stairs toward the yard.

"If we pick up the toys fast, we get ice cream!" the girl says, excited. "Mommy promised!"

"Ice cream?" her father asks with a grin. "Why didn't you say so? Let's do this!"

In the yard, my prey stiffens. The lone assassin watches as the two descend, and I wonder what he'll do.

Hell, I wonder what *I'll* do.

In the brief seconds after the glass door opens, my finger tenses against the trigger. I ache to pull it, to neutralize the threat that has already tried to take me down once. Everything in me, all of my training screams at me to kill him, witnesses be damned.

But if I do, I will scar that little girl for life.

To watch a man die in her own backyard—she will never feel safe. She will never feel whole. Every crack of thunder will remind her of bullets, and she'll never scrub the stain of a man's soul leaving his body from her memory. She will lose her last shred of innocence at an age when I was sparring blindfolded and learning to shoot my first rifle.

I can't do that to her. I can't take from her what I was never allowed to have in the first place.

With a frustrated grimace, I lower my gun.

The stranger below me grabs my dagger and bolts into the shadows, scaling the fence before the family has a chance to see him. As far as they know, the man was never even there.

And neither was I.

I pivot, peering out another of the fort's open windows as the stranger runs off into the night. The old me would have shot him without a second thought, but I'm not the girl I used to be, and the world isn't as it was.

I think of Levi, of Tucker and Drew, and even Jace —and I wonder what they would've said if I'd done it.

They would've been disappointed in me. After everything the five of us have been through, I want to be better. I want to deserve the love and trust they put in me, and sometimes that means making the difficult choices. The moral ones that put me at greater risk in order to save someone else.

Silently, I holster my gun.

I briefly debate going after the man and neutral-izing the threat like I was always taught, but this is a new world and a new life. I have to be more careful now than I was as a Spectre. Sure, he came after me, but I would be foolish to rush into danger unprepared.

I'm good, but I also have a lot more enemies now than I used to.

I knew coming to see Irena was a risk. I knew I stood the chance of being found. I didn't come out here for a joyride—I came to make peace with my sister, the person I would do anything to save, at the very real risk I'd be barred from seeing her again.

But to go after this guy now—that would be reckless.

The thought gives me pause, and I run my fingers absently over my arm as the little girl picks up her toys at the far end of the yard. It was so natural to think of my life as a Spectre in the past tense, to know I will never be sucked into that world again.

It makes me wonder if I can convince Zurie to come to her senses and make a truce with me, or if I truly am doomed to fight my former mentor to the death. After all, that woman's enemies don't tend to live long. There's no telling how long the fight will go on, even with my new magic.

As the little girl gets the last of her toys, she and her father race upstairs with their arms full, laughing all the way. I find myself smiling at their antics, at the way her father acts a little like a kid himself, at the way he carries seven toys to her one, but never once complains at doing most of the work.

Funny, I've never been envious of a child before.

As my eyes trail upward, scanning their house for other snapshot moments, I notice a hulking shadow on the roof. I draw my gun on instinct as the dragon lifts his head to face me, breaking the five-hundred-foot rule in a human zone. Most of all, I'm astonished that he could have snuck up on me.

It takes me a moment to recognize Levi.

I let out a sigh of relief and holster my gun yet again. Of course Levi got the drop on me—no one can out-maneuver that dragon, curse him.

Once the family is inside, I climb the deck and use it as a leg up to climb the water drain to the roof. With a few quiet grunts, I step onto the shingles of the house, my hands on my hips as I study my ice dragon.

"It's rude to stalk people, you know," I quip.

Levi rolls his eyes and snorts, a plume of frost shooting from his nose as he lets me know exactly what he thinks of *that*.

I smile and set my palm on his forehead in greeting. His brilliant blue eyes shift toward me, stunning as ever. As we touch, our connection opens, and a surge of protective energy rushes through from him.

I know, I tell him silently, before he can berate me. *You don't like that I left the dojo. But you don't understand—*

And? he asks impatiently, interrupting. A swirl of

annoyance burns through our connection, a blend of worry and anger that bubbles and froths.

And what?

He huffs in frustration. Instead of answering, he tugs at me, and I feel the unnatural pull at my navel that means he's trying to yank me into his mind.

Levi, don't.

I'm hit with another surge of his impatience. No words, just his irritation. His anger. Without so much as a pause, he tugs at me again, stronger this time.

It's not safe, I say. *There's someone out here, someone who—*

I saw. He's gone. It's secure. The ice dragon presses his head harder against my palm, pushing me back a few steps with his sheer strength. *Please.*

I sigh and indulge him, giving in to the pull.

My world goes dark as I'm drawn into his mind, past whispers of fading gray memories. I catch a silhouette here, a voice there—but it's all rough and echoing, like quick sketches of life that lack the color and depth of a real memory.

It hits me, then, just how quickly Levi is fading. How quickly his feral dragon is taking over the human trapped inside.

In a rush, I'm in his human arms. Now that I'm safely in the last recess of his mind that he controls, he holds me tight. His hand presses against the back of my head as he holds me to his hard chest. Despite the gravity facing us in the world outside, I smile and lean into him, wrapping my arms around his muscled torso.

"You need a hobby," he says with a chuckle.

I laugh. "What, like knitting?"

"Anything," he says, pulling back to study me with those piercing blue eyes. "Anything at all that keeps you out of harm's way." His loose strands of dark hair fall into his face, tempting me to play with them.

"You dragons." I smirk and shake my head in mock disappointment. "Always trying to lock me in a tower."

"Not lock you away," he says, his smile fading. "I just want you to be safe. I don't want you to be miserable. Just… alive, Rory. *Alive.*"

"I know," I say with a sigh. "I know. I wanted to check on Irena."

He crosses his arms, studying me with a disbelieving frown. "You realize you can't lie to me when you're in my head, right? I can see through it."

I groan in annoyance. No, actually, I hadn't realized that.

"You're not just putting yourself or Jace in danger when you leave the dojo," Levi adds. "You're risking Tucker, me, and Drew. We would all come for you if anything happened."

Truth be told, I don't really know what to say to that.

Levi winds his arms around me once again, holding me to him, and leans his jaw on the top of my head. "I know you don't want to be locked away," he says softly, like he's sifting through my memories and appreciating each one he sees. "You're worried for Irena. You don't know what to expect of the future. There's so much unknown in your life, and you feel like you're losing control."

The painful truth in every word eats away at me. It corrodes my resilience, setting me on edge and plucking at the strings of anxiety in my chest. I want to shut down, to do anything other than feel, but that's not an option with Levi.

Here, in the recesses of his mind, everything is so damn *raw*.

He lifts my chin, and I can't help but look into his sapphire blue eyes. He holds me there, suspended, stirring the emotions in my soul until I can't even speak.

Without a word, he presses his lips against mine. A delightful chill blisters through me, healing the wounds in my heart. For a moment, I feel like things will be okay. I feel like, as long as he's here, we'll figure it out together. I hold him tighter, grateful for him even if he does make me feel the things I try so hard to repress.

My body aches for him, and I wish I could somehow hold him closer. I run my fingers through his dark hair, drinking in every inch of his incredible body.

In a sudden and painful rush, he's ripped from me.

The world is dark again, and something is tugging

at my navel, dragging me from his mind.

In a split second, I'm on the roof again, kneeling to catch my balance as Levi snarls in front of me, a threatening rumble in his throat that builds like thunder. He glares off in the distance, his eyes dilating.

I've seen that look before.

His dragon is taking over.

"Levi," I say softly. "Levi, snap out of it."

His head whips toward me, his blue irises adjusting as he focuses on my face.

I hold my breath, hands raised as I try to rein in Levi's dragon. I swallow hard, bracing myself for whatever might come next, knowing I could never deal the final blow.

Not against Levi.

As I open my mouth to speak again, he rapidly blinks and shakes his head. When he opens his eyes again, they're normal, and he takes a few dazed steps backward as he gets his bearings.

"It's okay," I say quietly. "You're okay."

He watches me with a concerned look in his eye. A moment later, he nods, though he's clearly not altogether convinced.

"Let's get home," I say.

He nods again and lowers his neck, inviting me to hop on his back. I smile, never having had the honor before. Usually, my dragons get impatient and just carry me off in their claws.

For a brief moment, I debate saying no. He did just go feral for a second there, and it could be a disaster if he goes feral again while I'm on his back. But my voice snapped him out of it, and I can do it again. He and I have a connection that transcends even his feral nature —even his dragon listens to me. With someone chasing me through the neighborhood, this is definitely my best option.

I climb onto his back. His scales are surprisingly soft beneath my fingers as I settle in, and the muscles in his shoulders shift as he spreads his wings. With my hands around his neck, I'm safely situated.

He takes off into the sky, so silent he barely even rustles the trees nearby. My stomach lurches as he zooms through the air, silent as a ghost.

The lights below become blips along the distant ground as he soars higher. I lean my cheek against his neck as we weave through the clouds, the cool air sweeping along my face as he tilts this way and that.

I try several times to reopen our connection, but he never replies. Either he wants to focus on flying or, more likely, he just doesn't want to talk about his feral moment.

He never does. It's the only thing he won't discuss with me.

Levi can't run from this forever. He's quickly turning feral, and much to my horror, I still have no idea how to stop it.

CHAPTER THREE

Back in the dojo, I steal through the hallways.

The moment Levi crossed into the dojo's territory, we were flanked by four dragons. They kept their distance, each casting an occasional wary eye toward the semi-feral dragon in their midst, but none of them tried to attack. These were clearly just the guards to bring us in.

I knew Jace would be waiting for us in the court-yard, though, so I asked Levi to take a little detour.

Before I talk to Jace, I need to give Drew some fair warning.

The lock on Drew's door is easy to pick, and after just a few moments, I'm in without being seen. I gently shut it behind me, scanning the living room for any signs of him. One of my voids still sticks from the camera in the corner, and I shake my head in annoyance. With only a handful of those left to my name, I'm still not too happy he took a few from my pack.

Impressed, yes. But not happy about it.

I quickly scan the other rooms—his office, his bathroom, his bedroom. I pause as my eyes drift over the bed, smiling a bit as I remember all of our fun between his sheets. A quick burst of heat creeps up my neck at the memory of his hands gripping my thighs, of his thick cock riding me through the night, of the bursts of ecstasy as he dominated me again and again.

With a few shakes of my head, I shove aside the thought so I can focus. One thing is abundantly clear—Drew's suite is empty.

Running a hand through my hair, I pause in the middle of the hallway and wonder what I'm missing. He can't be far, not in the dojo. With as much as Jace hates Drew, the man can't go anywhere in the embassy without a few cameras following his every move.

As I'm debating where he could be, the door creaks open and quietly shuts. I take a few silent steps and peek into the living room, only to find Drew with his back to me, wearing nothing but a pair of cargo shorts as he steals quietly into his own suite. The hard lines of his back perfectly accentuate his muscle, and it's a little too easy to let his body distract me.

I smirk and lean against the wall, arms crossed as I wait for him to notice me.

He turns on his heel, freezing the moment his gaze

lands on me. There's a fleeting look on his face of a child caught stealing cookies, and that only makes me grin wider.

"Gotcha," I say, tilting my head knowingly.

"I don't know what you mean," he replies, the corners of his lips tilting upward knowingly.

Before I can help myself, my eyes scan the hard muscle in his chest. The solid pecs. The thick biceps. The broad shoulders and washboard abs. He's built like a tank, made up of nothing but tantalizing muscle. I feel the heat rising again in my cheeks as I imagine him pinning me against the wall and having his way with my body, but now's not the time to let my imagination run away with me.

Besides—I just pieced it all together.

Barely any clothes means he shifted recently and probably had a pair of shorts on hand to wear after he shifted back. Sure, modesty is more of a human invention and dragons don't care about seeing each other naked, but there's probably still something vulnerable about the son of the Darrington Boss stealing naked through another family's embassy.

I gesture to his shirtless body. "You were following me, weren't you?"

"No idea what you're talking about." That mischievous smirk of his breaks along his handsome face, and in that instant, it's abundantly obvious.

I shake my head, disappointed in myself for not noticing him. "How far did you get?"

He sighs in defeat. "All I got is that you probably went to the hospital to visit Irena," he admitted. "You're a damn good sneak, Rory. Too good."

I set my hands on my hips, satisfied with that. I'd given Drew a run for his money, yet again.

"You've got to stop leaving," he says. "It just—"

"I know," I said with a wave of my hand, cutting him off. "I've been over this with Levi. This was the last time I'm leaving the dojo through the tunnels."

Drew pauses, studying me as if he can't quite believe what I just said. "It was? For real?"

I nod. "That's what I came to talk to you about."

He tilts his head quizzically, clearly trying to piece this together. "Why do I get the feeling this is not going to end in my favor?"

I grin. "Your intuition is pretty spot on, Darrington."

He chuckles and shoots me a playful glare at the mention of his last name. I technically broke a dojo rule, mentioning his family name on neutral ground, but it was all in good fun.

"I'm telling Jace about the tunnels," I say simply.

Drew's smile fades. "He already knows about the tunnels. He's the master of this dojo, Rory. You think he's unaware they exist?"

"He didn't know the Darringtons infiltrated the

dojo," I pointed out, not backing down for even one second. "He might figure out how they did it, or he might not. And I suspect he doesn't know you've been sneaking around down there. Clearly, there's a blind spot in his security—a blind spot that can be exploited again unless he's made aware of it."

"There are protocols," Drew says, exasperated. "They run through a checklist and change the codes any time there's an incident like—"

"An *incident?*" I interrupt, incredulous. "An *incident,* Drew? Is that what you think the Darringtons breaking into the building and knocking everyone out with gas was? Is that what you call the order your father gave you—to turn me over to him? You think it was some kind of *mishap?*"

Drew sets his hands on his hips and shakes his head in annoyance, not answering me as he slowly paces the rug near the door.

"You found a loophole, Drew, like you always do," I say, genuinely impressed with his abilities. "But this exploit you found in the tunnel security system? It puts this entire dojo at risk as long as it exists. If you found it, someone else can, too. You have to admit that."

"He's already changed the codes," Drew says, gesturing toward the door as if that addresses any of my concerns. "He's already run through the protocols, Rory. You're safe."

I rub my face in frustration. "It's not just about me,

Drew. It's about everyone here—and no, we're not all safe. Not as long as that loophole exists. Can't you admit that, at least?"

"It's too risky," he snaps. "If we tell Jace about the exploit, then you're trapped here. You have no way out. Ever. Is that what you want?"

"Of course not." I set my hands on my waist, determined to make him see the bigger picture in all this. "Drew, I've been reviewing the options here and assessing the risk nonstop since your father and brother invaded this place. Do you really, for one moment, think they didn't pull code from the access panels while they were here? Are you sure they didn't run some tests to crack through the system, or plant any viruses?"

Drew crosses his arms and leans against a nearby wall, watching me with a grim expression and a squared jaw. His eyes narrow, and I know him well enough by now to understand what that face means— he isn't sure, and he has no answer.

"What if next time isn't so peaceful?" I say, pacing the living room as I study the Darrington dragon in front of me. "What if, next time, your father decides to bring a few more reinforcements? Or to use lethal gas? To flat-out declare war?"

I pause, letting that little thought settle between us. He knows his family better than me, and he's probably debated those options as well. I, however, am not so willing to sweep aside the risk—not after the way his father stared so hungrily at me after he saw the full brunt of my power.

That was the look of a man who will kill to get what he wants... and he's made it clear he wants *me*. A man that hungry will compromise his morals, and he knows Drew as well as Drew knows him. They'll try to play each other, and each man could easily make a mistake as he tries to assume what the other will do next.

I gesture toward the door, same as Drew did just a few moments ago. "I won't let the people here be slaughtered from access tunnels they think they control just because I want a way out of this place if I get upset with their superior."

"And how will you leave if Jace traps you here?" Drew says, lifting his chin in challenge.

"The front freaking door," I snap.

Drew pauses, like he legitimately hadn't considered that as an option. "What?"

"The front door," I repeat, pointing in the vague direction of the bridge that I crossed when Tucker, Levi, and I first came here. "Drew, I left today to visit Irena because I might not get the chance again for a while. Maybe ever," I add after a slight and painful pause. "Jace and I are going to have a little chat tonight, and at the end of it, we're either going to have a truce or a hostile split. It's all or nothing."

"Are you sure that's a good idea?" Drew tilts his

head to the side, a look of genuine concern cracking through his stony exterior.

I take a deep breath, pausing once again to reflect on my choices, but I already know. "Yeah," I say with a nod. "I'm sure."

Drew sighs and leans his head back against the wall, his shoulders relaxing somewhat as he thinks over what I said. "So, you didn't come here to convince me to turn over my intel to him."

"What? No." For a minute, I'm confused. That thought never even crossed my mind. "You two can work your own messes out. I just came to give you a fair warning about the tunnels."

"Thank you," he says with a somber nod of his head. "I suppose I can't change your mind, but I'm not a fan of giving up my way out. He might throw me in a cell again, but he can't keep me long without political repercussion. But he absolutely *can* lock *you* in the embassy."

"No, he can't." I chuckle humorlessly. "One video posted publicly about how the master of the Fairfax embassy is holding me against my will, and every dragon Boss will be personally standing outside that gate."

Drew laughs. "You're merciless."

"Only when cornered." I smirk. "Hopefully, Jace is smart enough not to corner me."

"He is," Drew admits with a shrug. "If it comes down to you leaving, where will we go?"

I grin. "I love how you just assume you're coming."

"Well, of course I am." Drew closes the gap between us, his hands teasingly grabbing my hips and pulling me closer. "A dragon has to protect his woman, after all."

"Oh, is that so?" I lift my eyebrows playfully as his fiery touch simmers on my skin. I try to ignore the way his hands ignite the craving within me, but I can barely contain the way my body aches for him. Heat shoots between my thighs, and I'm oh so delightfully tempted to wrap my legs around his waist.

"So?" he prods. "Where to, princess?"

"Princess, huh?" I roll my eyes as I debate how to answer his question. "I don't know," I eventually confess. "Any ideas?"

He leans toward me, and my eyes flutter closed impulsively as his lips graze my neck in answer. His warm breath rolls across my jaw seconds before he kisses it, his rough stubble scratching against my skin. "I might have a few mansions my father doesn't know about. Tropical island, palm trees, the works."

"Spoiled rich boy." I laugh.

"You like it."

"Maybe a little," I admit.

He peppers kisses along my neck, down to my shoulder. With a rough tug, he pulls aside the fabric of my shirt as his lips press against my skin. He's already completely comfortable exploring my body, and I don't want him to stop.

"You should also consider Castle Ashgrave," he says between kisses.

That momentarily snaps me from my lustful daze. "Isn't that the castle of the dragon gods?" I ask. "It's just legend."

"Apparently not," Drew says, pressing hard on my hips and guiding me toward the wall. As my back presses against the wallpaper, he leans in, towering over me. "From the moment you fused with the gods' magic, I've had people looking for it. Slow going, so far, but I might have a location pinned down. I've been a tad distracted, what with all the rescues," he adds, lifting an accusatory eyebrow at me.

"Hey, you didn't *have* to come," I point out. "Either time."

"You're welcome," he says, his voice deep and growly as he brushes his nose across mine.

"So, this Castle Ashgrave," I say, curious. "Isn't it just ruins? How could it possibly still be useful after so many centuries?"

"They say it's enchanted," Drew says with a shrug. "I never believed that until I saw what you can do, and now I'm not so sure. The texts we're finding even make it sound like it has a personality, though I don't know how much of that I buy into. It's supposed to be intact. Or, at a minimum, easily repairable."

"I highly doubt that."

"I guess we'll see. The manuscripts I'm finding are all immensely difficult to translate."

"Can I see them?" I ask, tenderly running my fingertips along his thick and muscled arms. I bite my lip just to play with him, knowing it'll drive him wild.

"You tease," he says, leaning his forehead against mine. "You're going to have to work harder than that to get your way, though."

I laugh as he sees through me. "You're no fun."

Drew studies my face, his broad grin slowly fading as the minutes slowly pass. After what feels like an eternity, he just watches me in silent concern. After several moments, his eyes drift to my lips, like he's struggling to find words.

"Are you going to tell Jace I have the codes?" Drew eventually asks. "That it was the Darringtons who attacked the dojo?"

I sigh. This was the one question I didn't quite yet have the answer to, yet. "I won't tell him about the Darringtons. I know that would force him into a war, per dragon law. If a dragon family is infiltrated like that, they must retaliate."

Drew told me as much right after it happened, but I looked into it a bit on my own. He was absolutely right, and this is something I have to keep to myself.

"And me?" Drew prods.

"What would happen if I did?" I ask, genuinely curious.

Dragon law is still so foreign to me—most of what I know is just the brutality of all of it. The rigid law and brutal enforcement.

"I would be put on trial for treason," Drew says calmly, studying my face for a reaction as he speaks. "I would face death for espionage, and should it look like things won't turn out in my favor, I would be forced to return to Darrington lands to avoid sentencing."

"Jace could pardon you," I point out.

"Not me," Drew says with a few shakes of his head. "Jace would love to be rid of me. You haven't even seen the beginning of his hatred for me, Rory."

"He can be an ass, but he's still an honorable man, Drew. I don't think you're giving him enough credit."

"Maybe," Drew admits. "But are you willing to bet my life on that?"

I hesitate, simply watching his face as he intently stares into my eyes.

No. No, I wasn't.

"Besides," Drew continues, "Even if he wanted to, Jace can't pardon this. If my father hadn't infiltrated the dojo, I would've gotten some jail time at most. But he would be forced to seek the harshest penalty after what happened. It would implicate me in the invasion. Worse than that, Jace would follow the breadcrumbs and realize what actually happened. He would still be forced to go to war with the Darringtons. If he knows I'm involved with the tunnels, it's just a matter of time before he figures everything out."

With a deep sigh, I lean my head against the wall and shuffle through this new information. I've never been fond of politics—it's just not my thing—but it's pretty clear I have to compromise my morals on this one.

To keep Jace, Drew, and the dojo's soldiers safe, I need to omit Drew's involvement in the tunnels.

"I'll cover for you," I say. "This time, and *only* this time. If you obtain access to the tunnels again, I won't cover for you like this." I look him intently in the eye to drive my point home.

"No, you don't have to do that." He smiles warmly, with almost a smitten expression on his face. "I'm a grown man and will accept the consequences of my actions. I just wanted you to know what's coming, Rory, and to be prepared. You never have to cover for me."

My lips twist into a soft smile, and I run my fingers affectionately along his hard chest. Even as he lights me ablaze with desire, I find myself endeared by this man. He's honorable, strong, and resilient.

"Don't be such a noble idiot," I say with a chuckle.

He laughs. "I confess, that's not the answer I was expecting, but—"

"I mean it," I add softly. "I don't want you, Jace, or the dojo hurt over something as stupid as pride. I'll take the hit this time, so to speak."

Drew sighs and wraps me in a tight hug, cradling the back of my head with his powerful hand. "You should never have to take the punishment for my decisions. I can't allow that, Rory."

"Tough shit. It's what families do," I say with a laugh as I hug him back. "We look out for each other, even when one of us does something stupid."

He chuckles and kisses the top of my head. Even though I can't see his expression, he holds me a little tighter. I wrap my arms around his warm body, grateful for the fire dragon in my arms.

These men—they *are* my family, every bit as much as Irena. They've fought for me, protected me, and challenged me to be better. A better fighter. A better person.

Even if I don't get away with things nearly as much as I'm used to, I still love these men—and I love who I'm becoming because of them.

CHAPTER FOUR

I n the darkness of Jace's private suite, I sit on the couch and brace myself. There's no telling how this conversation will go, and yet it's arguably one of the most important I'll ever have in my life.

Stupid *feelings.*

I try to go over the words in my head, rehearsing all the things I want to say, but the thoughts crumble away like sand through my fingers. No idea stays for more than a moment, and in the end, I'm left grasping at straws.

Truth be told, I don't know how to do any of this. Communication, healthy relationships, compromise— Zurie never taught me how to approach any of them. She was too busy breaking my bones or throwing daggers at me while I was blindfolded, to teach me to trust my other senses.

You know, a quality curriculum.

The doorknob turns, and I stiffen on impulse. With my arm draped over the back of the sofa, I'm sure I look far calmer than I feel.

The door to the hallway swings open, and Jace walks in wearing only the loose slacks of the dojo uniforms. He rubs the back of his neck, muttering under his breath as the door shuts behind him.

Still as a stone, I barely breathe. When faced with the master of the dojo, I'm just not sure what to say.

He stiffens, his eyes scanning the dark as his eyes adjust. His hand balls into a fist, and electricity instantly crackles across his skin. I marvel at the ease with which he summons his magic, the effortless power he exudes, and I have to confess that I'm rather envious.

Jace's eyes land on mine, and he instantly relaxes. With a few shakes of his hand, his magic dissolves into the air. "Jesus, woman. Why is it so hard for you to simply knock on my door?"

I chuckle. I can't help it. "Well, that's just not any fun, is it?"

He smirks and walks closer, taking confident strides as he examines me. I can see that he has a lot to say, too—see it in the way he hesitantly opens his mouth and shuts it just as quickly, in the way he pauses, just a foot or two away, with his hands in his pockets.

His gorgeous rock-hard body teases me, so close

and yet forbidden. If I indulge in my physical desire for him, the mate-bond could take us over. It could drive us to finalize the connection we share, the one neither of us fully understands, and one moment of indulgence and passion could lead to a lifetime of being connected to each other in an even more permanent way.

In the silence, we each wait for the other to speak. He studies my face, occasionally looking off toward the windows to rub his neck, and I wonder where he's been. He's shirtless, so I suspect he was shifted, off hunting for something.

Probably me.

I clear my throat, deciding to bite the bullet. "I left the embassy."

He laughs. "I'm well aware of that."

"The hospital alert went off?"

"It did," he said with a nod. "My codes, used at every door." He crosses his arms, shaking his head in mild disappointment. "Do you have to pick up on *every* little detail?"

I grin. "Of course."

"So, you swiped my codes by looking over my shoulder the last time I took you in," he says, piecing it together. "In order to go back later. Alone," he adds with an annoyed sidelong glare.

"I did," I admit.

"Do you like toying with me?" he asks with a shrug,

looking legitimately confused. "Is it just—I don't know, fun?"

"No," I say softly. Genuinely.

"Then why do you like putting yourself in danger, Rory?" he asks, frowning, his expression intense and accusatory.

"I don't enjoy it," I snap. "And today was a calculated risk. If you didn't like it, you could've locked me out of Irena's room," I pointed out, tilting my head in curiosity. "Why didn't you?"

"And have you hate me?" He snorts derisively. "No, thank you. I'll pass."

He's a bit upset, but I can't resist a little smile at that. Beneath the asshole exterior, he truly does care. Even if just a little.

Jace lifts one eyebrow. "You think this is funny?"

"Endearing," I correct.

That disarms him. His anger briefly melts away, and for a moment, he's left speechless.

I sit a little straighter in my seat, preparing myself for what I need to say. "Not too long ago, before we saved Irena, you said you were my mentor now—and that I need to do what you say."

His jaw tenses, as if he's fully aware of what's coming next. "Knowing what I know now, I admit that was a very poor choice of words."

I watch him hesitantly, not entirely sure I like where this is headed. "What do you mean?"

He sighs and grabs a remote from the nearby coffee table. Aiming it toward the television, he presses his thumb on the buttons. The screen pops to life, revealing security footage of me sitting at Irena's bedside, my hands on my knees.

"How did you get this?" I ask incredulously, standing. "I disabled the camera. I—"

"I hid multiple," he says. "The one you found was a cleverly placed decoy. The others are the real cameras, meant to protect her from Spectres. I have two dozen of my most elite soldiers in there, ready to take on a Spectre at a moment's notice. Nurses, patients, even visitors—those are the real soldiers. The armed guards are just the decoys." He pauses, glancing me over. "I didn't take any risks, Rory. Not with someone you care this much about."

I should be angry that he caught my private conversation on camera, but I'm mostly just fascinated at his ingenuity. Hands on my hips, I give him a brief once-over. "Well aren't you clever."

"A little." He smirks.

Though I'm gob-smacked and speechless, I'm suddenly deeply grateful I never told Irena about Drew or the Darrington invasion.

"I didn't want anything to happen to her because it would destroy you," Jace adds, his voice gentler now. "I couldn't watch you lose someone you love, not this close to seeing her finally get well. I just wouldn't know what to do, or how to help you if that happened."

"Thank you." I smile, genuinely grateful for him. He cares about me, even if he doesn't always show it in the most refined ways. It would seem I've been underestimating his capacity for compassion, if only a little.

"I would do just about anything for you, Rory," he admits, still keeping his distance. With his arms crossed like that, he looks equal parts intimidating and reassuring. It's such an odd combination, but on him, it somehow works.

This man surprises me, sometimes—there seems to be no halfway with him. It's all or nothing, *always*.

"If you would do anything for me, would you also stop trying to control me?" I ask, legitimately curious.

His jaw tenses, and a small dimple appears in his cheek. For the moment, it seems like that's the only answer I'm going to get.

"You know what I grew up with," I say, gesturing to the muted security footage on the television as it plays in the background. "You know who controlled my life. What she made me do. Who she made me kill. You know she's trying to drag me back to that. I finally have freedom, Jace. Why do you think I would just blindly obey you?"

"Because I *know* this world," he snaps, suddenly furious. "And you have *no* idea how to handle any of this."

Oh, *hell* no.

I bristle, my fury burning deep within me at the wildly inaccurate statement. I didn't live a life under Spectre rule to be brushed off as an idiot girl in over her head.

But before I can even open my mouth to retort, he lifts one hand and closes his eyes to quietly center himself.

The anger in his face softens, and he seems to rein in whatever impulse drove him to say that. "Sorry. That's not totally—it's—" He fights to find the words, tortured as he tries to figure out what he wants to say. "Look, Rory, you're brilliant. You're a skilled fighter. A fast learner. Of every student I've ever had, you're by far my favorite." He pauses, smirking briefly. "And not just because of the way the mate-bond screws with my body any time you're close."

Despite my brimming anger, that disarms me. I laugh, shaking my head, but I can't deny it. I feel the same any time he's near.

"But even Spectres die," he points out, his smile fading. "Even Spectres get killed. And you know why that happens?"

"Because you're better than them?" I ask, barely masking my contempt. It's such an arrogant thing for him to say.

"No," he says, throwing me entirely off guard. "It's because they're alone."

My shoulders relax, and for a moment, I don't know how to respond.

"They're alone, all of them." Jace takes a few careful steps to me, the rigid muscle in his arms bulging as he keeps them crossed over his chest. "They rely on favors instead of a vast network of capable intelligence officers working in tandem. They ask for submission instead of loyalty. They rely only on themselves, and that's why they fail. Every time one of them has come for me, I've seen the warnings a mile off." He pauses, barely a few inches from me now. "Every time, except for you."

I tilt my chin slightly, meeting his intense gaze. Those stormy gray eyes trap me, as they always do. As he leans in, my stomach churns with butterflies, and a crackle of desire snaps through me. A lightning storm of longing and hunger swirl suddenly to life in my core, and I never want to snuff it out.

And, deep within, my magic churns with its own desire for him. For his dragon. For our connection.

We stand inches apart, not touching even though my impulse is to run my fingers along his jaw. I resist, waiting for him to finish his thought, refusing to allow myself to be distracted no matter how gorgeous Jace Goodwin is.

"Rory." His voice is like a rush of air, rough and growly, and he reaches for me as he speaks. His fingers wrap around my arms, tugging me gently closer, and he looks down at me with such an intense expression that I briefly wonder if I've lost him to the mate-bond. If he's consumed by otherworldly lust and devotion, right now, or if this is really him.

"You're not used to needing someone," I say quietly, speaking for him. "I get it, Jace. If I die, you go feral—but you have to remember the opposite is true, too. People want you dead, same as me. I think you might actually have *more* enemies than me. When you put yourself in danger as master of the dojo, you put me in danger as well. It's a two-way street."

"I know," he says.

"I didn't come here to sit on your couch in the dark," I continue. "I'm here to share my secrets, Jace. I'm here to give you what I can—and I can't give you everything. Not yet. So, in exchange for my honesty, I'm asking for a bit of trust in return."

My heart is in my throat. I almost can't believe I'm doing this—showing my cards—and to a dragon, no less.

But this is Jace. For all his faults, he's not a manipulator. He won't lock me away, or leverage Irena against me.

I hope.

The master of the Fairfax embassy watches me, silent and intense.

Waiting.

"My only price in all of this is trust," I repeat. "You

might be the master of the dragon dojo. You might be general to the Fairfax army. You might train the most brilliant fighters in the world, Jace, but I was raised in an organization that hunted dragons—successfully, might I add. When I first got this magic and was utterly alone, I still managed to evade capture even while the entire world hunted me. I disobeyed a direct order from the Ghost—a death sentence—to save you, Tucker, Levi, and Drew. I carry the magic of gods in me, and I took my first kill when I was only twelve. I'm not a damsel, Jace, and I'm not going to sit in my room while you fight my battles and live my life for me. I need to know you see us as equals."

His expression softens, and he tenderly sets his palm against my cheek. "You were only twelve?"

I swallow hard and quickly look away, trying to suppress the memory of my first kill. The screaming. The blood. The pain I caused a man who dared betray the Ghost, every strike I made done on Zurie's command.

I quickly force a cough to rid myself of the stinging knot in my throat, refusing to let myself feel the guilt. "Yes."

"Rory, it's—"

"I'm fine," I lie, standing a little straighter and looking him in the eye. "Are these terms you can work with, Jace?"

He sighs, frowning slightly as he studies my

features, and I can tell he isn't sure. He still sees me as in over my head, and the thought alone just pisses me off.

"What is it?" I finally ask. "What's holding you back on this?"

He groans. "Rory, I'm more experienced. I can handle two dozen dragons at once, can take on an army, can fight brutal men and live to see another day. I have a network of soldiers at my command, a literal army to protect you. Elite soldiers to guard you anywhere you go. I have a network of intelligence officers that can give you insight on nearly any location before you enter. I have seven soldiers right now whose *only job* is to listen for intel on *you.*"

Wow, that's amazing. Despite everything else, I'm kind of flattered he would put so many soldiers on that.

But he's missing the bigger picture here.

"Can you destroy entire buildings with your bare hands?" I ask simply.

He hesitates. "As a dragon, sure—"

"Your bare *hands*," I correct. "Not claws."

He frowns. "No."

"I can." I nod toward the mountains out the window. "I blew a hole in one of those not that long ago, remember?"

That annoyed dimple appears again in his cheek, and I can tell he's barely biting back a scathing retort.

"How much longer do you think you can keep up with me when we spar?" I ask, entirely serious. "My magic is growing every day. How much longer will your thunderbird match it?"

"Don't get cocky," he snaps, sounding more like a teacher than a lover for a moment.

He has a fair point, though—one I'm ready to counter.

"I'm not getting cocky." I shrug. "I'm entirely serious. This is the power of the gods, and I'm quickly mastering it. I'm not saying I'm better than you, Jace. I'm just saying this is earth-shattering magic, and a force to be reckoned with."

Yet again, he doesn't answer.

"We each have strengths the other doesn't possess, Jace," I point out simply. "We can complement each other or argue nonstop. What'll it be?"

After a few tense moments of silence, he finally sighs and sets his hands on his hips. "I'm getting there," he admits.

It's not the answer I wanted, but it's progress.

As the security footage continues to play in the background, I catch sight of the nurse and doctor. They enter the room seconds after the secret door closes, and the nurse leans over Irena's bed.

"I don't like her," I confess. "She asks too many questions."

"She really does," Jace says with a sigh, taking a

wary step backward and slipping his hands in his pockets. "After reviewing the footage tonight, I've had her transferred to another building and had her access to Irena revoked. She won't go near your sister again."

My eyebrow lift in surprise, and I study him for a moment in bemused silence. "Did we just agree on something?"

He chuckles. "It would appear we did, yes."

I laugh, enjoying the reprieve after such a heavy conversation. "How soon until we can move Irena here?"

"After the fourth dose, which will be roughly a week or so from now. By then, she'll only need a few vitals monitored, and a nurse or two should suffice. No one will even know she's here—especially not Harper," he adds with a frustrated shake of his head. "With Irena's positive reaction to the last few doses, she may even wake up shortly after the fourth one." He smiles reassuringly at me. "I've made the arrangements. It's just a matter of waiting at this point."

"Thank you," I say again, smiling with gratitude. He didn't have to do any of this, but he did.

For me.

"Of course, that would make for *two* Spectres taking refuge in my dojo," he adds with a wry grin. "Honestly, woman, can't I just have a bit of peace?"

I shrug playfully. "Nah."

He laughs and switches off the television. With a heavy sigh, he relaxes onto the couch and drapes his arm over the back of the sofa, taking almost the exact position I'd been in when he walked into the room earlier.

I sit on the coffee table across from him, propping one leg on my knee as I try to find a way to finish what I came in here to say.

For a while, we simply sit in awkward silence. The smiles fade. The tension grows. I don't know how to change his mind, and I wonder if delivering an ultimatum would just destroy this inelegant but surprisingly satisfying ceasefire we've somehow constructed.

"I have guards around the perimeter of the hospital," Jace abruptly says. "They noticed you leave and tried to trail you, but you were too fast."

"At least I'm not getting soft."

Jace frowns. "They were looking out for you. *Protecting* you."

"Why didn't they just approach me?"

"You're damn fast, that's why," he says with a sigh. "But I also told them to keep a distance, to just observe unless you needed help. I figured this might keep you out of trouble." He laughs, rubbing his eyes. "I'm astonished you escaped their notice, but I guess I shouldn't be."

I grin, taking that as a compliment. "You're really not going to like what happened next, then."

He lifts his gaze, watching me warily as his smile fades.

Time to bite the bullet. "Someone tried to tranq me a few miles out, while I was looking for a car."

"What?" Instantly, Jace sits upright, watching me with a fierce expression, like he's ready to break necks the moment I give him a name.

"I think it might have been a Knight, judging by the way he moved." I briefly let my eyes glaze over as I recall the evening, trying to comb through any clues I might have missed earlier. "An exceptionally good one, but he was no Spectre."

"A Knight went after you by himself?" Jace frowns. "That doesn't make any sense, Rory. They work in teams because they're not trained enough for single combat with a dragon."

I smirk. "I'm not a dragon, Jace. Not yet, anyway."

"You might as well be," he says matter-of-factly, standing to pace the living room as he silently processes this new information.

I tilt my head away to hide the beaming smile of pride. I've come a long way to take that as a compliment.

"I'll find out who it is," Jace promises, his shoulders tight and squared. "I'll find him and take him down."

"We'll take him down together," I correct.

Jace groans and shoots me an exasperated look over his shoulder. I'm tempted to dig into him, to drag this argument to the surface again, but I'm not sure if I should bother. We've said everything already, unearthed every point to be made, and neither of us can agree.

"I debated waiting to change the codes on the tunnels until you got back," he says in a transparent attempt to change the subject. He crosses his arms and leans against the wall, studying my face as he waits for my reaction.

He won't get one.

"Whoever attacked us came in that way," Jace continues. "The investigation revealed as much, though I still don't know how they acquired codes that suppressed even my private alerts." He shakes his head in disappointment, clearly aggravated.

"Do you know who it was?" I ask hesitantly.

His severe gaze shifts to me, and I can tell he's fully aware I already know the truth. "Is this one of those things you can't tell me?"

I sit a little taller, taking a deep breath instead of giving him an answer.

He nods, almost to himself, and pushes off the wall. With his hands in his pockets, he slowly paces the room. "Rory, I'm legally obligated to press charges. They violated a treaty, and I'm sure they came for you."

"Probably," I say, playing coy.

"Rory," he says, a warning in his tone. "If you know, you need to tell me."

"If I did, wouldn't that mean you would have to go off to war?" I ask.

He shakes his head. "Only if they resist submitting to the treaty's—"

"These people gassed your entire dojo—and we're lucky they used non-lethal gas, Jace." I stand and gesture out the window. "You think they're going to roll over just because you find out who they are?"

To his credit, Jace swallows his pride long enough to not answer.

"If I did know, let's just say I would keep quiet to protect you." I cross my arms. "To protect your allies. Harper. Your soldiers. To save all of them from a pointless war."

"I have to do this, Rory," he says tensely. "It's my duty."

"I guess it's a good thing I don't know who it was, then," I lie.

He rubs his eyes in frustration. "But you *do* know, Rory. My investigation turned up some interesting things in the logs. Unauthorized access that somehow didn't notify command of the tunnels' use. Strange times, and odd paths taken." He sighs, running a hand through his hair. "How did you do it, Rory?"

"I'm not sure what you're talking about," I say with a shrug as I examine my nails. "But you might want to hire a trusted hacker to test your security code for exploits. Someone new, who hasn't seen the code before and can give it a fresh look."

Truth be told, I don't entirely know how Drew found the exploit. A good ethical hacker would, though, and that's all I need to do to send Jace on the right path toward fixing this mess.

It stings to sit here and omit the truth because it feels like a lie. To hide Drew's involvement, to absolve the Darringtons of their role in all this, feels wrong. One way or another, I'm going to hold Jett Darrington accountable for what he tried to do—I just have to figure out how to play his game, first.

"An exploit..." Jace shakes his head in disappointment, his voice trailing off as his mind races. "I bet Durand... That code was fine, but he insisted—damn it."

Jace crosses to the window and stares out at the brilliant night sky. In the silence that follows, the silhouette of a dragon soars past. It's a fleeting blur of dark blue against the pitch-black night, and I'm briefly lost in the wild beauty outside.

The dojo is magical.

"Thank you, Rory," Jace says without looking at me. "I appreciate the nudge in the right direction."

"You're welcome."

"And I came with an olive branch of my own," he adds.

"Oh?"

"I created a unique code for you—one that opens the tunnels," he says. "I never revoked access. I don't want you to feel trapped here with me."

"You did?" I tilt my head in surprise, completely caught off guard.

He nods. "The code is the day we met. Six digits." He hesitates a moment. "Of course, you don't get access to *everything*, but it should be enough to satiate your need to sneak through my dojo."

"The day we met, huh?" I grin. "I didn't know you had a sentimental side."

He chuckles. "There's a lot you don't know about me, Rory."

I chuckle, unsure of what to say—and, when in doubt, I usually crack a terrible joke. "You just did that so it's easier to revoke my access if I piss you off, didn't you?"

He smiles and briefly looks over his shoulder at me. "Rory, by the gods, can't you give me *some* credit?"

I laugh, genuinely impressed by this man. Part of me wonders if there really is something soft in him after all.

After a few moments of silence, where we both simply watch the beautiful world outside the windows, he turns to face me.

And there has been a very clear, very distinct shift.

His expression is now intense and stoic, and all the laughter from before has faded. "I need you to tell me who you saw down in the tunnels. You *have* to tell me who is responsible."

I walk to him, quickly closing the gap between us as I study his expression. Tenderly, I set a hand on his arm. Sparks shoot up my fingers, but it's a delightful little burn. As I touch him, he relaxes slightly, but that intense expression of his never fades.

I lean in and lower my voice, intent on making sure he understands. "Let me shoulder this one, Jace," I say softly. "You have enough to worry about without letting your people die for honor and obligation. This burden is mine, and there's nothing you can do to change that."

His expression shifts, and I watch the internal battle rage within him—the fight between his desire to protect his people and his obligation to the law.

"I came here to make a truce with you," I add, trying to steer the conversation in a new direction. "For us to work together, instead of against each other. You don't control me, and I don't control you. That's what I want. I gave up the tunnels—my only way out—in exchange for your trust. Even though you gave me access, you could still take it away at any time. So, tell me—is trusting you going to be a mistake?"

He watches me with a tortured expression. Eventually, he shakes his head.

"I don't think so, either," I admit. "But I want to make one thing very clear, Jace," I add, my tone shifting. "If you push me away or try to lock me in this place, the next time I leave will be through the front door. And I promise you, I won't be back."

He tenses beneath my hand, like the idea horrifies him, but he eventually manages to sweep aside the impulsive reaction and relax. "Since you arrived, I hated that you didn't trust me. That you wouldn't listen. It's been infuriating to watch you slip through my fingers time and time again, only to put yourself in harm's way. But after that—" he nods at the television "—I finally understand why. That changed things for me. It took immense courage for you to give up the exploit in my tunnels' security system, Rory, and I appreciate what you did tonight."

I smile, gripping his arm a little tighter. That one little gesture seems to unravel his last shred of self-control, and his entire demeanor changes.

In one moment, everything shifts.

It's like a switch turning on. The mate-bond snares us both in the midst of all that intimacy and connection, trapping us at a moment of weakness and propelling us forward.

Even if we fight it, the mate-bond wants us to see this through. To explore each other. And it's very quickly becoming more and more powerful.

In an instant, my traitorous body pulls me closer to him as the mate-bond takes over. I don't know if it's my exhaustion or simply the growing intensity of our connection, but this time, it's hard to fight.

My fingers tighten around his thick bicep, hungry to feel his firm muscle pressed against my body, and that only eggs him on.

His gaze shifts to my hand, and his eyes trail up my arm. He watches me hungrily, and I feel as though he's undressing me with his gaze. He steps toward me, his hands on my waist, his rough grip un-tucking my shirt from my belt as he slowly walks me backward toward the wall.

"Jace, we shouldn't—*oh*—" My eyes flutter closed as his lips press hard against my neck, in the small space right against my jaw. His hands inch up my sides, pulling my shirt higher as his hot skin rubs against mine.

"Maybe you just need to see what you're missing." His voice is rough and deep, and I can tell he's as lost in the magic of our connection as I am. "Since you seem to enjoy Tucker's bed, I only know of one way to sway you into mine."

He presses his mouth against mine, and in the ecstasy of his touch, I don't want to come up for air.

Stop, a quiet voice says in the back of my head.

As the mate-bond burns between us, wild and rough, he pins me against the wall and lifts my legs so that I can wrap them around his waist. I weave my hands through his hair as the bulge in his pants rubs against my entrance, and I'm utterly lost in him.

Stop, the small voice says again.

While one of his hands holds my ass, pinning me in place, the other reaches for the closure on my pants. He tugs it loose and slips his fingers past the fabric of my panties. His fingertips dance across my sensitive folds, strong and absolutely sure of what he wants to do next.

My entrance aches for him, desperate for him, *needing* him.

STOP!

Deep within me, something churns. It's like part of my soul is ripped open and left to bleed. I gasp in horror, and for a moment, I can't breathe. With my hand against my chest, I gasp for air, and that alone snaps Jace from the wild lust of our connection.

He lifts me effortlessly and sets me on the couch, kneeling beside me as he stares with wide eyes at my face. He tucks a few loose hairs behind my ear, watching me with concern. "Rory, what are you feeling right now?"

"I don't—" I grimace as the sensation tears through me again. My chest arches upward, and once more, it's almost impossible to breathe.

"Shh, it's okay." Jace tenderly runs his hand along my hair, and for a moment, I don't recognize this man. This is the shifter who jumped effortlessly from a four-story wall, who easily beat Guy Durand to a pulp and walked into the lion's den with me to save Irena—and yet he's comforting me, calm and soothing despite a lifetime of war and battle.

"What is this?" I ask through gritted teeth as the sensation slowly fades. Below my hand, my pulse thuds against my palm.

"That's your dragon, Rory," Jace says with a hint of pride.

I squeeze my eyes shut as the painful sensation bleeds away into an overwhelming desire to shift. It's so urgent, so overwhelming—but I have no idea how. "What do I do?"

"Ride it out. You'll have quite a few of these before we can make any progress."

"I want to shift but I can't—I don't know how to—"

"You will," he says.

I open my eyes to find him smiling down at me. He's wearing that merciless smirk of his, and once more, I see the playful bad boy I met in the courtyard when I first came to the dojo.

It's a challenge.

One way or another, he and I are going to bring out my dragon. I'll be the first human in history to shift—and we're going to do this together.

He and I don't agree on much, but we can agree on *this*.

CHAPTER FIVE

I collapse into bed, exhausted, and sigh as I lean the back of my head on the blissfully soft pillow. I wanted to check on Tucker, but I know he's fine. I can see him in the morning.

As I drift off to sleep, my ear impulsively twitches. I hesitate, trying to pull myself back into the waking world long enough to listen through the stillness around me.

There—the creak of a door hinge. Someone's walking into my living room.

I sigh, wondering what fresh hell this is going to be.

With my body tense for a fight, I wait. Still resting my eyes, I set my little trap for whomever is sneaking into my room. The thud of familiar footsteps across the carpet in the living room catches my attention, and I smile as I recognize who it is.

"What are you doing, Tucker?" Eyes still closed, I can't suppress the wry smile on my face at the thought of him trying to sneak into my room.

"Oh, come *on*," he says, his tone mildly irritated. "How far in did I get before you heard me?"

I snort derisively. "You're adorable."

"Seriously? You heard me walk through the main door?"

"It's cute though." I chuckle, peeking at him through one eye. "Good effort."

"All right, bossy pants." He tugs his shirt off and flings it aside, grinning at me as he sets his hands on his glorious waist. His lean fighter's build and hard pecs draw my attention, tempting me despite my exhaustion.

Damn, this man is pretty.

"Uh oh," I say, grinning. "The shirt came off."

"You bet it did." He feigns a somber expression, but he can't hide the slight tilt at the corners of his mouth as he suppresses a smile. "You went off on an adventure without me, so I have to give you the appropriate punishment."

I lazily lift one eyebrow. "Do you, now?"

"Absolutely. The punishment for that is butt stuff." He rubs his hands together eagerly. "Turn over."

I laugh at this adorable idiot as he tugs at the ends of my pants. I can't help it. Even with how exhausted I am, he's just too much.

"You're ridiculous," I say as he climbs on top of me, his hands on either side of my face.

He grins, those stunning green eyes of his brimming with laughter as he stares down at me. "You mispronounced 'brilliantly funny' there, babe."

I laugh harder.

Oh, Tucker.

Never change.

Way earlier than I want to be awake, I sit in the private war room adjacent to Jace's suite. The dojo master rifles through some papers in a seat nearby, utterly consumed with his notes. In the peaceful stillness, I lean back in my chair, my head leaned against the back rest, and close my eyes.

In the light of our oddly formed truce, he invited me to discuss plans for the meeting with the Bosses.

It's—well, nice. I'm impressed.

The door opens abruptly. Both Jace and I tilt our heads toward the entrance as Tucker and Drew walk in together.

"Can I help you?" Jace asks sarcastically, lifting his eyebrows in annoyance. "This is a *private* meeting."

"I have the right to be here," Drew says firmly, taking a seat across from me. "If Rory is going into enemy territory, you need my help to keep her safe."

"And you don't hate me anymore," Tucker adds, taking a seat nearby. "So, yeah, I get to be here, too."

"That's not at all how it works," Jace says with a baffled frown in Tucker's direction.

The weapons expert shrugs. "Close enough."

I chuckle, still exhausted from the aerobics Tucker put me through last night when he joined me in my bed. He didn't get "butt stuff," as he so eloquently put it, but he certainly kept me up late. He shoots a flirty wink at me, and I just smile and shake my head.

"Get out," Jace snaps, his gaze shifting between the two men who just joined us.

"Jace, relax." I lean my elbows on the table.

"*Relax?*" The dojo master's intense glare drifts toward me, but I'm virtually immune to it at this point.

"Yeah," Tucker says before I can get a word in. "Relaxing, have you heard of it? The general idea is to chill out. You know, roll out your shoulders and loosen up the muscle—"

"What I *mean*," I say, interrupting before Tucker can get too carried away, "is just let them be here. They'll be with us at the meeting with the Bosses, regardless."

"Says who?" Jace snaps.

"Says *me*," I snap back, entirely unwilling to deal with this bullshit. "I want them there, and that's completely reasonable."

He frowns, staring me down, and I match his gaze.

His glare briefly shifts to Drew, and I realize that's the only part of this plan he isn't fond of.

"Fine," Jace snaps. "I'll allow it."

I lean back in my chair, letting him think whatever he needs to think in order to keep the peace. If he wants to believe he's allowing this to happen, that's fine by me.

"Irena is looking better," Jace says, shuffling again through the papers in his hands. "Vitals are good. The fourth injection of the antidote is scheduled for the last day of our meeting with the Bosses."

I lean forward in my chair, suddenly alert. "You said she might wake up with that one."

"She might." He nods. "That's why we'll be trans- porting her here, ideally right after the dose is given."

"But if I'm not there—"

"*Relax*, Rory," he says, that cocky smirk on his face as he uses my words against me. I narrow my eyes in annoyance, but he continues before I can get a word in edgewise. "The estimate for her to awaken is several hours after the injection, which gives us time to move her. If her vitals are shifting and it looks like she'll wake up early, we'll leave the meeting ahead of schedule."

"Won't that be suspicious?" Drew rests his bulky arms on the table, studying the dojo master's face. "The Bosses will want to know why, including Harper."

"Perhaps." A brief look of annoyance crosses Jace's

features at the sound of Drew's voice, and he doesn't look at the fire dragon even as he answers the man's question. "It's a risk worth taking if it means a panicked Spectre isn't running loose through my dojo."

"Fair point," I admit.

"What's your backup plan in case she doesn't wake up?" Tucker asks.

Jace, Drew, and I each turn our heads in unison to look at the weapons expert, who seems to be suddenly unsure of whether or not that was a good question to ask.

"We're not going to think about that," I say softly.

"Right." Jace clears his throat. "Let's talk about the bio-weapon instead."

"The Vaer still have it," Drew points out. "They could still use it at any time, and who knows why they even made it in the first place."

"True, but we also have the antidote," I add.

Jace sets down five of the papers in his hands and spreads them out on the table. "The entire chemical composition, deconstructed and reconstituted into a recipe. After our labs dissected the vial Rory *procured* —" He rolls his eyes, emphasizing his annoyance with my methods. "We own everything."

"We have to release it," I say, ignoring his little jibe. "We need to make this available to everyone."

"Already begun," Jace says with a roguish grin. "Harper and I are releasing the antidote to every pharmaceutical company in the world, patent-free. It will destroy any chance the Vaer have to use their artificial disease."

"Harper knows?" I lean forward, my heart skipping beats in my chest. "I thought you weren't going to tell her about Irena, about—"

"It's fine," Jace says in a soothing tone, though it's quickly replaced with the hard tone I'm used to hearing in his voice. "She only knows we discovered the Vaer bio-weapon and its antidote, not how."

Tucker leaned his elbow on the table and set his head against his knuckles. "Won't she ask?"

"Let's just say she has an alternate understanding of the events that led to us *finding* it," Jace says, hedging around the truth. "And leave it at that."

I frown. "Jace—"

"Trust me," he interrupts. "I don't want Harper knowing about a Spectre in my dojo any more than you want her knowing about Irena."

"All right," I say softly, still not happy with this at all.

"Are you going to tell them?" With his eyes on me, Jace nods toward the two men at the table.

For a moment, I just watch him, utterly confused. "Tell them what?"

Jace tilts his head in annoyance. "The Knight?"

"What Knight?" Tucker asks, all humor dropping from his tone. In a split second, his voice is chilly and serious, ready for war.

"Ah," I say with a nod. "Right. I was pursued last night by who I believe to be a Knight. He tried to tranq me."

"And you were going to tell us… when?" Drew asks, a deadly serious expression on his face.

I gesture vaguely to the room around us. "I'm telling you now."

Tucker's jaw tenses as he leans toward me, his expression dark and serious. "Who was this guy?"

"I don't know," I admit. "I only saw his face for a brief moment, probably not enough to even recognize him in a picture. He moved like you, Tucker. At first I thought it *was* you."

"I would never—"

"I know," I say with a soft smile.

Tucker's shoulders are still tense, and his hand balls into a fist as his gaze shifts to the window. I suspect he's trying to figure out who could be going after me solo—and why.

"We need to be wary," Jace interjects. "Any time Rory leaves the dojo, this guy might be close. I have some of my intel officers on it, looking for data."

"I'll do the same," Drew adds, his gaze shifting toward Jace.

Jace briefly catches Drew's eye, but neither of them add anything else. I suspect they'll have a tense conversation about this later, in private—and I'm completely fine letting that happen.

"Talk to me about this meeting with the Bosses," I say, desperate to change the subject.

"We leave in a few days." Jace reclines in his chair, absently rubbing the stubble along his jaw as he speaks. "All in all, we're slated to spend roughly three days in a neutral zone that's outside of any one dragon family's control."

"Sure," Drew snorts derisively. "If you can believe for even one moment that it's actually neutral."

"This one is." Jace's voice drops an octave, taking on a gravelly tone as he meets Drew's challenge. "I saw to it myself."

"Be ready for some unpleasant surprises," Drew says with a shrug, his gaze drifting to me. "That's all I'm saying."

"Why the hell are we going, then?" Tucker asks, incredulous.

"Good question," Drew says with a sidelong glare at Jace.

"Oh, don't *you* start," the dojo master impatiently snaps.

"They want to size me up," I answer, since those two are just arguing instead of contributing something useful to the conversation. "They probably want to test me. My skills, resilience, and strength. My power."

"They want to know if you're worth going to war to obtain," Drew corrects, his forceful gaze trained on me. "If you're worth stealing."

I frown, unsure of how to reply. He's not wrong, but I'm not going to shy away from this.

"Rory, seriously," Tucker says, leaning toward me. "Why are you doing this?"

I sigh.

I'm going for a lot of reasons, actually—some of which I can't share while Jace is nearby.

The Darringtons did something not many can do—they surprised me. They truly and completely caught me off-guard, and it's because I never had the opportunity to face off with a Boss before.

"I don't know what I'm up against," I answer. "*Who* I'm up against. Their abilities. Their intelligence. When I see someone for the first time, I can gauge them. I can see through them. Intel is great and incredibly useful," I say with a nod toward Jace. "But there's something about seeing someone in person—I can often figure out who I'm facing off with, what they want, and how to disarm them. I can see the kind of person I'm up against. More than that, I can draw the line. Since I acquired this power, they've hunted me. I think it's time they realized what exactly I can do to those who come after me."

Sure, I could stay holed up behind walls for the rest of my life, but I shouldn't have to lock myself away.

And I refuse to do so.

This meeting is the chance for me to make it clear what I will and will not put up with. I need to make plain what happens to those who come for me—like the Darringtons did.

They got away with it once, and I will never let it happen again.

"Well, damn," Tucker says, his eyebrows shooting up his forehead as he processes everything I said. "All right, then."

Drew sighs and leans back in his chair—his own form of resignation, and the only confirmation I'm going to get from him that he's on board.

"We need to review the dragon families who will be there," Jace says, flipping once more through his remaining stack of papers. "The most notorious ones are, of course, the Darringtons."

He tugs out a picture of Jett and Milo, tossing them on the table between me and Drew. Drew tenses as his eyes drift toward the pictures, and he shoots another sidelong glare at the dojo master.

"I know about the dragon families," I say, wanting to stop any tension from building before it gets out of hand.

Jace shakes his head and taps Jett's picture with his pointer finger. "Not in this context. They each want something from you, Rory, and you need to make sure you don't play into their hands."

"And what do the Darringtons want with her?" Drew asks ominously, a tense frown on his face.

The dojo master tilts his head toward the Darrington heir, his hand briefly balling into a fist as he no doubt suppresses all the things he wants to say to Drew. "To use her, of course." Jace's voice is growly and deep, brimming with chilly rage. "Like they use everyone."

Drew's scowl deepens, and the two men look moments from tearing each other apart.

"Jett and Milo Darrington," I interject, tapping the photos as I try to diffuse the tension with what information I do know. "They're the oldest and most powerful family. Darringtons are mostly fire dragons, and they control a network of natural resources, governments, and industries globally."

"Don't forget," Jace adds, sitting back in his chair. "They're notorious for thinking they're above the rules and that they can get away with anything."

"They usually do, don't they?" Drew asks, narrowing his eyes in a barely contained challenge.

"What do they want with Rory?" Tucker asks, his eyes shifting between the two dragon shifters who look moments from tearing out each other's spines. "How do they want to use her?"

"As a weapon, probably," Jace says, never taking his eyes off of Drew.

"Guys," I snap. "Cut it out."

In unison, Jace and Drew briefly look at me, cross their arms, and glare in opposite directions. It would be funny, if they weren't seconds from killing each other.

"Okay, so that's the Darringtons," Tucker says warily, no doubt trying to understand where their tension was coming from. With everything going on, I haven't had the chance to tell him about Drew's heritage. This probably looks strange and unsettling from his perspective. "Who else will be there? The Vaer?"

"The Vaer aren't coming," Jace says. "They break so many treaties that they're considered rogue. They're no longer welcome at events like these, and any Vaer will be killed on sight."

"Good," I say with a curt nod. "I wouldn't want to play nice with any of them, anyway."

"So that's the Darringtons and the Vaer," Tucker says, ticking them off on his fingers. "That leaves the Palarne, Nabal, Fairfax, Bane, and Andusk families."

Easy. I've studied all of them and recited facts and details for Zurie all my life.

Jace lays a picture of an elegant woman on the table, and I instantly recognize the Andusk Boss.

"Elizabeth Andusk," he says, tapping the picture.

Oh, I'm aware of who she is.

Zurie sent me off more than once on missions funded by this vain woman. I've stolen dozens of rare paintings, priceless statues, and glimmering jewels for her, though she never knew it was me.

The Andusk family are typically fire dragons who prefer warm climates. Easy to spot because they're the only gold dragons known to exist. They're vain, materialistic, and they hoard wealth.

They also tried to kidnap me once already, so I'm not altogether fond of them.

"The Andusk probably just want to show me off," I say, leaning back in my chair.

"Probably," Jace admits. "They would never be able to contain you, though. Their military isn't nearly strong enough."

I grin, taking that as a compliment.

Jace tosses two pictures on top of Elizabeth's—one woman with loose brown curls, and a man with cropped hair and a rifle in his hand. "Natasha and Victor Bane."

Ah, yes. These guys.

The Bane family are fire dragons who view laws as guidelines that hold others back. They deal mainly in illegal activities, and of all seven dragon families, Zurie tended to hand out assignments to kill the Bane more often than not.

Victor is the Boss, but I've heard his sister Natasha likes to bend others to her whims. Especially men.

"They probably want to sell you," Drew says with a scowl, glaring at the duo's pictures.

"Lovely." I grimace.

"No one will touch you, Rory," Jace says intently.

"I'll see to it. You have the entire Fairfax army to protect you."

I smile, appreciating the gesture even if it is overkill.

"Harper will also be there," Jace says casually. "So, you'll at least have one familiar face at the table."

I nod at the mention of his cousin's name, but I'm still not sure where I stand with her. She's the total opposite of Jace, and yet probably just as brutal on a battlefield.

The Fairfax family is the only family with thunderbirds. Even though they have natural magical ability, most of them prefer to think of life as a game. Zurie always warned me that, to the Fairfax dragons, adrenaline is more important than money—they're hard as hell to kill.

"Aki Nabal," Jace says, throwing a man's photo on the pile. His high cheekbones and dark hair give him an elegant and aristocratic air. His features suggest Japanese heritage, and his dark hair contrasts sharply with his light skin.

Ah, right. The Nabal.

They're wealthy fire and ice dragons who deal in information. They have an eerie knack for figuring out intel they shouldn't know anything about. No one knows much about the Nabal, and I suspect that's how they like it.

"They probably want to dissect me," I say with a

laugh, only half-kidding. "They like figuring things out, so I'm sure they'd love to know what makes me tick."

"That's super not funny," Tucker says with a grimace.

I shrug.

"And lastly, Isaac Palarne," Jace says, ignoring my joke as he throws one last picture on the pile. A familiar man stares back at me, his dark eyes intense. His chocolate skin is a warm contrast to the cool sky behind him in the photo, and his expression bores into me as intently as if he were sitting across from me.

"Yeah, we've met," I say simply, stiffening in my seat.

After my run-in with Isaac, I'm not sure how to feel about the Palarne dragons. They're supposed to be noble fire and ice dragons known for their honor and war skill, but he seemed a little too eager to get me to return to the capital.

And I have no idea why.

"Every one of these dragons will be there," Jace says intently, tapping his finger on the pile of photos. "They all want you for various reasons, and we need to make sure they don't get the opportunity to fly off with you in their claws."

"That would be nice to avoid," I say.

"I want you accompanied at all times," Jace continues. "You're not to go out alone during the event."

I tilt my head toward him, not bothering to mask my annoyed expression.

"What?" he asks with a shrug. "Do you want me to say please, or something? This is serious, Rory. These people are dangerous."

In answer, I just sigh and pinch the bridge of my nose in frustration.

"She shouldn't sleep alone, either," Tucker says with a wry grin, wrapping his arm around me and tugging me closer. "I'll do my part in this fight."

I shake my head and set my face in my hands, but I can't keep myself from laughing at this lovable idiot.

"As much as I hate to admit it, you're right," Jace says through gritted teeth. I lift my brows in surprise, but the dojo master continues before I can make a sarcastic comment. "It would be easiest for someone to sneak in while Rory is asleep."

Exasperated with how long it's taking him to grasp my capabilities, I just point to myself. "Do you even know how many traps I set before I go to sleep every night?"

"Eight," Tucker says with a confident nod.

I chuckle. "Tucker, that was rhetorical."

"Am I wrong?"

"Very."

"Damn. High or low?"

"Low."

"I'm not willing to take the risk, Rory," Jace interrupts.

"Fine," I say with a shrug.

He hesitates, as if he can't believe I agreed with him, but he only pauses for a moment. "We'll have to be cautious. The castle grounds themselves will look inauspicious enough, but the forests surrounding the castle will be teeming with soldiers. Everyone will bring their armies, just in case."

"In case of what?" I ask.

Jace studies me for a moment, as if debating whether or not to tell me the truth. "In case they can take you," he finally admits. "In case there's a moment —even just one—where they can get away with kidnapping you."

An uncomfortable silence settles on the room, and I let it sit there. I don't fight it. I want to make sure I don't sweep this aside or assume I can handle it solo. Even Jace can only take on twenty dragons or so at a time—and we're walking into a den of hundreds, maybe thousands.

Each dragon family wants me, and each will keep the other at bay.

For now.

Jace and Drew know this world. They've lived it, even fought on opposite sides. As much as it pains me to give up control, I'm going to let Jace and Drew steer on this one. Their advice matters. Their protection counts.

When we step onto the castle grounds, we're trusting a fragile truce between six families that have all been at war with each other at some point over the years.

Every movement and every word must be chosen carefully. And whatever we do, we're going to do it as a team.

The five of us—together. Whether Jace and Drew like it or not.

CHAPTER SIX

A few hours after our meeting about the Bosses, I finally got to stretch my legs and train.

After I let loose a blast of my magic, only a smoking crater remained of the boulder that had once sat on the edge of the small clearing Jace and I use for training.

"That's an improvement," Jace says with a proud nod. "At least you didn't blow a hole in the mountain this time."

I roll my eyes. "Har freaking *har.*"

"Yeah, babe," Tucker says. "That was impressive."

I peek over my shoulder to find him standing in a firing stance with a rifle pressed against the crook of his arm. A row of circular red and white targets lines the edge of the cliff in front of him.

"Those are for Rory," Jace says with a slight frown, crossing his arms.

Tucker shrugs. "She'll just blow them up."

"Hey, now." I gesture toward my body. "This is pure control and power over here, thank you."

"Don't make me regret allowing you to train with us, Tucker," Jace says with a disappointed tilt of his head. "Stop distracting her."

"Fine." Tucker returns his attention to the targets and instantly fires five shots, each one hitting a perfect bullseye. The modified silencer on the barrel subdues what would have been thundering booms to mere pops.

I whistle, impressed. "Show off."

Dashing as ever, Tucker flashes me a broad grin and winks at me over his shoulder, all without lowering his gun. "What should I shoot next, Rory? The rocket launcher?"

"Well don't you have a ton of fun toys," I quip.

"Yeah, because he keeps stealing them from me." A small grin tugs at Jace's mouth, and I'm surprised to see he's not nearly as frustrated now as he's been with Tucker's thievery in the past.

I set my hands on my hips, the corners of my lips twisting upward as I study the dojo master. "He saves your life *once*, and now he's suddenly on your good side, huh?"

"Hey." Tucker points two of his fingers at his own eyes and then turns his fingers toward me, as if he's saying he'll watch me like a hawk. "Don't ruin this for me."

I chuckle.

"Don't get cocky, Tucker," Jace chides, crossing his arms. "But yes, Rory. He saw something that I missed. That saved my life and kept you from fracturing—or possibly going feral even before your dragon emerges. So, I'll admit, he's redeemed himself."

"Nah," Tucker says with a wry grin. "Jace just thinks I'm pretty."

Jace laughs, shaking his head and setting his face in his hand. "You really are too much, man."

Tucker shrugs and once more aims his rifle at the targets. "I'm fun at parties."

"All right, Rory. Let's focus," Jace says.

I sigh and look at him, waiting for the next exercise.

"Control the blast this time," Jace says. "Restrain it, minimize it, and only permit a small ray of it through."

I lift my eyebrows, not entirely sure how to even begin.

Jace seems to sense my hesitation and gestures toward another boulder nearby. "Just try it."

"Okay," I say, dubious. "Here goes nothing."

I lift my hand and aim my palm toward the center of the boulder, dipping into the magic in my chest as I've done so many times before. Each time I touch the magic swirling in my core, it becomes easier to feel it. Easier to control.

And, to my delight, it becomes even more *powerful.*

But Jace has a point. I need to be able to rein it in just as much as I let it loose. If I can't limit the power of an attack, my magic still controls me, in a way.

Heat billows down my arm, and white light simmers above my skin. It glistens and shifts like the northern lights, hovering over my body as I bring it forth.

I let out a slow and focused breath as my eyes narrow in focus. My fingers tingle with the raw power burning within me. It aches to break free, to wreak havoc, to burn and simmer and boil whatever it touches.

It wants to set the world *aflame.*

"Shh," I say softly, soothing the beast within.

To my delight, the magic softens ever so slightly at my reassuring voice.

My arm trembles from the effort of restraining the magic that aches to break free, but I keep it contained.

Barely.

"That's it," Jace says with an excited tone. "Breathe."

I hadn't realized I was holding my breath, but I take that moment to suck in some air. Relief bleeds through my chest, but the tension remains in my shoulders.

"Do it," Jace orders. "Now."

I release what I think will be a tiny blip of light—and, instead, a towering beam of energy breaks free from my palm. It cuts through the world like a blinding ray of concentrated sunlight and slices through the boulder, kicking up dust.

Coughing, I bat at the air to clear the plumes of dust. It takes a moment for the air to clear, but once it does, I can see the perfect hole I carved through the middle of the boulder—one that's roughly the size of my head.

Not *quite* what I was going for.

"Well, it is *smaller*," Jace says with a shrug, examining the hole. "I mean, usually you just blow things to rubble."

"Thanks," I say dryly.

He looks at me out of the corner of his eye, the edge of his mouth tilting upward in a cocky grin as he seems to debate whether or not to toy with me.

Thankfully, he chooses not to.

"Let's call it a day," he says.

"What?" I gesture to the forest around us. "You're not going to make me do that a million times before supper?"

He hesitates, smirking. "Do you want me to?"

"No," I say quickly. "Duh."

He laughs. "I would rather we work on something else. Something more important."

He takes a few steps closer, and as he nears, my body instinctively leans toward him. My mind goes fuzzier and fuzzier the closer he gets, and I have to fight to stay coherent enough to understand what he's saying.

He presses his finger against my sternum, the gentle tap of his fingertip shooting electricity through my chest. "Your shift."

"It hasn't moved again," I say with a hint of disappointment. "Not even a little."

"That's fine," Jace says with a relaxed shrug. "I want you to reach for it, this time. See if you can make it stir."

I take a deep breath to brace myself and close my eyes. I listen, reaching inward and looking for the same frighteningly beautiful sensation I felt before, when I nearly collapsed on his living room floor. As painful as it was, it meant my dragon was coming to life—and if I don't take care of her, she might die.

"Shifting takes trust," Jace says quietly, his voice moving as he circles me. "It takes a certain surrender to give a bit of control over to your dragon. Dragons are wild creatures driven by impulse and hunger." His finger brushes the back of my arm, stirring a flurry of desire deep within me, teasing me with an alternate meaning of the word. "It will take time to build that trust."

Finally, there's a blip of life deep within. A twisting sensation that feels like something coiling around itself, deep within my core. I gasp impulsively, trying to resist the impulse to pull away.

"Good," he says. "Go deeper. Touch it. Tell it what you want."

I square my shoulders.

Shift.

Nothing happens.

Please, I add.

It twirls again, retreating further within, and slips from my grasp. I frown and open my eyes, frustrated.

"It's fine," Jace says calmly, setting his hand on my shoulder. "It takes time."

"I don't *have* time." I run my hands through my hair, resisting the impulse to punch something in frustration. "The Bosses are going to test me, the Spectres are after me, the Knights want me dead, and—"

"Rory," Jace interrupts, holding both my shoulders as he stares deep into my eyes.

His stormy grey gaze snares me once more, holding me in place, giving me a moment of stillness despite the tempest of emotions blowing through me right now.

"You can't rush these things," he says with utter confidence. "You have a dragon in you, and that's more than anyone ever expected. She's growing quickly, but you can't rush it. She grows when she grows—but the moment she's ready, you have to be there to catch her. Do you understand me?"

"I think so," I say with a nod. "Patience just isn't really my thing."

"Yeah, no joke." Jace flashes that cocky grin of his.

I playfully push him away as punishment for that little jibe, but the warrior shifter just laughs and effortlessly recovers.

"It'll happen," he promises, setting his arm around my shoulders. His touch ignites sparks of energy throughout my body, and I can't help but appreciate his confidence in me.

For him, it's not if I'll shift—it's when.

I may have grown up hunting dragons, but the thought of becoming one is dazzling. The power. The strength.

The *freedom*.

I can hardly wait.

CHAPTER SEVEN

I sit at the edge of a cliff, watching the sun set on another day in the dojo. With a deep sigh, I lean back on my palms and let my legs dangle over the ridge.

Jace's confidence in my ability to shift is endearing, but I find it hard to be patient. Every time I think of the Bosses, the Vaer, Zurie, or Diesel, I just want to give in to this aching need in my chest to shift. I want to show them I'm not to be messed with, that the dragon in me won't allow it.

But I can't.

I *can't* shift.

Not yet. My dragon's just not ready.

I groan and fall onto my back, staring up at the branches above me. The canopy inches toward the cliff, like the trees are afraid to look into the foggy abyss, and bits of the blue sky break through the leaves above.

In a blue, blurry rush, Levi's head leans over me. His nose dangles inches from my face, and he smiles a *very* toothy smile.

I gasp violently in surprise and instantly burst out laughing, my hand on my chest as my heart races from the shock of his sudden appearance. "Oh, gods. That must be how Tucker feels every time I sneak up on him."

A few huffing breaths escape Levi—a dragon laugh.

Only Levi can get away with this. Seriously, I have no idea how he learned to be so stealthy, but he surpasses even Zurie's ability to sneak.

I sit upright and lean one relaxed elbow on my knee, observing the ice dragon as he curls around me. His tail drapes over the ledge, and he sets his head on the ground beside me.

He growls with pleasure, his eyes fluttering closed, and he nibbles affectionately at my knee. His touch tickles, and I chuckle again as we love on each other. I adore the little things that remind me of the human man within this massive dragon.

Absently, I run my fingers along his forehead, happy to see him. In a rush, our connection opens, and emotion floods through my fingers and into my core.

Calmness.

Satisfaction.

Peace.

And, underneath it all, a steady hint of worry.

My smile falls, and I try not to think about it so that I don't stir up his own thoughts through our now-open connection. I know he's worried about being feral, about losing himself to his dragon, and it won't do much good to push him into talking about it.

What's bothering you? he asks.

"My shift," I admit. "There's this—this *urge,* this overwhelming need to do it, but my dragon isn't ready yet. It sets me on edge, Levi."

I remember those days. He lifts his head, and I slide my hand along his neck to maintain the connection as he looks out over the misty ravine below us. *The ache. I once leapt off a cliff to force it.*

"Really?" I peek at the ravine below us.

Don't you dare, Rory, Levi says, giving me a sidelong glare. A protective surge of energy bleeds through our connection, his warning against following in his foot-steps. *I was a dumb kid. It didn't work.*

"Fine." I roll my eyes.

I miss it, he admits. *That feeling.*

"Which one?"

Trust. He sighs and lays his head on the ground once more. *Trust in my dragon.*

My jaw tenses, and I don't know what to say. I run

my finger along his forehead again, trying my best to comfort him.

I've never really been good at comforting others, but for Levi, I'll try.

He won't let me shift back, Levi says, his eyes closing. *I hate him, sometimes.*

My heart twists at the confession. "Levi…" As I trail off, at an utter loss for words, I wrap my arms around his neck. He growls softly, leaning in to me, and a flood of sadness bleeds through from him.

Loss.

Pain.

Devastation.

Isolation.

"What happens when you try to shift?" I ask.

He's too strong. Levi sighs. *Blocks me.*

I haven't found much information on what makes a dragon feral, but what I have discovered doesn't bode well for my ice dragon. In moments of intense trauma, the dragon takes over as an act of self-preservation—and never lets go. It's a fracture, in that moment, where the dragon and the shifter no longer trust each other.

Shifters need balance to survive, Levi says, no doubt reading my thoughts. *We need each other.*

"You'll fix this, Levi. You can still heal."

Maybe. He doesn't sound convinced.

"What happened?" I ask, careful with how I prod

into this. "Can you tell me? We can work through it together."

He pauses, his eyes shifting toward me as he hesitates to answer.

"You don't have to," I remind him, even though I want nothing more than to help him through this. "Only if you want."

He sighs, and a flurry of snow cascades from his nose. *I was in an elite squad. Defense. Learned stealth from my teachers. Was the best.*

It hurts to hear the fractured thoughts and crumbling sentences. It's like he slips in and out of being totally coherent, capable of full thought sometimes and not others. It reminds me of how far gone he already is, but I cling to the fact that he's still here. He's still talking to me, so he's not gone.

I won't let him fade completely.

There's a rustle of leaves behind us as someone walks closer, but I ignore it. I don't want to lose this moment with Levi.

"Do you remember what made you feral? Maybe we can—"

He snarls, as if someone stabbed him. Instantly, he breaks the connection, stepping away from me as his wings spread wide.

"Levi, wait—"

He takes off without another word, the gust from

his wings violently tussling my hair. He roars into the sky as he dives into the misty ravine below, and just as quickly as he appeared, he's gone.

"Damn it." I rub my eyes, furious with myself for pushing him too far. I hadn't realized—

"Yeah, he does that to me, too," Tucker says from behind me. "Any time we talk about what made him feral, he up and leaves."

I peer over my shoulder to find Tucker with his hands in his pockets, watching the ravine as he leans against a tree. Our eyes meet, and I sigh in resignation. "He can't avoid this forever."

"No, he can't," Tucker says, joining me. As he plops down in the dirt where Levi sat moments before, he sets a comforting arm around my shoulders.

"Whatever happened must have been truly horrible," I say absently.

"Yeah," Tucker admits. "He's not usually one to avoid talking about the difficult things."

I shake my head in frustration. "He has to face this. He has to heal it, or we'll lose him."

"I'm looking into it," Tucker says. "But there's no recorded history of a dragon coming back from being feral. Ever."

Right. That's what everyone keeps telling me.

I tap my finger on my lips, deep in thought. "Maybe we need to change our focus."

"What do you mean?"

"Maybe instead of looking for someone else who's done it, we need to better understand what makes it happen in the first place. Is it really just self-preservation of the dragon? Or is there a way to rebuild the trust between the two of them? If we can figure that out, maybe we can reverse it."

"That's a good idea, babe," Tucker says, squeezing my shoulder. "I'll see what I can find out."

"Me, too," I promise. "Drew and Jace said they're looking into it, too. Between the four of us, we'll find something. We have to."

In fact, I think I know a fifth person who can help— though I'm not entirely fond of asking for a favor.

We sit for a while in silence, both of us lost in thought as we enjoy the lingering sunlight burning behind the mountains. Ribbons of orange and yellow light dance through the clouds as dragons fly by, seemingly immune to the beauty.

"Are you ready for all hell to break loose?" Tucker eventually asks. "With this meeting…"

"Yeah," I say with a grin. "I'll be fine as long as I have a badass like you at my side."

He grins and kisses my nose, all flirty fun once again. "Face it, you only like me for my guns."

"Sir, I am insulted." I feign offense and set my hand on my heart to really sell it. "I also like your body."

He laughs and pokes me in the side before smothering me with kisses. As I chuckle, enjoying this ridiculous man beside me, I can't help but be grateful. No matter what's going on, even if the world is ending, Tucker can always make me laugh—and remind me of the joy in everything.

Even when everything else feels dire.

CHAPTER EIGHT

Since we leave to meet with the Bosses tomorrow, I take the chance to sit on my roof one more time before we head out. This place helps me settle my racing thoughts, and I like it up here.

The sunrise is beautiful, as always, and I smile as I take a deep breath of the breeze billowing through my hair. I close my eyes as the first rays of sun finally peek above the horizon and hit my skin. Content, I drink in the light's warmth.

The clink of hands grabbing shingles catches my attention. Seconds later, someone hoists themselves onto the roof, and footsteps crunch toward me.

For a moment, I expect Drew—but this isn't his gait. It's too light. The gap between each step is shorter than his are. This is someone else.

I tense, unsure of what to expect.

When in doubt, I prepare for war.

I tilt my head over my shoulder, feigning a relaxed glance even as I curl my fingers into a fist and get ready to break a nose or two. I may look calm, but I'm prepared to punch this person hard enough to knock them off the damn roof if they try anything.

To my surprise, Harper walks toward me with a warm smile on her face.

I relax my fist, but only slightly. I like this woman, but I'm never quite sure what to expect of her.

Unpredictability must be a common Fairfax trait.

"May I join you?" the Fairfax Boss asks.

I nod.

She sits beside me, her hands around her knees as she looks out over the beautiful forest that surrounds the dojo. "Are you ready for tomorrow?"

I shrug. "Ready as I'll ever be, I suppose."

"I know you're not used to the spotlight," Harper says with a relaxed tilt of her head. "I figure this is going to be quite the challenge, but I know you can do this."

With a sidelong glance, I watch her for a moment. Up until now, I assumed she knows nothing about my past—but with that little comment, I start to doubt myself a little.

Jace is hellbent on Harper never knowing about the Spectre—soon to be *Spectres*—in his midst. Perhaps, however, Harper has her own means of discovering information.

But she continues to smile, and if she's bothered by any of it, she doesn't let it show.

Interesting.

"I'm sure you know I'll be there," Harper adds.

"So I've been told."

"I have to warn you," the Fairfax Boss says. "I'll be... well, different."

"How so?"

"I call it Boss Mode," Harper says with a playful grin, her gaze shifting toward me as she speaks. "No humor. No laughter. I have to look as though I'll go to war at any moment. If I'm my usual, jovial self at these meetings, the other Bosses get a little too comfortable with me. They push boundaries they know better than to push."

I grin. I can't help it. "The poor fools."

"Right?" Harper lifts her hand, clearly incredulous. "Thank you. You understand."

I shrug. "I know what it's like to be underestimated."

"Yeah, I bet you do," The Boss says teasingly as she returns her attention to the forests beyond. "That said, I can't let them realize we're friends. You can't seem to have picked sides, at least not yet."

I don't answer. I'm still ruminating on the word *friends*, so casually tossed into the conversation, as if it's already fact. As if my lifelong training hadn't taught me friendship is a weakness to exploit. As if I even know how to let my guard down long enough to have one.

I'm not sure if I like it, or if I agree. I mean, I enjoy Harper, but she's still a Boss. She has the resources, opportunity, and authority to *truly* destroy my life and everything I love.

Technically, she walks among my enemies.

"Jace gave me the antidote breakdown," Harper says, continuing without so much as a pause. "I'm sure he's given you the rundown on what happens next. Even though it will take time to disperse and produce it, we're giving it a little financial push. The antidote will be on the market in three to four months."

I frown. "Is that soon enough?"

"I don't like it, either, but it's the absolute fastest we can do," Harper admits with a frown. "If something happens sooner, the companies will expedite production on governmental orders. We're just waiting on the red tape to clear, and I have some production going on as we speak to help offset the risk. As soon as the bureaucracy is over, there's going to be four crates of the antidote in every hospital worldwide."

"Good." I take a deep breath, my shoulders relaxing a little at the thought of disarming Kinsley. "Will the Vaer have notice?"

"None." Harper curls her thumb and pointer finger together in the shape of an "O." "Big fat zero. Everything is done under the radar. As far as Kinsley is concerned, she'll wake up one day to a useless bio-weapon."

I smirk. Serves her right.

"Unless the other Bosses tell her, of course," Harper adds with a frustrated sigh. "But they all hate the Vaer as much as you and I do, so that's a minimal risk."

"Kinsley can still make more," I point out. "New variations. New styles."

"Maybe," Harper admits with a nod. "I guess we'll cross that bridge when we get there, huh?"

The Fairfax Boss smiles knowingly at me, and I have to confess—despite the raw power she wields, she somehow manages to be utterly endearing.

I don't know how she does it. It's like a radiant, adorable superpower.

"Did you just come to check on me?" I ask, tilting a skeptical eyebrow. "Or is there another reason you're here?"

Harper chuckles. "Not everyone's out to use you, Rory."

"It's a fair question."

The woman sighs deeply. "There is one thing, yes."

My smile fades, and I tilt my head away to hide my disappointment. Before she has the chance to ask anything of me, there's something I want to ask of her. "First, I'd like a favor."

"Oh?"

I was going to wait until the meeting, when I knew

I'd see her, but now is a safer time to get this ball rolling. Fewer possible witnesses. "I need information on how to get a dragon back from the brink of being feral." I pause, careful with how I phrase my words. "As well as what causes the fracture in the first place."

"Ah." In the corner of my eye, Harper nods knowingly. "You're worried about Levi."

I don't answer. It's not necessary. At this point, I would rather she think whatever she wants, as long as I get my intel.

"I'll see what I can find, Rory." Harper adjusts her weight, getting more comfortable as we sit together on the roof. "I have some very capable people on my staff."

"I'm sure you do."

It's why I asked her. A Boss has access to things even a General doesn't. If anyone can get me the information I need, it's Harper.

The problem is—what will it cost me?

"I realize a favor needs to be repaid," I say cautiously. "I reserve the right to say no to what you ask for."

To my surprise, Harper laughs.

And she laughs *hard*.

I tilt my head in confusion as her face lights up with amusement. She covers her mouth with her hand, and after a moment, her bright eyes flit toward me. When she sees me entirely serious, her laughter starts to fade a bit—but the smile remains.

"What?" I ask, genuinely baffled.

"Rory, you don't owe me anything," Harper says, still chuckling. "It's so adorable that you're always this —I don't know, straight-laced and serious."

My eyes narrow. I'm skeptical, now. "Why wouldn't I owe you anything?"

Harper tilts her head away from me, like she's studying something fascinating. After a moment's hesitation, she grins. "You're new to friendship, aren't you?"

I chuckle humorlessly, draping one arm over my propped knee as I look out at the growing sunrise. "Maybe."

"I'll help you out, then," Harper says, leaning back on her palms. "Friends do things for each other not because they have to, but because they want to see each other succeed. Keep that in mind the next time you ask for a favor, okay?"

"Okay," I say with a smile, still not entirely sure I believe it. But if it means Levi gets saved, I'm happy. "What did you come to talk to me about?"

"I came to warn you, actually," Harper corrects.

In the brief moment of silence that follows, I marvel at this woman next to me, surprised that she actually didn't come to get anything from me at all. It's a surreal feeling to have a dragon Boss looking out for me—at no cost.

Harper shrugs sheepishly. "Yes, I wanted to check

on you before the meeting, but you need to be extra careful moving from one location to the next. We detected chatter on one of the leading threats against you, and he's moving in."

I sit up a little straighter, focused now. "What chatter?"

"We don't have a ton to go on yet, but someone is hunting you. A loner, from the sounds of it, but I think he's working on someone's behalf. When they behave like this, they always are." She frowns, her jaw briefly tensing in disdain.

I'm reminded, then, of just how much Harper has seen in her life. The blood. The betrayal, probably. She's not some sweet young woman with a bubbly personality—she's a warrior.

Only someone with a death wish would forget that.

My mind wanders back to the man I nearly shot in the little girl's backyard. This threat coming after me— my gut says it's him. "Who is this guy?"

"We don't know yet," Harper confesses. "We're working on it. What we do know is *not* good, Rory. This man has some serious connections to dangerous people. We're getting every shred of intel we can, but it's become evident that he has the means to intercept you in transit. Stay alert."

"I always do," I say. "But thank you for the warning."

"Jace knows, too," the Fairfax Boss adds. "He's

building in extra layers of security. Various cars, decoys, the works."

"Yeah, he's great with decoys," I say absently.

That damn second camera in Irena's hospital room. I almost can't believe I missed it—but Jace is far more skilled than I sometimes give him credit for.

"Stay safe, Rory." Harper stands, brushing off her shirt as she heads back to the window. "And stay wary. A lot of people want you dead, and many more want far worse."

I snort derisively. "What's worse than being dead?"

Harper pauses, studying my face with a somber expression. It's clear she's struggling with something internally, as if she's debating whether or not she should tell me what she knows.

"I know you're not some normal human girl," Harper eventually admits, her voice deadly serious. All the laughter and light is gone, for the moment. "Even before you became the vessel, you were a warrior. I can see it in the way you move and in your guarded demeanor. You've seen terrible people do vile things, haven't you?"

I don't answer. It isn't really a question. It's fact—one I'm impressed Harper picked up on.

"Imagine what those people would do to you now, Rory," Harper continues, gesturing to me. "These new people hunting you? Well, they're a lot more creative than anyone you've met thus far."

I impulsively tense, my hand coiling into a fist as my imagination begins to run away with me.

"Be careful." With a deep breath, Harper sets a reassuring hand on my shoulder. "Have as much fun as possible, and try not to die. I don't want to have to put my cousin down if he goes feral—or vice versa. You hear me?"

Shoulders tense, I nod.

"Good." With that, Harper turns her full back to me —a sign of trust. Moments later, she hoists herself over the edge near the window, and disappears into the window below.

Now alone on the roof, I can no longer enjoy the sunrise. Zurie is pretty damn creative, and her cruelty is the stuff of Spectre legend. Briefly, I wonder if Harper was talking about my former mentor—or if there is indeed someone far worse out there, gunning for me.

CHAPTER NINE

A s our bulletproof SUV rolls along a winding road surrounded by a thick forest, I anxiously tap my foot against the floor.

"This feels like overkill, Jace," I say with a glance upward through the back window at the dragon-filled sky.

Jace sits to my left, while Drew sits on my right. In the front seats, Tucker sits shotgun—with a literal shotgun in his lap—as a Fairfax chauffer takes us to the neutral zone for the meeting with the Bosses.

Overhead, hundreds of dragons soar through the air. Neutral zones like this lift the five-hundred-foot rule, and thus there are dragons everywhere—the trees, the edge of the road, the clouds.

And every head is fixated on the SUV. On me.

They know I'm here.

"We're in too deep at this point to turn back, Rory," Jace muses, casting a tense glare through the window. "And with your safety, there's no such thing as being too careful."

Levi maintains his position above our car as we speed toward the neutral zone. The casual flaps of his wings gently shake even the massive car, and it's reassuring to have him so close.

As we round the next bend, the road ends in a wrought iron gate. The delicate iron curls along the barrier tremble as it opens automatically for us, and I figure there must be cameras planted in the trees around us—no way does this gate let just *anyone* in.

As we pass through the entrance, the asphalt of the road is replaced by carefully laid brick that hums beneath the tires.

For a while, all we see is a brick driveway and the upward curve of a hill. After another sharp bend, however, we're treated to a beautiful sight.

The tree line ends abruptly in the perfectly manicured grass of a massive yard. Lines crisscross the endless yard, interrupted only by the beautiful brick pavers of the drive.

A castle looms into the sky at the top of the hill, overlooking the surrounding lands like a lighthouse watches over the sea. Easily ten stories tall, the fortress's light gray stone gently reflects the sunlight, giving it a soft and polished appeal.

"Wow," I say under my breath. "We're meeting in a castle?"

"Neutral zone seventeen," Drew says lazily, as if he's been here a dozen times before.

Hell, maybe he has.

"You admit it's neutral, then?" Jace says, lifting a skeptical eyebrow as he surveys the Darrington heir.

"He's harder to buy out than the others," Drew admits, not really answering the question. "But everyone has a price."

"What's yours?" Jace asks, his eyes narrowing in distrust.

Drew glares at the dojo master over me, and yet again, they look inches from tearing each other's throats out.

"Guys," I snap. "Stop it!"

Both men return their furious gazes out their respective windows, turning away from each other before they can cross the thin line between unspoken hatred and an all-out brawl.

The brick driveway passes by the two-story tall wooden doors, and we quickly reach the main entrance. As we do, the doors swing open, and a pudgy man steps out onto the grand front porch. The thick columns obscure his face at first as the car rolls to a stop. It's not until he begins to walk down the half-dozen steps to the brick driveway that I can get a good look. Though short and quickly balding, the middle-aged man smiles broadly in welcome as the car parks.

"Reginald Greaves," Drew says before I can ask the question. "Owner and caretaker."

"Let's go say hi," I quip.

Jace throws the door open. In seconds, he's standing on the brick, surveying the world around us as if Reginald isn't even there. Apparently satisfied, he offers me a hand, never once looking my way.

Jace is in full fighter-mode. It seems like conversation will have to wait.

I take his hand, mostly just to indulge him, and hop out of the car. After such a long ride, I take the moment to stretch my neck as I take in the sky full of dragons above me. There are easily three hundred, and it's eerily reminiscent of the swarm above the pit when I first acquired my new powers.

Oh *joy*.

"Welcome!" the caretaker says cheerily. "My name is Reginald Greaves. Please, though, call me Reggie," he insists, shaking my hand and affectionately setting his other palm on top of our joined fists.

The corners of my mouth tilt upward as I survey the caretaker. It takes a strong man to not be fazed by hundreds of dragons swirling overhead. I suspect there's more to Reggie than meets the eye.

"Nice to meet you, Reggie," I say with a polite nod, surprised that I mean it.

Drew's door slams shut, followed shortly thereafter by Tucker's. The men join us at the front entrance, and Jace signals for the SUV to carry on. It rumbles to life and drives off.

Tucker's shotgun rests casually against his shoulder as he looks around at the expansive castle grounds and whistles, clearly impressed.

"Oh, sir, no—" Reggie gestures to the gun. "I'm afraid weapons are not permitted on the grounds."

"Are you joking?" Tucker grins and gestures toward Drew with his thumb. "Then you're not letting this guy on the property either, right? I mean, just look at him."

"I'm not as easy to win over as Jace is," Drew says, though he doesn't bother hiding the smirk on his face.

Reggie frowns. "Sir, you don't understand. I must insist—"

"Reggie. My dude." Tucker lowers the gun, pointing it toward the grass. "I am a human in an ocean of dragons. There's no way in *hell* I'm going in unequipped."

"Oh!" Reggie's eyebrows shoot up his forehead. "You're human? Well of course! Come, come. Let's get you all situated."

Reggie trots up the stairs, and I smirk. "That was easy," I say under my breath.

"Yeah," Tucker admits with a nod. "I thought I'd

have to smuggle them in. I should've brought way more."

I laugh.

Without a word, Jace sets his hand between my shoulder blades and ushers me up the stairs. His eyes scan the world around us as if he's expecting an army to charge us at any moment. Pushy and impatient as he is, I resist the impulse to bat his hand away.

He's stressed. We all are.

The four of us follow Reggie at a short distance as he charges through the main hall of the opulent castle. Though Tucker is instantly captivated by the golden chandeliers and priceless artwork set on display every ten feet or so, I scan the building for weaknesses.

Exits. Entrances. Possible secret doors. Obvious doors. Windows.

The works.

My training kicks in, and I strain my ears to listen for any hints of activity in the vast building. The clatter of pans filters through a crack in a nearby door, and I catch the roiling flame of a massive stove. The sweet smell of cakes wafts through the opening, and I figure they're preparing for quite the feast.

After all, there's more than a few officials here. I wonder if Reggie has to feed the armies hiding in the forests, too, or if that's the responsibility of each Boss.

Hell, I wonder if he even *knows* about them.

"We've prepared our most elegant villa for you,

Miss Quinn," he says with a reassuring smile over his shoulder.

My smile, however, falls.

He knows my last name.

My jaw tenses impulsively as I look away, frustrated. So much of my life is public, now. Commonplace and well-known.

Harper was right. I prefer my shadows to the spotlight.

"I'm trusting you two," I say quietly to Jace and Drew, who walk on either side of me.

"It's well-placed trust," Drew assures me, carefully surveying the walls around us. "In me, anyway."

"Cute," Jace snaps, not bothering to look at the Darrington on the other side of me.

I sigh.

Just focus, Rory.

I can do this.

"As I'm sure you know, this is a unique location." Reggie grins as he gestures to the grandeur around him with a broad sweep of his arm. "We are one of the few truly neutral zones in the world."

Drew and I share a doubtful glance.

"That's lovely," I say, trying my best to imitate regal women I've seen on television before.

It comes out a little more *sarcastic* than *regal*, but I guess it'll do.

Jace elbows me in the side, a slightly annoyed

expression on his face—so, no, I guess it didn't work after all.

I blow an annoyed raspberry and look away. I guess I'll just stick to my cutting sarcasm, then.

Reggie truly doesn't seem fazed by anything, however. If he even heard me, he doesn't acknowledge my tone. He leads us to a set of elegant double doors at the end of the hall, their glass panes covered with white silk. The sunlight outside shines through, illuminating the soft fabric like the sun through a cloud.

He pauses, smiling at us over his shoulder. "Welcome to my home."

As Reggie throws open the doors, he reveals a sprawling estate that rivals any king's palace. The balcony leans out over an elaborate rose garden littered with fountains and paved walkways. The rolling hills beyond seem to go on forever, only ending at least a mile away in a dense forest. Ten villas dot the expansive landscape, each at least three stories tall and built from the same soft stone as the main castle.

To my surprise, two hundred soldiers in the dojo's black and yellow uniform line the stairs leading down to the gardens below. They salute as Jace walks onto the balcony, each of them standing at attention as their commander joins them.

"Wow," I say under my breath.

I didn't think this place could be any more beautiful, but I was clearly wrong. Though Tucker and I share the same astounded expression, Drew looks bored. Jace surveys the landscape, tensed and ready for war.

"Please, this way," Reggie says with a gesture toward the stairs. We follow him down to the gardens, toward the primary villa at the center of the field.

Oh, fantastic. I'm in the middle of the damn field, where there's absolutely *no* chance of going anywhere undetected.

Freaking delightful.

"While you're here, you have full access to the castle," Reggie explains as we walk past the immobile soldiers. Looking at him, you'd think this was just a normal Friday for him.

Well, given his line of work, it very well may be.

"Meals are at eight, noon, and seven," he says casually. "However, you are my most valued guests, and the kitchens will happily make you anything you desire at any time, day or night."

"Oh, man," Tucker says with a grin, patting his stomach in anticipation. "You shouldn't have told me that."

"Tucker," Jace chides.

"My one request," Reggie adds, "is that you not go into the north wing. That's my private residence." The caretaker smiles warmly over his shoulder as he nears the villa closest to the castle.

"Jace, why didn't you give *me* a whole wing?" Tucker pouts. "All I got was a suite."

I grin. "You're really pushing your luck with him right now. You know that, right?"

Tucker winks at me.

Oh, he knows.

"Here you are." Reggie types a code on a small pad by the doorknob, and I instinctively watch him to get the combination.

Old habits.

A little light on the pad flashes green, and an embedded lock slides loose. He holds open the door to the villa for us. "Your private codes are on the kitchen counter, along with a few small tokens of our appreciation for staying with us."

The door opens to a massive foyer and a golden chandelier overhead. Farther into the enormous cottage, I find an elaborate kitchen and sprawling living room, ending in a sliding glass door currently draped with more glowing white silk. Doors branch off on either side of us, likely bedrooms or other sitting areas, and a set of stairs in the far left corner curls upward to the second floor.

On the kitchen counter, gift baskets filled with chocolates and cheeses offer a wide array of delicacies I've only dreamt of up until now. Tucker heads there first, digging through the baskets almost without a moment's pause.

"This will do," I say under my breath, resisting the

impulse to whistle in delight at the sheer beauty of the place.

I can't be won over with a few baubles, though, and I instantly begin to scan for cameras or hiding places.

None of us can be too careful, even in a supposed neutral zone.

"Thank you," Jace says curtly once the rest of us are through. "That'll be all for today, Mr. Greaves."

"Of course, sir," Reggie says with another broad smile. "Festivities begin tomorrow morning after breakfast."

I laugh humorlessly. "Festivities, huh? Is that what we're calling them, now?"

For the first time, Reggie's smile falters, and his confused gaze shifts between me and Jace. "I'm sorry, what?"

"Nothing," I say with a tense sigh. "Never mind."

"Very well." He tries to don his smile again, but this time, it's obviously forced. He takes a quick bow and shuts the door behind him.

Once the man's gone, I lift one eyebrow at Jace. "Festivities? Really?"

"It's the largest contract of his career," Drew answers before the dojo master can get a word in edgewise. "He doesn't know the details—just that this is a big deal."

"For him to remain neutral, it's best he know as little as possible," Jace adds. He scans the living room, shoulders tight with nerves. "Tucker, check the house and make sure it's secure. Drew—"

"I'll watch over Rory," Drew interjects.

Jace shoots a wary glare at the Darrington in our midst, but Drew isn't fazed. He relaxes casually against the kitchen counter and sizes up the dojo master, as if daring him to disagree.

After a brief moment of tense silence, Jace's gaze drifts to me. "Are you all right with that?"

I nod. Drew isn't going to do anything to me. Well, nothing *bad*. He has the libido of a teenager, and if he had his way, we would never leave his sheets.

"Fine." Jace frowns, clearly not happy with the arrangement. "I'll secure the perimeter." He walks briskly toward the front door, but pauses beside me. He sets a comforting hand on my shoulder and gives me a tense smile before his gaze shifts to Drew. The moment their gazes meet, Jace's smile disappears. The dojo master walks out the door, slamming it behind him.

"I'll go check for bogeymen," Tucker says, hoisting his shotgun over his shoulder. "You ladies just relax, now. Let the men do the work."

I laugh. "Shut up, Tucker."

He blows me a sarcastic kiss and begins opening doors, scanning each room as he clears them one by one.

"The woods are already filled to the brim," Drew

says in a quiet voice, nodding toward the sliding back door. "Everyone else got here early."

"Surprise, surprise," I mutter, leaning against the nearby wall. "I'm starting to wonder if this was a bad idea, Drew."

"It's not," he promises with a confident shake of his head. "This needs to happen."

"But your father is here," I point out, my gaze shifting toward him. "After he—"

"I know," Drew interjects, nodding curtly without letting me say anything more. He sighs and crosses his arms, watching the back doors warily. "I know."

"First floor is clear," Tucker shouts as he heads toward the stairs. "I was kidding though. You guys can totally help."

"Nah," I say with a shrug. "You've got this, honey."

He chuckles, shaking his head as he scales the stairs. Gun lifted and aimed into the hallway above, he briefly pauses at the top of the stairs before continuing. His footsteps thud above us, and I shake my head in disappointment.

Stealth, Tucker. We've been working on this.

"I have three emergency evacuation plans," Drew says, snaring my attention. "Four if they have a helicopter pad."

I smirk. "You *know* they have a helicopter pad."

He grins. "Four, then."

"I have a few, as well," I admit, absently scanning the

living room again even though I'm confident it's clear. "I just don't like how busy the skies are."

"Most of those were Fairfax dragons," Drew assures me, leaning his elbows on the black marble kitchen counter. "They aren't a concern."

"All it takes is one spat in the forest for everything to blow out of proportion," I remind him, leaning my head back against the wall. "You dragons sure know how to hold a grudge."

"Us dragons, huh?" He grins playfully. "You don't get to be selective about when you're one of us and when you're not."

I laugh. "I don't really feel like a dragon, yet."

"What'll it take?"

"Shifting," I say. "Easy."

"Well, hurry up, then," he says, snapping his fingers. "Chop, chop. Shift already."

"Oh, you think you're cute." I tilt my head, but it's hard to hide my charmed smile.

He grins and closes the gap between us, sparking butterflies in my chest the closer he gets. He gently runs his knuckles across my cheek, smiling a little as he leans in. Heat blasts through me at his touch, igniting my core, and I resist the impulse to weave my hands underneath his shirt. I want nothing more than to feel the hard lines of his muscle beneath my fingertips, but Jace doesn't know about us, yet—and given the way he and Drew always look seconds from killing each other, I'm not sure I want him to.

"You look tense," Drew says, leaning over me.

"Can't imagine why," I joke. "It's not like there's six dragon armies surrounding me right now or anything."

He grins, his eyes drifting to my lips. "If you need help relaxing, I might have a few ideas on how to take your mind off things."

I laugh as he grabs my hips and presses my ass against the wall, pinning me in place. His lips graze my neck, teasing me, but it's now fairly clear why he offered to "watch over" me.

"Go patrol or something," I say, smacking his hard abs. It's like hitting my hand against a rock, however, and touching his firm muscle only makes my heart beat faster.

"Jace said you're not to be left alone for any reason," Drew reminds me, his voice low and deep as he leans in toward my ear. "I'm just doing my duty to protect you."

His strong grip on my waist tightens, and my eyes impulsively flutter closed as I imagine the things he'd like to do to fill the time. I grin at his flimsy excuse to stay close, but I roll with it. "Well, if it's to keep me safe…"

"That's the spirit." He plants his lips on my neck, and tendrils of warmth spiral through my body with each of his kisses.

We could at least have a bit of fun before all the stress begins.

This meeting will be difficult. It will test us in every way, but I'm ready. Ready to face the Bosses. Ready to draw the line in the sand.

But the moment Irena wakes up—I'm gone, and I don't care *who* that offends.

CHAPTER TEN

Roughly an hour after we arrive, I sit on the luxurious sofa with my hair splayed across the back of it. Eyes closed, I sigh deeply with pleasure.

This thing feels like a freaking *cloud.*

With a smile on my face, I sink a little deeper into the plush cushions, wriggling until I'm perfectly comfortable.

In the kitchen, Drew fiddles with something metallic. Spoons scrape and glasses clink, and I wonder what the hell he's up to.

Tucker, Jace, and Levi are on patrol—something I've been told they'll be doing a lot of while we're here. I wanted to join, of course, but *oh, no*—I have to stay here and just be *bored.*

My four men seem to have agreed to some kind of

pact to watch over me and secure the surrounding area, and honestly, I'm just not going to fight it.

If it makes them feel more comfortable, let them do it. Besides, I like having a bit of added security in the midst of all the craziness outside.

The door beeps, the knob rattling as it turns, and I peek through half-closed eyelids as it swings suddenly open. In seconds, Drew is at the corner by the kitchen, a butcher's knife in his hand as he glares at the opening.

After a blinding flash of daylight, the door closes again, and Harper peeks outside through the eyehole without even looking back at us.

"What trouble are you getting into, Harper?" I ask with a wry grin on my face.

She looks at me over her shoulder and laughs. "All kinds." Her gaze shifts to Drew, her eyes darting briefly to the knife in his hands, and she lifts her eyebrow in challenge. "You going to put that down, cowboy?"

He frowns but relaxes and tosses the knife on the counter before returning to whatever he'd been doing.

Harper trots over to the couches and sits next to me, her hair splaying over the plush backrest in much the same way as mine. "Aren't these divine?"

"They sure are." I close my eyes and take another blissful breath.

"I think I'll try to buy the ones in my suite, but gods

help me. Reggie never lets me get away with *anything* here."

I chuckle. It seems like Reggie can, indeed, hold his own among dragons, then.

"I wanted to check on you," Harper adds. "How was the trip over?"

I drum my fingers absently on the cushion beside me. "Uneventful." I grin and steal a quick look at Drew before continuing. "And cramped."

He chuckles, but the towering, muscled man doesn't look my way.

"One of Jace's decoys wasn't so lucky," Harper admits.

I sit upright, now giving her my full attention. "What do you mean?"

"I mean they were intercepted," the Fairfax Boss says with a grim frown. "The car flipped four times, and a masked gunman shot both the driver and the decoy soldier riding in the back."

"What?" Drew demands, his smile fading as he towels off his hands and storms toward us at the news.

My fingers curl into a fist, and for a moment, I can't speak as my heart thuds against my chest. I'm disgusted, both with the hitman and myself. I never want someone to die for me, to—

"Rory, relax," Harper says, her eyes shifting between mine as she studies my face. "They're dragons, which means they're far tougher than they look. They're fine. Hurt, but alive."

I let out a shaky breath of relief.

"This guy has a death wish," Drew says, his voice dark.

"He does," I agree.

"When you leave, you need to be extra careful," Harper says, her gaze shifting between me and Drew. "Even more decoys. Disguises. I'm honestly not sure if it's safer to go without soldiers to avoid suspicion, or go with them in their human form to have back up. This guy—he's good."

"He's not *that* good if your people survived," Drew points out.

"Thanks for caring." Harper shoots Drew an annoyed glare. "He didn't realize they had dragonscale armor under their clothes. If they'd been without it, they'd be dead."

"He won't make that mistake again, then," I say, leaning back against the couch to process this news.

"Probably not," Harper admits.

"Lovely."

"It doesn't matter," Drew says with a confident shake of his head. "Not right now."

"How so?" I ask dubiously, not agreeing in the slightest.

"Rory, you need to focus on what's in front of you."

Drew points at the white curtains covering the sliding glass door in the rear of the house. "Those dragons are the immediate threat. We'll worry about this guy when we leave. No loner is going to make it here in one piece, not with this many armies on the property." He pauses, taking a deep breath. "Focus on one thing at a time."

"The Darrington is right," Harper says with a nod.

Drew lets out a frustrated groan and glares at Harper. "You're lucky she already knows."

"Oh, do you?" Harper lifts her eyebrows as her gaze shifts to me. "Good! I was worried he'd kept his secret from you somehow."

"Are you trying to get him in trouble?" I ask with a nod toward Drew.

"I just want to make sure you're prepared, Rory." Harper says with a shrug. "You need to know who you're up against, and technically, we're not in the embassy anymore. I can call him whatever I want."

Drew wrinkles his nose in annoyance.

"So, do you know what to do?" Harper asks, as if she hadn't just tried to reveal Drew's secret. "Tomorrow?"

"During the 'festivities?'" I ask with a chuckle. "Yeah. I'm set."

"Good. Keep your cards close to your chest, though I'm sure you're already familiar with that." Harper gives me a fleeting once-over glance, a knowing glint in her eye.

Yet again, I wonder how much she knows about me —and if she knows the truth, why does it seem like she doesn't care?

"I have news for you on the favor you asked of me," she adds, leaning in as her voice lowers.

"Oh?"

Drew frowns, his gaze shifting between the two of us, but he quietly walks away to give us space.

"The feral fracture happens during a mental break," Harper says quietly. "In eighty percent of cases, it came at a loss of life. It happens when a shifter loses someone close to him, someone special—usually, someone he protected."

Oh.

Oh.

It clicks for me, then. Levi's pain.

All the clues he's sprinkled across our conversations, probably not even realizing what he was telling me.

Levi lost someone dear to him—and when I saved him from the trap, he found someone new to protect.

It could very well be that his drive to keep me safe is the only thing that has kept him sane. It's proof to his dragon that he *can* protect others. That he's capable. That he's trustworthy.

He said that he and his dragon no longer trust each

other. Whatever happened to him, it left his dragon doubting his ability to keep control. To protect not just those they care about, but also each other.

"How do I fix this?" I ask quietly, more to myself than Harper.

"How does anyone rebuild trust?" she counters, leaning her head back against the couch with a sigh. "Slowly. Over time. Bit by bit, showing you've changed. Proving that you still care."

But Levi doesn't *have* time.

"If anyone can do this, Rory," Harper says with a smile, "it's you."

That disarms me. "Why are you so... *nice?*"

Harper laughs, arching her head against the plush sofa. "You really *aren't* used to friendship. Oh, gods."

I keep waiting for the catch. For the trick. For the young woman to show her cards and reveal herself to be a manipulator, like everyone else.

And she just... doesn't.

"We girls have to look out for each other, Rory." Harper winks at me and stands. "I admire your determination and strength. There aren't many who can take on Jace, after all."

The Fairfax Boss heads for the door with a sarcastic little nod in Drew's direction, and the fire dragon watches her warily as she leaves. I study the thunderbird shifter before me, wondering if this is, in fact, someone I can trust.

It feels too strange, too surreal to say I have a friend —but my life has gotten so bizarre, lately, that I'm at least open to the idea.

It wouldn't be the weirdest thing I've done in the last few months, after all.

CHAPTER ELEVEN

I sit upright in the darkness, my nerves suddenly on fire as I'm shaken awake by something I can't see.

Beside me, Tucker snores lightly with his head buried in his pillow. Moonlight illuminates the soft white curtains, the dim blue light casting a soft glow through the room. Tucker's weapon collection lies in neat rows along the hardwood, leaving only just enough room to get to the door.

My ear twitches, and I wonder what my subconscious picked up on that jolted me out of my sleep.

I grab my gun from under my pillow and lightly slip out of bed, walking toward the door without a sound. I press my ear against the wood, craning my neck as I listen.

Silence.

Every fiber in my body, however, warns that we are not alone in the little cottage.

Quietly, I remove the three traps I have set around the door—a few daggers in the gaps between the door and the frame that will drop if someone opens the door from the other side.

With the exit disarmed, I twist the doorknob and sneak into the dark hallway. Gun trained on the space ahead of me, I carefully make my way toward the main living area, passing shadows and checking rooms as I go.

Clear.

Clear.

Cl—

As I tilt my head into the living room, I spot a collection of silhouettes in the darkness. Twelve people, and I'm guessing they're men judging by their builds.

My eyes dart toward Drew's room across the open expanse, wondering if he's okay. If Levi's okay outside. If Jace, who's on patrol, even knows what's happening.

"Rory, how good of you to join us," a familiar man's voice says from the darkness. "We were just coming to get you."

Jett Darrington.

Damn it all.

I have enough bullets to take out ten of the men, but I doubt Jett would go down with a traditional bullet. I'll need to come up with something clever to disarm both him and target number twelve.

Time to dance, I suppose.

"Jett," I say as if we're old buddies. "How good of you to drop by."

I take a few cautious steps into the living room, always careful to keep my exits in the corner of my eye. Front door. Hallway behind me. Drew's room. A window in the kitchen.

It's habit, more than anything else—I'm not leaving this place without my men.

All of them.

Jett steps forward, his face slowly coming into focus despite the low light. Beside him, another familiar face appears—Milo, Drew's big brother.

"Milo's here, too, huh?" I ask, smirking even as I have my gun trained on them both. "Isn't this a treat?"

Jett grins, eyeing my weapon as if it's a toothpick. "Aren't you going to scream for help?"

I laugh. What a blatant power play. He should know better, frankly, and I'm disappointed he thinks something like that would shake me.

"What's so funny?" he asks, tilting his head curiously. "I could take you, little girl, and no one would know where you've gone."

"That's cute." I grin, not willing to let this jackass think for even one second that he has the upper hand.

"If you really could whisk me away, Jett, you'd have done it already."

His arrogant smile falters ever so slightly.

A conceited man like this—he wants to prove how superior he is to everyone else. He wants to live and remain above others, and that means it'll be fairly easy to pluck at the strings of his ego.

Time to play.

"Let's stop wasting time, shall we?" I prod, eager to get this over with. "What do you want? And I mean really, Jett. Most people want to turn me into some kind of weapon, and others just want to show me off. Are you as boring as they are?"

His jaw tenses, and I notice his shoulders square off. Oh, man. He was almost too easy to rile up.

Instead of answering, his eyes narrow slightly. I see the glint of intention, of calculated planning, and I have to confess I don't like that one bit.

Perhaps there's a bit more to Jett Darrington than I anticipated.

"The last time we met, I got away with it," the Darrington Boss points out, carefully sidestepping an outright confession of his involvement in the dojo invasion. "What makes you think this will be any different? I get what I want when I want it, and I want you to behave."

"What's next, then?" I shrug, as if he's boring me. "If you try anything, five armies will be at your throat in an instant. How much longer do you think you can hang out in here with me and not get caught?"

To his credit, Jett chuckles. "I have to admit, kid, I like you. In another life, you would have made an excellent daughter-in-law."

I catch the subtle reference to Drew, and the implication is clear. I am not an equal, not to his man, and he doesn't condone what Drew and I have. Since Jett has every intention of dragging Drew back to him, he will do whatever it takes to destroy Drew's affection for me.

Now, I'm more curious than ever to find out what he wants with me. If he doesn't want to parade me around, what *does* he want?

Behind them, Drew's door creaks open. The towering Darrington shifter walks through the cluster of men, each of the faceless soldiers cowering away from him as he strides confidently through their ranks.

Jett merely watches his son cut through his midst, while Milo looks on with a furious scowl. His disdain for Drew is obvious, and it makes me wonder why Drew would take the blame for Jace's brother's death when it was all Milo's fault.

This coward hardly deserves that kindness.

Drew walks calmly. Confidently. Eventually, he stands resolutely in front of me and crosses his arms. Chin raised in defiance, he stares down his father, and the unspoken ultimatum is delivered. Without so much as a word spoken, he makes it clear whose side he's on.

Mine.

Jett frowns, his eye twitching with anger, and opens his mouth to speak—only to be interrupted as the front door swings violently open. It slams against the wall. Jace storms into the cottage, his body brimming with barely contained fury as he glares at the Darringtons across from us. Electricity crackles over his arms, and I can tell it's requiring all of his self-control not to let loose on them right this moment.

"Get the *fuck* out," Jace demands.

For a moment, no one moves. I wonder what will happen—if this cottage will end up in flames, perhaps, as a war begins right here.

Eventually, Jett smirks and nods politely toward me. "We'll continue our conversation later, young lady."

Oh, I'm suddenly not a *little girl* anymore. I'm a *young lady*. How adorable.

I'm tempted to let loose a colorful string of all the things I want to call him, but I abstain. Consider that self-restraint my contribution to diplomacy. It's about as much as anyone will ever get from me.

Jett Darrington and his soldiers walk casually out the front door, and Jace seems to barely refrain from punching them all in the face as they leave.

When the front door finally shuts behind them,

Drew lets out a slow breath. "I hate how brazen that man is."

Jace points an accusatory finger at Drew. "It won't be long until the world loses its patience with your family's bullshit." He pauses, his gaze shifting instantly to me. "Harper told me you know about Drew?"

I nod.

"Of course you do," Jace says, shaking his head in disappointment I don't fully understand.

I cross my arms, staring after the Darringtons and wondering what else was up that man's sleeve. As if sensing my thoughts, Drew sets a hand possessively on the back of my neck, squeezing it lightly to comfort me.

Jace scowls at our silent exchange. "I'm going to check on Levi and then have a little *talk* with Greaves." Jace's biceps flex in his anger. "The fact that the Darringtons got in is inexcusable."

"I'll join you," I say. "I want to make sure Levi's okay and figure out how Jett—"

"Don't." Jace shakes his head. "Just—just stay here." With that, he storms out the back door, sliding it closed with almost enough force to break it. I'm astonished the glass doesn't shatter.

"That was kind of rude." I set my hands on my hips. "Even for him."

Drew rubs his eyes unenthusiastically. "As much as I

hate to make excuses for that jackass, he hasn't slept since we got here. No one's sleeping well."

A few thundering snores escape Tucker's room, and I just point in the vague direction of our resident weapons master.

As the former Knight continues snoring, Drew just chuckles and rolls his eyes. "Well, most of us."

CHAPTER TWELVE

In the brilliant sunshine of the next morning, I grimace and run my fingers along the silk frills of the royal blue gown currently weighing on my shoulders. With a sidelong glare at Jace, I point to the lace-covered bodice. "But it's a *dress.*"

He grins, rubbing the exhaustion from his eyes. "You're very observant, Rory."

"Why do I have to wear a *dress*?" I tug at the bodice, trying to breathe in this damned thing. "It's *itchy*."

The sliding glass door along the back of the living room sits open. Levi's great blue head rests at the entrance as he growls softly in approval.

"Oh, don't *you* start with me," I chide, even though I'm unable to hide my flattered smile.

Drew and Tucker sit on the cloud-soft couch nearby, their eyes drifting time and again to my gown's plunging neckline, while Jace leans against the wall nearby. All of them watch me as I fuss with the frills, none of my men able to hide their smiles.

To my surprise, Drew's grin is the broadest of everyone's. His eyes rove the bodice and land on my ass, and I figure his imagination is getting the better of him right now.

I glare at the Darrington man in our midst. "You wouldn't be laughing if it was *you* in a dress."

"I would," Tucker says with a resolute nod. "Hands down, no question."

Levi and Drew chuckle, and even Jace lets out a short laugh as he watches me fiddle with the ball gown. "Have you really never worn a dress, Rory?"

I stare at him incredulously and point to myself. "How many times a day do you forget how I was raised? It's not like we had formal mixers during assassin training."

In answer, Jace just laughs. "Touché, woman. Touché."

"You look hot, babe," Tucker says, reclining against the couch and tucking his hands behind his head. "Seriously, total stunner."

I set my hands on my waist and study his wide grin, trying to fight the flattered smile slowly dawning on my lips. "Really?"

"Twelve out of ten." He nods toward the full-length mirror in the corner. "Go look."

I indulge him and float toward the mirror—which is really the best explanation I can offer for the odd way this dress makes me move—and I'm astonished to see a proper lady in my reflection. She's regal, her skin glowing like it was gently kissed by the sun, the royal blue fabric practically radiant in contrast to her dark hair that curls around her face.

And that cleavage. Wow. This bodice is so tight and restricting, but it's incredibly becoming.

"Whoa," I mutter, tilting my body as I examine the dress from a new angle.

"Told you," Tucker says.

Levi growls appreciatively, and this time, I shoot him a flirty little smile.

As I study my reflection, my initial instinct is to rip the damn thing off. I mean—yes, it's beautiful. The fabric cascades over my body like a river. The folds of the dress gently flutter with each of my movements, and I have to confess I feel like a princess.

But I'm a battle-hardened assassin raised in blood, pain, and war. I'm not supposed to like frilly things.

Still, I can't help but look at the gown lovingly as I sway gently back and forth at the mirror.

"All right, men, let's move out." Jace claps his hands together and ushers Drew and Tucker off the couch. "You two know what to do."

"Aye, Captain." Tucker feigns a mock salute and jogs

toward the open doors, giving me a quick peck on the cheek on his way out.

Drew follows suit, his hand gently weaving around my waist as he leaves. He winks as he exits through the backdoor, that dashing grin of his on his face. It's like he knows his touch left fluttery goosebumps along my skin.

A soft rumble in Levi's throat catches my attention, and he leans his head into the room. Gently, he brushes his nose against my hand before taking off into the sky.

With the rest of them gone, Jace walks up behind me and sets his hands on my shoulders. His head rests against the back of mine as a gentle, electric current buzzes along my skin from his touch. He presses his lips against my cheek.

I grin. "Since when are you cuddly?"

"Since I've gotten two hours of sleep in the last three days." His grip tightens on my shoulders, and he sighs heavily. "You smell like roses. Is that a new perfume?"

"Oh, so we're friends again?" I tilt my head back to look at him, not willing to let him off the hook so easily after his little episode last night.

He sighs and buries his face in my hair. "It's just hard to see you and Drew so—close."

And there he is—the possessive shifter who wants me to choose just one of them, to go against my culture and belong to only one man. I've been over this before with him, and I suspect we'll go over it again.

I sigh, not willing to push these buttons right now.

"I had a talk with Greaves," Jace continues, running his finger absently along the back of my hand, swirling up all the desire and affection I feel for him despite me being angry.

In the end, his adorable, sleep-deprived demeanor wins me over.

"What did Reggie say?" I ask.

"It looks like the front door codes were hacked. One of his people sold the code to the Darringtons." In my periphery, Jace grimaces, the full fury of his rage burning briefly in his eyes. "Suffice to say, I was not pleased with that news."

I pause. "Did—did you kill Reggie?"

"No," he says with an exasperated sigh. "We *talked* Rory."

I hesitate. "Does your version of 'talking' involve blood, or—"

"No, damn it! I didn't kill him," Jace snaps.

"Okay," I say with a resigned wave of my hands. "Because I like that bald little dude."

Jace chuckles. "When he doesn't screw up, I like him, too. I've checked the house and removed the four bugs the Darringtons managed to plant before you found them."

"Good move," I admit.

Jace nods in thanks. "Greaves tried to give us some money back, but I told him all I care about is security. He's spent all that he was going to refund us on extra hired guards, designed specifically to protect you."

"Good man." I'll admit, even if they're just humans, extra guns on my side won't hurt.

Jace kisses my neck, the buzzing sensation getting stronger as he explores my skin. "I had a present built into your gown. Tucker helped," Jace adds with an exasperated sigh and an eye roll. "He wanted assurances that I would tell you he was involved."

I chuckle. "What is it?"

"A few surprises," Jace answers cryptically. His hands slide along my back and to my waist, his fingers brushing the smooth silk of the bodice along the way.

Even though I'm slightly annoyed with him, his touch makes my heart sing. As our intense connection burns between us, my imagination begins to run away with me.

I imagine him throwing me on the nearest bed and hoisting up the four layers of skirts on this thing. I dream of him running his hand up my thigh as the petticoat scratches my skin. I can almost feel the warmth of his fingers as they slide past my panties and toy with my entrance, aching to enter and fill me.

My face flushes with need, and I take a few deep breaths to clear my racing thoughts.

It doesn't work.

Jace gently nibbles my ear as his fingers brush one of the folds of the skirt. "There's a gun hidden here. Fully loaded. Twelve rounds."

I grin. "You sure know how to sweet-talk a girl, Jace."

He chuckles, and his other hand slowly weaves down the skirts on the opposite side. "A dagger here." His strong hand shifts a few inches to the left. "And another here."

Jace sets his strong hand against the skirt, gripping my thigh through the fabric. The hard outline of a dagger presses against my skin, sandwiched between his palm and my leg.

Heat rushes through the space between my thighs, and I don't even know any more what's the mate-bond and what's our raw attraction to each other.

I reach my hand over my shoulder, cupping his neck with my fingers. A low growl escapes him, rough and almost feral, and he gently bites my jaw in response.

"Trust me, Rory." His voice is gravelly and coarse, thick with lust. "I want nothing more than to throw you on the couch and rip off the dress it took you an hour to get into. I want to ride you until you scream my name."

Oh *gods*. He's such a tease.

"But when I finally take you," he continues, "I want it to be because you chose it." He pauses, brushing his mouth against the back of my head as if it's taking all his willpower to say this. "I don't want it to be because we got lost in the moment."

My body aches for him so badly, it's hard to breathe. I close my eyes to settle my racing heart as he slowly—in such a tortured way—lets go of me. He takes a few steps back, and my body is suddenly cold.

The mate-bond seems to get more intense every day, and I wonder how much longer I can resist it... or if I even want to, anymore.

CHAPTER THIRTEEN

Roughly two hours after Jace and I had our little *talk*, I sit at the head of a table in one of the castle's many rooms.

In the silence, all eyes are on me.

Six dragon shifters sit around the rectangular wooden table, three on either side of me. A dozen people line the walls behind them, and despite the sheer number of shifters in here, it's still surprisingly spacious.

A row of windows draped with elegant red curtains line the wall to my left, while gilded doors to who-knows-where line the wall to my right.

There are a ton of exits, but no real way out—not considering how tightly monitored every square inch of this complex is. I peek at the camera blinking in the corner of the room, its little red light on as we wait in silence, and I wonder who's watching.

Jace, Drew, and Tucker stand behind me, framed by a massive marble fireplace large enough for me to stand in, but I resist the impulse to look back at them.

After all, this is the moment of truth. The moment we've all been waiting for.

Quietly, I survey the six faces before me—six of the seven ruling Dragon Bosses. Only Kinsley Vaer is missing.

At the far end of the table, Harper's expression is stony and calm. There's not even a hint of her inherent humor or charm, and I figure this is the legendary Boss Mode she told me about. Her eyes narrow as she watches me with cold calculation, and I can't help but wonder how much of this is show and how much is real. Two men stand behind her, likely her guard. I was surprised to see Jace stand behind me instead of her, and for the first time, I'm struck by the political implications of the Fairfax General having a mate-bond with the dragon vessel.

For him and his cousin both, it must feel like he's picking sides.

Elizabeth Andusk sits beside Harper, her elegant head tilted toward me as she studies us all. I peg her as roughly thirty-five, and she seems to be aging well. Her eyes drift behind me, and I wonder what's going through her brain as she sees that two of the world's most powerful dragon shifters have already sided with me.

Jett Darrington sits next to her, closest to me, and I'm honestly not surprised he weaseled his way into a nearby seat. I barely give him or Milo—who stands with his back to the wall—a passing glance.

Isaac Palarne sits on the other side of me, his elbows resting on the table as he leans his chin against his knuckles. Oddly enough, he looks younger than I expected him to—only about thirty. He watches me quizzically, though there's no hint of calculation in his gaze. Two men I don't recognize stand at attention behind him, their gazes locked on the wall ahead of them as if the rest of us don't exist.

Aki Nabal sits beside Isaac, reclined in his chair. The forty-something-year-old ice dragon absently rubs his pointer finger and thumb together, his eyes narrowed in focus as he studies me. I wonder if he's trying to dissect me from afar, to glean what he can from me without even a word spoken between us. I'm none too fond of the wickedly smart glean to his eye, and I'm instantly wary of him.

Victor Bane sits beside him, and I surprisingly can't read his expression. He covers his mouth with one hand, his eyes only slightly narrowed as he studies me, and he's not quite what I expected. I was ready for a crass man who made snide comments—not a silent shifter who simply observed the world around him.

His sister Natasha rests her back against the wall of windows behind him, however, and she's *exactly* what I expected. She props her heel against the windowpane, her bare knee slipping through a high slit in her dress. Unsurprisingly, her attention is focused on the men behind me, and a seductive smile plays at her red lips. My shoulders tense impulsively at the thought of her sizing up any one of my men as some kind of plaything.

The door to the hallway swings open, and Reggie enters with a broad smile on his face. "Welcome, welcome! I apologize for the delay. Let's begin! My staff and I are so honored to have each of you here this fine day. Miss Quinn, I would like to introduce you to—"

"I know them," I say with an indifferent wave of my hand. "Thank you, Reggie."

I don't like to be dismissive to such a kind man, but every move I make must be a power play. Knowledge. Authority. Control. I must exude all of that and more at any given moment, and I must never back down from any challenge.

Not with *these* dragons watching.

"Ah, well," Reggie pauses for a moment, clearly trying to skip a few bits of his rehearsed routine. "In that case, I will leave you all with a few parting rules, and then you may begin your—*deliberations*."

I resist the impulse to smile as he avoids the word "festivities" this time.

His gaze passes over the many faces in the room. "This is old hat to many of you, so I thank you for your patience as I repeat the laws of the castle. Please, no shifting within the buildings. All dragonish activities must take place outside." He nods toward the windows. "As my staff and I are all human, please do not engage with any of us in a physical manner, or I'm afraid I will have to immediately remove you from the property. Multiple infractions may result in a lifetime ban, so I ask that you not tempt fate on that one! And, lastly, no fistfights in the castle halls. Everything must be taken outside. On the grass, you're free to do as you please. However, I implore you to please not light my forest on fire!" He chuckles, but no one else laughs at his joke.

Honestly, in this political climate, it's probably a real risk.

Reggie pauses, scanning the faces before him. I figure this is his attempt to get us to agree to the rules, but no one speaks. He nervously clears his throat.

"I'll take my leave, then," he says with a hesitant bow. "The cameras will turn off momentarily." As he casts one last fleeting glance toward me, he walks into the hall and gently shuts the door. Almost instantly, the red light of the camera in the corner flickers off.

And just like that, we can begin.

The moment the caretaker leaves, Jett Darrington opens his mouth to speak.

I beat him to it.

"The Vaer have a bio-weapon, one capable of rendering humans unconscious," I say, diving in to the most prominent thought on my mind. "I've—shall we say, *acquired* its chemical composition, as well as the antidote."

Behind me, Jace lets out an annoyed little sigh, but I resist the impulse to smirk.

"I've partnered with a few distribution centers to distribute the antidote globally," I continue, barreling through the over-simplification with a wave of my hand.

None of them need the details, anyway.

Jett leans back in his seat, an arrogant smirk on his face as he gives me a once-over. "And how did you discover this nefarious plot, exactly?"

I lift one eyebrow. "Don't worry about that, Mr. Darrington."

He frowns.

Elizabeth Andusk tilts her regal chin thoughtfully. "I would like my own copies of this antidote, as well as the weapon." She smiles warmly. "Purely for study, of course."

My eyes flit briefly to Harper, who nods almost imperceptibly.

"You can have the antidote," I say. "But not the weapon."

The barest hint of a scowl crosses Boss Andusk's face, but she recovers quickly. "I understand. I imagine you want to keep that information for yourself."

I smirk at the jibe, but I don't indulge her by responding. She's just trying to put me on the defensive. I can't even remember how many times Diesel has pulled this stunt on me—it just doesn't work anymore.

Aki Nabal clears his throat, smiling a bit as he adjusts in his seat. "As I'm sure you can tell, Miss Quinn, none of us are particularly fond of each other, but we despise the Vaer far more. I'm grateful for what you've done." His smile falters. "Kinsley doesn't need any more power than she already has."

"I agree," I say with a nod.

It feels damn good to dismantle something the Vaer have worked so hard to build.

"Yes, yes," Jett says, waving his hand dismissively as if none of this matters in the slightest. "I believe there are other things of more importance, however. Such as you, Miss Quinn." He sneers as he says my name in a slightly mocking tone, clearly just trying to toy with my patience.

Before I can help myself, I grimace.

"Tell us what you can do," Victor Bane orders, finally breaking his silence. "What does it mean to be the dragon vessel, exactly?" He lounges in his seat and sets the heel of his boot on the elegant table before us as he watches me with a hunger I've seen before. The overconfident smirk, the relaxed shoulders, the not-so-casual spreading of his legs—he's observing me with barely contained lust, and he's likely debating all the things he would do to me if he could have his way.

"Yes," Elizabeth says, the thin line of her cleavage exaggerated as she leans subtly forward. "We're quite curious."

"That's a shame," I say with a cocky grin.

I've never seen so many people frown in unison. That clearly was not the answer they came all this way to hear.

"We have a right to know," Victor Bane snaps.

"She is the dragon vessel," Isaac says, the last of the Bosses to break his silence. His voice has a distinct accent to it, though it's difficult to place—I didn't hear it when he spoke to me in his dragon form, but it's unmistakable in his human body. "She owes us nothing, Bane."

Victor scowls at the Palarne Boss before him. "The noble warrior comes to the maiden's rescue, huh? Let the girl speak for herself."

"Show her *respect*," Isaac snaps. His voice booms through the air like thunder, thick with authority and control.

Victor narrows his eyes in disdain, but he doesn't say anything more.

"Perhaps you're worthless," Jett says with a lazy shrug. "Perhaps all of this pomp and pretense was for nothing."

"Perhaps," I say with a wry smile, matching him at his game. "Perhaps you all wasted your time over some silly legend. I'm just a harmless human, after all."

Behind me, someone shifts uncomfortably—Tucker by the sound of the boots. He's likely wondering what the hell I'm doing, but he's thankfully not going to undermine me by asking in front of everyone.

Good, because this is all part of my plan.

"Or," I continue, eyes narrowing on the Darrington Boss before me. "Perhaps you know damn well what I can do, and you're trying to make the others care less about figuring it out for themselves."

With that, I set my finger on the wooden table before us and summon my magic, never once breaking eye contact with the Darrington Boss. White light blisters over my skin, casting a soft glow across the room. Elizabeth and Aki both gasp, though everyone else manages to contain their excitement.

Electricity can carve intricate patterns into wood. So, either my magic is going to do something truly breathtaking, or I'm going to blow this table to bits.

Either way, I win.

With a sudden jolt, I reach into the depths of my magic and channel a measured blast of power through my finger. The magic crackles through the table, burning golden lines into the wood that splinter in different directions like the roots of a tree.

When I lift my finger and lean back in my chair, the table before us smokes. Golden lines crisscross the grains of wood, as fine and beautiful as if a craftsman put them there intentionally.

Oh—oh *crap.*

Though I maintain my stoic expression, my heart skips a beat at the thought that perhaps this wasn't just some table—perhaps it was a custom build, or worse, an heirloom.

Shit.

I'm going to have to apologize and maybe even replace it.

Damn it.

Careful to maintain my composure, I gently adjust in my seat, getting comfortable as I smile knowingly at Jett Darrington.

His eyes finally snap away from mine to assess the table before us, and his scowl deepens. "Impressive."

"Impressive?" Victor Bane asks with a skeptical laugh. "Don't try to undervalue this. The lines—the gold—and so *fast*! That's more powerful than any old thunderbird." The Bane Boss sneers as he runs his finger along the gold grains.

"Thanks," Harper says dryly.

"I figure we'll be discussing quite a bit over these next few days," I say, doing my best to sound casual.

"But I want you to know one thing for certain, all of you." I pause, waiting for each gaze to drift back to me before I continue. "I am not afraid of any of you. Not your armies. Not your powers. Not your resources. You do not scare me, and I am *not* for sale."

A few hours later, Reggie stands at the open door, his mouth gaping as his fingers claw at his remaining hair. "By the gods above, what happened to the table?"

"Ah," I say, trying not to grimace with guilt. "That was me." I give the caretaker an apologetic nod, even as I try to maintain my composure in front of the Bosses.

"But—how did—*you* did that?" He blinks rapidly, at a loss for words.

"I take it lunch is ready?" Jett asks in an irritated tone.

It takes a moment for Reggie to shake himself from his daze, but he eventually manages to nod at the Darrington Boss. "Uh—yes, sir. Yes, it is."

"Good." Jett's chair scrapes over the hardwood as he stands. He leaves without another word, and several of the other Bosses follow silently behind.

We're all exhausted from several hours of interrogation, and I am beyond relieved for the break. As the Bosses turn their attention away, I feel a comforting hand grip my shoulder. I look up to see Jace nod approvingly at me and gesture for me to follow the rest of the dragons filing out of the room.

There's something I need to do, first.

I clear my throat. "Reggie, can I have a word?"

The castle's caretaker tilts his head curiously but indulges me by walking over as the last of the Bosses step into the hallway. "My dear, if this is about the, er, *intrusion* last night, I cannot even begin to express my utter apologies to—"

"No, consider that forgiven." Jace had already run him through the ringer, and I wasn't about to do it again. Instead, I nod toward the golden lines now wrought permanently into the table. "Sorry about that. Can I pay you back, or—"

"Not at all!" Reggie laughs. "My dear, you just made that table priceless. Touched by the dragon vessel herself? Miss, I'm fairly certain you just allowed me to double my daily rate for use of this room!"

I laugh at his candor. "In that case, I get to stay for free in the future, right?"

"Absolutely, my dear." He grins and offers me his arm so that he can lead me to the buffet. "Shall we?"

I chuckle and take the balding man's arm. I have to admit, I'm rather fond of Mr. Reginald Greaves.

As for the Bosses, however—I'm sure most of them were expecting a frail little girl in over her head, faking and bluffing her way through the meeting.

I, however, don't have to bluff. I have the guns to protect myself and the trigger finger to fire should the need arise.

Back arched, I join the Bosses in the next room as Jace, Drew, and Tucker flank me and Reggie. One morning down—only two and a half exhausting days left.

CHAPTER FOURTEEN

A s the day wears on, I'm left dog-tired.
But I figure that was the point: wear me down. Ruffle my feathers. Make me break and reveal something crucial—something they shouldn't know.

Fat chance.

I slip into the restroom as we break for dinner, eager to have a moment to myself. Jace tried to follow me in, but damn it all, I will get *one* moment of peace and quiet.

As the door shuts behind me, I press my back against the elaborate designs in its wood, take a deep breath, and survey the ornate room to make sure I'm alone.

Unsurprisingly, there are no cameras in here. An elaborate sink with a gilded mirror covers one wall. A few reflective trays in each corner of the wide counter offer lotions, rolled towels, and perfumes to guests. An elegant black chaise rest against the other wall, and I wonder if anyone has actually sat on it—or if it's more for show. White marble covers everything from the floor to the sink to the ceiling, and I figure the phrase "tone it down" was never mentioned when the architect built this place.

There are two separate doors in here, and I figure the builder added two toilets for increased capacity. The door to one of them is open, though the other is closed. Despite the utter silence in here, I frown, wondering if I'm alone after all.

To my surprise, the knob turns almost instantly.

Moments later, the door to the second water closet opens, and Elizabeth Andusk walks into the elaborate restroom. When our eyes meet, she gasps in surprise and sets a hand on her chest.

"Oh, my," she says with a light chuckle. "You startled me."

"Sorry," I say, my moment of peace shattered. "The door was unlocked, so I didn't realize the room was taken. I'll leave."

"No, nonsense." She waves her regal hand to dismiss the idea and smiles warmly as she heads to the sink. "I'll be done in just a moment."

As the beautiful woman gently bends over the ornate counter to wash her hands, I take the moment to survey her skeptically.

I don't believe for one moment that this was accidental, and she's a fool if she thinks this worked.

"Since you're here," Elizabeth says as she daintily lifts a rolled towel from one of the trays on the counter. "I have a surprise for you."

"No, thank you." It's tough to be polite when I want to punch pretty much everyone in the face, but I force myself to grin and bear it. I only have two more days of this nonsense, after all.

As I turn the knob to leave, she clicks her tongue in disapproval. "Honestly, Rory. This is a *fun* surprise."

Uh huh. Sure.

Before I can even open the door, Elizabeth whips out a velvet box from a hidden pocket in her dress. It's roughly the size of my pistol, and for a moment, I wonder if she actually got me something useful.

Not that I'd *take* it, but still. It's the thought that counts.

She lifts the lid to reveal a dazzling diamond pendant set on a crisp black satin pillow. The center stone is as large as my thumbnail, and it glistens with brilliant facets in the warm light around us. Four smaller diamonds, each equally dazzling, trace their way up the golden chain.

"It's a trifle," Elizabeth says with a smile as she lifts the necklace from the box. "Someone as beautiful as you should be doted upon, don't you think?"

The Andusk Boss sets the box aside and raises the

necklace, wordlessly offering to clasp it around my neck, but I lift a hand to stop her.

"Do you really think I'm so easily bought?" I ask, raising one eyebrow in annoyance.

"I—I don't know what you mean." Elizabeth watches me with a wounded expression, and she takes a wary step backward.

But I see through the act.

"Did you think I forgot about the attack by the cliff?" I take a step toward her, squaring my shoulders as I look her dead in the eye. "Did you think I forgot you sent your people to kidnap me? Back before I went to the dojo? Back when you thought I didn't know how to control my powers?" My voice lowers as I near her, and I don't bother to mask the icy chill in my tone. "I remember, Elizabeth, and I will *never* forget."

For the first time since we met, Elizabeth drops the phony warmth she's so good at faking.

Her nose wrinkles slightly as she studies me with a disdainful expression, and she lifts her chin in defiance. "Those are some bold words."

"They're not just words," I promise.

The Andusk Boss chuckles humorlessly. "You are *property*, little girl," she says icily, her tone shifting dramatically from the honey-smooth kindness she's spoken with all day.

I bristle at the insult—at the insinuation I can be

owned and *tamed*—but I grit my teeth to keep from saying something I'll regret.

Elizabeth lifts the beautiful stone in her hand, studying it as the light glints brilliantly off its facets and casts small rainbows around the room. "You're like this diamond, in fact. Beautiful. Rare. Commanding. But, ultimately, you're just another thing for me to obtain." Elizabeth smirks, the sultry tilt to her eyes brimming with confidence as she speaks. "You can fight me, you can be shackled and controlled, living a miserable life in a cell. Or you can simply *obey* me and live in comfort. It's your choice."

I scoff. "Even if it's comfortable, it's still a prison."

"You don't know what we can do to you, child," Elizabeth warns, her voice dropping to a harsh whisper as she slowly closes the gap between us. "The ways we can break you, the ways—"

As she nears my face, entirely too close, I've finally had enough.

Before she can even blink, I whip out one of the daggers hidden in my skirts and hold it to her neck.

"You're done talking." My voice is cold. Harsh. It leaves no room for interpretation or doubt.

Elizabeth stiffens as my blade presses against her neck. Her beautiful brown eyes narrow as she glowers at me, but it's several moments more before she finally steps backward.

"You're a fool," she snaps. "And you will regret this."

She slams the diamond necklace into my palm in a fit of disgust. Without another word, the regal woman storms from the restroom.

When the door clicks shut behind her, I tilt my head slightly to stare after the regal woman. I simmer on everything she said, on all those hollow threats, and I wonder if any of them had any substance.

It's hard to tell with her. One moment, she's frail and elegant; the next, it's like I'm looking at a totally different woman. A vengeful one, someone who would go to the ends of the Earth to settle a grudge, if that's what it took.

Curious, I lift the diamond in my palm, examining the beautiful stones on the glimmering golden necklace as the room's soft light dances through the facets. I've stolen necklaces like this before, though nothing quite this beautiful, and I suspect it's easily worth hundreds of thousands of dollars.

But a woman like that—she has an ulterior motive. They all do.

Carefully, I flip over the pendant and pick at the settings with my dagger. A few of the stones pop out, totally clean, and I briefly wonder if I'm wrong—if she really did just hand over something worth hundreds of thousands of dollars in a transparent attempt to buy my loyalty.

A moment later, though, I pop out the fourth stone. A small tracker nestles against the diamond, hidden in a brilliantly clever placement along the base.

Without removing the stone, I never would have found this.

For a moment, I stare at the gems in my hands, at the necklace, astounded at the brazen attempt to both buy and track me, all in one.

The fools.

Frowning, I toss the necklace in the trash. Elizabeth Andusk is going to have to try harder than *that*.

CHAPTER FIFTEEN

W hen I walk out of the bathroom and into the ornate hallway of the castle's east wing, I find Jace with his foot raised in the perfect fighting form. His gaze is locked on the doorknob, his hips angled perfectly to deal a deadly blow—and I'm fairly certain he was about to kick the bathroom door down.

"Well, hi," I mutter, deeply entertained by whatever the hell I just walked in on.

"Thank the gods," he mutters, grabbing my arms and pulling me close. He lets out a sigh of relief as he holds me to his rock-hard chest, and I can't help but blush a little at his overt display of affection.

Usually, he would never do this in public—any snuggly moments I get from this guy are behind closed doors.

This poor man is *exhausted.* Far more so than even I realized.

"Jace." My voice is slightly muffled as he holds me to his shirt. "You really need some sleep."

"I'm fine," he says, clearing his throat as he releases me. "Momentary lapse of judgment."

"Uh huh," I watch him warily, wondering if I need to sedate him to force him to get some shut-eye.

"This place is becoming more dangerous by the moment," he says, dropping his voice to a bare whisper as he leans in. "I can't leave you alone anymore. That's final."

I cross my arms defiantly. "If I'm on the toilet, I don't have an audience. That's my rule."

"Rory, this is *serious.*"

"You think I'm not?" I gesture over my shoulder at the restroom as the door softly shuts behind me. "I had it handled, Jace, but thank you."

He tilts his head, lips tight with annoyance. "This is about more than a private chat with the Andusk Boss," he says. "There have been brawls in the forests. Blood drawn. One of the Nabal soldiers nearly *died.*" He stiffens, his brooding glare roving the halls around us as he leans in. "The armies are getting riled up, and it's getting worse and worse the longer they're here. Only my people and the Palarnes are keeping level heads, and just barely at that." He grimaces. "I'm not sure how much longer before those forests erupt in an all-out war." He pauses, his intense and stormy eyes passing over my face. "Dragons know how to hold a grudge, Rory."

Hmm. "What if—"

Jace stiffens, his attention suddenly focused down the hallway to my left, and I pause to follow his gaze. Drew stalks toward us, casting a brief look over his shoulder as he nears.

Yeah, dragons certainly *do* know how to hold grudges.

I sigh, wishing the two of them could get along with more than a tense armistice, but I suppose I can't blame Jace. As far as he's aware, Drew killed his brother— very few people know it was really Milo.

I wish I could tell Jace the truth, but honestly, this isn't my secret to share. He and Drew need to work this out—hopefully *soon.*

More than that, I wonder how much longer Drew is going to be willing to protect his big brother from getting some much-needed justice.

"We need to leave," Jace says firmly as Drew approaches. "Immediately. We've done what we need to do, and—"

"Absolutely not," Drew interjects, much to my surprise.

"She's in danger," Jace snaps, gesturing toward me. "This is worse than we anticipated. If the armies brawl, it could turn ugly. Fast. What's to stop someone from kidnapping her in the chaos?"

"If it gets ugly, we fight," Drew says simply. "If we leave now, she will appear weak. Scared. This is our one chance to make an impression, and they need to know they can't scare her off after one little meeting."

"Little?" I rub my tired eyes. "That went on for eight *hours*, Drew."

"Oh, you sweet summer child," Drew says with a dry laugh. "That's barely a taste of the tedious interrogations of dragon politics."

I grimace. "I'll pass on future invitations, then."

"That's why I prefer settling things in the arena." Drew grins and cracks his neck. "Way more exciting."

"Listen closely, Darrington." Jace jabs Drew's chest with a finger. "While you've been comfortably situated up here, I've been patrolling. I've watched the deals made behind closed doors. I've seen the soldiers out there, shifted and roaring, ready for blood. I know what's at stake, Drew. You *don't*."

"I know what's at stake up here, and it's just as deadly." Drew nods in the vague direction of the Bosses clumped together in the lavish dining room not too far away. "I know what my father will think if she leaves tonight. I know what the Bane will do. I know what the Nabal will say. I've lived my life among these people, Jace, and I know how the conniving assholes think. Give me some damn credit."

"Here's a thought," I interject, gesturing to the hallway around us. "Maybe we don't have confidential discussions out in the open, hmm?"

Jace and Drew each turn their intense gazes on me, but only Jace shows any emotion. While Drew watches me with that same stony expression he always wears in public, Jace gives me a curt nod. With a huffy sigh, he waves for me to follow him. "We'll get you back to the villa."

As we leave, I can almost feel the gazes of the Bosses on my back. I wonder how many cameras have been planted through the castle, or how many secret recording devices I may have missed. It's hard to scan a room to make sure it's secure when everyone's eyes are locked on me. Worse than that, the elaborate dress I'm wearing limits movement.

In this castle, I'm the center of attention, and I despise how little freedom I have to move.

I ache to sneak. To slip unseen, if only for a few moments, through the shadows. But it doesn't look like I'll get that here—and if Jace has his way, I may never get to do it again.

CHAPTER SIXTEEN

When I'm back at the villa, I can finally put on something more comfortable. As beautiful as the dress is, I can barely move in that thing.

With Drew and Jace off somewhere arguing in hushed tones, I stretch my aching arms and walk into the living room as my tired muscles hum with relief. Getting out of that dress is like taking off weights strapped to my chest and legs.

I can finally *breathe.*

The house is quiet, and after a few moments of straining my ear in the silence, it's clear I'm alone. It's hard to believe they left me unsupervised, but there's a chance they simply forgot in the heat of all their bickering.

That same aching need to steal through the

shadows thrums through my chest, and my lip curls mischievously as I debate indulging it.

Just a little.

Safely, of course.

No one will even know I was gone.

I'll be smart about my target. It's not like I *want* to get caught, and I realize the dangers this place poses.

I purse my lips as my mind wanders. Maybe I can pop into the castle and scope the hallways for hidden cameras. Though I kind of want to sneak into the forest and see the six armies for myself, I resist the impulse to go. That would truly be tempting fate, and I'm no idiot.

The castle it is, then. Maybe I'll stick to the employee areas, or the vacant parts. I don't need to gather any intel—I just want to stretch my legs. Staying in the bits of the palace that dragons aren't allowed in will keep me out of trouble.

Probably.

Carefully, I slide open the back door and pretend to gaze out at the night, in case any of my men are watching. I survey the darkened grounds, eyes narrowing as I study the villas with lights in their windows.

Hmm.

Perhaps the other Bosses have some surprises hidden in their villas, something I can steal—

A rush of wings and air flies at me. Before I can so much as pivot to see who's coming, a giant claw rushes out of the dark night. It pins my chest to the wall of the villa, and I instantly summon my magic to defend myself.

If someone's going to be brazen enough to attack me in the open, he's going to die a painful death.

White light coils and curls around my fist as I lift it, taking aim, only to find Levi's beautiful blue face before me. He snorts a blast of frost across my cheeks, a furious tilt to his eye as he glares at me.

"Damn it, Levi," I snap, shaking my hand to release the magic I nearly used to take him out. "Don't surprise me like that."

I grab one of the toes in his claw to open our connection, and his emotions instantly bleed through.

Fury.

Impatience.

Disbelief.

You were leaving, he accuses me. *Here, surrounded by the enemy.*

"It was a walk, at best," I lie, knowing full well I've been caught. "A little—"

Rory, just stop, he snaps, a low growl building in his throat.

A flood of energy bubbles through our connection from him, the sensations bleeding together in a confused flurry. Devotion. Lust. Desire. Love. The ache to protect.

Every sensation is choppy and rough, blurred and

barely stitched to the next one. The feelings funnel into me like waves on a beach, ebbing and flowing, never consistent.

"Fine," I snap back at him. "I'll just stay here and be *bored*."

Levi presses his massive blue head against my forehead, and for a moment, the world stutters. There's a tug at my navel before I realize what he's doing, and he instantly drags me into his mind. The color around me fades.

Within seconds, I'm in his human arms, in the depth of his mind once again.

There are no words—only feelings. He cups my face and kisses me fiercely. Frantically. His lips are cool against mine, like the air when it snows, and it steals my breath away.

As quickly as it began, it's over, and I'm once more pressed against the exterior wall. My chest rises and falls as I struggle to breathe. His brilliant blue eyes snare me as he softly growls, and a moment later, he releases his hold on my chest.

What. Was. *That*.

For a moment, I just stare at him, blinking as I try to get my bearings. It was all so raw. So real. I had startlingly little control over any of that, and it concerns me how impulsive he's becoming as his dragon slowly takes over.

"I'm sorry," I confess. "I was just bored. I didn't

mean to—"

Levi snorts impatiently and nods toward the open door back into the villa.

I set my hands on my waist, annoyed at his pushiness. "You've been hanging out with Jace too much."

Levi snaps at the air far above my head, growling a bit in frustration, but he takes a few steps backward and nods once more to the door.

I roll my eyes and indulge him, looking back over my shoulder as I slide the door shut. He stares intently, watching me like a blue ghost in the night, just waiting for me to leave again.

His head shifts abruptly, and he snarls at something I can't see. Instantly, he soars over the roof, toward the front door.

Moments later, the doorbell rings.

I narrow my eyes in suspicion, but cross to the entrance and peer through the peephole.

A beautiful Asian woman, maybe eighteen at most, stands on the porch in a stunning green dress that clings to her hips. Her elegant black hair is pinned artfully to her head, and she waits calmly for me to answer. A wrapped present sits in her hands, the ornate bow taking up most of its surface.

I scan the open field behind her, wondering where Levi has gone, but he's likely on the roof preparing to pounce. The wide stretch of grass between us and the castle is empty, and it's clear she came alone.

Carefully, I draw my gun and hide it behind my back, tilting my body so that the woman won't be able to see it when I open the door.

The door creaks slightly as I confidently open it—after all, I don't want to peek through a slit in the door like some terrified little girl. I'm armed, and there's a dragon on the roof—if she tries anything, she'll get a painful reminder of where my boundaries lie.

The woman smiles warmly as our eyes meet. With a slight bow of her head, she offers me the gift in her hands. "My name is Jade Nabal. It's a pleasure to meet you, Miss Quinn."

Oh, well isn't this interesting.

Aki's daughter is here on my doorstep with a beautifully wrapped present, and I wonder just what kind of tricks the clever Boss is trying to play.

The easiest explanation is that he suspected his gorgeous daughter would appear non-threatening, but I know enough about her to be wary. She's an ice dragon, like her father, and just as powerful. I've even heard she's as quick with a weapon as any Spectre, and I don't for one moment trust her.

"What can I do for you?" I ask dryly.

"Nothing at all," Jade assures me. "I've simply come with a small token from my family. Something to let you know you're not alone in all this chaos."

Honestly, I'm tempted to shoot the box while she's still holding it to make my opinion on presents from *any* Boss well known. I don't want that damn thing anywhere near me—because I don't trust anyone here.

"That's not necessary," I say instead.

Instead of dropping her guard or frowning at me, like I expect, her smile only broadens. "I understand how this must seem. I told him not to do it."

I chuckle. "He should listen to you more often, then."

"I'll make sure to relay that advice." She laughs, the sound warm and relaxed.

"You can give it back to him," I say with a nod to the box. "Sorry to waste your time."

"Not at all, Miss Quinn," Jade says. "But if I may make a suggestion?"

I quirk a skeptical eyebrow. "Yes?"

"Even though you have every right to be skeptical, I believe you will want to see this." Effortlessly, she lifts the top on the box, revealing that it wasn't wrapped at all—it was nothing more than a cleverly disguised lid.

I tense, ready to shoot her in the face if I have to. I expect a flash of light, or smoke, but inside is a simple manila folder. She lifts it effortlessly and sets the now-empty box lightly on the porch beside her.

"Take it," she says with an elegant nod toward the folder, offering it to me.

Curious, I cock the still-hidden gun with one hand and reach for the folder with the other, never taking my eyes off the woman before me. She never stops smiling and barely even moves as I slowly retrieve it.

"You'll want to look at those alone." Jade nods to the folder with a knowing smirk as she retrieves the box from the ground beside her. "Not all of us are enemies, Miss Quinn," she adds as she begins to walk away, back toward the towering castle behind her.

There's not a single piece of tech I know of that could hide in plain sight on paper. In theory, it should be safe to at least look. I still briefly debate incinerating the folder in my hand, letting my magic burn it to ash, but I refrain.

The Nabal trade in information—and it would seem they just gave me some, for free.

Levi drops onto the grass outside, snarling as he monitors Jade's retreat toward the castle. The young woman walks with calm confidence, her hips elegantly swaying in the moonlight. A low thunder builds in Levi's chest, and I figure he was none too happy with her visit. After a moment, he tilts his head toward me.

I shrug, not entirely sure what to make of the young woman, either.

He soars back to the roof, and I close the door. After holstering my gun, I spread the papers out on the counter—and to my surprise, there are only five sheets.

They're files—on me and my men.

I grit my teeth, eyes narrowing as my nose wrinkles in disdain. The unspoken threat is clear. He knows who I love, and he knows things about them he shouldn't.

I scan each of the files. They knew Tucker was part of a secret organization, but they couldn't guess which one. There's a shortlist of ideas beneath his picture—CIA, Knights, Interpol. They have a surprising amount of detail on his technical ability, but they seemed to have missed his connection to the General.

Thank goodness.

Drew's file is slim, but everything on it is accurate. Darrington family line. Lone wolf. Seemingly endless web of connections, resources, and wealth. It also mentions one mansion in Malibu, so I make a mental note to let him know to sell that one.

Jace's file is similar to Drew's, and it's clear they want me to ask for more. They give the barest highlights, lists of battles fought and medals won. His ascension to master of the dojo, and the dragons he had to best to get there. It even includes a string of lovers he's had in the past, which just feels like a low blow.

I roll my eyes at Aki's attempt to stir up drama.

My file is empty, nothing but my picture and a blank page. The photo looks like it was taken while I was on the run, back before I went to the dojo. The snapshot shows smudges on my face as I look cautiously over my shoulder at something off camera.

I grit my teeth at the thought of them following me.

They were aware, very early on, of who I was—and where I was going.

Sure, the Nabal tend to do that. They find out things they shouldn't know, but I don't like this one bit.

The last page is Levi's file, and much to my surprise, his is also blank. His name is in bold at the top—Levi Sloane.

Interesting. I never learned his last name. Yet Aki Nabal seems confident he knows who Levi really is.

Only a picture of his face covers the otherwise empty page.

His *human* face.

It would appear the Nabal *do* know who he is.

Handwritten scrawl covers the bottom half of the blank sheet, the blue ink sharp and neatly drawn.

Miss Quinn—

Mr. Sloane's file is the most interesting of them all. I would be happy to give it to you in exchange for a favor. Any information you need, you have but to ask. We will not chase you. We will not corner you. We will not trap you. We don't need to resort to such measures because our allies come to us willingly. Just remember that, when you do reach out to us, our help does not come cheap.

—Aki

I frown, deeply annoyed. Anything they want from

me wouldn't be good, and I don't like the idea of owing a man like Aki Nabal a favor.

It concerns me how much they know—and how close they are to finding out my men's biggest secrets. I find it hard to believe they have nothing on me, and the curious itch to know more burns within.

If they find out I'm a Spectre, I'm screwed. Even worse—what if they share that little bit of data with the world?

I would be dead, and anyone defending me would die at my side.

Furious, I summon my magic into my fingers. As I hold the papers, they burn to ash in my hands. The edges crumble as I destroy everything the Nabal gave me.

I've memorized it all, anyway.

This was a power play, and it worked. They left me feeling unsettled, my mind buzzing with the possibilities of what this could mean. What they know. What they might do with that information.

They know who I care about. They know some of our weaknesses and may be close to learning others.

And, what's most worrisome of all, is they know who Levi really is—even as he slowly forgets.

CHAPTER SEVENTEEN

As the night wears on, I can't sleep.

I sigh and rest my head on Drew's shoulder as I lay beside him. Tenderly, I press my ear against his warm skin as his strong fingers trace the curve of my spine.

"You're still awake, huh?" he asks.

I nod, my eyes stinging a little with exhaustion as I rest against him. Each of his breaths soothes me, assuring me that somehow everything will be okay as long as we're all together.

The five of us.

"The Nabal papers?" Drew prods.

Though in the past I would have kept something like that to myself, I decided to share what I'd learned. Part of me wished I hadn't burned the papers in my anger, but I was still able to recite everything effortlessly.

Jace was… *displeased.*

Drew wasn't too overjoyed with any of it, either, but he immediately texted his realtor to sell his mansion in Malibu.

I run my finger over Drew's hard pecs. "Do you really think the Nabal have something on Levi?"

"I wouldn't be surprised."

I pause, simmering on what to do. "Would he have information on how to turn Levi human again?"

Drew sighs and grabs my waist, lifting me effortlessly on top of him. I chuckle as the powerful shifter maneuvers me into position, my legs spread across his hips. He adjusts himself, not-so-subtly pressing his hips against mine as he flashes me that trademark smirk. I lean my weight on my palms, one on either side of his head as he holds my hips firmly in place. My hair cascades over one shoulder as I study his handsome face, wondering what exactly he's up to.

"Nothing Nabal has is worth what he charges for it," Drew says, his smile faltering as he stares deep into my eyes. "The man is smart, but whether it's money or favors, he asks for too much. Every time."

I sigh, tilting my head as I shake the temptation to ask anyway. Levi just doesn't have much time, and I would do just about anything to save him.

"Rory," Drew says again, his voice more urgent than

before. "I mean it. Anything he has—it would be incomplete at best. It wouldn't help you."

"Maybe," I admit.

"It's going to be fine," Drew says with a weary sigh as he pulls me to his chest. He cradles my head with his powerful hand, and in this position, I feel like I could finally sleep.

My eyes slowly drift closed as Drew holds me tight, his strong fingers weaving occasionally through my hair while I lay on top of him.

"You need to demonstrate a bit of your power tomorrow," Drew eventually says, his deep voice almost booming through the silence.

I yawn, barely able to stay awake. "What do you think the bit with the table was for?"

He chuckles. "I mean your fury. They need to know you can kill. That you're *willing* to, if they push you."

"Why?" I prod, lifting my head to study his face. "What have you overheard?"

Drew's jaw tenses slightly as he presses his lips together, refusing to answer. He simply watches me, that all-too-familiar expression on his face—the one that makes it clear I'm not getting a word out of him.

I tilt my head, eyes narrowing slightly in annoyance. "Oh, you want to play that game?"

With a coy smile, I inch my knees a little farther up his body so I can get some leverage. I lean back and gently rock my entrance along the bulge in his pants, knowing full well the best way to torture him for information is to tease him mercilessly.

He groans and looks away, trying to hide the smirk on his face as I toy with him.

"Oh, you don't like this?" I ask, sitting upright. The movement presses the warm space between my thighs right against his hardening cock. The layers of fabric between us are barely enough to restrain him.

"Rory, play nice," he chides me.

"I *am* playing nice." I slowly lift the edges of my shirt, revealing my abdomen inch by tantalizing inch as I hint at what else he might get to see—if he behaves.

The man loves to be teased, and right now, this is utter torment.

"Tell me what you know," I demand, grinning. "Tell me, and maybe I'll reward you for your trouble."

Instead of answering, a rough and almost primal growl escapes the fire dragon underneath me. He grabs my hips and flips me onto my back in one powerful motion.

Instantly, he's above me, his hands on my knees. Without a hint of effort, he pries my legs open and tugs me toward him, until my entrance presses against the thick cock in his pants.

I click my tongue in mock disappointment. "You can't have your way with me until you spill your guts."

He lets out a frustrated groan and laughs. "Gods, you're a master at this."

I wink flirtatiously.

"Curse the power you have over me, woman." His voice is dark and deep, and he lays on my chest. His forehead presses against mine, and I feel delightfully dominated by him as he sandwiches me between his muscled body and the mattress.

"You like it," I whisper in his ear.

"A little." He chuckles and leans his mouth against my ear. "You want to know what I've overheard?"

"Very much so."

"The Bane have begun to orchestrate a kidnapping attempt and are looking for one of the staff they can buy off to help them." Drew's grip on me tightens possessively. "Obviously, Greaves has been forewarned."

"What did he say?"

"That he would personally shoot whoever sells him out," Drew says casually.

I'm surprised—I knew Reggie could hold his own, but that seems brutal for a balding and overweight middle-aged man.

Drew chuckles. "Greaves is a badass, Rory. Don't underestimate him."

"Note to self," I say with a bemused shrug. "What else?"

"The Andusk have been trying to figure out how to whisk you away, but they fear they lost their chance."

"The bathroom?"

"Yeah," Drew nods. "Something about a tracker?"

"She gave me a necklace, and I figured it out before I even left the bathroom."

"I'm not surprised." Drew grins down at me with pride in his eyes.

I smile, loving the way he looks at me. "Anything else?"

"My father wants to carry you off in his talons, of course," Drew says with an aggravated eye roll. "I've heard rumors he's holding a contest to see who can bring you in first, but there's nothing confirmed."

"Wouldn't surprise me," I admit with a huff. "One golden ticket for whoever can manage the task."

Drew chuckles.

"I guess that's why Jace is okay with this?" I ask, gesturing between us.

The fire dragon on top of me nods. "He doesn't want to think about it, and I'm sure he likes to imagine I'm spending the night on the floor. As long as you're safe, he's happy."

"He's going to go crazy if he doesn't get some sleep."

Drew snorts derisively. "The man is already crazy."

I playfully smack Drew's shoulder. "Be nice."

"I'm always nice," the fire dragon says with a wicked grin.

"Ha! Right." I relax my head on the blanket beneath me, my eyes briefly glazing over as I think about tomorrow. "What should I do?"

"To demonstrate your power?" Drew shrugs. "Can you shift, yet?"

I frown and tilt my head away, frustrated with the answer.

"It's fine," he assures me, gently brushing his nose against my cheek. "If you can't shift, just blow something up."

I grin. "Now *that* I can do."

CHAPTER EIGHTEEN

The next day, I dress in a far more comfortable outfit. A black shirt clings to my curves, the sleeves hanging off my shoulders with an elegant droop. My boots crunch over the grass as I march through the field in black tights, my gun strapped to my waist.

Between my gun and the hidden daggers along every inch of my body, I'm armed to the teeth and ready for whatever the day has in store.

A few boulders line the edge of the woods, the largest of which sits closer to the field where the Bosses are gathered. If I blow *that* up, I won't catch the forest on fire.

Lovely. Time for a little show.

Drew, Tucker, and Jace walk calmly beside me, while Levi soars overhead. The Bosses and the select few chosen to join each of them already wait in the field, just as I asked Reggie to orchestrate.

"Care to explain why we're outside?" Jett Darrington snaps impatiently, his glare trained on me as I near.

"What's the matter?" I ask calmly. "Allergic to the sun?"

He tilts his head in annoyance, but doesn't bother replying.

As I join the shifters in the field, Aki Nabal catches my eye. He watches me with an odd expression I can't quite place—somewhere between expectation and curiosity.

He must be waiting for some sign that I read his note, or some unspoken request to talk more later.

The Nabal Boss won't get it.

"I've decided to offer a little demonstration," I say to the gathered crowd. "It's come to my attention that some of you think I can be holed away or taken." I glare briefly in Elizabeth's direction, and my eyes flit just as quickly toward Victor Bane. "I wanted to set the record straight."

Jett scoffs. "And how do you—"

Before he can finish, I raise my palm and aim toward the boulder sitting nearby. My magic courses instantly through my blood, earth-shattering and over-whelming as it burns through me.

In a blinding bolt of light, I release a blast of my magic at the rock, shattering the giant stone to rubble.

The boom echoes through the field and forest. A moment later, the canopy shivers—and I'm fairly certain that's not from my blast.

It would seem the soldiers in the woods are itching to see what all the commotion is about.

As everyone gapes at the destroyed boulder, I catch the barest hint of a proud smirk on Harper's face. It's gone in a flash, almost instantly replaced by her stoic mask, but I'm a tad grateful I caught it.

It's nice to know she doesn't think of me as something to control.

"I'm not a trophy," I say simply to the gathered leaders. "I'm not a prize. I don't want this to become anything big. No battles, no blood. I just want to be left alone, but if any of you come after me, it will be war."

In the silence that follows, each Boss's gaze slowly drifts back to me. Harper and Isaac Palarne don't betray a single emotion. Victor Bane and Elizabeth watch me warily, but Jett Darrington and Aki Nabal look almost—*eager*.

Oh *that's* just *great*.

I briefly glare at Drew, frowning at him and wondering if he gave me bad advice, but he doesn't move. He continues to scan the Bosses before us, his face stoic and unreadable as ever.

With an annoyed sigh, I return my attention to the

leaders. "I would be willing to build alliances over time," I continue, walking through the rehearsed speech Drew and Jace helped me create last night. "Maybe even—"

"How about a little duel?" Jett interrupts, grinning as he rubs his hands together. "Just a lighthearted match, nothing serious. Nothing at stake."

Oh, there's something at stake. There always is during any interaction with a dragon shifter.

"Just you?" I ask, admittedly confused.

"No, no." He waves the thought away. "All six of us. I know how to share," he adds with a sneer.

I frown, slightly baffled by the suggestion. I'm not even sure what a duel with dragons would look like, since I can't shift.

Besides, this is just a bad idea all around. If I take them on while they're in human form, they would detect my lifetime of training, same as Harper did when she spotted me sparring with Jace back at the dojo. And if I fight them in their dragon forms, I'll have no choice but to use my power—all of it.

They could see too much. I can't let them know my limits or weaknesses.

"That's not necessary," Drew barks from behind me, his voice curt and even more intimidating than usual.

"Nonsense. That sounds delightful!" Elizabeth Andusk says, clapping as if someone offered to go get cake instead of instigating a full-on sparring match. "A little duel, just the seven of us."

"What a joke," Harper snaps. She saunters between Jett and Elizabeth, wrinkling her nose with disdain as she glares between the two of them. "Did you not see the blast just now? She has nothing to prove to us."

"Of course *you* think that," Elizabeth huffs. "You've already seen what she can do. She's been at your embassy, after all."

"I've kept myself at an arm's length, and you *know* it," Harper snaps back, her body tensing.

"I agree with Boss Fairfax," Isaac Palarne says solemnly. "The dragon vessel owes us nothing, much less such a brutish—"

"No one cares," Victor Bane rudely interrupts, his voice dismissive. "Face it, Palarne. Your little attempts to butter up the Quinn girl aren't working."

"You'll do well to shut your mouth," Isaac says sternly, arms crossed as he glares a dire warning to the Bane Boss.

I stiffen, not entirely sure what's happening right now. All I can tell is this will get ugly if left unchecked.

Jace appears beside me and sets a hand on my shoulder while the six of them bicker. "I will absolutely *not* allow—"

"What are you scared of, Goodwin?" Victor Bane grins, apparently eager for an excuse to look away from Isaac. I can practically feel the smarmy arrogance rolling off of him. "Afraid we'll break her that easily?"

"I challenge you, Rory Quinn, to a formal duel," Jett Darrington interjects, squaring his shoulders as he smirks at me. "It'll be nothing more than a friendly little scuffle. Scouts honor." He winks.

It would seem I'm outnumbered.

If I say no—if I walk away from a challenge with dragons—it's the equivalent of painting a target on my back. They'll jump on the chance to call me weak. Afraid. They will have no respect for any boundaries I set, and I will walk away from this whole mess in a worse situation than when I started.

If I say yes, they will use the opportunity to size me up. Learn my weaknesses. Assess and discover things about my fighting style they shouldn't know.

Damned if I do, damned if I don't.

"Rory, don't do this," Jace says quietly into my ear. He leans forward, his hand still firmly on my shoulder. "This could end badly."

"It will end badly either way," Drew interjects softly on the other side of me. He leans in, his voice low. "She can take them, Jace."

"They're six *Bosses*—"

"And she's the dragon vessel," Drew interrupts. "Give her some damn *credit.*"

"Guys, stop." I wave them away, not able to take

their bickering right now. "Drew, give me a rundown of the rules."

"Sparring match, basically." Drew leans toward me with his hand covering his mouth to hide what he's saying from the Bosses still bickering in front of us. "One on one. They'll take turns. Nothing below the belt, no death blows. Dragons play rough, though. People get hurt in these fights."

Hmm.

I lift my hand, delicately placing it over my mouth so that none of the Bosses can read my lips. "Jace, what is the worst case, here?"

"You *die*."

I roll my eyes. "Then they won't get my magic," I point out, trying to make him think rationally. "Tell me the real worst-case scenario."

"One of them flies off with you."

With a shake of my head, I dismiss it. Doing that to a guest of the Fairfax embassy would mean instantly declaring war—not to mention the implications of stealing me away when everyone else wants to do the same thing. Each of them is chomping at the bit for any reason to duke it out with each other to control me.

That alone gives me an advantage over the rest of them.

"Can a blow from one of them kill my dragon?" I ask, catching Jace's eye.

He sighs deeply, and I see him debate whether or not to answer. "No," he eventually admits.

"I came here to find out who I'm up against," I remind him, my gaze never wavering. "I think it's time I finally do just that."

Jace frowns. "This is a dangerous way to do it."

"Was there ever a safe way?"

He lets out a frustrated sigh, but doesn't answer.

"You know I can do this," I add, watching his face for any tells of a lie.

For a moment, he simply studies me, deep bags of exhaustion under his eyes. A second later, however, he nods.

I smirk.

Victory.

"This all sounds delightful," I say to the crowd gathered before me, interrupting their arguments. "Shall we get started? Now works for me."

To my surprise, Jett's smile falters as I accept his challenge. It takes me a minute to realize he was hoping I'd back down. Jett already knows a bit of what I can do—I suspect he wanted to hide my true potential from the others. He figured I would tuck tail and run, effectively hiding my power from the rest of them.

Oh, the poor fool.

To his credit, the Darrington Boss recovers quickly. "As this is a test of *natural* ability, you'll need to remove your weapons."

"Of course."

And you know what, I make a show of it— just to mess with him.

First, I unbuckle the gun's holster at my side and gently let it fall to the ground. A few of the daggers in my boots are next, and one by one, I toss aside each weapon I have hidden on my body.

It takes a while.

I never break eye contact with the Darrington Boss. In fact, I'm careful to over-exaggerate every movement to remind them all I'm more than a damsel to carry off in their claws.

As the last dagger falls to the ground, I nod to him. "Your turn."

"With pleasure." There are no smirks this time. No arrogant tilts of the head.

Right now, it's all business.

Though I expect a few guns to be tossed aside, the six Bosses spread out along the field. The handful of generals and advisors who joined each of them quickly retreat to a safe distance.

Before long, the six Bosses all stand a fair distance apart, each of them facing me.

And, in unison, they shift.

The ground rumbles as their forms hum with energy. Their skin shifts color. Their bodies blur. Clothing rips apart as they grow into the beasts that live within each of them.

In moments, six towering dragons loom over me, glaring down with glowing eyes. Several shake their bodies to loosen up after the shift, while others stretch their wings. A few of them roar into the sky as they sink into their dragon forms.

The roars seem to trigger a cascading ripple of energy through the woods behind them. The forest rumbles. The trees quake. The crack of snapping branches barrels past us as the tension builds, and I wonder if this time, the armies waiting on standby won't be able to resist anymore.

For a moment, the world goes quiet. The breeze ruffles my hair as I wait, my body tense, for chaos to erupt.

I'm not disappointed.

All at once, dragons soar into the sky from the woods. Hundreds of them. Thousands, maybe. The flurry of wings hitting the air drowns out all other sound. It's a never-ending torrent of dragons and wings and claws, and they quickly block out much of the sun.

The world around me darkens as hundreds of dragons swirl overhead, casting blurred shadows across me as they rumble through the sky.

In the swarm above, dragons snap at each other and growl in warning as others come too close. At any moment, a full-on brawl could erupt through the armies, and this entire estate would end up as nothing but ash and ruin in their wake.

Most people would cower and run.

Most people would regret their decision to accept this "little duel."

But I just grin with gleeful mischief. I think this is going to be quite a bit of *fun.*

CHAPTER NINETEEN

This swarm is far worse than the one that appeared in the sky when I first got my magic.

When I was kicked into the pit and refused to die.

There are easily a thousand dragons here, if not more, blocking out the sun.

Preparing for war.

The Bosses scream into the sky, and the dragons above seem to hear some kind of command that I miss. One by one, the thousands of shifters drop to the ground and land behind their Bosses.

Before long, the six fully-shifted armies fan out across the grassy field like spokes on a wheel. They bob their heads, growling and adjusting their wings as they all focus on the center of the circle of dragons.

On me.

I briefly look over my shoulder to find Drew,

Tucker, and Jace standing in a row behind me, each glaring at the populated field around us. Arms crossed, each man surveys the gathered shifters with a grim expression. Levi towers behind them, thunder rumbling in his chest as he protectively scans the dragons around us.

And, to my surprise, the dojo's army fills the grassy field behind Levi. Behind *me*.

The dojo has made its declaration—they honor and protect me, so long as Jace orders them to do it.

The ground shakes beneath us, and to my surprise, I find Isaac Palarne stalking cautiously toward me through the makeshift arena we've created in the grass.

My first challenger.

The dark green dragon digs his claws into the ground with every slow and purposeful step as he sizes me up. The powerful muscles along his arms tense against his scales.

He's going to charge, and the admirable dragon is giving me quite a bit of warning.

The spikes on his wings glisten sharply in the sun as he coils, ready to spring. His square head angles toward me, his gaze focused and calculating.

I square my shoulders and clench my fists, summoning the white light along my skin.

Let's do this.

Isaac darts at me like a bullet out of a gun, and I roll easily out of the way. Recovering is easy, and I calmly walk the edge of the arena as I survey my opponent.

As he and I circle each other, I notice the Bosses watching me thoughtfully, studying my movements.

I'm not worried. I'll get to do the same to each of them in just a moment. They're going to betray their own secrets today, no matter what they think they'll glean from me.

Isaac thunders along the ground with the practiced grace of a seasoned fighter. Every step is made with intention. Every tilt of his head has purpose, and he never once leaves any part of his body exposed. The muscle in his legs and neck ripple slightly with every thundering step, and a low growl builds in his throat as he prepares for his next blow.

He's brilliant, and I would never want to truly face off with him in a battlefield.

Thankfully, this is all just a test. Today is about pushing boundaries. Assessing skill. This little match of ours isn't about drawing blood or breaking bones, but I figure the less noble of the Bosses won't be as opposed to that as Isaac is.

Let's see how fast he can be.

I let loose a shot of my magic, aiming loosely for his head. Before it can reach him, he effortlessly ducks the blast.

Hmm. He's even faster than I thought he would be.

I'm tempted to aim at his chest, to see what his

response time is in closer quarters when the target is bigger and the risk is worse.

However, I refrain. I don't want to hit anyone else by accident when he inevitably avoids the blow.

I decide to bluff, instead.

I summon another surge of white light into my hand, training my eyes on his chest as if I'm going to fire. He growls and charges toward me, closing the gap almost instantly.

I could roll out of the way, but I don't.

This time, I decide to meet him head-on.

A dragon like Isaac? He can take it.

Instead of jumping, instead of darting out of the line of fire, I cock my arm and meet him halfway.

My enhanced dragon strength lets me do what would crush a normal human—and I punch a dragon Boss in the face.

My fist hits his forehead, and a thundering boom cuts through the air from the impact. The muscles in my arms scream in protest, but I hold my form. The force of the mighty dragon before me resisting my blow drives my heels into the ground. With my knuckles practically embedded in his skull, he pushes against me, sinking my heels deeper into the grass.

Dirt and rubble kick into the air, casting a thin fog around us. When the dust finally clears, he and I both breathe heavily from the effort of our duel. My fist rests resolutely on his forehead, a bit of steam billowing from beneath my knuckles.

Our eyes lock, and the connection opens in a rush.

They will not play fair, he silently warns. *Prepare for blood, and do not die.*

I figured they would cheat, I admit. *But thank you, regardless.*

He nods and steps away, the last bit of steam dissolving with a hiss into the sky as not a mark is left on his face. He offers me a regal bow to signal he's done, and our duel ends in a draw.

One down. Five to go.

Before I can even relax, Harper barrels into the open arena.

The stunning thunderbird growls with anticipation, her shoulders tense as she sizes me up. Her gorgeous lilac scales are laced with glowing blue veins, and a beautiful symbol glows on her forehead—I've never seen it before, and I don't know what it could mean. Massive horns curl from her skull, arching gently above her as she sizes me up.

She dives playfully toward me, and I roll easily out of the way. Her tail swipes at me before I can recover, though, and it takes all of my strength to duck that as well.

I grin, looking over my shoulder at her. "Cheater."

A quick laugh escapes her before she charges again.

We duck and parry, each blow faster than the last,

and honestly it's just plain fun. Harper is a beast—fast and powerful, every bit as skilled as I imagined. She tests me, pushing my boundaries, but there's no challenge here. There's no threat.

I lose track of what I wanted to test in her ability, and I just let myself enjoy the match.

In fact, I haven't had this much fun since Irena and I last practiced our swordplay together, just before the Vaer tried to steal her from me.

I grit my teeth to shove the thought from my mind. Even in a lighthearted sparring match, I can get seriously hurt if I don't pay attention.

Harper swings her spiked tail at me. I flip backward to avoid the blow and land effortlessly on my feet, the fingers of one hand resting against the ground for balance as I kneel.

Judging by the excitement in her glowing eyes, she's as lost in the match as I am.

Her throat hums, the looming echo both ominous and thrilling, and a quick burst of purple light shoots impulsively from her mouth.

At me.

I don't miss a beat—hell, I don't even think about it. I lift my hand and fire a small blast in response, doing my best to match the size of hers.

They hit, our aim perfect, and a blinding flash of light cuts through the air. I shield my eyes with an arm to protect my vision, and when the smoke clears, Harper roars excitedly into the sky.

"Show off," I mutter, but I can't hide my playful smirk.

Briefly, my gaze flits toward Jace—only to find him scowling at his Boss. Electricity crackles across his skin, and I suspect he's none too happy that she and I got carried away like that. I can tell he wants to tear into her, but to do so here would undermine her rule.

Oops.

Though Harper and I square off to continue, a massive black dragon jumps between us. He spreads his wings, blocking my view of the purple dragon across from me. The new contender roars, fire building in the back of his throat as he stares me down. The snarling scream pierces the air as it rolls over me.

Victor Bane.

He snarls, his red eyes blazing as he stalks slowly closer to me. Everything about his dragon is jagged and rough. Spikes like black ice stick from his face. Hooked claws protrude from the end of his wings. The serrated, uneven scales look sharp as knives, and they even glint ominously in the sun.

My smile fades. It would seem my pleasant little duel with Harper has been cut short.

As the Fairfax Boss slowly retreats to the sidelines, she snaps impatiently at the air. Her body brims with anger, nearly shaking as she aches to sink her teeth into

Victor. Instead, she paces along the front lines of her army, and I tense for my third battle of the day.

Unlike Harper and Isaac, Victor isn't going to play fair.

Without missing a beat, he lets loose a stream of fire. This close to him, I can't avoid it. There's no room to move. No room to roll out of the way. My choices are to block the fire, or die a crispy death.

On instinct, I do the only thing I can think of.

I fire back.

Blinding white light shoots from my palms as I meet his attack. The flames billow around me, heat nearly boiling the air as his molten breath rolls past me. Sweat pools along my face and neck. It takes everything in me to not double down. To not blast a hole through his chest. I actively fight the urge to concentrate more energy into my counterattack, to straight up kill him for trying to pin me like this.

These assholes are going to play dirty, and I need to meet them head on.

The stream of fire stops, but I take the chance to drive home how little I care for his methods.

I pause my beam of energy only long enough to take aim—right for the bastard's face.

I fire again, and my magic shoots into the air. He roars and ducks out of the way, but he's not as fast as Isaac—or *me*.

The blast grazes one of his horns, shattering the tip.

He roars in pain, baring his knife-like teeth as he snaps at the air mere feet from my face.

"Bring it!" I demand, virtually roaring back at him in my rage.

He charges me, and I dive easily out of the way. He swipes at my head with his claws, and I evade him —barely.

His talons dig into the earth where I was only moments before.

Smoke billows from his nose as he lowers his head, pausing to reassess his next move. The black dragon slowly circles me, growling aggressively as he decides what to do next.

My muscles begin to scream at me. My body is being pushed to its limit, far more so than any session with Zurie, but I can't get tired now.

I still have three Bosses left to duel, and I'm not quite done with Victor.

Behind me, another dragon roars—the pitch of her voice a bit higher than the others I've heard so far today.

Careful not to turn my back on either of them, I tilt my body until I can see them both.

Elizabeth Andusk stalks into the ring, apparently ready to take her turn against me. She doesn't strike me as a fighter—more of a princess—and I'm astonished to see her actually join the duel.

Her golden dragon is radiant, the scales shimmering like the sun's rays. Every step is graceful, like a dancer on a stage, and her tail slinks delicately from side to side as she walks the edge of the arena.

A black stripe runs from her forehead clear down her spine, and I find it odd that some Bosses have this line along their backs—while others don't.

Victor Bane snaps at her, apparently not done with me yet, and she lifts her head in defiance. Her wings instantly spread open, dazzling and bright as they reflect the sun. Bane winces, squinting as the light blinds him, and slowly backs toward the edge of the arena, giving up his place in the fight.

Now unchallenged for her place in the ring, Elizabeth lowers her wings and circles me. Her jeweled eyes glint in the sun, seemingly a dazzling array of colors. Every step is smooth and fluid, and the way her tail coils behind her reminds me of a snake.

I had assumed Elizabeth was a woman of comfort and elegance, and I suspect she won't be able to hold her own very long against me.

Elizabeth charges me, blindingly fast, nothing but a blur of gold in the sunny field. I roll out of the way, but her wing clips me.

The force sends me rolling across the grass, and I grimace as I push myself to my feet. It'll take more than a little love tap to keep me down. I summon my magic, daring her to try it again.

It would seem she's been paying attention to my other fights.

She struts, a self-satisfied smirk playing at the edge of her mouth, and I can see her getting cocky. This is why she's combatant number four—she quite intentionally let others go ahead of her, to test me and see what my limits are.

Little does she know I've only just begun.

She snarls, backing away from the white glow of my skin as if she's allergic.

"Scared?" I ask, smirking.

She shouldn't have shown her cards. As vain as Elizabeth is, I wouldn't be surprised if she's merely afraid my magic will leave a scar on her pretty face.

I know she's fast, but I want to test her reflexes. I aim a bolt of magic at her head, and she barely ducks out of the way in time. She snarls, furious, and quickly slinks back toward the sidelines.

"Done already?" I taunt.

Before she can even respond, a towering gray dragon steps in front of her, the silvery sheen of his scales almost on par with hers for sheer brilliance. A bright blue stripe runs down his spine, visible only briefly as he snaps at her to back away, and a trail of frost billows from his nose as he returns his attention to me.

Aki Nabal.

His dragon—by the gods, it's something else, unlike

anything I've ever seen.

A row of spikes lines his chest like spear tips, and he puffs himself up as he studies me. The effect makes him seem even larger, somehow even taller, and it almost hurts my neck to look up at his face as it looms in the sky above me.

Unlike the others, Aki isn't one for games.

He instantly charges. His jaws snap at the air, second after second, driving me backward as I barely duck out of the way each time. With each crack of his powerful jaws clomping the air, too close for comfort, it takes everything in me to avoid the blows.

I'm barely an inch away from a broken arm. Broken leg. Broken femur. Every time, I only *just* avoid a gruesome injury, and I realize I misjudged Aki.

He's a clever, cunning man—and quite an adept fighter. This man is *fast,* and it's clear he's been studying my movements more closely than anyone else thus far.

With every shift of my weight, every change in direction, he's there with a counter. His tail whacks me hard in the stomach several times, throwing me onto my back. My head hits the ground hard with each blow, my world spinning even as I force myself to roll out of his reach.

Panting, I try to put some distance between us so I can catch my breath. It doesn't work, and I look up only to find him charging toward me once more.

Adrenaline boils through me. Deep in my core, my dragon stirs, trying to come to my aid. But she's not ready—and I need to focus on the dragon Boss before me instead of coaching her through this moment.

I barely dive out of the way in time. I long to land a blow on him, but I never get the chance. Aki has me on the defensive, and I hate it.

Though I'm not getting much of a chance to test his physical limits, I am learning a lot about how he learns. What he looks for.

Based on his attacks, I can start to paint the picture of what he's trying to do. He only picked up on a few of my habits—the way I frequently feint to the right, the way my elbow cocks when I'm about to bluff my way through an attack.

Those are little things, and they're easy to change.

In fact, I will never allow myself to do any of them again. He just made me a better fighter, and he probably doesn't even realize it.

As focused as I am on our duel, I tune the world out. It's just me and him, just the repetitive motion of rolling out of his reach. I get tunnel vision—I have to, or else he might take off my hand.

A shrill roar cuts through the air, and a breath of smoke rushes past us. I cough, shifting my attention briefly, only to find Jett Darrington's massive face barely ten feet from my own.

Gods above, I hate it when someone gets the drop

on me—especially when that someone is Jett Darrington.

Staring into the Darrington Boss's eyes is like gazing into hell itself. His body glows like molten lava, the sharp spikes along his neck sizzling as if they could melt off at any second. His mighty wings slowly stretch above me, spreading with slow and ominous intention. Small holes appear along the edges, no doubt scars from the many battles this shifter king has fought —and won.

Damn it all to *hell*. I let Aki get the best of me, and while I was distracted, Jett decided to make his move.

Though I sort of expect the two to team up, to break the rules and take me on at once, Jett Darrington turns his slow and furious gaze onto the silver dragon.

Aki snarls, lifting his wings defiantly as he bares his teeth, and for a moment it looks as though the two of them are going to face off instead.

After a tense moment, Aki slowly backs away, leaving the arena to Jett.

The fiery Darrington Boss snarls and turns his attention back to me. Thunder rumbles in his chest as he stares me down, closing the gap between us with crashing steps. I back away as his claws dig into the ground, tearing up grass by the roots.

Everything about him radiates power, and it's suddenly abundantly obvious where Drew gets his own natural authority.

On Jett Darrington's next breath, flames roll over his teeth.

He's—he's going to spit *fire*.

The moment after I realize what he plans to do, the flames tear from his mouth. The grass beneath us burns away, roasted by the heat.

I summon all of my energy, all of my magic, and counter in the only way I can—by firing a blistering beam of my magic, straight into the flames. The white light burns against the inferno trying to roast me as I pour myself into my attack. My muscles scream with pain, but I press through.

I lose track of time.

It feels like I'm there forever, sweat dripping down my arms and neck as I fight the colossal dragon before me.

My body aches for rest, but I can't indulge it.

I can't stop.

Not yet.

When the flames finally end, I wearily lower my hands. The blinding white light of my magic disappears as black smoke billows before me. I can't see Jett, but I barely have any energy to move. To find cover. I've been pushed to the limit, pushed almost to my max by each of the most powerful dragons on the planet.

I'm exhausted, and Jett Darrington *knows* it.

The molten dragon barrels through the flames as

the last of them dissolve into the sky, using his own attack as cover to charge me.

I lift my hands again to fire, but he's too fast—and I'm too exhausted.

I expect him to smack me with his head, to send me barreling across the field. Maybe he'll swipe at me with his claws to draw a bit of blood. To mark me.

It'll hurt, but I'll live.

As I summon my magic to protect myself, his teeth dig into my torso. It's the ultimate low blow, tearing into a human who can't bite back. I bite back an agonizing scream as pain rips through me. Blood streams down my body from a half-dozen holes.

And by the gods, it *hurts.*

I've never felt pain like this. It's like my skin is slowly ripping apart, slowly tearing open. My world goes fuzzy. I can't see. I lift my hands through it all, desperate to counter, desperate to do more than sit in his jaws and let him crush me.

I fire a bolt of my sizzling magic directly into his mouth.

He shrieks in misery. With a sudden thrust of his head, the enormous dragon tosses me clear across the field.

I roll for several feet, grimacing with agony as I slowly come to a stop. Everything in me screams for me to stand. To fight. To end this, to see it through.

But, for a moment, the pain is just too much.

"Rory!" Several familiar voices yell my name from somewhere far off. Their voices are distant and almost watery, and I figure I probably have a mild concussion.

But I don't care.

This asshole just pushed me too damn far.

The ground shakes beneath me as a blurry shadow looms over me once again.

Briefly, I wonder if Jett is trying to kill me—and if he could truly get away with that, given all these witnesses. It seems so far-fetched, so impractical given how hard he's fought to kidnap me, but he's a Darrington. They can get away with anything.

It takes a moment for my blurry brain to piece together the truth.

He wants me to forfeit. To give in. To admit defeat, but only to him. To crown him the winner of this little duel.

But biting his human prey and throwing her across the field is hardly a fair blow, and I figure he broke the rules.

That means he's fair game.

As the thundering ringing in my ear begins to fade, replaced by the furious roars of the dragons around me, I figure I'm not the only one who thinks so.

Jett Darrington won't care, though. To him, a win is a win—no matter how it's acquired.

"Rory, tap out!" Tucker shouts over the din.

"You've done enough!" Jace adds.

No, I really haven't.

I'm just getting *started.*

Jett Darrington roars, his face coming suddenly into focus only about fifty feet away, and I furiously summon my magic. My power hums across my skin, vast and infinite, an electrifying reminder of who I am. Of *what* I am.

He's going to regret ever meeting me.

As my body ripples with light, I lift my palm and aim straight for Jett's ugly face.

And I *fire.*

He ducks, and in my fury, I'm almost faster than even him. He barely maneuvers out of the way, leaving everyone behind him to duck as the beam soars over their heads.

As I force myself to stand, I clench my fists and dig into the last of my willpower. The world around me glows white as I summon every shred of my magic, knowing full well I have to tap into the deepest reserves to pull off what I plan to do next.

I don't care.

I am so *done.*

The Darrington Boss snarls, apparently furious that I won't give up. It'll be a cold day in hell before I do, and he'd best get used to that.

I'm ready to end this.

Without hesitating, I fire several beams of light at his head. His chest. His feet. His wings. One after the other, I drive Jett backward, never giving him a moment of respite. He ducks and dodges them all, slowly making his way toward me as we set the field on fire. Smoke billows into the air from every gray patch of ground I hit.

And still, he stalks closer.

Even still, he won't stop.

He roars, barely twenty feet from me now, and I decide to end this. Once and for all. Drew survived a direct blast of my magic—maybe his father will, too. At this point, I don't really care either way.

In my raging bloodlust, I don't even care if that means killing a Boss.

It's time I *really* test Jett Darrington. Because at this point, he's practically begging me to break him in half.

I summon the full force of my magic. Every drop. Every ounce. It reminds me of the powerful surge I felt when Ian tried to break me—just as I did back then, I feel my feet gently lift off the ground. I surrender to the magic within me, to the power in my blood, and my world goes fully white.

All I can see is Jett barreling toward me, glowing like the open pit of a bubbling volcano.

He roars, summoning flames in his throat.

But I don't need to snarl into the sky to be powerful.

His flames billow toward me, and I unleash the full force of my magic on him. It bleeds from me in a beam of light twice as tall as I am as my toes hover several feet above the grass.

In the blazing glory of the moment, a calm stillness sweeps over me. It's a confident knowing, of sorts, and I feel as though it's not really mine. As if these are the feelings of something else, something powerful taking over me.

I know, then, that his dragon-fire doesn't even stand a chance.

Not against me.

I cut through the flame effortlessly, and my aim is perfect. My bolt hits him square in the face.

He screams with pain. Black smoke billows into the sky. It shrouds us, hiding everything, enveloping us all in the darkness.

In the aftermath of my blow, the world is eerily silent. A piercing ring in my ear is the only sound for a time—that and the thunder of my pulse.

As the smoke finally begins to clear, the first thing I see is Jett's glowing right eye. He glares at me, huffing and exhausted. A radiant white scar covers his left eye, and he can't even open it. The scar smokes like a bonfire, and even on a dragon like him, it must hurt like hell.

A stream of black smoke billows from his nose as he growls, but he doesn't attack me again. It seems like he's very much done.

And *pissed.*

That makes two of us.

He played dirty to get me to quit. He pushed me to my limits and tried to break me. The bastard even tried to literally snap my body in half. Yet again, he felt as though he was above the rules.

And I am so freaking *done.*

Done with Jett. Done with Milo. Done with these Bosses who look at me like a plaything.

Because they're wrong. I'm anything but a toy—I'm a warrior, and I have the magic of the three dragon gods in my core.

My blood boils—from the utter rage, from the buzz of battle, from the unrestrained hum of the raw power in my veins.

Deep within me, my dragon stirs again. She's as furious as I am, as lost in the anger and rage as me. As I grit my teeth, my body covered in blood and bruises, I feel something overtake me. Something unquestionable, powerful, and undeniable. I feel a surge of energy unlike anything I have ever felt before, and my skin glows with the unrestrained magic in my blood.

It fills me with *fire*.

"I want to make one thing clear," I shout to the gathered horde of dragons around me. It's like something has possessed me with the fury of the gods, and I want nothing more than to decimate the world around me. "We can be enemies, if you want. I'll fight you, tooth and nail, until my dying breath." The words roll effortlessly from my tongue, and I'm almost surprised to find I mean it. Every word comes from my heart, and every sentence is an honest and bloody promise. "I swear to you all—if you *fuck* with me, if you so much as *threaten* anyone I love, I will *end* you. Everything you've built, everything you worship, I will set it on fire. And I will make you watch as it burns to *rubble*."

As the rage flames on within me, several of the Bosses bristle at my threat. Their necks arch in defiance. Their eyes narrow in hatred. They growl, the quiet thunder of their voices thrumming in their chest, and the seven of us stare each other down with our armies at our backs.

But no one attacks.

No one challenges me.

Because they know I'm right—and now, thanks to what I just did to Jett Darrington himself, they know I'll follow through.

Diplomacy is about negotiation. You state the terms you desire and allow the other side to discuss alternatives from there.

But dragons—we're different.

Today, I drew the line in the sand. The boundary. The one rule I have for all of them...

Leave me the hell alone.

And I *dare* any of these fools to cross it.

CHAPTER TWENTY

What a crazy day.

I sit on the roof of the villa, surprised at how much I miss my view from the top of the castle back in the dojo. For someone who always jokes that my men are trying to lock me away in a tower, the irony is not lost on me that one of my favorite places in the world is sitting on top of one.

But hey, the roof is different.

That's what I tell myself, anyway.

Levi curls protectively around me in the growing dusk, surprisingly comfortable to lean against despite the steep slope of the shingles. Though the light is quickly fading, I feel utterly comfortable curled up against him. He supports my weight, locking me safely in place as I stare out over the castle grounds.

A searing pain shoots through my side, and I wince

in agony as my wounds heal. Something about my new magic lets me heal faster than a human or a dragon—no one's really sure why, of course—but I don't mind it. I should be better by tomorrow morning, and Reggie's on-hand nurse kept assuring me that I might not even have a scar.

Pity, though. I hope I get a big one. Scars are beautiful proof you're a survivor.

As Levi and I survey the world around us, all I can think about is how right Drew was—how *different* life is outside the dojo. How strict. How pretentious. Ruled by duplicity and lies.

I see, now, why Jace enforces the embassy rules so fiercely. It makes the place feel like a home, rather than another political arena.

Part of me wants to ditch this meeting and go see Irena. To give these assholes the finger and just leave.

After today, I feel like I earned the right to do just that.

As Levi breathes beneath my head, his chest rising and falling in a smooth cadence, I run my fingers lovingly over his scales. He growls happily at my touch, his eyes closed.

Our connection opens as my skin brushes his scales, and I smile as the flood of his emotions streams through to me. Satisfaction. Peace. Devotion.

And, always, that surge of protectiveness. Possessiveness.

Love.

I press my cheek against his body, the scales soft and soothing, and I sigh with pleasure.

It's nice to get a bit of peace.

I'm tempted to ask him questions about being human, about what I can do to help him turn back, but I don't want to press him. He's given me everything he can, and now, it's up to me to do the rest.

He inches his head toward me, curling around his body as he presses his nose oh-so-gently against my chest. I grin, grateful for how gentle he's being with my wounds and aching muscles, but I decide to poke fun all the same. "I'm not a porcelain doll, you know."

A few huffing laughs escape him. *You're strong.*

"Darn right I am." I grin playfully.

He takes a deep breath and presses his head a little harder against me. Without warning, I feel a sudden tug at my navel. An invitation to join him in his mind.

Despite the castle grounds brimming with dragons, I let him tug me in. Jace, Drew, and Tucker are watching over us. Besides, after today's little stunt in the grassy arena, *no one* is getting within a hundred feet of me tonight.

The darkness swarms me yet again as he pulls me into his mind, and within moments, I'm in his arms. He holds me close, his grip almost desperate. The way he cradles my head, it's almost like he's afraid I could fade away to dust at any moment.

I lift my chin, studying his gorgeous blue eyes and loving the way his dark hair hangs in his face. "What did you want to—"

Before I can finish, he grabs my jaw and kisses me roughly. A delightful chill snakes through me, as his strong fingers slip toward my neck. He holds me tightly, his kiss filling me with a soothing kind of joy I didn't know I could ever feel. His hands sink lower, along my shoulders, down my sides, exploring me. Before long, he grabs my waist as he presses me backward. Almost instantly, my back flattens against a wall.

But most of all, I feel his *soul*.

A channel opens, stronger than any I've felt before. It's a floodgate of sorts, and it's like everything he wants to say, everything he feels so deeply but can't express—it all pours into me in a rush.

I love you.

I would die for you.

I will do anything to keep you safe.

To make you happy.

The words flutter through me, and I'm not sure if they're mine or his.

Levi's mouth explores mine, eager and hungry. His hands sink to my ass, and he lifts me effortlessly into the air.

The wall behind me disappears, and I fall abruptly backward.

The world shifts around us, and I'm suddenly

falling onto a bed. In his mind, I guess he has free rein to do what he wants—and he apparently wants to be inside of me.

Levi leans over me, pressing one arm into the mattress for balance as his other hand roams my body. His strong grip chases up my leg, across my thigh, and brushes across my entrance.

I gasp quietly, grinning at his brazen lust, not entirely sure what's come over him—but I like it.

In this raw moment fueled by his passion, he snares me completely. Heart and soul. I can see nothing, think of nothing but Levi. His intense blue gaze hovers over me, his eyes charged with desire and longing.

"This is what I want to give you." He pauses, his voice rough and deep as he catches his breath. "I want to show you every possible way your body can feel pleasure. I want to bring you ecstasy again and again." His smile falls. "Before it's too late."

"It's *not* too late, Levi." I lean toward him, resting on my elbows as I bring my lips inches from his. "It's just not, and I won't give up on you. I refuse to. We can do this in person—when you're human again."

"I can't—" He groans, looking sharply away.

A knot tightens in my throat as I watch his tortured expression. "I'm going to fix this, Levi. I promise you. I will never give up on you, do you hear me? Not for one minute. And I need you to believe in me. I need you to trust me."

His head snaps toward me, his jaw tensing as his blue eyes drink me in. Something I said triggers something deep within him—something he's not sharing. His eyebrows tilt upward, and it's clear he's fighting a bloody internal war.

In a sudden rush, the bedroom disappears. The dusty swirls of his last lingering memories flit by me as he kicks me out of his mind.

"Levi, don't—"

Just like that, I'm on the roof again, leaning on my hands and knees as I cough, trying to breathe past the agonizing wound in my side.

He growls gently, sounding more wounded than angry, and stands. His nose presses softly against my back, a comforting gesture to help me catch my breath.

"I'm fine," I assure him. "But I mean it. I need you to—"

Apparently satisfied that I'm okay, he doesn't let me finish. The rush of his wings tussles my hair as he takes into the sky. I look over my shoulder to find his blue form retreating into the clouds, and I sigh in defeat.

His dragon takes over more and more every day.

I just don't have *time*.

In an instant, Jace lands on the roof beside me, the breathtaking thunderbird watching as Levi retreats. He's tense and ready for war, wings arched as he prepares to give chase.

"It's fine," I assure him, wincing as I hold my side.

His gaze shifts to me, and he growls softly. With a tender nudge on my back, he inches me toward the window I used to climb out here in the first place.

"All right, all right," I mutter, waving him off. "Pushy dragon."

He chuckles, waiting until I lift the window before he takes off into the sky again. But as I climb back inside, I pause and stare off after Levi's retreating form. As he disappears into the clouds, I wonder what on Earth I'm going to do.

Save him, obviously. But—*how*?

When I climb back into the house, I'm surprised to find Harper waiting for me downstairs on the cloud-like sofa. Drew fiddles with something in the kitchen, banging and making a mess of things. Tucker sits on a barstool, cleaning one of his guns.

"Hey, babe," he says with a flirty grin. "Wait until you hear what the big bad Fairfax Boss is calling these sofas." He nods toward Harper. "Go on, tell her."

"I decided to call this the bliss-couch." Harper says with a happy sigh as she sinks into the cushions.

"That sounds like a sex thing," I admit.

Tucker and Drew snicker, each returning to their

work as I apparently lay bare what they were both thinking.

Harper groans. "Great, now you ruined it for me."

"You're welcome."

The Fairfax Boss sits up and studies me, a proud little smile on her face. "Sparring with you was fun."

I grin. "The feeling is mutual."

"That bolt, and the way you blocked my magic? Just —*wow*." Harper falls back against the couch and splays her arms out beside her, like she can't believe what she saw. "Amazing. We should do that again sometime when we don't have to hold back."

"I think I'd be down for that."

The Fairfax Boss waggles a finger at me. "I knew you were good, but I didn't know you were *that* good. It seems my cousin has been keeping secrets. I mean you—girl, you're a force to be reckoned with."

"Thank you, thank you." I feign a sarcastic little curtsey, though a sharp pain in my side from the wound means I can't move quite as far as I would have liked to.

"What's on the agenda for tomorrow?" Tucker asks.

"Palarne requested a formal meeting," Drew answers. "The only one to follow protocol," he adds with a not-so-subtle glare at Harper.

"Oh, go away," the Fairfax Boss mutters, waving her hand dismissively. "I don't have to do that stuff if I've already met her."

Drew rolls his eyes.

"I think it's time to leave," I say. "I'll send Isaac a note explaining the situation, but I don't want to stay just for that. Technically, I've already met him, too."

"That doesn't count." Drew sets down a plate of chicken and broccoli and leans his elbows on the counter as he picks at the food. "You could learn something useful from him."

"Like what?"

"What he wants with you." Drew shrugs. "Why he's trying so hard to get you to his Capital."

I shake my head. "He's been pretty good at stringing me along. I don't see how tomorrow will be any different."

"Yeah." Harper nods. "I've enjoyed hanging out with you, Rory, but you've done more than enough for these Bosses. I think it's fair if you head home early."

"It's not just that," I admit. "I want them to know how, even with their armies around me, even though I'm literally sitting in the middle of an open field, I can get away from them at any time." I grin wickedly. "That I can slip through their fingers with ease."

"Huh." Harper lifts her brows in surprise, eyes momentarily glossing over as she thinks through my idea. "Yeah, actually. That's brilliant."

"I'm down." Tucker screws the last bit of his gun into place and slings it over his shoulder. "Let's get the hell out of here."

"Drew?" I ask, curious to hear his thoughts.

It's still odd to me—having a team. Asking for input before I make a decision. But it makes us stronger, and I would be a fool to just disregard their advice.

"After today, yes," he eventually admits. "I think you have a valid point. I still think you would benefit from staying and talking with Palarne, but you can always meet with him another time. There's nothing especially important about it happening tomorrow."

"Good." I smirk. "I doubt Jace will mind, so let's pack up."

And thank the gods—because like Tucker, I can't wait to get the hell out of this dragon den.

CHAPTER TWENTY-ONE

I n the dead of night, once only a few lights remain on in the main castle, we leave in a silent stream of cars.

There were some *heated* deliberations—to put it mildly—on how best to make our way back to the dojo. The sheer distance we need to travel, combined with zero-tolerance regulations on human-owned dragon neutral zones, like Reggie's, ironically enough meant we can't fly. Turns out dragons can shift all they want on Reggie's property, but any flights into or out of the land are strictly prohibited and closely monitored by the humans nearby.

That leaves us stuck on the ground. Not the best option, by any means, but we have to make it work.

Given how there's a lone hitman after me, off

shooting cars in an effort to track me down, quite a few tempers flared. Including mine.

In the end, we went with keeping the element of surprise.

This hitman knows we're aware of him, and he's going to expect us to have extra guards. To deal with that many soldiers, he might use explosives or jeopardize human bystanders in an effort to throw us off our game, and I want to keep one step ahead of him.

That's why I'm going to do the thing he least expects—hop in a gaudy limo with no obvious guard.

Is it my favorite choice? Hell no.

Is he going to be looking for me in one of these things? Also no.

That's why Jace and I settle into the back of a stretch limo, the windows tinted nearly to black.

Twelve cars roll out of the castle grounds at once in a nearly silent procession down the main road. Once the single roving road out of the castle branches off into side streets, the decoy cars begin to take off in different directions. We have everything from limos to SUVs to even a taxi with one *very* confused driver making his way toward the airport. I made sure to put an extra guard with him, since I didn't want him hurt on my behalf.

Every unit has two vans of reinforcements on standby, following at a short distance to swoop in if anything happens. Within moments, any lone gunman targeting the cars will be overwhelmed and, ideally, dead.

There's still risk, of course. I wanted more cars. More decoys. More reinforcements, but we ran out of unmarked vans. I also wanted an army of dragons flying overhead as cover—but in the human-owned areas we have to pass through, the five-hundred-foot rule was still in effect.

All boots have to be on the ground, in their human forms and armed to the teeth. That seriously limits our choices. Especially given how last-minute our departure was.

"It's a good plan, Rory." Jace takes a deep breath, his eyes closing as he leans his head back against the headrest. "There's risk, but my team can handle this. Stop worrying."

"Stop worrying?" I grin, giving the dojo master a once-over. "Who are you, and what have you done with Jace Goodwin?"

He chuckles, the bags under his eyes worse than ever. "I'm so glad we're out of there."

I nod, smiling a bit at how adorable he is when he gets this tired. "I bet you'll sleep for days to make up for this sleep deficit of yours."

"That sounds pretty good," he admits.

The limo goes over a bump in the winding country road, and Jace's head rolls toward my shoulder. As his temple brushes my neck, he sits abruptly upright and clears his throat, trying to look alert.

I chuckle. "It's almost over, Jace. Hang in there."

In answer, he yawns. "I just want to get home, where I know you'll be safe."

"I wouldn't mind that, either," I admit. "I'm ready for a bit of quiet." I adjust in my seat, the thick gauze around my abdomen restricting my movement. My muscles are stiff and sore as I recover, and a sliver of pain slices through me as I move. I grimace, holding the injury on impulse.

"What's wrong?" Jace leans in instantly, his hand on my abdomen as his eyes rove my torso, probably in search of blood. He lifts my shirt, checking the wrappings before I have the chance to bat his hand away.

"I'm fine." I laugh and shoo him off, adjusting my shirt to cover all the gauze. "I'm mostly just sore at this point."

"Really? Just sore?"

"There's a bit of pain, but it's not terrible." I shrug. "I've had worse."

"Wow. You heal faster than even I do," he says, impressed. "That's incredible."

"Yeah, well, I'm not at a hundred percent yet," I remind him. "So that means no training for, what, a week?"

He scoffs. "You're lucky if I give you an afternoon off."

I grin. "Hardass."

He smirks at me, giving me a playful sidelong glance, and lifts a small communications device to his mouth. "Units, check in."

"One, clear," Drew's voice chimes through the transmitter.

I grin at the fire dragon's voice—he was none too happy about Jace joining me in the car, instead of him. I'll probably get quite an earful later, but we all decided it was better to fan out. It would confuse the hitman and hopefully trip him up.

"Two, clear," Tucker chimes in. He only agreed to take another car if I convinced Reggie to let him have the castle's brand-new Jeep.

"Three, clear," one of Jace's soldiers chimes in.

One by one, the eleven other cars sound off. Thus far, everyone is fine. No suspicious activity. No gunfire. Not even a roadblock to redirect anyone.

"Have you seen anything, yet?" Jace asks the elite dojo soldier disguised as our driver.

"Nothing, sir," the man replies. He briefly glances into the rearview to catch his superior's eye, the visor on his chauffer's cap blocking a good bit of his face. "I'm keeping an eye out."

Jace sighs and leans back into his chair. "Good work, Russell."

"Thank you, sir."

"Can you relax, now?" I ask, reclining against my seat.

"Not until we're home."

"And then?"

Jace's stormy gray eyes shift to me, and he grins mischievously "I'm going to drag you into my bed and fall asleep with you on top of me."

I laugh. "Such a romantic."

He shrugs. "I try."

"What if—"

"Unit seven under fire!" a woman shouts into the transmitter. "He came out of nowhere. Gods— requesting backup. Repeat—"

A resounding boom interrupts her, and her voice abruptly cuts off.

"Reinforcements assigned to unit seven, engage!" Jace shouts into the transmitter. "Move, damn it! Cover them!"

"Alpha team engaging, sir!" a man shouts.

Somewhere nearby, several vans filled with his warriors were already in pursuit, speeding off to take out the threat.

Though I'm concerned for Jace's soldiers, he promised to only pick the best of the best—the ones who have been in situations like this before. They can handle this, and so can I.

Satisfied with my plan, I smirk. Whoever this lone hitman is, he fell for our decoys. By the end of the day, we'll have him outnumbered and outgunned.

"Do not hesitate to eliminate the target," Jace orders into the device. "I repeat, I want this motherfucker *dead*, do you hear me?"

Whoa.

My eyebrows arch along my forehead as I stare at Jace in amazement. He's never spoken like that before. In my surprise, I simply observe every detail of his face. The wrinkling along his nose. The deep scowl. The look of utter hatred directed at the floor as he barks orders to his soldiers.

Just like that, the General in him broke free. I've never gotten to see this side of him. The authority. The control. The commander, leading his army.

And, despite the danger, I can't help but lose myself in how freaking *hot* he is.

My blood boils with desire for him, at knowing the lengths this man would go to in order to protect me.

To protect *us.*

"Sir, we have movement," Russell says from the driver's seat. "Two black SUVs at our six. Possibly engaging. Standby."

Jace draws a gun from a holster hidden under his shirt and cocks it. "Risk level?"

"Unknown, sir." The warrior up front tightens his grip on the steering wheel, his eyes glued to the side mirrors. "Continuing to observe."

"Unit four under fire!" a man shouts into the transmitter.

"What?" I frown, confused. "Four is several miles from Seven, Jace. There's no way this guy could—"

"Damn it." Jace aims his gun out the back window, eyes trained on the two black cars behind us. With his free hand, he lifts the transmitter to his mouth again. "All reinforcements, deploy to your assigned units immediately. Repeat, *all* units. Move!"

I curse under my breath and draw my gun from the holster at my waist, carefully twisting in my seat so as not to tear open the still-healing wound on my abdomen. I aim at the cars behind us, trying to get any details on their faces that I can.

"I don't think this is a lone wolf, Jace," I mutter. "Was our intel bad? How could—"

"I don't know," he interrupts. "Stay low and don't engage, Rory. Let me do this."

"Right, as sleep-deprived as you are, I'm sure your aim is golden." I snort derisively. "Maybe *you* should sit this one out."

"Rory, just *listen*." He glares at me, his voice deep and rough. "I've trained for situations like this. No amount of sleep-deprivation can—"

"Sir, they're leaving," Russell says with a sigh of relief.

Jace and I return our attention out the back window as the two black cars turn down a side road.

In the silence that follows, I keep my gun trained through the back window, scanning for threats. It would be lovely if the danger had passed, but I don't let myself believe it. Still, I can't help but wonder if we got worked up over nothing. If, perhaps, those two SUVs were just tourists, or maybe locals driving home.

The limo screeches suddenly to a halt. I'm thrown forward, rolling across the floor as Jace falls on top of me. Bolts of pain tear through me. Something in my side rips. I groan in agony as hot blood bubbles from my torn skin.

Russell swerves. "Mother of—"

Whatever the soldier was about to say, he never gets to finish.

A car races toward us out of nowhere, catching us off guard as it hits us square in the side. Unable to avoid the impact, Russell's head jerks violently to the side.

To my dismay, the limo flips.

We jostle through the cabin, tossed this way and that. Everything's a blur. Somewhere, glass shatters. A man groans in agony. We roll and roll, until the limo finally lands upside down.

The first thing I feel in the aftermath is blood seeping from the dozens of scratches in my arms.

I grimace, my world still spinning as I slowly lift myself onto my hands and knees. My palms rest against what was once the ceiling, and shards of glass scattered beneath me threaten to slice open my fingers. The sleek black leather is ripped nearly to shreds.

Dazed, my arms shake as I try to get my bearings.

The limo is empty. No Russell. No Jace. All that remains of either man is a huge hole where one of the windows used to be.

"Jace!" I yell. I can barely hear myself over the ringing in my ears. I stumble, trying to stand, trying to rush to him and make sure he's okay.

I don't make it very far.

The door behind me opens, and blinding light streams through. I squint, trying to summon my magic to defend myself, but my body hasn't caught up yet. I can barely sit upright, much less fight.

A shadow looms before me, cutting through the blinding light. A man's form, judging by the broad shoulders. For a second, I wonder if it's Jace—but then he grabs a fistful of my hair. His fingers nearly dig into my scalp, and with a sharp tug, he drags me from the wreckage.

The splitting pain coursing through my body is almost too much to bear. My head. My arms. My side. Blood seeps over everything, and my fingers are slippery from the hot liquid rolling over me. I reach for my gun, but for several moments, I just snatch at the air.

After a crash like that, my coordination is shot to shit—and everything is still so damn *blurry*.

My hand finally reaches my holster, but it's empty.

Damn it.

Not one to waste time, I switch gears and look for a knife. After a few moments of struggling, I finally manage to grab one of the daggers in my boot, but I'm too late. Two strong hands grab my waist and hurl me through the air. I land on something hard, and instantly, the light fades.

Vibrations float through me, disorienting, and the fluttery dread in my chest starts to turn my blood cold.

But I'm a fighter.

I've been through worse than this.

Survive, Rory, I tell myself. *Whatever it takes, survive.*

I squeeze my eyes shut, giving myself only a second or two to clear my head.

To focus.

To fight.

It works. The ringing fades. My vision clears enough that, despite the darkness, I see the dim glow of a red taillight filter through a gap in what looks like metal. My fingertips massage the ground beneath me— cheap carpet.

I'm in a car.

Correction—I'm in a freaking *trunk.*

Oh, this asshole is going to die a painful death.

The floor beneath me lurches, and I slide across the cheap carpet as the car speeds off. With each twist and turn, I'm jostled and thrown around. It's tough to keep my balance, but I manage to lie on my back with my hands on the roof of the trunk to stay still. It only kind of works, however, and I still slide along my back as the car screeches around the next bend. A sliver of pain shoots up my spine from all the injuries, but I grit my teeth through the pain.

He's driving—which means he's distracted.

Only a fool turns his back on someone who trained as a Spectre all her life—even if he thinks he has her safely stored away in his trunk.

With my enhanced strength, I kick out the carpeted wall opposite the red glowing light. The goal is to get into the car's cabin, and sure enough, my boot and the decimated fluff that was once a seat cushion lands in the backseat.

A dark forest whizzes past the windows as the car races down an isolated road. A man sits in the driver's seat—dark eyes, light skin, dirty blond hair. His furious gaze in the rearview mirror is focused on me, instead of the road, and I hope he realizes how badly he just screwed up.

The risks here are obvious—either he's armed and tries to shoot me, or I take him out and we end up wrecking his crappy car.

Or both.

To hell with it. I've already survived one crash today, and getting in another one doesn't faze me. Especially not if it kills this guy.

He lifts a gun, angling it toward me over his

shoulder, and I effortlessly kick it away. I figure he wasn't expecting me to get my coordination back, but that's the perk of people underestimating me—it's easier to kick their asses once they let their guard down.

The gun clatters to the floor and slides beneath the passenger's seat. Without even giving him a chance to reach for it, I lean my chest against the back of his seat and wrap my arm around his neck to choke him.

My injury screams in protest as I lean against the back of the driver's seat. Stitches rip. Blood seeps through my shirt. I can already feel the wound ripping open again.

But I do *not* care.

The stranger gasps for air, clawing at my arm as he desperately tries to get me off of him. His nails gouge the full length of my forearm, but I grit my teeth through the pain and use it as fuel to grip him tighter.

In a desperate move, he spins the wheel sharply to the left.

The momentum throws me off of him, but he can't recover in time to keep the car from flipping off the road. We roll, the world spinning around us. In the chaos, my back hits one of the car doors, and the force of the impact knocks it open.

As my world tumbles, I can feel a thick rush of something warm seeping through my shirt. Something sharp stabs my shoulder. I grimace in agony, impulsively biting back the scream of pain as Zurie always taught me to.

When I finally stop rolling, everything hurts. It takes a long while for me to groggily lift my head, and for a moment, I don't dare move. I just can't. I lay in puddle of blood, beaten and bruised, and I almost can't tell which parts of me hurt worst.

Not far away, the man groans in pain.

Guess I can't tend to my wounds, then.

I force myself to my feet, squaring my shoulders as I stare him down. Blood drips in a steady stream down my thigh, but I try to ignore it. I can figure out what's bleeding later.

The stranger climbs out of the wreckage. Considering how twisted the engine and trunk are, I'm astonished he survived.

For a moment, he's nothing but a silhouette in the dark woods around us. The moon cuts through a gap in the canopy above, casting a spotlight on the dead leaves between us. As the man drags himself out of the car, I catch a glimpse of his face.

Rough stubble lines his jaw, and his wild, dirty blond hair frames a rugged face. He glares at me, the thick muscles in his arms flexing as he tries to get his bearings.

I have no idea who this guy is, and that just pisses me off even more.

"You must have a death wish," I say, a dangerous chill to my voice.

"Quite the opposite." The man stands, teetering as he tries to catch his balance. "You're my ticket to a better life, and you're coming with me even if you barely have a pulse when I drag you in."

"Death wish it is, then." I crack my neck, running on the fumes of my fury and adrenaline. "Let me help you with that."

CHAPTER TWENTY-TWO

With my injuries, it takes everything in me just to stand. My knees threaten to give out. My neck aches, and the steady drum of a thumping headache pulses through my brain.

But, as always, I persevere.

Blood rushes down my abdomen and pools in my boot. A bout of dizziness shakes my brain, and for a moment, everything goes blurry.

Not once, however, do I let the man standing before me know that.

My fingers curl against my palm as I try to summon my magic, but it sputters and fades. I have almost no energy left at all, and it takes most of my effort just to remain on my feet.

Looks like I might have to kill him the old-fashioned way, then.

"Do you know who I am?" he asks, chest heaving.

I resist the impulse to roll my eyes. He's trying to buy himself some time to recover from the accident, and his little ploy is just so painfully transparent.

As wounded as I am, though, I need to conserve my energy. As much as I would love to simply charge him and end this, any and all movements must be kept to a minimum.

I need him to come to me, which means I need to indulge him. For now. I have to use this moment of respite to figure out his weaknesses. His insecurities. I need to rile him up, throw him off guard, and trick him into making a mistake.

"Never heard of you." I glance him over like he's an insect, just to rile him up. "I don't bother myself with minions."

His nose wrinkles in hatred, and he stumbles once as he impulsively leans toward me. His emotions almost get the better of him, but he manages to rein them in.

Good. It looks like pride is one of his faults, then.

With slow and careful precision, he pulls a long knife from a sheath strapped to his thigh. The case is so smooth, so thin, that I didn't even notice it at first.

But once the knife's out, I instantly recognize the subtle curve of the blade. The way the handle tilts at the end. The custom angles to the dagger, all designed to kill with a single, devastating blow.

That's a Spectre weapon.

Shit.

In a flash, I piece it together. I'm his ticket to a better life, apparently, but I'm to be brought in to his masters alive—and the only Spectre who wants me alive is Zurie. This guy is good, but he's sloppy, so he's not among the ranks of Spectres. Not yet, anyway. A Spectre never would have put me in a trunk I could escape from.

That means he must have made some sort of deal with Zurie, and I'm pretty sure their agreement won't work out in my favor.

"You like it?" he asks, his gaze shifting to his dagger as he arrogantly smirks. I'm sure he thinks he's about to drop some massive secret on me. "Zurie sends her regards, by the way."

"Is she taking on charity cases, then?" I tilt my chin, smirking as I feign a bored expression. "She's sunk to a new low."

He scowls, his arrogant charm gone in a flash. Without another word, he thunders toward me.

I grit my teeth and block his blow as every inch of me screams in protest. As he swings again, I duck out of the way, careful to minimize my movements.

Time and time again, he swipes at me, the blade sailing inches from my face. He's a tad careless, but he makes up for it by being *fast*. I can see why Zurie chose him to hunt me down—he shows promise, and with maybe six years of training, he could pose a real threat.

"What did she promise you?" I counter one of his blows and kick him hard in the thigh. Bones crunch beneath my boot. "I hope it's worth the trouble I'm going to cause you."

He yells in agony as he limps quickly out of my reach, lifting the dagger once more to keep me from following him.

It was almost too easy to fracture his leg, and I'm suddenly reminded of how far I've come since I bowed to Zurie's will.

If he's truly her new protégé, he's in for a rough life.

"You lost your chance with her," he seethes between clenched teeth, glaring at me. "You had everything, and you squandered it. For what? For dragons?" He nods toward the road somewhere behind us. "Where are your precious dragons when you need them, huh?"

I nod to his fractured thigh. "I can take care of myself."

He grimaces, clearly trying to push through the pain. I want to charge him, to finish this while he's weakened, but he's still armed and I'm very much not. I can barely stay on my feet, and even as we both pause to catch our breath, I feel myself teeter off balance.

I dig my heels into the dirt, settling into my stance in an effort to stay upright.

"I don't care what it takes," he says, standing a bit

straighter. "I can bring you back without a few pieces if I have to. You just need a pulse."

"Good luck." I crack my knuckles, inviting him to continue our dance.

Tires screech over an asphalt road nearby. Gunshots ring through the air, and the crunch of footsteps through the underbrush interrupts us. A bullet whizzes past the stranger, nearly hitting him in the back of the skull.

The stranger hesitates, and I can see the battle raging in his mind. Run, and lose his chance to take me down? Or try to take out this new threat with a possibly broken leg?

Hell, I'm not sure of what to do, either. We have no idea who this newcomer even is. I limp toward a nearby tree, ready to take cover should the need arise.

I'm quickly running out of options.

To my delight, however, Tucker storms through the shadows in a haze of bullets. His gun and a deadly glare are trained on the stranger. Their eyes lock, and Tucker's eyes widen briefly in surprise.

In recognition.

In that brief moment, the stranger bolts.

Tucker snaps out of it, now scowling with hatred, and fires rapidly after the stranger. Three shots hit—two in the arm and one in the side. The stranger groans in pain, but the injuries only seem to propel him faster into the darkness.

"Damn it," Tucker says under his breath. "With all the tree cover—I can't believe I *missed*."

My knees shake as I lose far more blood than any mortal should. I lean against the nearby tree, smiling with relief and gratitude that Tucker barged in when he did.

"Get him," I say breathlessly with a nod after the stranger. "You can have my kill, just go. I slowed him down for you."

Tucker pauses, a deadly serious look on his face as he studies me. His gaze briefly shifts toward the darkness where the man disappeared, but he doesn't move.

"Tucker, go!" I point in the vague direction of the man who tried to kill me. "He's getting away!"

"Sorry, babe," Tucker says with a deep sigh. "We need to get you to a hospital before you bleed out." He holsters his gun.

"Kill that asshole, and do it now!" I shout, furious that he would let the man who's been hunting me disappear into the night.

"If you can resist me, gorgeous, then I'll do whatever you want," he says with a laugh as he sweeps me off my feet. My body trembles with the sheer depth of the pain rattling through my body, and a stream of blood rolls down my arms as he carries me toward the road.

I can feel myself nearing a blackout. My world spins, and I try to yell at him to go back. To chase the man down. I try to tell him that he's wrong, but I can't even form the words.

"Tucker—damn it—"

He grins as my world darkens. "Love you, too, honey bun."

CHAPTER TWENTY-THREE

The first thing I feel when I wake up is a pounding headache.

I groan, sitting up in bed as I cradle my temple. A bout of nausea burns in the back of my throat, but I manage to hold it at bay.

There's a soft golden light filling the room around me. A window on my right. A white curtain on my left. A closed door in the wall nearby. Something soft presses against the backs of my knees—sheets, maybe. I peek around to find myself lying in a bed, with a heart rate monitor hooked to my chest. I quickly rip off the sensors as I lean forward.

And—in the chair across from me—Drew leans on his elbows with his face in his hands.

"How long was I out?" I slur a little as I come to.

His head snaps up, and he watches me with grateful

disbelief. Instantly, he storms over and wraps his arms around me.

"Ow," I mutter, craning my neck as I try to hug him back.

"Sorry." He takes a deep breath and puts his hands on my shoulders, studying my face like he has so much to say and doesn't know where to start. "You've been out for twelve hours. How do you feel?"

"Like I got hit by a bus," I admit, grimacing.

Everything hurts.

"Yeah, that's what happens when you flip, what, eight times in one night? Between the two cars?"

I shrug. "I'm an overachiever."

He chuckles and kisses me lightly. I can feel him restraining, and I know how badly he must want to have his way with me, to dominate me like he usually does.

This must be torture, to hold back.

He tastes amazing on my lips—like apples and happiness. I sink into the kiss as my memories slowly crawl back to me. The crash. The knife. The stranger.

"Jace!" I shout, suddenly breaking the kiss as I grab Drew's collar. "I couldn't find Jace after the crash, and Tucker—"

"They're safe," Drew promises, holding my hands tenderly. "Everyone's safe."

"Even Russell? The way his head—"

"Everyone," Drew promises. "Russell's got one hell

of a headache, but you definitely got the worst of the injuries."

I sigh with relief.

Drew reaches past me and pushes a small green button on the wall. "As much as I always want to keep you to myself, Jace threatened to literally throw me in a cell if I didn't tell him the moment you woke up. Jace, Tucker, and I took shifts looking over you, since we weren't sure when you would wake up. Levi about lost his damn mind, Rory. Jace almost had him tranqued."

"Oh man." I rub my eyes. "That didn't go at all to plan, did it?"

"Not a bit," Drew admits with a chuckle. "But hey, we can't predict the future. We did all right, knowing what we knew then."

I shake my head. "This guy who hunted us down, he—"

The door swings open, and Jace barges into the room with a thick bandage over his head. The moment our eyes meet, his expression softens, and he jogs to the other side of my bed. "Thank the gods."

I wrap my arms around his neck and hold him close, grateful I didn't lose him. "I was afraid the car rolled on you, or—"

"It'll take more than that to kill me," he says with a chuckle. "You, however, certainly tempted death." He holds me tightly, sighing into my hair, and I wonder if he's had a chance to sleep at all.

Knowing him, probably not.

"Where's Tucker?" I ask.

"On his way," Jace promises, watching me with an odd expression. It's something between relief and gratitude, and on his usually hardened features, the gentle expression seems out of place. "First, I have a surprise for you."

Without waiting for me to guess what it is, he walks to the white curtain and pulls it back to reveal Irena, sleeping soundly in the bed next to mine.

I smile, relieved. Her cheeks have color. She breathes normally, and a single heart rate monitor beeps softly in the corner.

I throw off the blanket and swing my legs over the side of my bed.

"Wait, Rory." Drew raises a hand, gesturing for me to stop.

I wave him away. "I'm fine."

My world spins briefly as my toes brush against the floor, but my head quickly clears. My aches all begin to fade as I get my blood moving, and I suspect a lot of my pain is just from sitting still for so long. I absently pat the wound on my abdomen to find fresh bandages beneath the shirt. Even through the gauze, I can feel the distinct ridge of a scar.

Score.

Carefully, I stand while both Jace and Drew hover nearby, ready to catch me if I fall. I shake my head, chuckling a little at their antics. I wish I could make them stop fawning over me, but I take it as a compliment.

They care.

Having people who love me is still pretty surreal, given how I was raised.

As I stand, I impulsively stretch my arms as far as they'll go. The pleasant sensation goes all the way down my back and into my legs. My muscles hum with delight, and I can almost feel my magic fizzing through my body. Repairing me. Healing me.

"Oh man." I stretch my neck, rolling my head back and forth to limber it up, lost in the ecstasy of the quickly releasing tension.

"That's unbelievable," Drew mutters. "How are you standing right now?"

"Anyone else would be dead, Rory," Jace adds with a subtle nod as he watches me, incredulous. "You're lucky to be alive."

"I probably wouldn't be without you guys." I smile gratefully at them before returning my attention to Irena. "When does she wake up?"

"She got the fourth dose this morning," Jace says. "She gets the last one in a week, but honestly, she looks better than ever. I wouldn't be surprised if she woke up before the next dose."

I smile with gratitude, almost unwilling to believe we've made it this far with her health. We're *so* close.

"You need to lie down." Drew sets his hand gently on the small of my back, trying to usher me back into the bed.

"Hell no." I laugh and bat his hand away. "That's the last thing I need. My muscles are tight as hell." I stretch again, trying to limber them up.

With a few careful steps, I slide the curtain back to give Irena some privacy.

The thunder of boots in the hallway catches my attention, and I set my hands on my hips as I wait for the familiar footsteps to reach us.

Moments later, Tucker sticks his head in, chest heaving as he tries to catch his breath. "Sweet Jesus, you're awake." He elbows past Drew and wraps his arms around me, holding me tightly.

"Hey, Tucker." I chuckle and hug him back. "If you hadn't shown up when you did—"

"Nah," the weapons master interjects. "You would've beat his ass one way or another." Tucker waves his hand flippantly, like he hadn't found me bleeding out and at death's door in the middle of the woods.

"You know him, though," I say, tilting my head so that I can see Tucker's face. "The stranger."

It's not a question because I already know. The expression on Tucker's face—that was undeniable recognition.

Tucker sighs, his smile fading, and his gaze shifts

across the other two men in the room. "Are you seriously going to sit there and let her *work* right now?"

Drew scoffs. "You try to stop her, then."

"I'm serious," I say sternly, trying to get them to focus. "The man in the woods—"

"Carter Holt," Jace interrupts, much to my surprise.

I hesitate, tilting my head in confusion. "How did you—"

"Tucker told us everything." Jace gestures toward the weapons expert and casually leans against the wall. "The man you fought is a Knight named Carter Holt."

"I used to train with him," Tucker says, crossing his arms. "Brutal and *very* good at what he does. Hates me with a passion. As much as I despise that man, I have to admit he's easily one of the best Knights alive."

I frown, rubbing my jawline as I try to stitch all of this together. "If he's a Knight, then why did he have Spectre tech?"

"He had Spectre tech?" Drew asks incredulously.

I nod. "A knife. This Carter guy told me he's working for Zurie." I pause, my training warning me to keep the rest to myself. This is a new life, though, with new allies. I try to ignore the impulsive warning to keep secrets. Doing so would only hurt us all in the end. "He said his job is to bring me in."

"Damn it." Jace squeezes his eyes shut and rubs the bridge of his nose in frustration.

"Oh, man," Tucker says, his voice a bit dazed, as if he just realized something massive.

"What?" I prod.

"Carter always talked about the Spectres. Knights idolize you guys, you know," Tucker gestures loosely between me and the curtain where Irena still sleeps. "It's the ultimate dream, to ascend into the Spectres."

"Was it your dream?" Jace asks with a quirked eyebrow.

"Hell no," Tucker scoffs. "I just wanted out, like any *sane* man would."

"Spectres always talked about Knights with disdain," I admit, crossing my arms. "As disposable."

Tucker laughs. "Ouch."

"Not me," I correct. "Obviously. But Zurie, Diesel— all of them despise the Knights. Working with them is a last resort."

"At least we know who the mysterious vigilante is," Drew says.

"But he didn't work alone," Jace points out. "And Spectres almost always work alone."

"He's still technically a Knight," Tucker points out. "And a high-ranking one at that. Maybe he called in some backup."

"That would make sense," I admit. "Zurie won't like it, of course, but this changes everything. If Zurie's recruiting, that means she's desperate."

"Isn't that a good thing?" Jace asks. "Desperate people make mistakes."

"Not her." I shake my head, eyes glossing over at all the memories of watching Zurie get backed into a corner. "It is definitely *not* good for us. A desperate Zurie does horrifying things, Jace."

The three men around me stand in silence, each of them lost in thought as they process the news.

"Oh, man," I mutter as another thought comes to me. "If she's recruiting, I wonder... I wonder if... I mean, it would break *so* many rules..."

"Rory," Jace says curtly. "You're doing that thing Tucker does."

"Look hot?" Tucker interjects.

Jace chuckles and shakes his head, rubbing his eyes as he tries to ignore the joke.

I slowly pace the hospital room. "With me and Irena out of the picture, Zurie has no heir. No one to take over her role as the Ghost. That means the role passes to Diesel—unless she takes on a new soldier to mentor."

"You think she's training Carter to be the Ghost?" Tucker asks, his eyebrows nearly in his hairline.

"I'm saying it's possible," I admit. "Though he would have a long and bloody string of challenges to prove his legitimacy. Taking me out would be one of those."

"But he was told to bring you in," Drew argues.

"I know," I say, admittedly confused by that little detail.

As my mind puzzles over this new information, trying to make sense of it, a shot of intuition spears me through the gut. I stiffen, lifting my hand in warning for the others to listen for danger.

All three men pause, their wary eyes surveying the room. The bolt of intuition hits me again, like a knife through the back, and I pivot on my heel. The only thing behind me is the curtain hiding Irena's bed, and yet I feel like I should prepare for war.

I just don't know *why*.

All I know is something's wrong. Very, *very* wrong.

CHAPTER TWENTY-FOUR

I n the silence that follows my hit of intuition, I barely breathe. I can't allow any noises to interrupt us. Detecting the slightest huff of air or shuffle of a boot on the tile could be the difference between life and death.

There are no footsteps. No rustling fabric. No movement. And that's when I realize what set me off.

The heart rate monitor is silent.

Irena.

My heart in my throat, I rip open the curtain—

—and nearly get a fist to my face.

I barely duck the blow. My forearm slides against my opponent's torso as I redirect the attack. My world briefly blurs as my body reacts on impulse. My hands and legs run through familiar routines I've practiced hundreds of times before.

That's when I realize it's Irena.

Irena just tried to punch me.

In the *face.*

She stares at me, glaring with the fury of a sun, her once-brown eyes now bright green. Her dark hair flows around her face, the loose curls as wild as her expression.

There isn't a hint of recognition in her expression. Not one moment of clarity.

Just fury.

As I pause, trying to figure out what the hell is going on, she effortlessly grabs my arm. Her foot sweeps my leg, trying to kick out my knee and trip me. It's an old technique we've tried on each other a hundred times, and I effortlessly hook my arm around her shoulder to counter. With a sharp grunt of effort, I use her own body weight against her as I throw her off balance to avoid the blow.

But she doesn't stop—so, neither do I.

Our dance is fluid and deadly. We never once pause. Bits of it remind me of old times in the sparring ring, of the way we would joke and tease each other as we fought. If she recognized me at all, I would even call this fun.

She cocks her arm to land another blow, this time aiming for my jugular.

"Irena!" I shout, trying to snap her out of this.

Trying to fully bring her back.

For the first time since I pulled open the curtain, she hesitates. Her now-green eyes search mine, a hint of understanding slowly dawning on her face. She blinks rapidly, her eyebrows tilting upward.

"Rory?" she asks quietly.

"Yes." I smile so broadly my face hurts as relief blisters through me. "Irena, you're safe. Stop trying to kill me, already!"

"Oh my god." She sighs with relief and pulls me closer, hugging me tightly as she presses her cheek against mine. I hold her to me, drinking in the soft and familiar scent of her hair.

To my surprise, her grip is tighter than it used to be. After a few moments, I feel pins and needles down my arm as she cuts off circulation.

I grab her shoulders and hold her at a short distance so I can study her face.

Those *eyes*.

"What happened?" I ask, trying to piece it together. "What—"

Her gaze shifts behind me, and she gasps in horror. "Rory, look out!"

I look over my shoulder as she shoves me behind her, putting herself between me and my men. Irena lifts her hands, ready for battle, and subtly eyes the door as she no doubt plans our escape.

Jace tenses. Drew squares his shoulders, frowning.

Tucker reaches behind him, his shirt shifting as he no doubt wraps his hand silently around a hidden gun.

"They're friends, Irena," I assure her. "They're—"

"They're *shifters,*" she snaps, her eyes flitting briefly toward me. "I'll take the big one. Can you handle the other two?"

"The big one?" Drew huffs, mildly offended.

I set my hand on her back to soothe her. "Irena, stop. Calm *down.*"

She doesn't.

In the roiling surge of adrenaline that's still burning through her, the deadly assassin charges her prey. Drew settles instantly into a fighting stance, his shoulders loose, and I know he'll take her down if he has to.

If he can.

I have to stop this.

I grab her arm and pull her backward with all my strength. We topple to the ground, hitting the tile *hard.* Tangled together, we slide along the floor as I take her down. She falls, and I instantly lock her arm in an arm bar. For added security, I wrap my leg around her waist and hold her tight.

The whole thing is over in less than a second. We lay on the ground, Irena utterly immobilized beneath me. Our chests heave, and we glare daggers at each other.

"God *damn,*" Tucker mutters, his eyebrow lifting in surprise as he surveys my handiwork.

"Yeah," Drew agrees, finally relaxing.

"Rory!" Irena snaps, trying twice to elbow me in the neck. "Stop this! What are you doing?"

"They're safe, Irena," I say through gritted teeth. Jolts of pain shoot through me from my still-healing injuries as I use every ounce of my strength to keep her in place.

She's so damn *strong*. Way stronger than she used to be.

"Who are you?" Irena practically growls, glaring at me from the floor. "What happened to my sister?"

I sigh in disappointment. This is going to be so much harder than I thought.

"Irena, you've been out for a long time," I say, trying my best to keep my voice calm even though I want to scream at her. "I almost lost you. You and Zurie were—"

At the mention of my former mentor's name, Irena wrinkles her nose in disgust.

I hesitate, noticing the subtle shift in Irena's features, but I need to calm her down first before I start interrogating her. "You were both taken, and Mason tried to kill me."

As I pin her to the floor, I tell her everything. The pit. The magic. The swarm. My men. Our budding family, our newfound alliance. I tell her I've quit the Spectres, and that Zurie is after us both.

I tell her everything.

The longer I speak, the less she struggles. With every new development, her breath begins to even. Her lips settle into a thin line as she studies me, ruthless and calm, her eyes slightly narrowed as if she can't entirely believe what she's hearing.

When I'm done, I let silence settle on the hospital ward. I'm tempted to keep talking, to fill the aching quiet with something other than her disbelieving glare, but I force myself to wait.

It's her turn to speak.

For quite some time, however, she doesn't say anything. She just watches me, as though she's analyzing a stranger.

"Let me up," she eventually demands.

"Swear to me you won't touch them," I order.

"Rory," she snaps. "Get the hell off of me!"

"Swear it," I say calmly, not once wavering despite her cold tone.

Irena grimaces, clearly furious. After a moment, though, she finally groans in defeat. "Fine. I won't."

Cautiously, I release my grip on her arm. She instantly slides out of my hold and gets to her feet. As she runs a hand through her beautiful dark hair, she quickly paces the far wall. Her eyes glaze over, and I suspect she's simply trying to think through everything I just told her.

"A dragon," she mutters. Her green eyes flit to me and narrow with a hint of doubt. "The dragon *vessel*, in fact."

I stand and square my shoulders. "Yes."

"You've taken in shifters," she says with a nod to the three men behind me. "And a Knight."

"Yes," I confirm.

"I should k—" She can't finish the sentence. Her voice breaks, and she chokes on her words. Her eyebrows tilt upward, and for a baffling moment, it almost looks like she's going to cry.

"You should kill me?" I finish for her.

In my periphery, Jace stiffens. I can see him shift into warrior mode, fully prepared to end this if he has to. Tucker still holds his gun behind his back, and Drew has been ready for murder from the start.

But she won't do it. That's the only reason I told her all of this—because I know her better than she sometimes even knows herself.

Even though she doesn't realize it, even though she's fighting it right now, she can handle this.

I know one thing for a fact, however—the moment I get Jace alone, we need to have a little chat with the doctor. Because whatever happened during Irena's coma, she has definitely changed.

The eyes, her new strength—we might have brought her back, but it's clear the bio-weapon did something else to her.

"You would never hurt me, Irena," I say calmly,

stepping in front of my men as she paces. "Not in a million years."

She pauses with her back to me, her hand on her neck as she sighs deeply.

Irena is gifted. Brutal. Deadly. She could probably get Tucker's gun off of him, and all of us would have at least one bullet hole in us when she left. She's cleared dozens of rooms full of talented shooters and left nothing but corpses in her wake.

I know because I've watched her do it.

I know because she killed all those men, over a decade ago, to save me.

To save me after I screwed up on a mission—after Zurie tried to push me into the field long before I was ready.

That's what sisters do.

That's who we are.

"I love you, Rory," Irena says, her voice tight and sad. "You know I would do anything for you. But this? Dragons?" She turns on her heel and glares at me. "After *everything* we've been through?"

"They'll surprise you," I promise, speaking from experience.

Irena's gaze shifts behind me, no doubt studying each of the men standing, ready for war, at my back.

Her shoulders relax, and she sighs in defeat. "Show me," she demands, her green eyes shifting to mine. "Show me everything."

CHAPTER TWENTY-FIVE

"It's beautiful," Irena admits.

She leans her elbows against the railing of a balcony as we look out over the rear end of the embassy property. Her eyes flutter closed, and as she takes in a deep breath of the mountain air, she hums with delight. For the first time since she woke up, a small smile plays at the edge of her lips.

Ah. *There's* the sister I know.

"I can't believe how much I've missed," she says sadly, rubbing her face. "I'm jealous that *you* got to kill Mason."

I wink. "Beat you to it."

"This is… it's…" She looks out over the misty ravine as dragons dive into its depths. Others soar in tight formation across the sky, surveying the land below, and we are quite literally surrounded by shifters.

"Overwhelming," I admit.

She scoffs. "You *think?*"

Standing here with her, it feels like old times. Like it hasn't been ages since we've spoken, like I haven't gone without her for far too long. We're close again, and just like that, the world is a little better.

I smile.

"You look beautiful," Irena admits, scanning my body. "Did the dragon magic do that, too?"

"Yep." I adjust my bra. "Bigger boobs and everything."

She laughs and pushes me in the shoulder, throwing me slightly off balance with her oddly enhanced strength. She hesitates, her smile faltering as she stares at her palms with a wary and slightly concerned expression.

"Look," I say softly. "Irena, the Vaer tried to kill you with something no one understands. I guess it's only natural for there to be some... side effects."

She lifts one eyebrow skeptically. "Side effects? You call these side effects?" She points at her brilliant green eyes that nearly glow, a beautiful contrast to the dark hair that pours over her shoulder.

I shrug, searching for an alternative word. "Uh... complications?"

She laughs and nudges me with her elbow. "Shut up."

"It's good to have you back, Irena." I loop my arm in hers and lean against my big sister's shoulder. "I missed you."

The hardened assassin chuckles. "Who are you, gooey fiend, and what have you done with my baby sister?"

"Oh, shut up and enjoy the moment."

She laughs and leans her cheek against the top of my head. "You're so damn bossy. You get one little hit of god magic and suddenly you're in charge, huh?"

I chuckle. "Yeah, pretty much."

After a while, I feel her slowly begin to stiffen beside me. It's a gradual thing, like the heavy weight in the air that builds before a storm, and I eventually lean away so that I can study her face.

She's staring at her hands, frowning, her eyes glossed over with deep thought.

"What's wrong, Irena?"

"Is there a safe place to talk?" She casts a wary eye around us at the dragons on nearly every ledge.

"Is it, uh, *mentor* talk?"

She nods.

Ah.

"Yeah, follow me."

I lead her expertly through the halls, already familiar with every route thanks to the number of times I've stolen through the corridors. I'm not *entirely* sure where we should go to discuss such a sensitive topic, but I have a pretty great spot in mind.

As I hoist myself onto the roof where I like to sit and think, Irena deftly follows. As her hands grip the black stone shingles, however, she crushes a few of them in her palm. Black dust billows into the air as a gust soars past us. Irena frowns, a confused look on her face, but she pushes through it and follows close behind me.

We sit together in the warm daylight, our arms around our knees as we look out over the forests beyond the embassy.

"I'm still not on board with all the dragons," Irena admits. "But I see why you like it here."

"All the hot men?" I ask with a teasing grin.

She chuckles. "You sure know how to pick them, Rory." She whistles softly. "Kinda jealous."

I smirk, giving her a playful sidelong glare. "Well, don't get any ideas."

She rolls her eyes. "Oh, please. Sisters don't double dip."

I laugh. "That's just crass."

Chuckling at her own stupid joke, she blows me a sarcastic little kiss.

"So what did you want to talk about?" I ask. "I've told you pretty much everything I know about Zurie's current plans. She's still after me, and she told me you were dead to her. She told me…" My smile falters as I trail off. As I absently fiddle with my nails, I don't even want to finish that sentence.

"What?" Irena presses. "Tell me everything."

I brace myself to dig into the memories I want to ignore, but I can't avoid this. She needs to know. "Zurie told me you betrayed us." I laugh humorlessly and shake my head in disgust. "The very idea. I *knew* it was a lie."

To my surprise, Irena is completely quiet. I expected an indignant huff, or at least a humorless laugh at the news. When I turn to study her face, she hangs her head in shame, her shoulders tense. There's a grim frown on her face.

I know that look.

It's… *guilt.*

"Irena…" I don't really know where to start. For all intents and purposes, it seems kind of like she just admitted fault here.

But… that's impossible.

"I have a lot to tell you," Irena admits, staring off into the forest. "You might hate me for it, but I need you to promise me you won't leave this roof until I've told you everything. And if you hate me—" Her voice breaks, and she roughly clears her throat to recover. "Well, I wouldn't blame you if you hate me for it."

I can't speak.

I have no idea what to say.

My heart thuds in my chest, the sinking dread tumbling through me like a cold fog as I wait for her to continue.

"We've been in the Spectres for our whole lives, Rory," Irena says softly as she stares out at the forest. "You were too young to remember life before Zurie, but I remember our mother."

I impulsively stiffen with surprise. She's never told me this before.

"It's just little bits," Irena admits, studying the criss-crossing lines in her palms as she speaks. "A voice here, a face there. Her smile." The ends of Irena's mouth tilt upward briefly, but she sighs as she looks back out over the woods. "She was a good woman, Rory, and a brilliant fighter. She and Zurie were both mentored by Marcus Anderson, one of the most brutal Ghosts to ever live."

"Why didn't you ever tell me this?" I ask.

"Because I didn't know much of it," Irena confesses. "Not until Zurie was preparing me for my final initiation a few months ago. I was about to have everything. Power. Wealth. Control over the assholes who made our lives hell. When Zurie died, I would be Ghost. After a lifetime of preparing me for it, I felt ready." Her nose wrinkles as a look of pure loathing passes across her face. "But then I found the files."

I watch her cautiously, fairly certain I'm not going to like where this is headed.

"I found out what they did to our mother," Irena says. "She just wanted a better life for us, Rory. We were young, and they were already training us to follow in her footsteps. The tests they put us through, and so young..." Irena squeezes her eyes shut as if she's trying to scrub the images from her mind. "I found footage of some of the tests they gave you, Rory, and they made me so furious that I shot the screen."

"I don't remember any of it," I say, as if that's going to make it better.

"You do," she says. "That kind of thing burns into your subconscious. Deep down, it's there, and nothing I can do will ever heal it." She shakes her head sadly. "Deep down, they scarred you. They scarred us both." She rubs her face. "Our mother wanted a new life for us. All she did was try to smuggle us out, but she was caught. Marcus ordered her to hand us over and kill herself, but she refused. She disobeyed the Ghost. The notes on the fight itself are fairly brief, but she ended up killing Marcus, and Zurie dealt the final blow to her. She didn't die on a mission, Rory. She was killed trying to give us a better life."

I frown and stare off at the distant mountains, my eyes slipping out of focus as I process this new information. To think, we were so close to escaping the Spectres—so close to never having lived this life. My imagination toyed with where our mother would have taken us. A cottage somewhere distant, maybe, or hiding in plain sight in a busy city.

But from the very start, Zurie was always trying to drag us back to her.

"And then I found *your* file," Irena says, her voice tense. "I found Zurie's plans for you."

I frown in confusion. "Plans?"

Irena nods, the look of loathing now bleeding into one of utter fury. "Who do you think betrayed us to the Vaer, Rory? If you had to guess?"

"Diesel," I admit without a pause. "If Zurie, you, and I die, he becomes the Ghost."

"Yeah." Irena nods. "That's what I wanted everyone to think."

I watch her for a moment in horror as I process the deeper meaning of what she just said.

"You…" I can't even form the words.

"What Zurie did to our mother was horrible," Irena says, not really answering me. "But what she wanted to do to you was *unforgiveable*."

I can't speak. I just gape at my sister, utterly astonished at what I'm hearing.

"There's a little-known program in the Spectres called the Gold Ones." Irena runs a hand through her hair. "In the Spectres, initiates are sometimes primed for the program with brainwashing and obedience so they can be sold to the highest bidder to fund the orga-

nization." Her jaw tenses. "An assassin for sale, basically, alleged to be utterly obedient to whomever *owns*
them." Her nose wrinkles in disgust. "The younger they
are when they're brought in, the easier they are to
indoctrinate."

"Zurie wanted to *sell* me?" I ask, still not quite able
to process all this.

Irena hesitates, still as a statue, but eventually nods.
"That's why you never got an ounce of freedom, Rory.
Zurie didn't want you to develop a taste for it. A Gold
One, trained by the Ghost herself? She could have
asked any price for you. You were supposed to become
a mercenary to be sold off, and if she had gotten away
with it, I never would have seen you again."

The surreal shock of this news hits me hard in the
chest, and for a few moments, I can barely breathe. I
stare at the tiles beneath my feet, my eyes slipping in
and out of focus as my brain races a mile a minute.

"My world imploded," Irena says softly. "I couldn't
bring myself to work for these people anymore. If I
waited until I became the Ghost to change things, I
would lose my chance to save you. She was months
away from selling you off, Rory. *Months.* Zurie already
had three buyers lined up." Irena shakes her head,
furious and wounded. "I didn't have much time, but the
only people who can take on the Spectres are dragons."

"So you made a deal," I finish for her. "With the
Vaer."

"They were the only contacts I had," she says softly. "I didn't know they go back on their deals. I didn't know they couldn't be trusted."

My eyes shift warily to her. "What was your deal?"

"I give them Zurie and the Spectres," she says. "You and I were to be pardoned and allowed to disappear. Mason became my point of contact, and he helped me orchestrate a fake mission to steal a bio-weapon from the Vaer. Just me and Zurie. I would lead her into a trap, and he would let me walk out of it. Zurie was practically salivating over the bait. It was almost too easy to lure her in—she trusted me so completely. But when I led Zurie on that fake mission, I learned the weapon was quite real." She rubs her eyes, sighing in disappointment and anger. "Mason promised he would wrap up the loose ends. After he injected me, when I was quickly losing consciousness, he told me he was going after you. I did everything I could to get out of there, but..." Her eyebrows twist upward, and as she squeezes her eyes shut in shame, she tilts her head toward the clouds above.

For several minutes, we sit in silence. It's almost too much to sort through. Too much to hear.

"Why didn't you tell me all of this?" I ask softly, a knot in my throat. "I could have helped you."

To my surprise, she laughs. It's a quick little sound, more surprise than humor, and she absently rubs her neck. "I knew it was risky, and I wanted to save you no matter the cost. If you were involved in any way, if they found out we were plotting something like this together, they would have killed us both." She sighs shakily. "If I was discovered, I wanted to at least know you would be absolved. That you wouldn't be hurt. Worst case, you would take my place and become the Ghost—and while life as a Spectre is hardly glamorous, at least you would've been alive."

As I sit on my roof, sifting through everything she just told me, I wonder if there's more to it than that. If she didn't trust me to handle it, much like Jace seems to think he needs to protect me from the world.

I hang my head as a tremor of betrayal rocks through me, shattering my heart.

"You must despise me." Irena says softly as her eyes scan the forests. "I won't blame you if you do. I caused this. All of it."

Do I hate Irena?

How could I?

I've done everything in my power to save her. To bring her back. To right a wrong and protect the big sister who has saved my ass more times than I can even count.

I could never hate her.

"You're my sister, Irena," I say softly as I battle the bone-deep hurt I'm feeling after her confession. "That means I love you, even when you do stupid shit."

She laughs and, without another word, wraps me in

her arms. This time, I don't care that the hug is too tight. I hug her back, and we sit there in silence for what feels like hours.

"Don't you ever try to save me again," I add with a weak chuckle. "We do this together from now on."

"Okay," she says with a shaky laugh, somehow making the hug even tighter. "I promise."

CHAPTER TWENTY-SIX

With Irena situated in her new suite two doors down from mine, I collapse into my bed.

Alone.

The soft comforter lumps beneath me as I stare at the ceiling, eyes drifting out of focus. I need to think. To spend some time by myself and sift through everything I've learned.

Irena betrayed the Spectres.

Irena.

The golden child.

And she did it to save *me*.

She gave Mason everything—houses, codes, secrets. The only things she kept to herself involved the two of us, but he somehow managed to get his hands on those on his own. He was never supposed to touch me, but the Vaer don't leave loose ends.

That's all I was to them—a loose end to tie up. They never expected the situation to spiral as it has. They didn't expect me to rise up against them.

As much as I hate the Vaer, I can't be angry with Irena. Not really. Not now that I understand why she did it and what Zurie had in store for me. But the whole situation is still so surreal—to finally get Irena back, only to discover her darkest, most brutal secret in the same day. Only to discover the traitor in our midst was none other than the person I had spent so much time and effort to save.

My mind buzzes like a hive, and I can't just lie here. I stand, pacing my room, looking for something to do. The gauze still wrapped around my torso itches, and I debate ripping it off—but Jace explicitly asked me not to, and I just don't feel like fighting him on this one. With the dojo master, I really do need to pick my battles, and a bit of itchy discomfort is not worth an argument.

To keep myself busy, I unpack one of the bags I took with me to Reggie's castle. A few shirts. A handful of modified pistols. Ammo. Some cargo pants. A few daggers.

The essentials.

When I'm done emptying the bag, it still feels suspiciously heavy. Like I missed something in one of the pockets.

With a curious frown, I throw it on the bed and rifle through the zippered compartments.

Empty.

Empty.

Em—whoa, *not* empty.

My hand brushes the cold metal of a tablet that was definitely not there when I originally packed my bag.

For a brief moment, I'm excited at the prospect of a mystery to sink my teeth into. How did it get here? Who does it belong to? Why did they want me to have it?

But if this made its way into my bag after the meeting with the Bosses, it probably came from one of them. After the high-stakes tension of the last few days, I have next to no patience for crap like this.

With a few tugs, I wrench it free and study it. Silver casing. Large screen. Camera embedded in the top. No branding. No markings. No notes. As I study the casing, it's easy to tell it's never been fiddled with. No explosives could be in there, so that's at least worth a sigh of relief.

This is just a normal, unremarkable tablet. If not for the fact that it was definitely put in my bag with intention, I wouldn't even bother myself with it.

My thumb taps lightly against the power button, and I wonder what will happen if I turn it on. Irena and Tucker are fast asleep. Drew—well, he *should* be sleeping, but who knows where he really is. Levi is out hunting. Jace is probably out cold, and I don't want to wake him up. The man needs to recover.

With a huff, I sit on my bed and turn the thing on, my thumb carefully covering the camera.

Just in case.

It's empty, without even the basic apps installed on this kind of model, and I wonder what purpose this could possibly serve. The only app is used for video calls, but the account has no contacts.

Weird.

After a few moments, a data connection pops up in the notifications tray.

Instantly, the tablet rings as an incoming call hits the device.

Nope.

Not in the mood.

I press my thumb against the power button and hold it, trying to turn the tablet off, but the device auto-answers the call on the second ring.

Damn it.

Out of morbid curiosity, I quickly glance at the video to see who this is before I turn the device off completely.

An elegant woman with dark hair and bright green eyes reclines in an elaborate leather chair with silver inlays along the edge. She wears a dark dress with shimmering silver metal scales sewn into the shoulders. Thin, silver chains embedded with green jewels weave across her hair, draping over her head like an expensive scarf.

Though I know she can't see me with my thumb covering the camera, her expression is still eerie. Her green eyes are piercing, and it's almost like she can see right into my soul.

"Hello, Rory," she says, her voice dark and sultry. "I believe it's time we had a little chat."

Wait—I know that face.

Kinsley.

The Vaer Boss.

A pop up appears on the screen, covering Kinsley's face as it asks if I want to end the call and power down the device.

I lift my thumb off the power button and sigh in frustration. After a brief deliberation, I click *cancel.*

"Don't I get to see your face?" Kinsley prods, a slight smile on her ruby red lips.

I don't answer. This is one of the most powerful women in the world, and easily the most vindictive. Everything I say needs to be calculated, and I'm tempted not to say anything at all.

"Fine," Kinsley says with a lazy flick of her wrist. "I prefer to keep these things short, regardless. Rory, it seems like we got off on the wrong foot. You and I don't have to be enemies."

"You've sent two of your best men to kill me," I remind her.

"Not *kill* you." The powerful woman rolls her eyes in annoyance. "I asked them to bring you to me and discover your abilities. I was *testing* you." She shrugs. "You passed. Let bygones be bygones, my friend."

Ha.

We are *not* friends.

"Since the other Bosses hate you so much, you didn't get to hear my little speech," I say coldly. "I'll give you the same warning I gave them. Leave me alone, and we'll be fine. Come after me, and—well, you've seen what I can do, Kinsley." I smirk, even though she can't see me. "You know what's at stake if you piss me off."

She frowns slightly, the elegant slope of her lips almost imperceptible as she does a fairly good job of hiding her irritation.

I'm tempted to rub my success in her face, to let her know I've made her bio-weapon useless, but I still need four months before the antidote disperses. I have to be patient, and unfortunately, that means I don't get to gloat.

"Bye, Kinsley," I say curtly.

As I reach again for the power button, she calmly leans forward. "Don't you want to know what made Levi feral?"

A bolt of icy dread shoots through me, and I pause.

"Don't you want to know how to fix him?" she asks, a nasty smile spreading across her face.

I don't answer. I can't. I can't let her know just how much that gets to me.

"I know how he got that scar, Rory," the Vaer Boss says. "Have you figured it out, yet?"

Damn it.

His scar is so subtle that I'm tempted to believe her. No one else has even mentioned it, and unless I'm standing right next to him, I can't even see it. For her to know it's there suggests that she does, in fact, know more about my ice dragon than meets the eye.

But this is a *Vaer.* They lie. It's what they do.

"He was a tracker," Kinsley continues, studying her fingernails with a bored expression. "One of the best, if not *the* best. Stealthy. Silent as a ghost." On that last word, Kinsley's eyes flit briefly toward the camera. Toward me.

I frown at the subtle nod to my Spectre heritage, but I force myself to remain silent. She must know she has my full attention, even if she can't see me. I'm waiting for this to all make sense, for the pieces she's slowly handing me to finally fit together.

She's certainly milking it.

"He never fit in, though," Kinsley says with an exaggerated sigh. "He was never really one of us."

Oh.

Oh, *gods.*

Levi is a Vaer.

In the silence that follows, I can barely breathe—

and I suspect Kinsley somehow knows it. She smirks, all cocky arrogance as she weaves her fingers together in her lap. "Deep down, a Vaer never changes, Rory. Do you still feel safe around your precious feral dragon?"

A knot tightens in my throat, and I truly do not want to believe this. Any of it.

I'm tempted to blow this tablet to bits, to simply end the call, but I force myself to take a steadying breath instead. I need to keep my cool, and if I do, I might be able to get more out of her.

"If that's all the information you have, it's hardly useful," I lie, as if she hadn't just splintered my world.

Kinsley falters, a brief expression of disbelief cracking across her face as her composure shatters. "He'll be dead any day, kid," her voice goes dark. Icy. "Just wait. He's going to snap, and when he does, I hope you have to watch as Jace Goodwin shoots him out of the sky." She sneers and leans toward the camera, glaring with the full force of her hatred and spite. "Tick tock, little ghostie."

The call ends.

I nearly throw the tablet at the wall in frustration. I nearly toss it out the window and fire a blast to destroy it.

The only thing that keeps me from doing both things—in that order—is the memory of how much I regretted disintegrating the files Aki Nabal gave me. Begrudgingly, I simply turn the tablet off, resolving to give it to Jace and Drew before my rage gets the better of me.

I toss the damn thing on a pillow and stalk to the window. With my palms on the windowsill, I take a few steadying breaths to calm myself.

If Kinsley was lying to rile me up, it freaking *worked.*

Or, worse, if Kinsley told the truth... Levi is a Vaer. The one dragon family who has relentlessly hunted me from the start.

As I stare out into the night, a familiar blue silhouette lands nearby. Levi perches on the wall below my window, scanning the night as he sits upright on a ledge.

I *know* him. I know his heart. The Levi down there would never hurt me, no matter what family he comes from.

But when he's human again—because I'm determined to save him—will he remain my lovable Levi?

Or will he become something dark?

CHAPTER TWENTY-SEVEN

I n the early morning hours close to dawn, I creep through the embassy. I don't need to—if any of the guards saw me, they would just say hello—but it helps me clear my head all the same.

A fiery tug in my chest stops me in my tracks, and I set my hand on my heart as the sensation settles. I can't tell if that was my dragon, or something else entirely.

But as it hits again, it begins to feel oddly familiar. There's a pull ushering me down the hallway, toward a balcony that overlooks the west side of the embassy. It's a call to be near someone, like something within me is craving a piece of my soul that's missing.

I follow the feeling and silently slip onto the balcony, scanning the horizon as the sensation gets stronger.

A conversation floats over me from somewhere

down below. Just to be a devious little twit, I crouch down to hide myself and decide to listen in.

"...and it's unclear if he can, sir," a man says, his voice deep and unfamiliar.

"The answer is *no*," Jace retorts.

The flutter in my chest dances again, and I chuckle at my growing dragon's antics. She must have been craving him.

I'm surprised he's awake, though. I debate getting the tablet, but as I rise to jog back through the embassy, I catch more of the conversation.

"He's getting worse," the first man says, his voice urgent. "Surely you've seen it."

I frown, wondering who they're talking about.

"Listen to me," Jace snaps, and I can imagine him leaning in as he scowls. "Levi is off limits. If any of you touch him, you answer directly to *me*."

I impulsively stiffen.

Oh, gods. This isn't good.

"Sir, he's begun snapping at the scouts."

For a breathless moment, Jace doesn't answer. Eventually, he sighs in frustration. "Is anyone hurt?"

"No, sir. Each time it happens, he seems to catch himself after the first few moments. This can't go on, sir. It's just a matter of time before he loses control. We need to do something before someone gets killed."

"Gods," Jace mutters under his breath. "This is bad."

"He's in the rear courtyard, sir," the first man says. "If a few of us surprise him, we can—"

"Shut your damn mouth," Jace snaps.

I smirk in victory, and a ripple of relief shoots through me at Jace's protective tone.

The soldier stutters. "Sir?"

"You will not kill that dragon unless I expressly order it," Jace answers. "You all are skilled warriors, and you can be patient. Levi is not to be hurt unless he becomes entirely lost to his dragon side."

"And when that happens?"

"If it comes to that, well…" Jace trails off, so I peek over the railing. His arms are crossed as he stares off at the ravine. After a moment, he lifts one hand to rub his eyes in frustration. "Then I hope Rory can forgive me for what I'll have to do."

"You mean when," corrects the guard next to him. "Not if."

Impulsively, I silently snarl at the soldier, wishing I could punch him in the face for that little comment.

Jace glares at the soldier, and the fury in his gaze mirrors my own. "Levi is stronger than any of you are giving him credit for. Stronger than you were when you first got here, in fact."

The soldier winces as if the comment cut him to the bone, and he quickly looks away.

"Focus on keeping the dojo secure," Jace commands. "Leave the feral dragon to me."

"Yes, sir." The soldier rushes off, and I suspect he was anxious to leave the conversation.

With a wary sigh, Jace walks beneath the balcony, no doubt into the embassy as he heads off to some other task. If he didn't feel me nearby, I suspect he's every bit as exhausted as I suspected he was.

I run my hand through my hair, biting my lip as I think about what the guards must want to do to Levi. They fear him. A feral dragon in their midst is a threat to all of them, and they must resent Jace at least somewhat for allowing him to stay.

Gods all freaking mighty, this just keeps getting worse.

Kinsley dangled how little time he has, and now even Jace is debating what he'll do if Levi forces his hand.

I quickly jog through the embassy, heading down a few stairwells on my way to visit my ice dragon. I need to see him. I need to come up with a plan, and I need to do it *now*.

As I jog down the steps toward him, he's curled in the rear courtyard. He lifts his head as I approach him, but quickly lowers it again without greeting me.

"Are you okay?" I ask, brushing my fingers along his back.

He snorts, mist swirling from his nose as he tilts his head away from me.

"What, you're mad?" I tilt my head in confusion. "About what?"

He groans softly, his blue eyes shifting toward me, and his irises can't seem to stay still. His pupils dilate and shrink in rapid succession, as if they can't quite focus on anything.

"Hey," I say as softly as I can, trying to soothe him. "It's okay. You and me, we're going to solve this. Right now."

He moans, dragging his head along the black stone tiles beneath him, and looks up at the sky.

"I mean it." I kneel beside him and press my hand against his chest. "I'm here for you, Levi. Always."

As my skin brushes his scales, the connection between us opens. Emotions flood through, practically overwhelming me with the sheer surge of energy. Urgency. Hunger. Sadness. Loss. Pain. Despair. Anger. Rage. Hatred. Lust. Fury. Grief.

The impending sense of doom.

It's almost too much to bear.

I grit my teeth, struggling to keep my sense of self despite the surge of his dragon's emotions. My first impulse is to break away—to snap the connection just long enough for me to regain my composure—but I refuse to make him go through this alone.

I refuse to let him go through this at *all*.

He and his dragon are at war, and we're going to settle the fight.

Today.

"Levi, listen to me," I say gently. "I need you to trust me. I need you to be willing to talk about what you've refused to—"

His eyes shift suddenly toward me, and he growls. His lips curl up to reveal his dagger-sharp teeth, but I'm not going to back down from his dragon.

Not when Levi's life is at stake.

There's a tug on my navel, and I debate whether or not this is a good idea. If I let my guard down long enough to go into Levi's mind, we might be able to think up a plan—but his dragon might not play fair in the meantime.

While I debate our options, the pull on my navel becomes a push. It's a concerning sensation, one I don't like in the least. It's like someone is trying to shove his way into *my* mind.

And he *succeeds*.

I can almost feel the fingers in my brain. It's a prickly sensation, like pins and needles through my temples. I feel like someone's sifting through my mind, picking at my memories.

"Cut it—" I wince as the memory of Jett Darrington biting into me resurfaces. "Cut it out!"

Levi snarls, his eyes dilating as his dragon takes over. The dragon pins my hand to his chest with one claw, and he only dives deeper into my mind.

There's Harper, sitting on the sofa in the cottage. Laughing.

I tug on my hand, trying to break the connection. "Stop!"

Another memory blurs into focus as Elizabeth glowers at me in the ornate bathroom. She shoves the diamond pendant into my hand and storms past me.

The memories blur together. Next thing I know, Kinsley's face smirks at me on the video call, those ruby red lips repeating the words that paralyzed me.

"He was never really one of us."

As Kinsley's wicked grin spreads wider across her face, Levi freezes. His body practically hums with anger.

Only, this isn't Levi. It's abundantly clear that his dragon has completely taken over—and, try as he might, Levi is no longer in control. The dragon finally releases my hand and stands, snarling.

I lift my palms and splay my fingers in front of me, trying to placate the beast who now controls one of the men I care so much for. "If you—"

He roars, and I never get the chance to finish.

Fast as lightning, he's in the air. His wings cut through the sky, kicking up a gust that blasts through my hair. And just as I think he's going to disappear again, he dives.

At me.

I curl my fingers into fists, summoning my magic

on impulse. The white light floods across my skin, ready to devastate whatever it touches.

But I can't.

I just can't hurt *him*.

Levi's talons wrap around my waist, kicking the air from my lungs as he soars off with me in his claws. He holds me so tightly that spots dance along my vision as the circulation slows in some areas.

"Rory!" It sounds like several men shouting at once, from multiple directions. I can't figure out who's speaking.

Seconds later, a red dragon races toward us—Drew. He snarls, fire building in his throat as his gaze narrows on Levi. Barely a breath or two behind him, Jace's thunderbird cuts through the sky, his brilliant blue magic glowing in his wings and mouth.

But Levi's dragon is faster.

He ducks and weaves, snarling as the two fighters tail him. He spins, and my world tumbles as I lose all sense of what's up and what's down. His natural skill and lifetime of training kick in, and he's running purely on instinct.

Levi's dragon dives, and my stomach flies into my throat. After a moment, my world stops spinning—just as we disappear into the misty ravine. The cold fog hits my face like an icy breath.

Within moments, we break through the fog—only to encounter a craggy floor. Rocks as sharp as spears jut out across the ocean water below us as it carves between the island and the mainland. Levi maneuvers expertly through the stones, doing everything in his power to lose the dragons behind us. A bolt of fire shoots through the fog above, dispersing some of it, but it's not enough to clear the thin cloud cover.

Levi and his dragon know these lands. Ever since they came to the embassy, they've been exploring them. Memorizing them. Little did Levi realize that would just give his dragon fuel to evade the very people trying to save him.

As he dives into a hairpin turn, sliding expertly into a thin gap between two rocks, the wind bites at my face.

When we land—*if* we land, and I don't get hurled into the rocky sea below instead—I don't know what Levi's dragon will do. But I know Levi is still in there, and I'm going to do everything in my power to save him.

I have to give this one more try.

For Levi.

CHAPTER TWENTY-EIGHT

With an ear-splitting roar, Levi's dragon lands on a rocky cliff overlooking the ocean. His grip on my torso finally loosens, and I gasp as I suck in grateful breaths of air. The pins and needles begin to fade as my circulation returns to normal, and I lean on my elbows as I try to recover.

I have no idea how far we are from the embassy. I've never seen the mountains now surrounding us, and as far as I can tell, there's not even a path up to this ledge. It's a platform that sticks out over the rolling thunder of the waves a hundred feet below, and that's going to be one hell of a fall if I get knocked off balance.

His dragon paces along the far end of the wide ledge, snarling at me with all the pent-up fury of a tiger locked in a cage. His wings curl around his sides, tense and ready to spring, and his tail slides aggressively back and forth behind him.

"Levi," I say softly, lifting my hands to gently soothe him. "Levi, I know you're still in there."

The dragon snaps at the air, growling.

"You would never hurt me." I smile warmly, unafraid. I've battled dragon Bosses and the Ghost herself—facing off with a feral dragon doesn't scare me.

But the thought of losing Levi is *terrifying*.

The dragon before me relaxes, if only slightly, at my gentle tone. He still paces, watching me warily, as if he suspects I'll charge him at any moment.

"You attacked an entire Vaer fortress just to *help* me," I say, doing my best to remind him of who he is. "You did it *twice*, Levi, and both times, you gave me the cover I needed to go in and save someone who would have otherwise died."

Should I have let Zurie die? Yeah, knowing what I know now, that probably would have been the best move. But at the time, it made the most sense to save her.

Lessons learned, I guess.

Levi's dragon pauses midstride, watching me with narrowed eyes. He's still as a stone, barely breathing, but I know he's still aware of me. I know he's still listening.

If anything, he seems slightly distracted.

With a flicker of hope, I wonder if Levi is trying to take over once again.

"You make me feel when I want to shut down," I admit, doing everything I can to connect with the heart of the man who I so fervently adore. "You make me look inward. You make me want to be a better person. To deserve you."

The dragon snarls, shaking his head like he's trying to knock something out of it, and I can see the internal battle take hold.

"This war has to end, Levi," I say softly. "You two have to heal. You can't fight each other anymore."

The dragon's eyes snap toward me, and without wavering, I hold his gaze.

"I mean it." It's clear I need to shift gears and talk to his dragon, if only for a moment. "You need each other. You can't live without him, and Levi can't live without you. Do you understand?"

A soft growl builds in the dragon's throat, and he shrinks away from me ever so slightly. His body tenses, and his wings inch open. Like he wants to fly off.

If the dragon flies away, he and Levi are done. They'll keep fighting, and they'll never heal. If they take off now, I'm going to lose them both.

I'm not really one for feelings. It's never been my thing. But if it means saving Levi, I'll rip my heart out, crack it open, and lay everything on the table if that's what it takes.

"Wait," I say gently, taking a careful step toward him. "Wait, okay? Stay here. Stay with me. Let me help you. You don't need to do this alone, all right? You don't ever have to be alone again."

The dragon coos softly, the sound tortured and hurt, and he gently lowers his head as I walk nearer. He keeps flinching, like something's rattling around in his brain.

This is it.

Every second here counts.

Every movement, every breath, every word matters.

"Let me help you," I repeat softly as I set my palm gently against his forehead.

His eyes snap open, furious and full of rage, and I briefly wonder if I'm about to lose my hand.

But his expression eventually softens.

And, after a moment, he leans into my palm.

There's a pull at my navel, and with a grateful sigh, I instantly give in to it.

The world darkens around me as I'm pulled into Levi's mind. There are no fading memories anymore— just the endless black around me as I float through the vast nothing.

Before I can so much as call for him, two powerful arms hug me from behind.

Levi.

Thank the freaking *gods*.

I tilt my head backward to see Levi in his human

form. He looks down at me with a tormented expression, like he has a hole through his gut. Eager to help him in any way I can, I twist in his grip and wrap my arms around his neck in relief.

"I thought I lost you," I say softly.

He holds me tight, but he doesn't reply.

"You can't run from this anymore," I whisper into his ear. "Tell me what happened."

"Rory, I—" He sucks in a deep breath and presses his forehead against mine. "It's too painful."

I lean back and hold his face until he looks at me. When he does, when I'm sure I have his full attention, I kiss him.

Fiercely.

We stand there for who knows how long, locked together until I finally force myself to pull away. I gaze deep into those beautiful blue eyes of his, trying to find the words to tell him how much this matters to me.

"If it's too painful," I say softly. "Then let me face it with you."

He squeezes his eyes shut and sighs. After a moment, he takes my hand in his and gently kisses my palm. "I'll try."

A hazy blur appears in the darkness before us. It's a dim swirl of shadows among the black, barely visible. As we watch, they brighten, until they're gray swirls of light in the nothingness.

They begin to take forms—people I don't know,

faces I don't recognize. Soldiers, by the look of their dark uniforms.

Vaer.

"This ends today, Sloane," the tallest one says with a sneer.

"She can't even shift!" another one chimes in. "What are you *doing*, kid?"

In the swirling void, more shadows pop to life. A house. A window. A few pieces of overturned furniture. A terrified young woman, probably eighteen at most, curled and trembling in the corner.

The tall man grabs her by the hair and drags her out the door as she screams. She twists in his grip, doing her best to wrestle herself free as she claws at his arm, but she's frail. I can practically see the bones in her arms. She resists, trying to kick and bite him until he lets her go.

This girl is a fighter at heart.

She's just not strong enough to deal a blow.

The scene shifts, and we're suddenly outside on a patch of dirt. The man throws the girl to the ground, and she whimpers in pain as she hits the earth. She looks back at him, scrambling to get away, but he stalks toward her.

And, as the memory stretches out before us, more soldiers appear.

Fifteen.

Twenty.

Thirty.

Fifty.

"My entire battalion came to our house that day," Levi says softly. "Vaer Team One, the Boss's personal hit squad. The best of the best." He squares his shoulders defiantly, watching the scene before us. "To kill my sister."

I gape at the memory, speechless with the horror of it all. "But why?"

"She makes you *weak*," the tall man says again, interrupting us. "You should never have been allowed to keep her."

"Like she was some *pet*," Levi says with disgust.

I hold him tighter, trying to ease his pain in any way I can. "This is awful."

On the ground in front of us, a thick plume of smoke juts into the air and takes the form of a man on his knees. Thick shackles cover his hands as he fights the six men keeping him down.

Levi.

"Touch Daisy, and I'll kill you!" the foggy memory of Levi shouts. "I'll kill *all* of you!"

A ripple of laughter bubbles through the crowd of soldiers, the sneering men and women in their crisp black Vaer uniforms totally unfazed by the threat.

"Now, that just won't do," the tall man says. "You can't threaten your Commander, boy."

"I just *did*," the memory-Levi snarls. "She's done

nothing to deserve this, Commander. Nothing! Let me take her to the hospital, let me *help* her!"

"She's done *nothing?*" The Commander looks down at her with disgust. "She's a disgrace. What Vaer can't shift? What Vaer lets their dragon die?"

"He was so full of shit." Beside me, Levi practically growls with his hatred. "She never *had* a dragon. Not all people born into shifter families even *do.* But stupid, vile people will always find someone to hate."

I study the terrified girl on the ground, a frail human among vengeful dragons, and I wonder what her life must have been like. My heart twists for her.

For Daisy.

The Commander kneels beside the shackled Levi. "How many times have you tried to smuggle her out to some other family's embassy, Sloane? Twelve? Today was supposed to be lucky number thirteen, wasn't it?"

Levi grits his teeth, struggling harder against the soldiers holding him in place. "Don't you dare touch her, you spiteful sack of—"

"I give the orders, boy." The Commander grabs Levi's jaw, his grip so tight that his thumb distorts Levi's cheek. "I'm tired of wasting resources monitoring your home, your devices, your movements. You're useful, kid. You're smart. You're fast, and you're nearly as good as me. I want you to be my protégé, boy, I've *trained* you your whole damn life. Someday, you could take my job. You're the best I have, but I've let you get away with far too much. We need you to focus on the cause and devote yourself to *us,* not some slimy mortal brat who doesn't have a dragon to her name."

"She's my *sister,*" Levi snaps back. "She's the only family I have left!"

"Family holds you back, kid." The Commander wrinkles his nose in disgust. "I mean, just look at yourself. On your knees, fighting the people who feed you, all so you can save some weak link in the food chain? You need to rework your priorities, kid. You need to learn some *respect.*" The Commander stands, glaring down at the memory-Levi with disdain. "I should've done this years ago. It's time you man up, Sloane, and I think this should finally do the trick."

"No," Levi says his voice panicked and urgent. "I'll do whatever you want, Commander. Please. Just don't touch her. Don't!"

The Commander cracks his neck, ignoring Levi's panicked demands, and shifts his attention toward the girl lying in the dirt.

"No," I say softly. "Gods, no."

As the real Levi's chest presses against mine, his hold around me tightens.

The Commander shifts, his form shivering and twisting as he lets his dragon loose. In moments, a massive black dragon snarls into the air, wings spreading wide as he glares down at the girl at his feet.

The crowd of soldiers around them jeers, anxious for a show.

The dragon growls, lowering his head ominously as the girl desperately tries to back away. The wisps of shadow roll off of her like water evaporating from a lake, irregular and rough as she stares at the dragon above her.

"No!" the memory-Levi screams. He fights with his captors, but more soldiers pile on to keep him at bay.

"How can he get away with this?" I ask in horror.

"He was Kinsley's lover, at the time," Levi says with loathing. "She let him do anything he wanted."

The Commander roars, and a thick stream of ice billows from his mouth. The girl screams. The shadowy Levi of the memory shouts in horror, pulling against the men holding him down. His adrenaline takes over, and he manages to drag them behind him as he tries to race to her aid.

He doesn't make it.

The ice hits her, freezing her instantly. Her look of terror is locked on her pale face, one arm lifted in vain to protect herself as the ice solidifies around her.

Moments later, the black dragon lifts both of his front claws and, with a mighty roar, crushes the icy block before him. It shatters, shards flying in every direction.

"NO!" the real Levi shouts as he relives the memory that broke him.

Lost in his grief, he rushes into the wispy memory. The shadow swirls and twists around him as he drops to his knees, sliding the last few feet toward the dragon's claws.

The crowd laughs.

These fuckers *laugh.*

My heart in my throat, all I can do for a moment is stare in horror at the scene. At the moment that fractured Levi's soul.

Before us, the shadowy Levi of the memory begins to fade. He's shouting, but the words are muted and unclear. The shadows comprising his body quickly dissolve, and in moments, he's simply gone.

The laughter in the crowd quickly fades into worried chatter, and a moment later, screams.

The memory begins to shatter. The people in the scene begin to fade into dust, one by one, as the memory of the moment that made Levi feral starts to unravel. The soldiers all stare at the sky—at something I can't see.

And they run.

The memory quickly becomes nothing but the roar of dragons and the screams of victims. After a few moments, the final wisps of smoke disappear. Levi kneels in the middle of it all with his back to me, his palms on the ground as he grieves his sister.

"I killed them all." He doesn't move as he speaks. "I

killed all fifty-three of them, including the Commander. I left his corpse in the field by our house."

"I don't blame you," I confess. I kneel beside him and cradle him in my arms, letting him pour his soul out. "I would have done the same."

"That's why I was on Vaer lands," he continues. "I'm a Vaer. Kinsley was telling you the truth."

My heart thuds nervously in my chest, but I don't say anything. I just sit there as he leans into me, and I let him talk.

"When I was done…" He shakes his head, furious, hurt, full of hate. "When they were all dead, my dragon refused to give me my body back. It wanted more. More revenge. More justice. Nothing was ever enough. No amount of bloodletting would ever fill the hole. I decimated entire outposts and fortresses. Anything nearby became rubble. Any Vaer who crossed my path became dinner." His nose wrinkles in hatred. "Kinsley sent unit after unit to get revenge for her lover, but I slaughtered them all. She never stopped hunting me, and I never stopped evading her." He grimaces. "I guess my hatred kept my mind sharp for far longer than it should have. But I constantly felt myself slipping. I figured I was just prolonging the inevitable, and I nearly gave in. That day when the trap finally caught me, I thought this was it—if I'd managed to let my guard down enough to get snared, there wasn't much of me left."

He looks at me with those intense eyes, trapping me with his gaze, and his expression softens. "But then you saved me."

The knot in my throat is so tight that I can't even speak. I watch him breathlessly, not wanting to interrupt.

"You gave me another chance." He shakes his head. "One I didn't deserve. Not just a chance at life, but a chance to prove I could keep someone safe. You showed me not everyone was cruel, that some people were worth protecting. I felt like—" He pauses, grasping for the right words. "I felt like, maybe, my failure could be redeemed. You gave me purpose again, Rory, but I never expected…" He runs a hand through his hair, staring off into the darkness.

"What?" I ask softly, leaning in.

He tilts his head toward me, and after a moment, smiles warmly. "I never expected to fall for you as hard as I did."

I smile through the pain in my throat and sit on the dark ground beside him, running my hand lovingly along his back. I want to say something, but no words come close to expressing the way he makes me feel.

"And now…" Levi's shoulders droop as he stares into the darkness above him. "Now, I guess I'm trapped here."

"You're not." I shake my head violently. "This is

what you've needed to do all along, Levi. Face what happened—and forgive."

"I will *never* forgive that sack of—"

"Not him," I say with a shake of my head. "No, *fuck* him. I mean you. You need to forgive yourself—and forgive your dragon for taking over. Forgive its bloodlust."

He opens his mouth to speak, but his voice cracks before he can say a word. He rubs his eyes, gently shaking his head through the pain.

"You did everything you could," I say, tenderly holding the back of his head as I lean against him. "You are powerful, stealthy, strong, and a brilliant fighter, Levi, but you are not going to be able to save everyone every time. No one can. We might be dragons, but we're still mortal. All we can ever do is our absolute best. All we can ever ask of ourselves is to be better than we were yesterday." I suck in a deep breath as the words tumble from me, pouring from my heart. "Sometimes, the people we love are ripped from us, and no matter what we do, we can't save them. But you *cannot* hate yourself if fate gets the better of you."

He won't look at me.

"I'm proud of you," I add with a soft smile. "You did everything in your power to save her. You poured yourself into your revenge. But it's time to forgive." I kiss his nose. "It's time for you to come back. To the world. To me."

Levi gently lifts his head, his wounded eyes shifting back and forth between mine, and he takes a slow, steadying breath. He sets his palm against my cheek. "I don't deserve you."

"Yeah, you do." I grin.

Though his eyes are still watery, he laughs.

"I know all about revenge," I add, my smile fading a bit. "And if you want to avenge your sister, I'll help you take down Kinsley. But we'll do it together."

"I don't know if I can, Rory."

"Try," I say, brushing my nose against his. "For me."

He holds me tightly, and we sit in the darkness with only our breaths to keep us company. My heart hammers in my chest, and I know I've done all I can.

It's now up to him.

And I just hope I don't lose my Levi.

CHAPTER TWENTY-NINE

The warm sun beats against my skin as it rises over the ocean. For a moment, I don't know where I am.

Blinking rapidly in surprise, I glance around the rocky ledge, trying to get my bearings. I'm kneeling on the stone, and I run my hand through my hair in confusion. The ocean roars below as the horizon erupts with color. A cold gust tears past me, chilling me briefly to the bone.

"Rory," a familiar voice says, his tone oddly surreal.

I pivot to see who spoke. Levi kneels with me on the rock, and we face each other. He lifts his hands, studying his human skin in disbelief. His dark hair curls around his gorgeous face, every bit as handsome as it was when I saw him in his mind.

With a rough lining of stubble along his jaw and the

hard muscle covering every inch of his naked human body, his eyes go wide with shock.

"You did it," I say softly, almost afraid to believe what I'm seeing. "Levi, you did it!"

His blue eyes flit toward me, and he smiles broadly. "*We* did it."

Without another word, he grabs my face and kisses me deeply. We fall against the polished rock beneath us as my heart soars with gratitude and joy.

I lose myself in him, in the surreal happiness of it all. Weaving my fingers through his hair, I drink him in, almost afraid he might dissolve into dust beneath my hands.

His hands explore me with masterful strokes of his fingers, and I never want him to stop. My waist, my neck, my thighs—he investigates it all, his touch unrestrained and alluring.

The raw power of his embrace stirs parts of my soul I didn't even know I still had. A carnal yearning springs to life deep within me, surging through me like an ocean swell.

As our hot skin brushes together, I can almost feel his emotions. His joy. His disbelief. His love.

Wait—I *can* feel him.

She's perfect, he thinks. *I want her. All of her.*

Lost in the moment, he rolls me onto my back and straddles me. His strong fingers lift my shirt, tugging it off in a perfectly fluid motion.

"Levi, I can hear your thoughts," I say through the kisses. "How can—"

"Later," he interrupts. He nibbles my ear as he unhooks my bra and tosses it aside.

I grin, gasping with delight as he tugs on my pant leg. I suppose I can allow a little distraction. Within seconds, the pants and underthings fly off, and he gently sets me once more on my back.

His mouth tenderly bites my jaw, and my eyes flutter closed. I sink into him once again, lost and in love.

His thick cock hardens between my legs as he ravishes me with kisses. Every brush of his lips against my skin sparks a ripple of delight. Every time his hand grips my waist, my heart sings. His touch ignites me in ways no one else can, dipping into my soul and bringing me happiness I didn't know I was allowed to feel.

When I lay beneath him, naked and aching for him, he spreads my knees apart with his own. There's never a pause in his kisses, never a moment to breathe, and I love every second of it.

The tip of his cock presses against my entrance, and he gently leans into the thrust. I moan as his cock begins to fill me, bit by bit, almost tantalizingly slow at first. I'm delightfully sandwiched between his hard body and the cool, smooth rock beneath me. Tenderly, he sets his hand beneath my head to protect it as he presses himself deeper into me.

Impulsively, I wrap my legs around him as he fills me. In the moment, I utterly surrender to him. I want nothing more than his kisses, nothing more than his touch. I crave the way his love and devotion blur into me, until I'm not sure which emotions are mine and which are his.

Our souls meld as his cock burrows deeper and deeper, stretching me to my limit.

When his hips finally press flush against mine, he pauses briefly and brushes his nose lovingly over my cheek. "I promised to make you feel every pleasure known to man," he says, his voice rough and sultry. "Let me deliver on that pledge."

I grin up at him, lost in those blue eyes. "If you insist."

His mouth presses gently against mine as he pulls slowly out of me. As his bare cock slowly slides through me, it sends ripples of pleasure through my body. I ache for more. My eyes shut impulsively, and I arch my back as he has his way with me.

When his cock slides out, he drags the tip along my entrance. Sparks of delight blister through me, and I chuckle in ecstasy as he teases me. His cock presses hard against my clit, rubbing it mercilessly when all I want him to do is be inside of me.

His cock slips downward, wedging itself against my

sensitive folds. He holds it there for a moment, pausing to nibble lightly on my lip. I sink into the sensation of his mouth on mine, briefly distracted.

With a hard thrust, he thrusts his cock deep within me, filling me to the brim.

As I gasp in absolute ecstasy, he does it again.

And again.

And *again*.

He rides me as the waves crash below us, every masterful buck of his hips rocking me with pleasure. I moan as he takes me higher into the blissful sensation. His cock stretches me, pushing every button as it becomes my ticket to both physical bliss and soulful connection.

An orgasm builds within me, just out of reach, and he thrusts harder into me as it springs to life. Something about the way he curls his hips with each thrust keeps my climax at bay. His technique makes my orgasm build ever so slowly, promising to be truly mind-shattering once it hits.

He leans his mouth against my ear. "Come for me," he demands, his voice growly and rough. "I want you to come so hard you forget where we even are."

Oh *gods*.

He kisses me fiercely as I gasp and moan his name, unable to do or say anything else.

When the orgasm hits me, it rolls through my body like a tidal wave. The logical side of my brain shuts off, and all I can feel is the pleasure. The delight. The bliss.

I lose track of time as his cock continues to thrust into me again and *again*, riding me through the entire climax. My thighs tighten around his hips, and I grab fistfuls of his hair as I moan into his mouth. As our lips brush together, I can feel the seductive tilt of his mouth as he smiles in pride at his handiwork.

As the orgasm slowly recedes, I fall back against the rock. My breath races, my chest heaving, but I never let go of his hair.

He continues to ride me as I come down from my blissful, orgasmic high. Every thrust sends another little twinge of joy through my legs. I tilt my hips toward him, giving him full access, letting him do whatever he wants.

With a contented sigh, he stiffens and leans against my chest. He releases himself into me, the flood almost never-ending. The sensation nearly sparks a second orgasm for me, and I gasp as ripples of bliss shoot through me from between my thighs.

For a few moments, we simply lay there together in silence, gasping and trying to catch our breath. He holds me tightly, his cock still buried within me as he tenderly leans his face against my neck.

I love you, he says through our connection.

I smile and tilt my head toward him, kissing the bit of his ear I can reach. *Love you back.*

I don't know why we can hear each other's thoughts, or why the connection that's usually limited to dragon forms remains for us in his human form. It raises so many questions, but as we lie on a ledge hovering above the salty water, I figure we don't need to explore those questions now.

He lovingly nibbles my jawline. "Whatever happens, Rory, whoever you end up choosing—just know that I will be here to protect you. Always."

I laugh. These pushy dragons. They all think I'm going to pick just one man, and I'm not going to.

But I know Levi is here to stay, and that fills my heart with joy.

CHAPTER THIRTY

Though I'm tempted to spend the entire day on the ledge with Levi, giving him full access to every inch of my body, the others are probably starting to wonder if I'm dead.

I should probably go soothe some furious tempers.

As I yank on the last of my clothes Levi tossed aside earlier, I steal another glance at his gorgeously naked body. He stares off into the sunset with his back to me, the hard muscles in his shoulders flexing as he runs his hands through his hair.

"I'm alive, right?" he asks with a glance over his shoulder. "Or is this heaven?"

I chuckle. "How can you be both a fearsome warrior *and* totally adorable, all at the same time?"

He laughs and pulls me toward him, his strong arms warm and comforting as he holds me close. He peppers kisses tenderly along my neck, and I shiver with delight as his mouth passes the sensitive area along my jaw. I weave my arms around him, letting out a happy little sigh now that he's back.

Now that he's done the impossible.

"Do you know where we are?" I ask.

"Kind of." He frowns briefly and scans the ocean around us. After a moment, he surveys the steep cliff overhead, his head tilting backward as he cranes to see it all. "I've only traveled out this far a few times, but I can probably get us back."

"Well, that's quite the vote of confidence." I chuckle.

He grins, his gaze briefly flitting toward me before he returns his attention to the cliff. "Getting up there is going to be a challenge."

"We can do it." I cross my arms and study the overhang, making a mental note of the route I want to take.

Without a word, Levi runs his hands through my hair. When I look at him, he's watching me with a grateful smile, like there's so much he wants to say but he doesn't know where to start.

I open my mouth to tease him a little for the adorably goofy grin on his face, but the crunch of footsteps on the land above us interrupts me. Levi and I glare at the edge, both of us tensing at the same time.

This is *not* a place to be cornered.

The cliff is our only way off this ledge, and it involves climbing what could easily be fifty feet of sheer rock. Below us is a hundred-foot drop into a craggy ocean littered with rocks as sharp as spears.

If anyone starts firing on us right now, we're screwed.

Levi *just* turned back into his human form. I will not, under any circumstances, ask him to shift in order to fly us out of here.

We'll figure out something else.

I summon my magic into my hands, the white light flitting across my skin as heat and power surges through me with effortless grace. Eyebrows furrowed, I prepare for war.

To defend Levi.

To save us both.

I aim toward the ledge, preparing to fire the moment I see the barrel of a gun.

The crunching steps near, hesitating a moment as they reach the overhang just above us.

Moments later, a familiar head pops over the edge of the cliff, his loose brown hair dancing in the wind as he looks down at us. "Rory!"

Tucker.

I just about collapse with relief.

"Hey, babe!" I shout, shaking my hands to dismiss the magic from my fingers. "Man, am I glad to see you!"

"Guys, over here!" Tucker shouts over the gale of wind. He disappears for a moment before leaning back over the ledge. "Babe, how did you get down—" his eyes shift toward Levi, and even though he's fifty feet above me, I can see the vague hint of a confused expression on his face. "Do I know you?"

Levi laughs. "Yeah, man. You know me."

"Are you…" Tucker furrows his brow, his tone soft and disbelieving. "Levi, is that you?"

Levi just grins.

"Where is she?" Drew demands, his tone thick with the demand for an answer.

"Is she okay?" Irena asks a moment later.

Four heads lean over the edge, and I take a deep breath of relief as everyone checks in on me—Jace, Drew, Tucker, and Irena.

"You guys didn't even *try* to split up?" I joke. "I'm carried off in a dragon's claws, and you clomp through the forest as a single unit?"

"It's called a search and rescue, babe," Tucker says with a nod toward Jace. "His nerds locked your location, but this place is damn hard to get to. Too risky to fly through those waters. Honestly, Levi's lucky he even made it out here."

"It's called *skill*," Levi says with a confident wink.

"Who the *hell* are you?" Jace snaps, glaring at the man beside me.

"That's Levi," Tucker says, beating me to it.

"No way." Drew leans a little closer. "That would be impossible—"

I whistle sharply to get their attention. "Hey, are

you guys going to stare at his pretty body all day, or can you maybe give us a hand out of here?"

"And you call *me* pushy?" Drew lifts an eyebrow playfully. "Let us appreciate the historic moment of a dragon reversing his feral nature, will you?"

"I'll go secure the rope," Irena says, disappearing for a few moments.

"See?" I point after my sister. "There's a clear head on that one."

Drew and Tucker laugh, but Jace's eyes simply narrow on Levi—like he doesn't quite believe it.

He will. I'm not worried.

A few moments later, two rope lines hurl over the edge, shivering as they fall toward us. They end a few feet short of the rocky outcropping we're standing on, so I take a running start and jump the seven feet to grab it. As I take hold of mine, Levi does the same—though, I notice, it's not nearly as difficult for his tall, lean body to reach his rope.

Together, we climb the fifty-foot precipice. Though we don't have harnesses, this is *so* much easier than it would have been without help.

I'm really starting to enjoy having a team.

When we reach the overhang, Irena and Jace grab my arms to help me onto solid ground. Beside me, Drew and Tucker hoist Levi onto solid ground. A few backpacks sit open nearby, their contents half-spilled over the grass. The ropes end in a large boulder nearby, the knots firm even as the frayed cables sway in the breeze.

Before I can even stand, Irena wraps her arms around me and holds me close. "I can't even take a damn nap without you getting into trouble anymore."

"Stop being dramatic," I say. "It worked out, right?"

Still, I hug her tightly back.

"I'm proud of you, man," Tucker says with a broad grin. The former Knight sets his hand on Levi's shoulder and squeezes.

"Thanks." Levi smiles and nods to me. "It was all her, though."

"Oh, take credit." I roll my eyes. "It was a team effort."

Irena frowns, her eyes drifting toward the forest as she avoids looking at Levi. "Can someone get this very naked man some clothes, please?"

Drew laughs. "What, you don't like the show?"

"Sorry," Levi says with a chuckle, trying to cover himself. His massive hands only hide some of his cock, however, and I blush a little as my eyes impulsively drift toward his crotch. I resist the impulse to bite my lip with pleasure at the sight.

"Here." Jace rifles through one of the small packs sitting open nearby and tosses Levi a pair of the dojo's uniform pants.

As Levi tugs them on, Jace zips up the pack and leans toward me. "We can't stay here," he says urgently under his breath. "This is Knights territory. We barely got here unseen—I couldn't even bring reinforcements. We need to move immediately, as some of the chatter we've picked up suggests they saw you and Levi flying out here."

I impulsively stiffen, and his warning is all I need to slip instantly into warrior mode. "Have you spotted anyone moving in this direction?"

"Possibly," Jace admits, his eye twitching briefly in frustration. "They've begun to develop camouflaged movements. Sometimes they disappear from the scanners, and we can't always rely on those."

"You have units standing by?"

"Of course," Jace says with a grimace. "But the likelihood of them getting here in time is slim. This is just about the worst place Levi's dragon could have taken you."

"That's probably why he did it," I confess. "Isolation."

"Probably," Jace admits with a begrudging groan.

It's frustrating that Levi's dragon lugged us into Knight territory, but the primal part of his dragon was hardly thinking straight. That's what the human side is for—self-preservation, logic, and restraint.

Yet, here we are, and we need to make the best of this.

With a grim frown, Jace studies the ice dragon beside me. "Levi, can you shift?"

"Jace!" I scold, disappointed in him.

"Dude," Tucker adds, his tone a bit disgusted. "He *just* did the impossible. Can he breathe for two seconds first?"

"Tucker, you know where we are," Jace snaps. "This isn't the time for courtesy or emotion. We need to get the hell out of here."

"I can't shift, yet," Levi answers with a simple shake of his head. "I'm going to need some time, Jace. My dragon and I are better, but we're not totally in sync yet."

"Very well," Jace says with a disappointed sigh. "Drew, we can carry them." He smirks at the fire dragon. "Unless you're getting fat and lazy, what with all the time you've spent in my dojo, eating all my food?"

"Cute," Drew says dryly.

"Wait," Levi says chuckling in disbelief. "You want to carry me? In your claws?"

"Would you prefer a golden chariot?" Jace asks sarcastically. He quickly scans the forest behind him. "I wanted to find you both sooner, but flying out here would have attracted the wrong attention, and we didn't have time to waste getting into a firefight. Now, however, we need to get out of here as fast as possible, and that means we fly." He gestures at the spiky coast below us as another gale shoots over the cliff. "Those rocks are deadly, and the winds here can down even the best fliers. This is a dangerous spot, and we can't take any risks. If we keep to the land, we should be able to avoid the gusts and gales that could rip you out of our claws or sink us completely." He gives Levi a skeptical once-over and crosses his muscled arms. "Do you have a problem with that?"

"Yeah, I'm fairly certain I prefer death." Levi snorts, and even though he's joking, he bristles at the very idea of a dragon carrying him off.

I chuckle. Dragons can be such prideful creatures.

Jace sighs in annoyance. "We don't have time for this."

Levi calmly shakes his head, his hands on his hips as he stands a little taller in defiance. "Dojo master or no, you are not flying off with me in your talons."

"You literally just did that to her," Drew points out with a nod toward me.

"That's different." The ice dragon laughs, nervously scratching the back of his neck as he's called out on his dragon's behavior. "Besides, I said I was sorry."

I tilt my head. "Did you, though?"

He grins, his sexy blue eyes narrowing seductively. "Pretty sure I did, yes."

Heat rises along my neck, and I turn away to hide the blush as it creeps up my face.

Without another word, Jace tosses his pack to Irena. She hoists it on her shoulders, surprisingly at ease with being surrounded by dragons, and I wonder if the danger of the moment has convinced her to just play along.

Jace shifts. The rip of his pants tearing as his dragon takes over catches my attention, and a rush of air shoots by me as he stretches his wings. The beautiful black thunderbird towers over us, his body glowing with magic and light. He leans on his back legs and reaches for me with one of his talons, inviting me to come closer.

I sigh and lift my arms in defeat, letting him wrap his claw tightly around my waist. The injury from my fight with Jett is nearly healed, and the pressure of his grip only yields a slight discomfort.

Man, I *love* being a dragon.

Levi grimaces and takes a few wary steps backward. "Jace, there has to be a better way to—"

Apparently not one to banter, the lightning-fast dragon bolts toward Levi and grabs him in his other claw. I stifle a giggle as Levi wrestles in the thunderbird's grip, cursing silently under his breath.

As Jace banks over the water, a gust carries him suddenly higher. He growls in frustration and tilts back toward the forest, trying to keep from losing control on these wild and unpredictable winds.

As we recover, my cheeks flushed with a bit of nausea from the ride, a familiar red dragon bolts into the sky beside us. He holds Tucker and Irena in his claws, their legs dangling over the steep drop to the sea. Irena stiffens in his grip, glaring at the fire dragon above her with a blended expression of discomfort and anger.

Tucker, however, appears utterly relaxed. He leans his elbow against Drew's claw and rests his cheek on his fist. "I've been carried off by dragons a lot, lately," he shouts at me over the howling wind. "It's kind of emasculating, honestly. I need to wrestle a few bears after this."

As Drew and Jace groan at the stupid joke, I laugh. I can't help it. These men are ridiculous, and I'm so happy they're mine.

My family.

A gunshot echoes through the forest, and the chilling boom wipes the smile from my face. A second gunshot ricochets off the trees a few minutes later. A flock of birds takes to the air, screeching as they scatter.

Drew tilts his head toward me, a concerned glint in his eye. I nod, catching his silent request, and summon my magic into my fingers.

Just in case.

Since this is Knight territory, there's no telling how long they've had to mobilize. If they spotted Levi's dragon when he first dragged me out here, there could be a whole army on its way.

We have to get out of here.

Fast.

CHAPTER THIRTY-ONE

W e're being shot at—trapped between gunfire and a rocky cliff that might drag us to the ocean below.

Not great choices, but if I have to choose, I trust my men and their skill as fliers.

"Go higher!" I shout to Jace and Drew. "Go where they can't follow! You can handle this—I know you can!"

He briefly looks down at me, growling at the idea. With my magic still rushing over my hands, ready to fire at a moment's notice, I press my cheek against his leg to open the connection.

You'll freeze, he says. *If we go too high, you could pass out.*

A hail of bullets fly violently past us, and Jace spins

to avoid it. His wings tucked around his body, he plummets suddenly, and my head spins as the world tumbles around me.

His wings cut through the air again as he evens out, but the damage is done. Any second now, and I might hurl.

I groan, my eyebrows pinched together in a pronounced frown. *It's better than being shot!*

Jace nods and tilts upward. Seconds later, Drew follows suit. If we stay out of range, we can avoid any gunfire.

The key is getting out of range before they fire at us —because if they catch up to us, they might send us plummeting into the craggy rocks dotting the shoreline below.

An echoing symphony of thundering gunshots cut through the forest, scattering another flock of birds. I wait with bated breath to see if we'll make it—or if the Knights moved too fast.

Two dozen blistering shots of electricity soar from the forests on the edge of the cliff, all of them perfectly spread to maximize the chance of hitting their targets.

And, unfortunately, the Knights aimed at the sky above us, forcing us lower.

They're trying to head us off.

Jace growls in frustration, his magic building in his throat as he scans the ground below us. I lift my palms, trying to take aim, but the guns are too well hidden. There's no telling where the shots came from—or where the next ones will be.

I don't have to wait long.

The next round of thunder hits, but this time, it doesn't stop. I lose count after twenty-seven shots, and they just keep going.

This time, however, it's not bullets.

Every shot arching toward us is now a sizzling bolt of taser fire. They soar through the sky like flaming cannonballs. Even though I hate these things, it's better than bullets—a hit from one of these in the right spot can knock a dragon unconscious. In the wrong spot, they can still take one down.

Which says to me that they just changed tactics—capture the dragons alive.

The cannon fire rains on us, the arc of the shots soaring both above and right at us. They're trying to keep us low to the ground because they know we'll be out of reach if we get much higher.

Just as I feared, there really is an army here.

And they have come *very* well equipped.

Jace dives, and Drew narrowly avoids the onslaught. Between the two of them, they flip and spin through the sky with masterful control. If I were watching from the ground, instead of trapped in Jace's claws, I might even enjoy it. As it is, I'm about two seconds from passing out entirely.

My magic fades from my fingers, and it takes every-thing in my power to focus on staying conscious.

I look down at the rocky shoreline, and the thought of one of those spearing *anyone* on my team utterly guts me.

Furious, I summon my magic once again and release a thick blast of the blistering white light into the forest. I don't really care where it hits—honestly, since the thundering cannons don't seem to ever pause, I figure I'm bound to hit *something.*

The beam of light soars through the air, true to aim, and explodes against a row of trees a hundred feet below us. Trunks fly into the air as leaves and smoke billow into the sky. A second later, something else explodes nearby, and I think perhaps I got one.

One of *many.*

My attack doesn't even put a dent in the taser fire. The sizzling beams of electricity surround us like hail in a storm, somehow more intense and concentrated than before. Between the camouflaged weapons and Jace spinning and twirling to avoid the shots, I can't make any sense of where the enemy fire is even coming from.

I try to take aim, to fire back, but Jace ducks and weaves too quickly for me to get a clear shot. The red blur of Drew's massive body swirls in and out of focus, and I don't want to hit him by mistake.

We *have* to get out of here.

I set my hand against Jace's leg to reopen our connection, trying to talk to him and come up with a plan, but he's too focused on avoiding the blasts.

A beam of taser fire hits his side, and smoke billows from the wound. He roars in pain, dropping abruptly in altitude.

Levi and I yell as we plummet toward the rocky coast below. My stomach soars into my throat as we fall, but Jace recovers with a pained snarl—never once loosening his grip on me or Levi despite the sizzling crater in his shoulder.

Three blasts nail Drew in his neck, and he bellows in pain as he, too, loses altitude.

Jace snaps at him, roaring a command I don't understand, and the two of them bank in unison toward the forest. They angle away from the guns, trying to put as much distance as possible between us and the weapons shooting at us.

He's taking us *inland.*

This is either going to work brilliantly or be a spectacular failure. With so few options, there's just no in-between—and we are fresh out of other choices.

Damn it.

Part of me hopes we've gotten far enough that we're at the edge of the Knight's territory, but I know better than to rely on boundaries to hold the Knights at bay.

As we race over the canopy, more and more bursts of electricity soar into the sky. Though the trees are mostly just green blurs below my feet, I try to give Jace and Drew some cover. Whenever it's clear Drew won't get caught in the crossfire, I release beam after beam of my magic into the forest below.

I don't really care what I hit. I just want the blasts to stop.

Drew unleashes a torrent of flame on the forest, his powerful fire decimating everything in its path. It's like watching a volcano erupt, and for a moment, I'm simply dazzled by him. His power. His strength.

It's amazing to see.

Seconds later, however, more taser fire erupts from the other side of the forest. Drew has to duck and weave to avoid it, and the stream of fire ends.

Jace lets loose a sharp blast of his powerful blue magic onto the forest below. It gouges a deep scar into the earth, kicking up trees and dust, but we're all just guessing.

We're just trying to give ourselves enough cover to get out of range.

And we're close.

The taser fire is getting more and more sparse. It's easier to avoid. I fire another blast of my magic at the ground, and a powerful explosion rocks the forest. Branches fly into the air, followed by a tire.

Score. I must have hit one of their anti-dragon vehicles.

I lift my palms to take aim again when a hailstorm

of fire erupts from behind us. It's ceaseless. There are easily fifty blasts, all headed for us at once.

Shit.

I refocus my attention, firing the beams of my magic at the taser blasts in an attempt to disperse them. I hit seven, but I'm just not fast enough.

Two hit Jace square in the chest. Four more hit Drew, one of them in the head. An instant knock-out.

The two dragons plummet to the ground, as do those of us in their claws.

As my heart rises to my throat, I scramble to think of a plan. Jace's wings beat through the air as we tumble toward the ground. As dazed as he must be, he's trying to regain his balance, but his world is flipped.

Drew just falls.

"No!" I scream. "Irena! Tucker! DREW!"

In a sudden, panicked rush, Drew's wings snap to attention. He recovers, if only barely, moments before he crashes into the canopy. I watch in horror as he pivots onto his back, cradling Tucker and Irena in his arms to protect them.

As Jace, Levi, and I plummet to the ground, I feel Jace's grip on me tighten. He rolls onto his back, taking much the same position as Drew just did.

"JACE!" I scream, more worried for him than me.

"Rory, hold on!" Levi shouts, grabbing the talons around his waist as he prepares for impact. "This is going to *hurt!*"

Branches snap as we break through the canopy. Leaves scratch my face. We hit the ground with an earth-shattering thud, and my world goes black.

CHAPTER THIRTY-TWO

I open my eyes to a swaying canopy. The sunny gap in the branches above me shifts every time I try to move my eyes, and nothing is quite in focus. It's just color and light—greens, whites, browns.

I blink rapidly to clear my head. Someone's talking, but their words just echo uselessly through my brain. Dazed, I try to stand, but my knees give out on me.

"Get up," a strange man barks at me.

Calloused hands grab my arm.

Oh, right.

Oh, *shit.*

The taser fire. The anti-dragon guns.

People were after us.

They *are* after us.

I squint, trying to see who's looming over me. His face blurs, and I can't make out any detail. Whoever grips my arm hauls me roughly to my feet. I limp along, trying to stand upright, pushing against him as I try and fail to summon my magic to defend myself.

Stupid *concussion.*

He throws me on my knees, and I land on my palms to keep my balance. Something about the violent movement resets me. Maybe it's the adrenaline, or the rage. I'm not sure, but my world finally clicks into place, and I can see again.

Irena and Tucker kneel to my left, their palms pressed against the back of their heads in reluctant surrender. Four soldiers guard each of them, and every uniformed Knight has a gun trained on their heads.

To my right, Levi glares up at the four soldiers who have their guns trained on him. His hands are also behind his head, and I feel someone grab my hands to force me to do the same. I resist, impulsively tensing to kick them in the balls, but a gun barrel presses flat against my forehead. I glare up at a stranger as he scowls down at me, daring me to give him a reason to shoot.

The crash of footsteps through the underbrush gets my attention, and a dozen soldiers join us. They throw Jace and Drew onto the dead leaves of the underbrush, both men unconscious.

I stiffen, wanting to run to them and see if they're okay, but one of the soldiers behind me presses a second gun against my skull. I curse under my breath, glaring at him, ready to rip out his spine.

We're easily outnumbered twenty to one. Through the gaps in the trees around us, I spot at least thirty Humvees armed with anti-dragon guns.

This is *bad.*

"Imagine my delight," a familiar man says from somewhere nearby, "when I got word you left the embassy."

Carter Holt brushes aside a low-hanging branch as he steps into the clearing. He sneers down at me, an arrogant smirk on his face as he leans his rifle against his shoulder. "Carried off by a dragon, no less. I figured they would all come for you, Rory, and I got *ready.*"

I groan. Not this asshole again.

"Didn't I kill you?" I ask, feigning boredom.

His nose wrinkles briefly in annoyance, but that doesn't seem to faze him as much as I hoped it would.

"I figured you would bring me this one," Carter says with a nod toward Tucker. "That's why I waited." He squats in front of Tucker, smirking as the former Knight glares bloody daggers at him. "You're lucky your daddy put a bounty on your head, bro, or you'd be a corpse in the ocean right now."

"Go to hell, Carter," Tucker snaps.

"I don't get you two," Carter says absently, gesturing between me and Tucker. "You both had everything given to you on a platter. You were each set to seize control, and yet you both squandered it." He scoffs. "You deserve each other. Really."

He stands and continues surveying his prizes, only to pause when he notices Irena. "Well, now," he says softly, almost in disbelief. "Providence truly shined upon me today, didn't it?"

Irena scowls up at him as four gun barrels press harder on her forehead to keep her in place.

"That's right," he says with an arrogant smirk. "Don't you try anything, Irena. You're disposable."

"Don't *touch* her," I snap.

"Oh, I don't need—"

A scuffle catches our attention, and as I tilt my head toward the rustle of boots and leaves, the gun barrels leave cold indents in my forehead.

Jace and Drew are on their feet, naked and furious. Drew launches to his feet and snaps the nearest soldier's arm in a beautifully fluid motion. At the same time, Jace kicks out another soldier's knee. As the man falls, the dojo master kicks him square in the jaw. The man slumps to the ground, unconscious, and Jace snatches his gun. In moments, he and Drew are armed, their weapons trained on the circle of soldiers around us.

But they're outnumbered, and no amount of grit or gumption is going to get them out of this.

Eyes wild, their chests heave with the effort of their fight. They look at little dazed, and I figure they aren't even sure what's going on. They probably just woke up.

Carter clicks his tongue in disappointment. "Put down your guns, gents." He cocks his rifle and aims it at my head. "Now."

Drew's brows knit together in hatred, his furious gaze trained on Carter. Jace, to his credit, doesn't betray an ounce of emotion. He simply glares at the man holding a gun to my head, his eyes narrowed and calculating—but it's a bluff. He's trying to act disinterested, but the Knights aren't going to buy it.

Neither of them would ever let anything happen to me, and Carter knows that.

After a moment, both men drop their weapons and raise their hands behind their heads. A dozen soldiers rush to kick out their knees, and my powerful men fall to the ground in surrender.

For now.

Carter and I started this dance back when he tried to tranquilize me outside the hospital, but I know more about him now. I'm learning who he is, what he wants, and what he fears.

There's only one way to disarm a man who has me this vastly outgunned, and that's to play the strings of his insecurities.

I scan the dozens of soldiers and tanks around us. "You realize Spectres don't ask for help, right?"

Carter's gaze snaps furiously toward me, and the barest hint of a scowl rolls across his face.

"Oh, do they not know?" I feign a loud whisper, knowing full well the rest of the soldiers can still hear me. A small smirk plays on my lips as I toy with my prey. "Was that supposed to be our little secret?"

"Shut your mouth," Carter warns, his voice low and dangerous.

"You can't go running off to the Knights whenever you're in over your head," I point out. "First the botched castle heist, and now this?" I mockingly click my tongue in disproval. "A Spectre handles his own mess. Surely Zurie told you that?"

"Shut up!" He backhands me, his knuckles landing a painful blow across my face. My head snaps to the side from the force, and for a moment, my world goes fuzzy.

The blow sparks a frenzy of chaos.

"I'll kill you!" Levi snarls, wrestling with the soldiers holding him at bay. Four more rush over to help their comrades keep him in line, but they're having a hell of a time of it.

"Don't *touch* her!" Tucker shouts as he punches a soldier clear in the jaw, trying to get to me. Someone hits him in the temple with the butt of his gun, taking him to the ground. I tense, worried for him, but he winces moments later, already getting up again to continue the fight.

Jace and Drew thrash against the dozen guards holding them at bay, their words muffled as they fight against the men restraining them.

It looks for all the world like this place might erupt into a battle royale, and every man here is going to be gunning for Carter.

As the stinging fades, I lift my head defiantly to look Carter dead in the eye. He sneers down at me, daring me to speak. Daring me to add any more flippant comments. Practically *begging* me to say something so that he can hit me again.

In the corner of my eye, Irena casts a curious glance across my men. There's a brief hint of surprise on her face at how fiercely they want to defend my honor, but she doesn't allow herself to simmer on it for long. Her gaze quickly returns to Carter, and she's once more ready for battle.

Like me, she's focused. We're both in murder mode, waiting for the chance to strike.

"Aw," I say gently, as if his attempt to hurt me was more of an adorable attempt than anything else. A thin trail of blood leaks from the side of my mouth, but it's nothing I can't handle. "That was a cute little love tap, Carter. Sorry, though. You're just not my type."

Carter kneels and roughly grabs my face, pinning me in front of him until his furious glare is all I can see. "You're really testing my patience."

"Oh, no! Am I really?" I taunt in a mocking tone. "Whatever will I do?"

"The only reason you're even alive is because Zurie wants to kill you herself," he snaps. "The *only* reason—"

"I sense a pattern here, Carter," I interrupt. "I mean, look around us. Do you really think Zurie approves of *any* of this? You're no Spectre. You'll never be a Spectre. You're too much of a coward."

His grip tightens on my jaw to a painful degree, but I smirk through the pain.

"You hide," I continue. "You wait. You plot. You ask for *help*," I say the word with disdain, as I know Zurie would, just to get under his skin. "You could never face me at full power because you're *weak*. You know you would lose, so you do everything you can to stab me when I'm not looking." I lean toward him despite his rough grip on my jaw. "It's going to be delightful to watch you break once Zurie tells you the truth."

"What are you talking about?" he asks, his eyes shifting warily across my face.

I grin. Oh, this poor fool—he doesn't realize he's being used. If I'm right, Zurie's dangling a dream in front of him. By promising him a life as a Spectre, she can ensure she has a loyal drone to do her bidding. At best, however, he's a backup plan. She doesn't want to train someone new, not after she poured a lifetime into training someone who's still alive.

She wants me.

"I guess you'll see," I say.

He groans in disgust and throws me to the ground. I recover my balance quickly, never one to stay down long, and watch as he storms toward one of the Humvees. "And get the savages some pants, will you?" Carter adds with a repulsed nod toward Jace and Drew.

"Why?" I prod, smirking. "Jealous of what you see?"

He glares at me and storms back toward me, the fury burning in his eyes. I can see how much he wants to put a gun to my head and pull the trigger. I can see the tunnel vision, the roiling hatred burning in the back of his brain.

It won't be much longer until I completely break him.

Carter kneels until we're face to face once more. He grabs a fistful of my hair, drawing me painfully closer to him, and his hot breath rolls against my face. "The moment I get the kill order," he says in a harsh tone, "a bullet's going to go through your brain. The less you *annoy* me, the less *painful* that's going to be for you."

As my scalp screams for mercy, his grip only tightening the longer he holds me, I force myself to sneer in answer. "I guess we'll have to see which of us has the faster trigger finger."

After everything he's done to me and the people I love, I'm really going to enjoy killing him.

He releases me and stands, gesturing to the soldiers around him. "Move out!"

"Rory," Levi says gently, trying to lean toward me even as the soldiers drag him to his feet. "Are you okay?"

"I'm fine," I say softly. "Just stay alive."

His jaw tenses as the soldiers drag him away. We share a brief and breathless gaze as they lug him out of my sight and into a nearby Humvee. One by one, they drag my team away.

Things look dire, I won't lie—but my plan is working. Soon, Carter will be putty in my hands. He'll make a mistake, and I'll pounce. I, however, don't play with my food.

I go straight for the kill.

By the end of the day, that's what he's going to wish he'd done to me.

CHAPTER THIRTY-THREE

Carter has each of us thrown into a different Humvee. I sit in the backseat, my hands still on the back of my head as eight men train their guns on me. Even the soldier in the passenger's seat up front twists in his chair, his pistol aimed between my eyes.

I could get out of this, though I would probably get shot in the process. I might even flip the car, and then I would have a harder time figuring out where Carter took the others. Injured, I would have a harder time rescuing them, and he could easily dangle their lives as bait to get me to comply.

For the moment, as much as I hate to do it, I have to play along.

As the vehicle charges through the forest, its tires bounce over the rough terrain. Each jolt throws me off balance, and with my hands on the back of my head, it's tough to sit upright. More than once, the barrel of a gun jabs me sharply in the face, but I don't let my annoyance show. I can't. I remain focused on the road ahead, never so much as flinching as I search for clues on where we're going.

My primary concern is for Tucker and Irena. Drew is an important political figure, worth a ton of money in a hostage situation. Same for Jace. They won't kill Levi without knowing more about who he is, given the stature of the other two dragons he was found with.

But Irena—she has a target on her back. Zurie has openly admitted she wants Irena dead.

And Tucker—well, I listened in as Tucker's father essentially disowned him. Either the General will try to reprogram Tucker's insubordination out of him using Zurie's methods, or he'll shoot my beloved weapons master in the face.

I grit my teeth, tensing at the thought, and my mind buzzes as I grasp for ideas on how I can get us out of this one.

That said, my other three men are all dragons. The Knights aren't historically fond of the dragon race, so their lives aren't exactly *safe*.

Really, we're all in hot water here.

The vehicle jostles as it hops onto a road. Dust kicks from the tires as it speeds onward, faster than before, toward a giant tunnel carved into one of the nearby mountains.

Oh, joy.

We're going underground.

I suppress the intense desire to roll my eyes in frustration. This just keeps getting better. Underground means fewer exits—and fewer chances to escape.

After roughly ten minutes of meandering through tunnels, the vehicle screeches to a stop. The soldiers grab my arms and drag me out of the car, throwing me onto the stony ground as they bark orders.

Their voices overlap each other, and try as they might to hide it, I can hear the terror in their voices.

Good. They *should* be scared.

I take a moment to scan my surroundings. The ceiling stretches above us, arching high overhead. This must be a natural cavern within the mountain, though its walls have been carved into stairways and buildings. Roughly five levels of windows face the center of the giant cavern like the stands of a giant, rocky stadium. The only light comes from rows of fluorescent bulbs embedded every ten feet or so in the rocky wall.

With a shuddering boom, another row of spotlights in the ceiling high above us turn on. It's like turning on the sun itself, and a flood of light pours down on the center of the room. It cuts through the shadows, revealing a platform that had been shrouded in darkness before. Four polished steps lead to the platform, and I wonder what it could possibly be used for.

The new row of lights reveals a few more details

that were shrouded in shadow before. A tidy row of Humvees lines the walls on either side of me, each of them armed with an anti-dragon rifle. To my left, a collection of propane tanks line the wall, roughly twenty feet from the nearest Humvee.

I take in every little detail, hoping something here will be useful later.

First, I need to get my hands on a weapon. A few of the soldiers nearest to me seem like decently easy marks, but the trick is going to be grabbing one of the guns without getting shot by the others in the process.

Seven Humvees pull into the cavern, their engines revving. The barking orders of dozens of soldiers flood the room as the rest of my team is brought in.

I square my shoulders, bracing myself for what's going to come next.

They're shoved onto their knees beside me, the six of us in a line facing the platform. I scan their faces, my heart thundering as I look for new injuries. Each of them scans the room, just as I did, and we all look warily at each other.

There's a way out of this. There always is.

We just have to be clever enough to *find* it.

I could always bring forth my magic and unload the fury of my dragon on everything around me, but when I'm this vastly outnumbered—and still recovering from a hundred-foot fall into the forest—there's a high risk someone I love will be caught in the crossfire.

Or, worse, shot just to spite me.

I need a plan. A real one. And I'm running out of time to figure things out.

Another car engine revs through the cavern. The hum of tires over the stone gets louder as it approaches, and seconds later, a black sedan screeches to a halt near the platform.

The doors open—and, to my disappointment, Zurie gets out. The Ghost surveys me with cold and compassionless eyes, just as she's surveyed hundreds of prisoners before. It's always the same dispassionate look—the bored frown, the relaxed gait, the careless way she surveys the people dragged before her, like they're nothing but insects to squash. It's all designed to intimidate, to make her prey revere her like the Reaper himself. I've seen grown men grovel before her, begging for mercy, before she even opened her mouth to speak.

I've always been at her side in these situations, a step or two behind as she takes command. It's strange to be on the other end—to be on my knees before her.

I don't feel the cold dread I thought I would. I don't feel fear.

Because I see *through* her.

Sometimes, I wonder if she remembers I can see through her games, or if she thinks these sort of tricks still work on me.

The fact is, however, she got here much faster than

I figured she would. That does *not* bode well for us. I figured we would have at least a little time to organize ourselves before she swooped in to ruin everything.

Damn it.

Moments later, a man I've only ever seen in photographs walks around the car from the passenger's side door. His furious gaze scans the row of prisoners before him and instantly lands on Tucker.

General William Chase.

Tucker's father.

Zurie's gaze, however, shifts toward me. If she's excited about this little reunion of ours, she doesn't show it. Her lips remain in a grim line, and her cold gaze barely moves. Her eyes do flit briefly to Irena, but again, she shows no emotion.

She never does.

"Bring Rory here." Zurie snaps her fingers as she stands in front of the platform. "And bring the device."

Oh, fabulous. There's a device involved.

This ought to be fun.

Carter grabs my arm and drags me forward, barely letting me get to my feet as he rushes to obey his new master. I stumble for a moment but manage to catch my balance, standing without his help as he guides me toward my former mentor.

Zurie takes a wide stance and crosses her arms as I near, studying my face for something more than just injuries. If I had to wager, I'd say she's wondering if my magic has fully fused with me yet.

She's wondering if she can yank it out of me—or if she needs to kill me.

The General doesn't join Zurie near the platform. He instead stalks toward his son, who has three rifles pointed at the back of his head. The two glare at each other, and I can see Tucker barely restraining a few choice barbs.

I hope he can hold them back. On top of everything else, we really can't deal with a General's bruised ego right now.

"Have you had your fun?" the General asks. "Are you bored of your sex toy yet?"

Tucker's jaw tenses as his eyes narrow with hatred. He looks like he wants to throw a punch at the man's face—and I figure he might, if not for the fact that the rest of us are being held at gunpoint.

"Why aren't they shackled?" the General shouts. "Who dropped you idiots on your heads when you were kids? Get the cuffs, morons! You can't have loose dragons, *ever*!"

"Yes, sir!" two soldiers nearby say with a salute.

I shake my head in disappointment. Great leadership.

Zurie grabs my jaw and tugs, forcing me to look at her. I indulge her, barely able to restrain how much I want to skewer her with a dagger. I know my hatred shows on my face, but in this heated moment, I just can't bring myself to care.

"Has it fused?" she asks softly, almost impossibly quiet. "Is it too late?"

I honestly don't know.

I hope so because I would never give up my dragon or my power.

Even though I don't answer, Zurie lets out a relieved sigh. She seems to read something in my face that I didn't mean to give away, and that gave her all the reassurance she needs.

Which is *very* bad for me.

"What are you doing, Zurie?" I ask disdainfully, trying to stoke the fires between her and the people helping her. "*Knights?* You despise them."

"You're right," she says under her breath. "Look what you made me do, child. All to drag you back before it's too late."

"Before it's too late?" Carter asks, studying Zurie with a confused expression.

"Silence," she snaps, not even bothering to look at him.

I smirk, casting a sidelong glance at Carter. "She means before my magic fuses and becomes permanent. She wants me, idiot. Not you."

"Maybe," Zurie interrupts with a frown. "If you cause me any more trouble, Rory, it won't be worth it."

"Bullshit," I say, calling her out. "You spent a lifetime

training me. He's sloppy at best," I add with a nod toward Carter. "You need, what, six years to train him to be even mildly capable? Minimum?"

Zurie's lips purse in disappointment, confirming I'm absolutely right. Carter's grip on my arm tightens, enough to cut off circulation as his fingers dig deep into my bicep. Pins and needles bleed into my palm, but I don't care. It's worth it to rile him up. It's worth it to throw him off his game.

"You didn't think you were getting *her* job, did you?" I ask him, grinning.

He scowls at me, his right eye twitching as he no doubt refrains from backhanding me again.

Zurie snaps her fingers to interrupt us. "Carter, get the device like I *told* you to."

"Yes, ma'am," he mutters through gritted teeth. He leaves me with Zurie, knowing full well he has enough ammunition trained on my team to kill them if I try anything.

Moments later, he brings a large black box toward us and sets it on the platform behind Zurie. I frown, studying it, wondering what could possibly be inside. It's barely two feet long, with no detail or symbols of note on the box at all.

He opens the hinged lid, and before I can even look inside, I feel like my soul is being dragged from my body. I groan in agony as my heart skips anxious beats.

Breathless and gasping for air, I fall to my knees, my limbs suddenly weak.

"Yes," Zurie says, excited. "Beautiful."

"What are you *doing* to her?" Jace snaps.

Men grunt, and the metallic clunk of a gun hitting skin cracks through the cavern. I hear several guns cock, and I can practically hear them pressing on their triggers.

"Jace, stop fighting them," I plead through gasping breaths. "It's fine. I'm—I'm fine," I lie.

I squeeze my eyes shut, trying to fight the surging nausea of whatever this box is doing to me.

Though I feel weaker with each second, I grit through the pain and force myself to my shaky feet.

"Impressive," Zurie admits, scanning me as I stand. "My contact said you wouldn't be able to move, but I figured you're too damn stubborn to stay down." She sighs, tapping her finger on her jawline as she studies me. "Don't worry, Rory. This will fix you. I will do what no Ghost has done before, and I will pardon your ridiculous behavior."

"You can shove your pardon up your ass," I mutter through gritted teeth, trying my best to remain on my feet.

She sighs with disappointment. "You've always been a fighter, Rory. Too obstinate for your own good. I broke you of that once, though—I can do it again."

I glare at her, hating her too much to speak.

"I've come too far to stop now," she admits, leaning in. "Did you think I'd given up? I bet you were a tad relieved to not see me for a while, weren't you?" She laughs humorlessly. "Why do you think I had to find the boy to track you down, Rory? I had to go off on a *treasure hunt*. I had to cash in dozens of favors. Do you *know* what this cost me?" She nods at the black box on the platform behind her. "You will pay off everything I've spent recollecting you. It will take you *decades.*"

Spots dance along my vision as the box drains the life from me—as it drains my magic. My beautiful dragon.

Though I can't see much of what's inside the box from this angle, I *have* to figure out what could possibly have such a powerful effect on me.

I take a few uneasy steps, stumbling until I'm close enough to catch a glimpse of what's inside. A simple, faceted crystal the size of my head lays on a thick bed of black silk, the soft fabric tucked neatly around it like an elegant nest. The giant stone dances and shimmers with light. With magic.

My magic.

Zurie gestures behind me, toward Irena. "She betrayed us, Rory. She sold us out. She is the only reason any of this has happened. The only reason you were kicked into that pit. It's time we fix this." She pauses. "All of it."

My former mentor hesitates, her eyes shifting

across my face as she studies me. I think she's waiting for some kind of reaction or hint of surprise. She wants to see the hurt on my face, but she's too late.

Yes, the betrayal still stings.

But I won't let Irena die.

"Get to the *point*," I snap, furious that she's stalling.

She wants me as weak as possible when she gives me whatever inevitable ultimatum is coming. She wants me on my knees, with none of my magic left, so that my choice is made for me.

What she forgets is how fearsome I am, even without my dragon. She must think I've grown soft and dependent, relying on the power in my veins instead of my natural wit.

That mistake is going to cost her dearly.

The thought alone keeps me rooted in place. Though my knees shake with exhaustion as the crystal bleeds me dry, I force myself to remain on my feet.

"You have a simple choice to make," Zurie says in a chilling tone. "Give up your magic. Kill those men. Kill the traitor that nearly got us both assassinated. Do that, and you will be initiated as a full Spectre. Do that, and you will be deemed my rightful heir and the next Ghost." She hesitates, a small smile on her face. "It's everything you ever wanted, Rory."

Correction—it's what I *used* to want.

Standing slightly behind Zurie, Carter grimaces and looks quickly away, his nose wrinkling in disgust. I want to gloat at him, to goad him further, but with that crystal draining the life out of me, it takes all my energy to simply remain upright.

Zurie gestures to one of the soldiers nearby, and they hand her a close-range dragon rifle. At roughly three feet long, it's the smallest one that can kill a dragon at close range.

And, much to my surprise, she shoves it in my hands.

"Do it," Zurie continues. "Or die."

She snaps her fingers, and every weapon not currently trained on the five kneeling warriors turns toward me. A few red dots appear on my chest as my magic is rapidly drained from my body.

"Do it, Rory," Drew says from behind me.

I spin on my heel, baffled, only to find him watching me with a somber expression. His shoulders squared proudly, he simply waits, knowing he doesn't have to say anything else.

"Do it," Jace echoes, a sad tilt to his eyes. Our gazes lock, and his jaw tenses with all the things he wants to say to me. "You'll be safe," he adds with a weary sigh. "You can't go feral if you don't have your dragon."

The thought alone nearly shatters me.

"At least you'll be alive," Levi agrees, his jaw tensing as he fights to hide a tortured expression.

"Shut *up*, you three." Tucker grits his teeth, briefly looking down the line of dragons beside him before he turns his gaze on me. His father pops him on the back of his head with a sharp blow, and Tucker lets out a string of curses as he refuses to so much as look at the man. He and I lock eyes, and I can see the pleading request in his expression. He's silently asking me to do something, to give him a chance to grab a gun —anything.

My gaze shifts to Irena, and she simply watches me. Calm. Tensed. Ready. Her bright green eyes lock on mine, just waiting for the silent cue. Her shoulders relax, her fingers stretching as she limbers them for battle.

Irena already knows what I'm going to do.

My men are noble. I know in my heart they mean it —each of them would die for me, and that is not something I take lightly.

But it seems they don't know me as well as my sister does. Not yet, anyway.

As Zurie assumes I'm facing some difficult dilemma, I scan the world around me once more. The Humvees. The mounted guns. The propane tanks. The veritable sea of soldiers.

"You don't have to do this," I say quietly to my former mentor. "There's a third choice here."

She scoffs. "And that is?"

"Leave me alone," I say, exasperated. "I won't fight you. I won't destroy you. I won't even care what you do if you just leave me be." I point to Carter. "Train this little moron to replace me, for all I care. All I want is a truce, and if we have that, you and I can live in peace."

"Spectres don't quit, Rory." Zurie rolls her eyes. "That's the law. You return to me, or you declare war. These are your options. Now, choose."

I sigh, milking the moment as I stitch together the makeshift patchwork quilt that is my final plan. It's risky. I will probably get shot. A lot. It's going to hurt.

Hopefully, no one I care about dies.

"Easy," I say, lifting my chin with a prideful flourish, mimicking her in moments of difficult decisions. I want her to think I've given in to an older side of myself, the part of myself she used to control. It'll buy me time.

With that, I walk toward Jace and press the barrel against Jace's forehead.

He lifts his gaze, meeting mine as I stare him down. He looks resolute, like he's accepted his fate. Like he's silently grateful I'm going to kill him first, so that he doesn't have to watch what he suspects is coming next. I figure he thinks this is a suicide, of sorts—he must figure I want to kill him first so I go feral and wreak havoc on the place.

As he faces death, I subtly examine the row of twelve propane tanks behind him. It must take a lot of fuel to run a place this big.

That works in my favor.

It's astonishing, really—the very idea that I would ever hurt my men or my sister is ridiculous.

Zurie is about to see what happens to those who dare back me into a corner.

They die.

CHAPTER THIRTY-FOUR

As I press the gun to Jace's forehead, I lock eyes with him. The Fairfax General. The dojo master. A commander. Leader. Warrior. I'm proud of him for his strength, for the courage he's showing now.

But I wish the noble idiot would figure out I'm not going to shoot him.

I can't signal anything to him because Zurie will see it. Once I act on my hastily drawn plan, we're not going to have a ton of time to get weapons and cover. He, Drew, Levi, and Tucker will have to act quickly to avoid getting a headshot.

But this is the only choice we have.

I quickly assess the other options, just to be sure, but none of them are good enough. My next gunshot has to count, and it needs to buy me enough time to get my team to safety. Shooting Zurie would probably fail, since her speed is practically unparalleled, and the people I care about would get instant headshots. Not worth it. Shooting the General would yield the same result.

I need a diversion, one large enough to throw everyone here off their game.

As the seconds tick down, I carefully plan the sequence I'll have to follow once the diversion hits. The soldier behind Jace has a semi-automatic, and that'll make it easier to take out the guards holding my team at gunpoint.

Irena's ready. She doesn't need help, but my men might. My next job is to cover them until they have weapons and cover.

After that, I'm going to shoot the hell out of that damn black box. I'm getting my magic back, one way or another, and blowing that thing to pieces is probably the best way to do it. After that, I'll deal with Carter and Zurie if they haven't retreated by then.

I'll have, at most, two minutes to do all of this.

Fun.

As I fight another bout of dizziness and nausea from the crystal that's slowly sucking my magic from me, I flex the muscles in my core and prepare for battle.

In my periphery, the propane tanks loom like giant targets. I carefully track the one spot that will cause the largest explosion. I'll only get one or two shots off before the world around me erupts in gunfire, so I have to make this count.

All my life, Zurie taught me that failure wasn't an option. I had to be perfect, every time.

That's about to backfire for her.

I squeeze on the trigger, preparing my shot. Jace maintains his gaze, but for the first time since I raised the gun to his head, his eyes narrow slightly in confusion. His eyes drift briefly to his left, toward the propane tanks, and I wonder if he's pieced it together yet.

Hope so.

Fast as lightning, I lift the gun toward the propane tanks and pull the trigger. In the stunned silence following my shot, I manage to fire one more. Both shots hit my target, and the world around me erupts in the largest explosion I've ever seen.

All hell breaks loose.

Soldiers scream. A few run past, burning, throwing off the aim of anyone whose gun is trained on me or my team. Three of the Humvees explode, shooting debris in every direction. A tire takes out the guard holding Tucker in place, and he instantly grabs the gun from the dead man's grip. He aims it at his father, who counters with a few well-placed blows. A shattered door hurls toward them, and they both dive out of the way before it slices them in half.

In the seconds that follow, Jace instantly grabs the

gun I was going to go for. With a grunt, he flips the guard over this shoulder and shoots him in the head with his own gun.

"Switch!" I shout, throwing him my rifle as bullets tear past us. He tosses me the semi-automatic, and we quickly take out the soldiers behind our teammates.

In a matter of seconds, my team is free—and we're under heavy fire. A Bullet grazes my shoulder, and I wince as I duck for cover.

Racing toward the nearest Humvee, I do a quick scan to make sure everyone's okay. My men bolt after me, all armed and ready to recoup. But when I tilt my head to check on Irena, she's armed with three guns and surrounded by four bodies, kneeling behind a flipped car as she scours a soldier's pockets for more ammo.

Good.

I gesture for her to join us, and she obliges me. She stays low, gun raised and firing as she bolts toward us. I fire the semi-automatic in my hands to give her cover.

The six of us take refuge behind one of the Humvees that didn't explode. As Drew kneels next to me, he grabs me by the collar and kisses me deeply. It's quick and passionate, rough and beautiful.

Before I can say a thing, he releases me and cocks his gun, all business once again.

No words. Just action.

All right, I can work with that.

"We need to get out of here!" I shout to them as the fires rage nearby. Rivers of flaming oil weave around us, slowly expanding, and we can't stay here long. This Humvee is going to blow in five minutes, tops.

"There will be armored cars in the next garage over!" Tucker shouts back over the crackle of flames.

A hail of gunfire hits the Humvee as the soldiers recover, and I wonder how many we're facing now. The explosion took out a good chunk of them, but we're still in a freaking Knights fortress.

"Tucker, get a vehicle for us," Jace orders. "Levi, can you shift?"

Levi frowns, glaring out at the cavern. "I'll try."

"No!" I shout as another hail of gunfire hits the car. "Levi, please. Don't."

My ice dragon tenses, watching me with the stern and stoic gaze of a warrior who's willing to do what it takes to survive. He doesn't answer, and the sheer fury in his gaze sends my heart stuttering with dread.

"All right, Levi, don't do it," Jace reluctantly agrees. "We just got you back. I don't want to lose you again, buddy."

A slight smile tugs on Levi's mouth, and he nods gratefully to Jace.

The dojo master braces himself and hands Levi his gun. "Drew, you and I need to take out as many of these assholes as we can."

"For once, I agree with you," Drew says with a grin as he hands me his pistol.

He won't need it.

"I need to destroy that box," I say with a nod toward the device still sitting on the platform.

"And I need to destroy *her*," Irena practically growls, sneering with hatred as she peers around the Humvee.

At Zurie.

"Irena, don't." I grab her arm and tug sharply, forcing her to look at me. "When we get the chance, we'll do it together. You hear me? *Together.*"

Irena, much to my irritation, doesn't react or respond. She simply watches me, her expression somber and on edge, and I know that's not going to happen.

Damn it all.

"I mean it!" I shout as an explosion rocks the cave. Dust falls from the ceiling, and I wonder if another of the vehicles was just torn to shreds.

"No promises," she says quietly. "I started this, and I need to end it."

"Move out!" Jace shouts, apparently oblivious to our conversation. "This vehicle's going to blow! We'll give you guys cover, but you need to get *out*!"

He kneels and shifts, his body morphing and vibrating as his dragon takes over. Drew follows suit, and the two of them quickly tower over us. They roar into the cavern, a final warning to let anyone who still values their life to run away as quickly as they can.

The two dragons bolt into the gunfire, and I hear the delightful crackle of flames roasting everything they touch as Drew lets loose a storm of his dragonfire. The blinding bolt of Jace's magic carves through the cave, and the cavern trembles beneath their might.

"Rory, can you use your magic to cover us?" Tucker asks.

I try to summon the white magic, but it fizzles and dies along my fist. I finally got out of range of the box, but it took too much of my magic for me to use it. I can feel the dull and distant pulse of my dragon, but she's nearly gone.

Furious and practically boiling with hatred, I shake my head. "I need to destroy that box first."

"Damn," Tucker cocks his rifle. "Let's go, then."

The four of us dart into the fray, only to encounter utter insanity.

Flames coat most of the world around us, casting thick plumes of dark smoke against the ceiling. Jace and Drew soar through the air, unleashing hell on the soldiers that are trying to run for cover.

To my dismay, Carter and Zurie bolt down one of the tunnels branching off from the main cavern. Even worse, Carter has the black box tucked neatly under his arm.

Damn it.

A few bullets hit the ground at our feet as snipers try to take us out. We race toward the wall, taking cover when we can as Tucker leads the way to the tunnels.

"The garage is down that tunnel." Tucker nods toward the tunnel next to the one Zurie took. He lifts his gun and takes out two soldiers in the top rows of windows, relieving us momentarily so we can run into it.

Irena doesn't. Without a word, she takes off into the tunnel after Carter and Zurie, leaving the rest of us to sort out what happens next.

I get it. She doesn't want to let Zurie get away—but if she and I are going to win this, we have to face her together.

"You and Levi go!" I shout to Tucker. "Irena and I will destroy the box."

"I'm not leaving you!" Levi shouts to me.

"Dude, I *cannot* do this alone!" Tucker shouts at his best friend as he fires at a few lingering soldiers on the top level above us.

Levi groans in frustration as we near the fork between the two tunnels. He grabs my arm. "Rory, I would shift for you. I don't care what the consequences are. Even if I get stuck as a feral dragon again, I can't—"

"Cover Tucker," I say softly, kissing him. Our lips brush lightly against each other, the lingering buzz enough to settle my heart despite the chaos around us.

"Stay safe, Levi." With a doting smile, I walk backward a few steps before running into the tunnel after Irena.

"Hey, where's *my* kiss?" Tucker shouts down the hallway after me.

I laugh. "You'll get it after this is over, hot stuff!"

"I better!" He shouts back.

I race into the darkness, but Irena is startlingly fast. The tunnel is dotted with sparse lights, just enough to barely see, and I keep my gun trained ahead of me as I carve my way through the shadows. The explosions become more and more distant, muted and muffled, the farther I run. I can't even see her, and I have no idea how far she went.

Before I can reach her, I hear gunfire.

My heart skips beats, and even though I want to speed up to help her, that's a great way to get shot in the head. The tunnel curves sharply to the right, and I force myself to slow enough to peer around the bend.

Crates line the tunnel on either side, offering both cover and making for surprisingly little visibility, given the massive height of the tunnels.

Irena stands between Zurie and Carter in the center of the wide corridor, fending them off simultaneously. Each time Carter swings at her face, Irena counters and lands a devastating kick that throws him off balance. With each deadly blow from Zurie, Irena ducks, occasionally using Carter as a shield. Two guns lay on the ground a short distance off, and I see all three of them eyeing the weapons from time to time, judging whether or not they can dive for them.

With her enhanced strength, Irena lands a gut-wrenching kick to Carter's face. It launches him into the air, and he hits the wall hard. The black box under his arm drops to the ground, and he lands on his hands and knees, wheezing as he tries to breathe.

Poor guy can't even handle a love tap.

I cock my gun and aim at his head. Time to end this. First Carter, then my former mentor.

Zurie started this war, and Carter tried to take the reins. It didn't have to be this way, but I intend to finish what they started.

CHAPTER THIRTY-FIVE

With my gun trained on Carter's head, I fire.
And the bastard *ducks.*

I hate him with all the fury of a sun, but even I have to admit he has skills. He rolls out of the way, grabs one of the loose guns, and fires off three rounds at me. The shots whiz past as I duck for cover. He doesn't stop, and the gunshots get louder as the seconds tick by. It's clear he's walking toward me, trying to corner me and catch me off guard.

That's probably worked for him in the past, but it won't work against someone with Spectre training.

I squat as he rounds the bend and kick out his knees, taking him instantly to the ground. He recovers quickly and aims the gun at my face, but I don't give him the chance to pull the trigger. With practiced ease and a skillful twist of my hands, I disarm him. The gun slides across the ground, clattering against the far wall.

With practiced ease, I hold his chest down with one hand and aim my gun at his face with the other. He grabs the barrel as I fire, twisting out of the shot at the last possible second. The bullet ricochets off the concrete floor, burying itself in a wall as he wrestles the gun from my grasp. We fight for it, rolling over the ground as we try to get the advantage on each other.

In a last, desperate attempt to get it, he elbows me in the face. I take the hit, never one to back down, and knee him in the gut.

The gun slides across the floor to the opposite end of the hallway, and it looks like I'll have to kill him with my bare hands.

Irena grunts with pain, but I have to trust she can handle her fight with Zurie for now. In my weakened state, I have to be careful. Any distractions at all could give Carter the upper hand, and I can't allow that.

Still weakened and nauseous from the crystal's drain on my power, I hook my leg around his to root him in place and punch him as hard as I can. He ducks, however, and though I clip his ear, my fist hits the ground by his head. My knuckles ache with the mind-numbing pain of hitting concrete, and I grit my teeth in agony.

The crystal has totally warped me, far more so than I realized.

I can barely fight.

Carter bucks his hips and tosses me off of him. I roll, skidding the last few feet as he charges, not even giving me a second to recover. He flips me on my back and straddles me, shoving my shoulders hard against the concrete as he pins me to the ground.

His hands wrap around my neck, and he squeezes tightly. I claw at his wrists—not because I'm desperate for air, but because I want to distract him while I look for an opportunity to get him the hell off of me.

A knee in the back, a sharp punch to the throat—there's plenty I can do to weaken his grip on my throat, but I just need an opening.

Irena grunts with effort and agony. Seconds later, the splinter of wood catches my attention, and it sounds like she just sailed through a few of the crates lining the tunnel. I grimace, trying to decide what needs my attention more—my sister, or the man cutting off my air flow.

"Don't kill her, idiot," Zurie snaps, her footsteps nearing.

Oh *shit.*

I tilt my head backward to see her walking toward us, the box in her hands. As she nears, she opens the lid, and once more I feel as though my soul is being sucked from my body. The crystal glows vibrantly blue, and I wonder how much longer until my power fades completely.

I will *not* let that happen.

I will *not* let my dragon die.

Zurie drops the box next to my head, and this close, it feels almost as if I'm being stabbed. My heart, my throat, my eyes—everything stings. Within me, my dragon writhes in agony as she slowly fades to nothing.

Zurie kneels beside me. "You're not *special,* Rory. It's time to realize that." Her voice is low. Dark. Grating. "You're a Spectre, child. That's all you are. That's all you were born to do. It's all you'll ever be. You are nothing more than an assassin I created." She pauses, maybe to let her words sink in as her minion slowly chokes me to death. "I *own* you."

"You think you *own* me?" My voice grates against my throat, almost painful in my burning anger.

I narrow my eyes, watching her, realizing something deep in my core, something I've known for a while but was too stubborn to admit.

I once thought she saw me as a daughter. I thought, perhaps, her attempts to bring me back were in part because she cared, even if only in her broken, fractured way.

But I'm not her family. Zurie doesn't *have* family. She operates alone and loves nothing. To her, I'm not even human. I'm not worthy of rights or a voice. I'm a puzzle piece, the closest thing she has to a legacy. I'm simply the last card she has to play, and she's not going to let me out of this.

"You've never owned me, Zurie," I say through gasping breaths. I glare at her, and I don't have to yell or curse for her to understand how deadly serious I am. "And you *never* will."

Zurie's right eye narrows slightly, almost imperceptibly, so subtly that no one else could have possibly noticed.

But I did.

I know her, maybe even better than she knows me. This is the woman who raised me. She taught me to fight, to kill, and I know that face. That expression.

It's the one she makes when she's about to snap.

When she's about to kill.

And she's looking at *me*.

"Fine," she says simply.

That one, little word says everything.

It's the kill order.

She surrendered, and she knows she'll never reprogram me. I'm too far gone, and all of the favors she's cashed in have been wasted.

Now, it's about revenge. And Zurie is *very* good at revenge.

"When she's weak," Zurie says, shifting her attention to Carter, "kill her. Consider this your initiation."

A sadistic grin breaks across Carter's face. "With pleasure, ma'am."

Zurie casts one last disgusted look down at me—at her shattered legacy—and stands.

It hits me, then.

How badly I wanted this to work.

How much I craved the idea of her simply letting me go—and letting me live in peace.

Letting me. Like I somehow needed her permission.

I don't.

There will be no redemption for Zurie. No talking sense into her. There will be only war, blood, and death.

If it's her or me, that's an easy choice.

Irena coughs nearby. Thank the gods—I was worried Zurie had killed her. Even as spots dance along my vision from Carter's hands tightening around my throat, a sliver of gratitude floods through me that she's okay.

"How would you like to die?" Carter asks, sneering. He looms over me, a lock of his hair hanging over one eye as his wild gaze roams my face. "I've thought of so many fun ways to do it."

"I'm sure you have," I gasp through his fingers on my throat.

He's a fool chasing a dream, though. He doesn't have the experience I do. The Spectres would accept me as the Ghost, if begrudgingly so, but no Spectre would ever honor Carter's rule. He'll die the first week Zurie isn't there to protect him. Maybe sooner.

And Zurie knows it. She just wants someone to

exhaust me, to make me weaker and distract me from her battle with Irena so that I'm easier to kill.

Fine. I'll play her game.

As I dig into the last of my energy, I twist my hips and throw Carter violently off of me. He grabs my hair as a last-ditch effort to keep his grip, and with a painful tug, he drags me a few inches toward him as he falls.

I glare at the bastard, wondering who made him like this—how one man could be so full of hate.

In the end, it's just not my problem.

With my magic quickly seeping from me, I need to get to that box. I have to destroy it.

As we wrestle on the ground, throwing punches and skillfully avoiding each other's blows, I keep glancing at the box. The crystal grows brighter every second, and I know I'm quickly running out of time.

I knee him hard in the back, and he doubles over in pain. I scramble on my hands and knees for the nearest gun—his pistol. I reach for it, but he tugs on my ankle. My fingers brush the metal as he drags me away.

I pivot, twisting in his grip, and kick him squarely in the face. His nose snaps beneath my bloodstained boot. It sits at a crooked angle on his face, and he screams in agony.

"A Spectre never screams," I say through gritted teeth. For good measure, I kick him in the throat.

He coughs, sputtering blood and bile across the floor. I race again for the gun, but I'm fading. Fast.

Every movement is a chore. Every muscle aches. Every inch of my body is begging for me to just quit, to simply lie there, to conserve what little energy I have left.

But I refuse to just lay down and die.

My fingers wrap around the gun handle, but I can barely tighten my grip. My elbows shake, threatening to give out. I grit my teeth in frustration, aching to finish this. Aching to make this right.

"I'm going to break your bones one by one," Carter threatens, flipping me on my back. I groan in pain, gritting my teeth to bite back just how badly that hurt. He glares down at me, blood dripping from his nose and mouth as he wraps his hands once more around my throat. "I'm going to break every toe. Every finger. By the end of the day, you're going to *beg* me to kill you. And I won't." His grip tightens, and white lights dance along my vision.

My fingers grasp at the space behind my head, desperately grabbing for the gun. In his hate-fueled tunnel vision, he must not see anything but the color draining from my face as he chokes me to death.

"Maybe I'll drown you and bring you back," he continues with a dark and twisted laugh. "Maybe I'll chain you in a cell and let you starve." He shrugs, chuckling madly to himself. "Let's not get ahead of ourselves with how it ends, but I promise you, Rory— I'll film the whole thing, track down your men, and make them watch it before I do the same thing to *them.*"

Running on the fumes of my hatred for this man, I dig into my soul and find the last shreds of strength I possess. My hand wraps around the gun, and I lift it toward his face.

"No," I growl. "You won't."

Before he can so much as flinch, I shoot him between the eyes.

He falls backward, landing on my legs as he goes still. I gasp with relief as I can once more breathe. Even though I desperately crave air, I force myself to keep going.

Since he's basically solid muscle, it's a struggle to get out from underneath him. With a few strained grunts and lots of wincing, however, I manage to tug myself free.

When I finally shove him off my legs, I can barely think straight. My brain buzzes with exhaustion and the effects of the crystal in the black box. I can barely breathe. Every breath feels like a painstaking labor, and I wheeze as I struggle to stay conscious.

Chest heaving, I force myself to my feet. I stumble toward the box on the floor, focused on my singular mission to destroy it. I can feel the last of my dragon slowly dying, but I refuse to let her go.

She can't die.

I won't allow it.

With a shaky hand, I lift the gun and aim for the brilliantly glowing crystal at my feet. My world spins, my vision blurring, and I feel for a moment as though I might pass out.

I push through.

I have to.

My finger squeezes on the trigger. A bullet hits the black box, shattering the lid's hinge. I fire again, and again, hoping at least one of these will hit.

The third one does.

The crystal shatters like glass. A muted scream fills the air, and I wonder if that's Zurie or someone else. I can barely hear anything. Hell, I can barely even see.

I fall to my knees, having done all I could.

All I can do now is hope this works.

A steady trickle of energy seeps into my fingers. It's like my body is slowly defrosting. One by one, my muscles slowly spring to life again. My toes curl in my boots. I sigh with relief as my body relaxes, its energy slowly restored.

Warmth blurs within me, slow at first, but it steadily grows to something stronger. A gentle hum, like the essence of life itself, burning in my core.

And then she springs to life.

My dragon.

She curls within me, coiling with fury and might. Right now, she wishes she could shift—she pushes at my chest, desperate to break free. She wants nothing more than to tear holes through the person who did this to her.

The urge to let her take over is overwhelming, but try as I might, I can't do it. It's like we're hitting a wall together, and even though I want nothing more than to give in, I'm blocked.

The exhaustion slowly seeps from my muscles, replaced by power. Strength. Fury. Finally, I can stand. As I get to my feet, I practically feel like I could fly.

Soon.

When I open my eyes, two figures duel in the dark tunnel ahead of me. I lift my palm, and my magic instantly springs to life between my fingers.

I grin, narrowing my eyes as I focus on Zurie's face. Her gaze flits nervously between me and Irena, and it's clear that the tide just turned against her.

Zurie could have avoided all of this. I gave her a way out, and she should have taken it. But now, I need to end her.

Or she will *never* leave me be.

CHAPTER THIRTY-SIX

Brilliant white light cascades across my skin, simultaneously humming with the life of my renewed dragon and the destructive power of the gods.

With my palms trained on Zurie, my magic dances between my fingertips, desperate to wreak havoc. She and Irena dance across my still-clearing vision, their forms practically blurring as they each try to deal a deadly blow to the other.

The master, and the student.

Equally matched, and at war.

As I take aim at my former mentor, I'm struck by the surreal sensation of knowing I have to kill her. *Knowing* there's no other way. I face her as my undeniable enemy for the first time, and there's no turning back.

It's her or me.

Zurie is careful to angle herself behind Irena, using my sister as a shield to keep me from firing. As I prepare to join the fray, my gaze drifts briefly to the black box at my feet. A pile of shards is all that remains of the crystal that once drained the life from me, and it gives me pause.

If she found one, she might find others. I need to know what that thing was—and how to ensure no one ever uses one on me again.

"Stop," Zurie demands, jumping several feet backward as she holds up a small detonator in one hand. "Both of you, stand down."

Irena hesitates, body tense with bloodlust and the desire to finish this. I take a few careful steps toward her, until Irena and I stand shoulder to shoulder and face off with the woman who raised us.

"What do you have there?" I ask with a nod to the detonator.

"You know damn well what it is," she snaps, her eyes narrowing. "Rules twelve and eighty-seven."

Ah.

Rule 12 of the Spectres—always know when and how to escape.

Rule 87 of the Spectres—always have a failsafe.

"Where did you plant the bombs, Zurie?" I ask, never once lowering my palm.

From this distance, I could hit her with a blast powerful enough to kill her. She's wickedly fast, so I might only take out an arm, but it would be a devastating blow nonetheless.

What I *don't* know is what she plans to destroy with that small red button in her hand. Her thumb hovers over the trigger, ready to press it at a moment's notice.

If I fire, she will, too.

We're at a stalemate.

Damn it.

"You bore me, Zurie," I lie, trying to goad her. "You always run. You always give up. You're nothing but a coward."

Zurie scoffs. "You can't use my pride against me, child. I *taught* you that trick."

I shrug. "Had to try."

"Don't worry." She watches me like an insect she'd like to spear with a pin and stick to a wall as a trophy. "The next time we meet, it will be the last."

I shake my head, determined to end this. "There won't be a next—"

To my horror, Zurie presses the detonator.

The cavern violently trembles with all the force of an erupting volcano. It knocks me and Irena off balance, but Zurie is already running. I fire blindly at her as the world around us shakes, throwing off my aim. She stumbles, one of the bolts hitting her hard in the side, but she presses onward.

I try to stand, to follow, to end this and be done— but another explosion rocks the tunnel. A thick crack breaks across the ceiling above us, and massive chunks of the concrete overhead begin to fall.

"She's getting away!" Irena shouts, jumping to her feet. "Come on."

Above us, a massive chunk of the ceiling breaks free.

"Irena!" I grab her and yank her backward, away from her prey and—more importantly—away from a grizzly death.

We tumble to the ground as the concrete shatters across the area where she stood moments before. In a matter of just a few seconds, the way through is almost completely blocked.

More and more explosions rock the tunnel, caving it in, and I realize this was carefully orchestrated to ensure we couldn't follow. Irena didn't stop Zurie here —Zurie had stopped and *waited* for her.

For *us*.

"She can't get away!" Irena shouts as I help her to her feet. "There has to be another—"

The hiss of gas pouring into the tunnel interrupts her. In unison, we both groan in frustration.

Without another word of debate, we bolt back the way we came. Where there's gas, there's usually an explosion, and we would rather not die a crispy death today.

We race toward the cavern where we had been held at gunpoint. Our boots thunder over the concrete as we charge down the sparsely lit tunnel as fast as our feet will carry us. This entire tunnel could blow at any moment, and that would mean having a blazing inferno on our tail.

Irena and I pass a wide section in the roof that lets in daylight, and I briefly glance upward at the hundred-foot exhaust tunnel in the hopes of an escape. It's easily wide enough to fit a plane, but the steep walls would make it impossible to scale.

Damn.

The entire compound trembles again, more violently than ever before, and a hot rush of air blows past us.

The warning of what's to come.

"Shit!" Irena shouts. "Hurry!"

The inferno is on its way. I briefly glance over my shoulder, only to notice an orange glow reflected on the walls.

We don't have long.

With every step, I curse Zurie. I curse how she seems to always remain one step ahead. I curse how much she hates us, how she won't leave us alone. And, most of all, I curse how she just won't *die.*

The wall of fire quickly gains on us. Gusts of blistering air hit us hard in the back, as we barely maintain our lead. We're still a good hundred feet or so from safety, and I honestly don't know if we're going to make it.

I press on, regardless.

I won't give up.

Ever.

My breath stings in my lungs, biting and painful. My thighs scream for rest, but I force them to continue.

The roar of the flames quickly approaches, and I glance over my shoulder once more to gauge the distance.

Close.

Way too close.

A ripple appears in the flames, almost like a mirage. A shadow. It looms, closer and closer, and I can't believe this is how I'm going to die.

I refuse to accept it. I have to think of something—anything—to get us out of this. Maybe I can blast my magic into the fire, though I'm not really sure that will help. If I get enough of a head start, I might be able to cave in another section of the tunnel, but it probably wouldn't be enough to stop an inferno like this.

Think, Rory. Think!

With a wary glance backward, I once again check the inferno. This time, the mirage within the flame begins to take shape.

It looks almost like a... *head.* A face.

With teeth.

And wings.

Seconds later, Drew bursts through the flame,

propelled by his incredible speed and strength. He lowers his claws, talons stretched, and snatches us as the flames quickly overtake us. His hot scales sizzle against my skin, burning slightly, but it's a hell of a lot better than facing the inferno.

I want to thank him, to kiss him on his great big scaly face, but we're not out of this yet.

The fire dragon blasts through the tunnel ahead of the inferno, soaring through the air as he carries us through the crumbling remains of the main hall. The fortress shakes around us, and he dodges the rocks falling from the ceiling before diving into the next tunnel to take us out.

I set my hand against his leg to thank him, to ask him where the others are, to get any information at all, but he doesn't answer. He's entirely focused on his maneuvering.

Yet again, I have to trust.

I have to wait.

In just a few minutes of nail-biting maneuvers, he soars into the daylight. A plume of pitch-black smoke erupts after us, trailing off into the blue sky as the fortress implodes.

I expect Drew to slow and land, but he only flies faster through the air. He keeps low and bolts toward the forest.

Toward the sound of gunfire.

The distant crackle of Jace's magic tears through the

forest, splintering wood and setting off a series of explosions. A spiral of dark smoke rises into the sky, and I realize the fight isn't over.

It just relocated.

Out here, the battle rages on. But after Zurie's escape, I'm not in the mood to indulge any of this.

It ends.

Now.

As Drew breaks through the canopy and finally lands, the pops of gunfire grow louder. Through a break in the trees, I see Levi and Tucker hunkered down beside a blown-out Humvee. A bolt of brilliant blue light obliterates a patch of trees nearby, and several men scream as Jace takes out one of the units firing on them. I'm glad the three of them are okay, and for now, that's everything I need to know.

I don't waste a moment.

The *second* Drew's claws release me, I bolt into the forest. White light erupts over my skin, eager to burn off the energy I have so badly wanted to use against Zurie.

In my fury and rage, I spare no one.

Such is the fate of the fools who threaten the people I love.

Irena takes cover with Tucker and Levi, while Drew flies overhead. He unleashes a bolt of fire on the unsuspecting forest below.

As I step into the small clearing by Levi and Tucker's hideout, they both sit a bit taller with surprise. Their eyes widen, mouths opening to speak, but I don't pause.

I release the greatest blast I can manage, the beam casting a blinding white glow on the forest. It obliterates the woods before me—the trees, the canopy, the underbrush.

Everything.

And I don't stop.

I release blast after blast, letting my fury take over, giving into the rage that Zurie stirs within me.

Time blurs by, and I lose track of how long I destroy the world before me. I lose track of the number of white beams that burn the earth at my feet. I simply let loose, allowing my fury to take over for a time.

It feels *great.*

As the blinding white glow of my magic begins to fade, I stand in the middle of a charred scar in the woods. The blackened earth surrounds me for a half-mile in every direction, and only the Humvee protecting my team remains safe from my rage.

There's nothing else left.

A tire rolls by, still smoking, and lands on its side at my feet. For good measure, and mostly just because I'm still mad, I blow it to ash as well.

Behind me, Levi, Tucker, and Irena slowly stand, guns raised as they scope the obliterated landscape.

"Wow, babe," Tucker says with a slight chuckle. "I guess that'll work."

A ripple of white light races up my arm, and I squeeze my eyes shut to hold my power at bay. In the fury of nearly losing my dragon, it was so easy to give in to the thirst for vengeance.

I thought burning off the anger would make me feel better. Now that there's nothing left to destroy, however, I still feel a bit empty.

"Yeah," I respond. "It'll do for now."

CHAPTER THIRTY-SEVEN

"Dragon blood." Irena says flatly, her tone thick with disbelief. "The bio-weapon is made of... *dragon blood.*"

"Yes," Jace says simply.

We sit in his private war room with Tucker, Levi, and Drew. To my surprise, Jace actually *invited* them.

He insists it's just because he knew they would barge in mid-meeting, like they always do, but still. It's progress.

After the onslaught on the Knights fortress, we're exhausted. Wrapped in gauze nearly from head to toe, I have to confess we all look like burn ward patients who escaped their beds.

The full moon beams through the window behind Jace, and I know we should probably all be asleep, recovering.

But we're too damn stubborn.

On average, each of us has three bullet holes in us after our ordeal, but the dragons and I are all healing remarkably well. Tucker looks a little worse for wear, but he flashes me a flirty grin as I tilt my head to check on him.

In the silence that follows Jace's comment about the bio-weapon, Irena and I stare at him blankly. We wait for more detail, and he apparently takes the hint.

With a small shrug, he gestures toward the papers he laid before us a few moments ago. "I'm just telling you what's on the doctor's report," the dojo master says matter-of-factly. "It's marked as urgent, or we wouldn't be in this room talking about it right now."

"It's urgent because it's unprecedented," Drew adds. "No one believed this was even possible."

I lift the papers, scanning the obscure medical terms that barely look like real words. "Kinsley created a bio-toxin out of her own blood?"

"That's the best guess." Jace nods and gestures toward Irena. "Thus, the eyes. I don't know anyone else with her eyes."

"Especially ice dragons," Levi adds.

I pause and study him for a moment, appreciating that he's here with us. Inside. In the war room, finally able to join us at our meetings. I smile warmly, and he grins back.

It would seem he's glad to be here, too.

Jace abruptly clears his throat, dragging me—quite purposefully, I imagine—back to the conversation at hand. "It would seem, as a result, that the antidote possessed an odd blend of concentrated formulas that left Irena with, well—how did you put it, Rory?"

"Side effects," Irena answers for me, rolling her eyes.

I laugh. "Are you seriously *not* loving your super strength?"

"I just want to understand it," she says with a shrug. "And these," she adds, pointing to her nearly glowing eyes.

"The doctor had to get... creative," Jace says. "You were on death's door, and he didn't understand the antidote well enough at first. In his initial analysis, he made a few assumptions for the sake of time—especially when he discovered it would kill any human who came into contact with it. He had to make do."

"What does that mean?" I prod.

Jace sighs. "It's complicated. The initial antidote was rushed and imperfect. He isn't even sure how to duplicate that, to be honest. What you received, Irena, no one else can ever get."

I frown in confusion. "What version of the antidote is Harper giving out, then?"

"A refined version." Jace leans against the wall. "One that's been carefully tested, reviewed, and studied. One that will allow anyone who takes it to return to normal."

Irena massages her forehead in confusion. "And I, what? Got a botched version?"

"Kind of," Jace admits haltingly. "The Vaer had been running tests on you, Irena, and it seemed as though they might have been experimenting with other bio-toxins while you were unconscious." His brows knit together in anger. "Your blood is a very unique cocktail that I don't think can ever be replicated."

My grip tightens on the edge of the table, and the wood shifts slightly beneath my enhanced strength. I reluctantly let go of it, furious, not entirely sure how to channel the blossoming rage within me.

"Those bastards," Irena says softly. Her eyes squeeze shut, and her smooth face is perfectly stoic. Surprisingly calm. The only indication that she's upset is the slight curve in her eyebrow. As she leans back in her seat, she takes a shaky breath to steady herself.

I set a hand on her back, and she smiles weakly at me in gratitude.

"However, there is good news," Jace adds, though he casts a wary glance at Irena. "Well, I think it's good, anyway."

I cock my head to the side, suddenly suspicious of the way he's beating around the bush with this. "And that is?"

He hesitates, his gaze shifting between me and my sister, before pointing at her. "Irena is the *second* human-dragon hybrid to ever exist. Next to you, of course, Rory," he adds with a nod toward me.

My mouth drops open as I gape at the dojo master, because surely I misheard him.

Irena, to her credit, merely stares at him like he's grown three heads. "I'm a *hybrid*?" she asks in quiet disbelief.

"Yes." Jace hesitates, thinking over his answer, and shakes his hand back and forth. "Ish."

"Ish," she echoes skeptically, one eyebrow raised.

"It means you have enhanced strength of a dragon," Drew answers. "And possibly other traits, but no dragon within you." He hesitates. "Probably."

I rub my eyes in frustration. "You've got a lot of maybes in that sentence."

"It's all we know," Drew admits.

"So, what?" Irena asks with a bemused laugh. "I'm a knockoff dragon vessel?"

In unison, Tucker and I burst out laughing.

For a moment, no one else even moves. I snort at the very concept, lost in my laughter. Moments later, Irena shakes her head, unable to hide her smile anymore, and the laughter slowly bubbles through the rest of the room.

"Oh gods," I say, rubbing my face. "After what we just went through, I really needed a laugh like that."

With a big grin on her face, Irena shakes her head at me. "You're welcome, I guess."

As Jace launches into more notes on the bio-toxin, I lean back in my chair and survey the room. Drew catches my eye and smirks, that devilish smile igniting a burning desire for him that stirs deep in my core. Levi and Tucker are completely focused on Jace's words, their intense expressions endearing as they prepare for the next wave of the war with Zurie.

The final wave.

And Irena...

My sister briefly glances toward me and, despite the news of her newfound dragonish blood, smiles warmly. She's part dragon, now, same as me. A knockoff, as she described it, but part dragon all the same. It'll take time for her to really own that, but at least we can face it together.

As a team.

I close my eyes and sink into the blissful sensation of being home. Of being safe. Of being with the people I love.

My family.

Deep within me, a powerful surge of magic and life burns brighter than ever. My dragon is so close to the surface, already chomping at the bit and ready for her first fight. She's a warrior, same as me, and I love her fire. Our ordeal ignited the thirst within her, too. She's nearly ready, and when she breaks free, there will be no stopping us.

In my heart, I know I'll shift—and I know it'll be

someday soon. When I do, my dragon will be absolutely breathtaking to behold.

The next time Zurie and I meet *will* be the last—because my dragon and I will kill her, once and for all.

Together.

Rory, Levi, Tucker, Drew, and Jace will return in *Age of Dragons*, available to PREORDER now.

Join the exclusive, fans-only Facebook group to get release news & updates.

Read on for a special note from the author.

AUTHOR NOTES

Hey, babe!

Man oh freaking *man* was this book was a ton of fun to write. I truly hope you enjoyed it.

I've loved watching Rory grow. She started out as a badass assassin hungering for freedom and autonomy —and what she found instead was confidence in herself.

In *Reign of Dragons,* for the first time in her life, she defied her master.

In *Fate of Dragons,* she learned how to give up a bit of control. How to compromise.

And in *Blood of Dragons,* fittingly for the title, she's learning what it means to have family. To trust, to let down her guard to her inner circle, and grow as a person.

All while remaining her beautiful badass self, of course.

Tucker continues to make me laugh nonstop—he's equal parts hilarious and dangerous. No one knows their way around a gun like Tucker.

Drew is every bit the prince he doesn't want to be. He's imposing, commanding, clever, and has a knack for learning things he shouldn't know, as well as being places he shouldn't be. As strong as he is, he really can get away with almost anything—except with Rory. And let's be honest, here. He loves that she can keep him in line.

Levi—oh, be still my heart. Raw, honest, and deeply in tune with the world around him, Levi is Rory's brutally efficient protector. Who *doesn't* want a Levi in their life? Good gracious. *(Fans self)*

And Jace—he'll come around. It's fun to watch him slowly soften his bad boy exterior, if only toward Rory. He never thought he would find love, never really cared for it until he saw her, and he's learning how to be the man she deserves. He's just… slow about it, I guess. And he has such an all-or-nothing personality, it's going to be interesting to see how he reacts once he and Rory finalize the mate-bond—if he can get his head out of his ass long enough to do it!

As for the universe of the Dragon Dojo Brotherhood? Rory's world lights me on fire.

Pun *totally* intended. (Sorry, I like terrible puns.)

This place is a dream for me. An absolute delight. I've loved to delve into the realm of dragons, to play in a world where there aren't dragon kingdoms, but basically dragon *mobs.* I mean, how fun is that?!

Of course, I couldn't play in this world so much if you didn't love reading it. So, from the bottom of my heart, *thank you.* Thank you a million times over. If I ever get to meet you in person, I'm going to give you *such a big hug.*

You truly are such a gift to me!

Okay, mushy time's over. I just had to get that out.

I know you're probably chomping at the bit to learn what happens next. To figure out what those conniving

Bosses have planned for our leading lady—and just how badly she intends to whoop them when they try.

Zurie is still after Rory and Irena, as is Diesel—and we know Diesel has ulterior motives. After all, he's not really the obedient little pet everyone thinks he is, is he?

Let's not forget General William Chase, leader of the Knights, has a vendetta against Rory for taking his son from him. And, you know, for being a dragon. Kinda. Close enough, for him. Did he die in the fortress implosion? Or is he still at large?

Rory killed Ian Rixer, a wealthy dragon lord with connections. Don't you think someone might come for a spot of revenge?

And Kinsley Vaer—the Boss of the Vaer family—is still out there, after all. That woman doesn't like to get her hands dirty, but when her minions continue to fail, she eventually bites the bullet. I have to tell you, it's not a pretty sight when she gets personally involved. But, for now, she has one more trick up her sleeve—you guessed it. Guy Durand. And if he fails... well, she intends to let all hell break loose.

My goodness, Rory has a ton of enemies.

Lucky she and her men are such brilliant fighters. They won't let anything come between them. Whatever lies ahead, they're ready.

Are you?

The next book will be available in six short weeks. Make sure you **join the exclusive, fans-only Facebook group to get the latest release news & updates.**

> Until next time, babe!
> Keep on being your beautiful, badass self.
> -*Olivia*

PS. Amazon won't tell you when the next Dragon Dojo Brotherhood book will come out, but there are several ways you can stay informed.

1) **Soar on over to the Facebook group, Olivia's secret club for cool ladies,** so we can hang out! I designed it *especially* for badass babes like you. Consider this as your invite! We talk about kickass heroines, gorgeous men, our favorite fantasy romances, and... did I mention pictures of *gorgeous men?*

2) **Follow me directly on Amazon**. To do this, **head to my profile** and click the Follow button beneath my picture. That will prompt Amazon to notify you when I

release a new book. You'll just need to check your emails.

3) **You can join my mailing list by going to** https://wispvine.com/newsletter/olivia-ash-email-signup/. This lets me slide into your inbox and basically means we become best friends. Yep, I'm pretty sure that's how it works.

Doing one of these or **all three** (for best results) is the best way to make sure you get an update every time a new volume of the *Dragon Dojo Brotherhood* series is released. Talk to you soon!

ABOUT THE AUTHOR

OLIVIA ASH

Olivia Ash spends her time dreaming up the perfect men to challenge, love, and protect her strong heroines (who actually don't need protecting at all). Her stories are meant to take you on a journey into the world of the characters and make you want to stay there.

Reviews are the best way to show Olivia that you care about her stories and want other people discover them. If you enjoyed this novel, please consider leaving a review at Amazon. Every review helps the author and she appreciates the time you take to write them.